M000309559

LONG LIVE THE KING

Book One of the Charlemagne Saga

By

GUY COTE

World Castle Publishing

This is a work of fiction. Names, characters, places, and incidents are products of the author's imagination or are used fictitiously and are not to be construed as real. Any resemblance to actual events, locations, organizations, or person, living or dead, is entirely coincidental.

World Castle Publishing
Pensacola, Florida

Copyright © Guy Cote 2012
ISBN: 9781938243790
First Edition World Castle Publishing July, 15, 2012
http://www.worldcastlepublishing.com

Licensing Notes
All rights reserved. No part of this book may be used or reproduced in any manner whatsoever without written permission, except in the case of brief quotations embodied in articles and reviews.

Cover: Kelly Cote & Karen Fuller
Photos: Shutterstock
Editor: Jeff LaFerney

DEDICATION

To my wife Kelly and everyone who supported me over the years
I am eternally grateful

GUY COTE

ACKNOWLEDGMENTS

While writing may appear to be a solitary endeavor, no one is a fortress unto themselves. In my many years of writing screenplays and this novel, I have been fortunate enough to have the support and encouragement of some very important people. First and foremost, I wish to thank my wife, Kelly. As of this writing, we have been married for just under a year. In that time, I have found her assistance and devotion to my endeavors to be tireless. I can honestly say that I have never had a greater advocate than I do with Mrs. Kelly Cote. I love you.

I would also like to thank my parents, Roland Cote and Earlene (Kitty) Chadbourne. The older I get, the more I realize what a rare commodity two loving, selfless parents are. Dad and Mom have always been there for me and have often been the first people I turn to for advice, encouragement, or simple reassurance. You are truly a gift and I thank God every day for you.

My brother Adam has also been a dedicated champion of my creative efforts. Through the many frustrating years I spent writing and trying to market my screenplays, I always knew I could count on Adam to bolster me up. You are more than a brother; you're my best friend.

I also owe my Aunt Linda Cote a great deal of appreciation. She has always been a second mother to me. From teaching me to ski, taking me on trips (most notably Europe), tutoring me in French and encouraging me in all my peculiar undertakings (remember my *Interview with Elvis* song?), you have always been someone I can count on. My life is infinitely richer for having you in it.

My grandparents have also been pillars of strength to me and never-ending sources of inspiration. Harvey and Yvette Cote are no longer with us, but are never far from our hearts. Earle and Betty Ahlquist are thankfully still with us and the bedrock upon which my mother's side of the family is built.

I would also like to express my gratitude to my in-laws, Randy and Judy Swails and Grandma Ruby Combs. Thank you for welcoming me into your family and for encouraging me with my writing. You are wonderful people and I consider myself very fortunate to be related to you.

I would be remiss if I didn't also thank Barbara Sandy for her many years of encouragement. We met at a screenwriting conference at Burt Reynolds' ranch but formed a friendship that transcended the entertainment industry. You are a special person and I am blessed to know you. Thank you for never being afraid to give me your honest feedback, even if it frustrated me from time to time.

I owe Kristina Schulz my appreciation for helping me with the German translations. Thank you very much.

Lastly, I wish to give a shout out to my close friends: Mark Boissonneault, Chris Harrie, Rob (Bob) Raymond, Tim Peddie, Dave Nadeau, Blair Hodge, Woody Krueger, Chris Zito, Zach and Shelly Lambert and my friends/relatives: Jodi and Cory Wilson, John and Kristin Savage, Gerard (Fafa) Savage, Lorraine Savage, Colette Petrin, Paulina Cote, Ted Chadbourne and my nieces and nephews: Jordan Wilson, Marli Wilson, Ana Cote, Audrey Cote, Mia Cote, Addie Cote, Michael Cote, Brady Savage, Reese Savage, Molly Boissonneault, Sara Boissonneault, Brady Boissonneault and Andrew Boissonneault.

I hope you enjoy *Long Live the King* (though I think it may be a while before babies Michael and Reese will be able to read it).

CHAPTER ONE

Josie had never been so tired. Of course, that wasn't true. She had undoubtedly been more tired some time in her twenty-one years of life, but she couldn't recall when. In one week, she worked a full six-day schedule, three of which included back-to-back shifts (doubles as they call them in the waitress trade). Her life seemed to be an endless loop of work, dinner, sleep, breakfast, and work again. To make matters worse, most of her tips were meager.

She slowly entered the stairwell of her building, and her heavy legs carried her step by step toward her second-story apartment. She passed holes in the walls and gaps in the stairs as if they didn't exist. Her feet shuffled past debris left by children, and she ignored a soiled diaper which sat at the top of the stairs. She was weary down to her core and wanted nothing more than to wash the day's grime off her body and collapse onto her mattress.

Sliding her key into its slot in the door handle, she heard the heavy drone of a television. Irritation simmered within her as she prepared herself for more of the same ritual she'd experienced almost every night for the past three months. She opened the door and, just as expected, found Steve Cousins, her boyfriend, sprawled on the couch with an army of crushed beer cans scattered around him. Age-wise, he was six years her senior. Maturity-wise was another story.

"Here's something you don't see every day," she mocked.

Steve acknowledged her entry with a nod of the head and a swig from his beer. His glossy eyes followed a World War II documentary that played on the television.

"I guess Bank of America didn't offer you that CEO position yet," Josie said as she removed her sneakers and knee-high stockings.

"Huh?"

"Did you get off your ass at all today? Look for even one job?"

"Didn't feel like it," Steve replied.

Frustrated and disgusted, Josie made a beeline for the bedroom and slammed the door behind her.

"Pain in my ass," Steve said and finished his beer. He watched fighter planes streak through a black and white sky, firing at the enemy below. The room's surround sound gave him the sensation of being in the action. The entire entertainment system was worth three times as much as anything else in the apartment and was bought by Steve on Josie's credit. But he knew how to protect his purchase from would-be thieves. He kept a loaded .357 Magnum in a drawer by the couch.

Josie collapsed onto the bed, stretching diagonally across the mattress. The hand-me-down frame creaked beneath her hundred and ten pound weight. She buried her face in a pillow and thought about how the night would play itself out. She'll be sound asleep and Steve will stagger into the room, crashing into everything and anything around him. She'll pretend not to hear him, but he'll drop onto the bed and talk incoherently for about a half hour. Then he'll become amorous. His breath will smell of alcohol and whatever spicy food he devoured. He'll clumsily press his body close to hers and grope her awkwardly. She'll resist, but in the end, what will she gain? If they don't have sex, he'll complain and throw things like an angry child. If she gives in, she'll be left feeling disgusted, unsatisfied, and even more sleep deprived for tomorrow's first shift.

Josie slid her face out of the pillow and said, "I can't deal with this shit again." She pulled a small tote bag out from under the bed and went to her closet. Her friend Gretchen would put her up for the night. Gretchen had two dogs, two cats, a daughter, and a husband, but Josie would rather deal with all that than her drunken boyfriend. She'd figure out what to do about Steve later. As she put a clean work uniform in the bag, she realized that something wasn't right in her closet. She always kept it neat, with everything in its place, but her black stilettos were now entangled in a once folded afghan that was balled up in the corner. She wasn't as concerned about those items as she was the treasure box that was hidden beneath them. It was a simple shoe box, but Josie had been decorating it with photos, clippings, and drawings since she was little. She gingerly raised the cover to see that all the contents of the box were present. To her relief, they were. Maybe she was just being paranoid. Just to be sure, she lifted the scarf which enveloped her most prized possession. It was gone! The scarf was wrapped around nothing but air.

She searched frantically for her precious item, but it was nowhere to be found. A scowl darkened her pretty face and she looked at the bedroom door where Steve lounged in the room just beyond it.

Josie threw the door open and charged into the living room with her shoe box in her hand. She found Steve sitting on the couch with a fresh beer in one hand and his .357 in the other. He mumbled something about "bad ass Krauts" and pointed his gun at German soldiers running across the television screen.

"Where's my...what are you doin'?" Josie exclaimed. "Put the gun down."

"Just watchin' the enemy, dear. Nothin' to worry 'bout."

This wasn't the first time she'd seen him idly wave his gun, especially when he was drinking, so she wasn't overly concerned. "What'd you do with my pendant?"

"Your what?"

"My pendant!"

"I dunno," Steve slurred. "Ask Heidi. She came by this mornin'. Brought me my beer."

"Of course she did," Josie snarled while looking at nearly twenty crushed cans.

The surround sound speakers suddenly filled the room with exploding bombs and gunfire as the documentary's narrator said, "The Waffen SS Charlemagne Division implemented the political will of Hitler by rounding up civilians with ruthless precision and defending der Fuhrer's bunker when the end came in April of 1945. Named after the medieval emperor who ruled over the First Reich in the eighth and ninth centuries, the Charlemagne Division destroyed Red Army tanks at a rate unmatched by any other division."

Steve was riveted to the action on the screen, and his pistol continued to track running soldiers.

Josie looked at her box of cherished items with the most important one missing. Then she gazed at Steve. She watched him idiotically point his gun at the television as if it were a video game and realized that he didn't take her pendant. He would have had no idea what it was or how valuable it was. In fact, he didn't even know it existed. As she observed him, she realized that he never looked more stupid than he did at that moment.

"Put the gun away," she ordered.

Rather than do as instructed, Steve squeezed the trigger. An explosion detonated in the pistol and sent a bullet hurling out of the barrel with sparks streaking behind it. The projectile shattered the television and sailed through the wall.

Josie screamed. Steve stared dumbstruck at his destruction and dropped the hand which held the gun onto his lap.

"You moron!" Josie exclaimed. "You complete freakin' moron!"

Steve turned slowly to Josie. "I hate Nazis."

Josie trembled with rage and a fair amount of fear. She looked back and forth between the destroyed television and her inebriated boyfriend. Her gaze settled on the gun sitting on his lap and pointing at her. "You're a total asshole," she declared and charged out of the apartment, slamming the door behind her.

Steve's eyes drifted back to the shattered television.

The front door opened enough for Josie's arm to reach back in, snag keys from a hook, grab her sneakers, and disappear again. Once more, she slammed the door.

***

Josie clutched the steering wheel of Steve's dented, twenty-year-old pick-up with the intensity of an Indy 500 driver. She still wore her work uniform, an ugly plaid skirt and olive green t-shirt with rolled up sleeves. Her decorated shoe box sat on the seat beside her, and the void left by its missing item fueled her rage. She told herself she wouldn't go to Gretchen's until she found her stolen treasure.

Businesses on each side of the road came to life to greet the night while others locked their doors to surrender the day. Josie's eyes focused on the pink and purple neon lights of The Pussycat Pavilion, which blazed ahead of her. She steered the truck into the lot outside the establishment and thrust the gear column into park.

Josie entered the club which seemed to be part carnival side show, part sex shop, and a complete testament to the male libido. She took her place in line behind a middle-aged man and a girl who was barely old enough to drink. In any other setting, they would have appeared to be father and daughter.

"Enjoy your visit," said a massive bouncer to the couple.

"What's up, Vince?" Josie asked coldly. "Is Heidi here?"

"Heidi?" he replied with a chuckle. "Yes. Your mother is in her dressing room."

Josie brushed past him.

"Be a good girl," the bouncer instructed. "I'd hate to haul you outta here again."

Josie didn't look back as she entered a neon-lit room which had plenty of shaded recesses for patrons and performers to mingle in relative privacy. Rap music with lyrics that overtly demanded sex filled the ears of all who occupied the premises. The main stage was marked by a shiny, over-sized silver pole. The principal performer for that song was a girl with an hour glass figure and breasts too large for most brassieres. To the right of the main stage, a lingerie-wearing bartender dispensed beverages from a neon station. Josie felt fingertips touch the back of her neck and gently glide down her side. "Hi, sweetie," a light-skinned African-American woman cooed. "Are you looking for someone special?"

"My mother," Josie answered irritably.

"Oh?" The woman's interest piqued. "Do you and your mother like chocolate?"

Josie looked at the woman with an expression that bore a hundred negative responses, but she said nothing and walked off. She scrambled past Walt Kennedy, the middle-aged owner of the club. He was known to personally test all the merchandise in his business and tried on numerous occasions to add Josie to his list of accomplishments.

Memories passed through Josie's mind as she entered the employees-only area. She had spent her adolescence in this environment. She remembered the dancers who watched over her while her mother worked—women who had since gone on to early graves, sugar-daddy marriages, and the few who found more legitimate professions. She grew up with the drugs, the fake people, the selling of favors, and an abundance of pretended affections. It was a terrible place for a young girl to spend her youth, and it was a career choice Josie was determined to avoid, even if it meant serving grub to people who tipped her with pocket change.

Josie found her mother's dressing room at the end of a corridor, marked by a sign that read "Heidi Seek". She threw the door open, and Heidi Jackson (her real name) looked up, not even slightly startled. She was in the process of sliding a fishnet stocking up her tanned, muscular leg, and she was naked from the waist up.

"Josie, what are you doin' here?" asked Heidi.

Josie closed the door and stared at her mother's freshly painted face. "I heard you stopped by my apartment today."

"I brought you groceries. I figured you wouldn't have time to shop this week."

"Really?" Josie asked. "That's all?"

"Yeah."

"You didn't come for any other reason?"

Heidi stood. "Josie Ersman, are you calling me a liar?"

From down the hall, they heard a bouncer say, "Five minutes, Heidi."

"Where's my pendant?" Josie demanded.

"What?"

"I know you took it."

"What pendant are you talking about?" Heidi asked. "*The* pendant?"

"I don't have any other pendants," Josie said coldly.

"Well, I don't have it," Heidi replied and resumed her stage preparations. "Maybe Steve…"

"Where is it?"

Heidi took a deep breath and made a deliberate, audible exhale. When she spoke, the tone she employed was one which befitted a martyr. "Okay. You know Chuck left us two weeks ago. I've got six kids to feed, clothe, and take to the doctors. And the tips aren't coming in like usual. No one's spending money now."

Josie narrowed her gaze upon her mother. "You sold it?"

"I took it to the pawn shop," Heidi confessed. "I'm sorry, but Cheyenne needs braces, Alexis needs medicine, David broke his thumb, and I'm short with the mortgage again."

"You pawned the only thing my father left me?" Josie shouted. "The only thing I have worth anything?"

"You didn't even know him."

"I can't believe you did that!" Josie exclaimed. "Go get it!"

Hypnotic, almost psychedelic music grew in volume to dissipate through the stage area and course through the entire building. The disc jockey announced, "Coming from Eastern stages with skills first practiced in ancient harems, please turn your attention to the main stage and Tucson's premier performer, Miss Heidi Seek."

Heidi added a black lace bra and a furry tail to her costume. "It's gone," she said.

"When did you pawn it?"

"I didn't pawn it. I sold it to the pawn shop before work," Heidi revealed. "But I felt bad and went back during my break. The owner said he already sold it."

"And why wouldn't he?" Josie asked. "It was priceless."

With the musical cue ending, the disc jockey repeated, "Miss Heidi Seek."

Heidi's facial expressions became sultry. Josie watched as she transformed into Heidi Seek, entertainer. When she spoke again, every word came out as a seduction.

"You look tired, honey. Go home and get some sleep. I promise I'll make it up to you." With that, the performer walked out the door and disappeared down the hall.

Josie heard the familiar sounds of applause and cat calls. The music became less psychedelic and more exotic. The seduction was underway. The show had begun.

Josie simmered with rage, like a tea kettle about to scream on a red-hot burner. Her mother sold the only possession she truly valued. It was the sole link to her father, a man she knew only through infrequent letters she received from her grandfather in Germany. It was irreplaceable.

Josie's thoughts turned to retribution. She considered destroying anything of her mother's she could find. Then it occurred to her: payback, literally. She scoured the room for the box she knew her mother kept hidden. It was a shoe box, similar to her own, and it was where Heidi kept her tips. Would it also include the cash she got from the sale of the pendant? Josie moved aside piles of costumes and sexy accessories. Sure enough, there it was. She lifted the lid and found it overflowing with bills.

"Slow tips, my ass!" She grabbed the money and fled the room. Left behind her was the box Heidi had painstakingly decorated with photos of her children. It was empty, overturned, and lying in a pile of sexually suggestive clothing.

***

Josie climbed into the pick-up and stuffed the money into her shoe-box. She didn't bother to count it, but it was a lot of cash. Was her mother telling her the truth? Josie started to feel guilty about taking the money. If it was really meant for the family…oh, what was she thinking? Her mother lied for a living, and she always lied to Josie. Even if it was intended for the family, what did it matter? Josie despised her family, if that's what it could be called. It was really a motley assortment of half-

13

siblings. Heidi Jackson (her most recent last name) had given birth to seven children, five of whom had different fathers. Josie felt no familial bond with any of them. In fact, that's why she moved out when she was seventeen. No, she decided. It was her money, and she was going to use it to buy back her pendant.

As she started up the truck, the driver's side door flew open. Two arms grabbed Josie, jerked her out of the truck and threw her onto the hard packed dirt and gravel. Todd Skinner, a stocky, red-headed redneck, stood over her while Steve swayed behind him.

"Todd…" Josie began.

Steve cut her off. "You left me to 'splain everything to the cops!"

Josie tried to stand, but Todd pushed her back to a sitting position. "Ow, prick!" Josie exclaimed. "Does it make you feel tough to beat up on a girl?"

"He's got a lot to say, and you ain't leavin' 'til he says it," declared Todd.

Josie leaned back and stretched her legs out in the dirt. "Go ahead. I'm all ears."

"All you do is bitch at me," Steve slurred. "Been callin' me lazy for the past three months. You don't know how tough it is to be outta work."

"It sounds tough," she replied. "Especially when you have to walk all the way to the kitchen to get a cold beer."

"The cops coulda run me in tonight," added Steve. "Then they woulda seen my record and I'd never see the light a day, what with my past in the Caroli Syndicate."

"Good thing my cousin's a lawyer and smoothed things out," said Todd.

Josie had heard enough. She grabbed gravel with each hand, prepared to use it if Todd tried to push her down again. But Todd didn't interfere as she rose to her feet. "First of all, your cousin isn't a lawyer," she told Todd. "He's a jackass who defended himself in court."

"He won."

"That doesn't make him a lawyer." Addressing Steve, she said, "And you've got as many mob connections as I do, and I don't know anybody."

"That's where you're wrong," replied Steve.

"You're pathetic," Josie said. "Pathetic. And I don't wanna have anything to do with your sorry ass anymore. I'm over it. I'm over you!"

She brushed past both men.

"Oh, no. It ain't that simple," Steve declared. "Todd…"

Todd grabbed for Josie, but she threw the gravel in his face. He stumbled back. Steve scrambled after her, but tripped over his own intoxication.

Josie ran to the idling pickup, climbed in, slammed the door, shifted gears, and floored the gas pedal. The truck's rear end fishtailed. Todd jerked Steve out of the way as the soaring back bumper missed his head by less than a foot. The truck's tires sprayed gravel and dirt over the two men.

"She damn near killed me!" Steve exclaimed.

"Get in the car," Todd ordered.

Josie looked back and saw them climb into an old red Camaro. "What the hell am I doing?" she asked herself, but she didn't have time to answer. The Camaro spit smoke and spun its tires. The chase was on, whether Josie wanted it to be or not. She kept the gas pedal pressed to the floor and jerked the steering wheel hard to the left. Her shoebox sailed off the seat and scattered its contents over the passenger side floor. Newly arriving patrons cursed and leaped out of the way as Josie sped between two parked cars.

"Get the bitch," Steve commanded. "This'll be a night she ain't never gonna forget!"

Todd didn't respond, but squeezed the steering wheel, kept his gaze fixed on Josie's taillights, and buried the gas pedal.

The two vehicles chased each other around the building, pelting cars and people with soaring gravel. Josie yelled for people to get out of the way, though no one could hear her over the roaring engines and spinning tires. The bouncer named Vince pulled a couple into the safety of the building and glared angrily at the vehicles as they raced by.

Adrenaline coursed through Josie's veins as she sped across the parking lot. Todd rammed the pick-up with his much smaller Camaro. The impact crushed his grill, put out a headlight and folded the front part of his hood like an accordion.

Josie searched desperately for a safe place to go. To her relief, the road opened up before her. She set it as a target and pushed the truck for all it was worth. A sports car suddenly backed out in front of her. She swerved to the right and barely missed it. She swerved back and the truck teetered.

With his eyes fixed on Josie's vehicle and anger over his damaged car boiling within him, Todd asked, "You got your gun?"

"I ain't gonna kill her," Steve replied.

"Guns can do more'n kill."

Steve considered his friend's statement and replied, "I didn't bring it. Go in front of her. Bet'cha can cut her off."

Josie saw in her side-view mirror that Todd was making his move. His car had a powerful engine and would pass her shortly. She realized that they were going to force her into a wall or a parked vehicle, anything to stop her. If she was ever going to make the road, now was the time. Color drained from her face and knuckles as she clutched the steering wheel. She leaned forward, willing the truck to move as if she and it were one organism. She was ten yards from the road...five...three...the sleek black front of a Tucson police car appeared before her! Josie jerked the steering wheel hard to the left. The side of her truck clipped the cop car, but sped past it and leaped onto the road.

"Look out!" Steve yelled, but his warning was too late. Todd's Camaro crashed head first into the driver's side of the police car. The sounds of crunching metal, crushing engines and shattering glass filled the night. Airbags exploded from the front of the Camaro and the front and side of the cop car.

Josie raced down the road, checking her mirrors repeatedly, but saw nothing because of the angle of her retreat. She finally moved her side mirror and saw the destroyed vehicles and the police car's red and blue flashing lights. She heard sirens and saw other police race to the scene as a crowd began to gather.

Josie continued driving. Her heart raced, but she had the presence of mind to slow the truck down to a normal rate of speed. The more distance she put between herself and her pursuers, the less her body shook from the adrenaline which coursed within her. Five miles from the crash site, she felt in control enough to pull to the side of the road. "Okay, okay," she told herself. "Get a grip." She took deep breaths and looked around. There was desert on each side of the road and few vehicles. She appeared to be in the clear. "Think, Josie. Think."

Ten seconds later, she pounded the dashboard with both fists. "What the hell! What...the...hell!" Her eyes darted about the cab of the truck. Then she let her head fall to the steering wheel. "Holy shit. What am I gonna do now? If they survived that crash, I'm dead." She rolled her head back and forth. In the glow of the moon, she saw her overturned shoebox. Trinkets, photos, a passport, and money lay about the passenger side floor. "And I'm a thief," she added. She sat back, her shoulders hunched with the weight of her predicament. "Where can I go?"

As if in answer to her question, sirens screamed from the distance. Josie looked in her mirror and saw flashing blue and red lights growing larger and brighter with each passing second. Adrenalized once again, she looked over her shoulder and saw that they were coming for her. No doubt about it. She shifted into drive and hit the gas pedal.

One tire squealed on pavement and another spun in gravel. Josie's pick-up streaked down the road. Now what were her options? She knew she couldn't outrun the police. She couldn't hide either. The road was a straight shot, but for one turn-off that she was quickly approaching. Surrendering didn't seem to be a viable solution because she had undoubtedly racked up a laundry list of offenses throughout the course of the evening. No matter how she looked at it, she was plain and simply screwed…then, like a beacon summoning the lost and lonely to safe shores, an illuminated sign told travelers that Tucson International Airport was one mile ahead on the right. Josie glanced again at the money and passport hiding in shadows on the truck's floor. She looked in the mirror to see that the flashing lights were approaching, but the police were still too far away to spot her. The airport was her only chance. Did she dare to hop a flight? Where would she go? She thought about the only place she had ever really wanted to visit, and nodded, as if to reassure herself. One last time, she forced the truck to flee with every ounce of speed it could muster.

GUY COTÉ

CHAPTER TWO

Josie passed the majority of her flight to London's Gatwick Airport by alternating between much needed sleep and contemplation of her current situation. She had a layover in the busy English hub that lasted almost two hours. In that time, she bought a sweatshirt and jeans to replace her uniform, ate fish and chips, and browsed the shops. Leaving Tucson was a new experience, and she was enjoying it…so far.

She sat on a second plane bound for Germany with thoughts of what might await her running through her mind. Her grandfather had asked her to visit him in Cologne numerous times, but she never did. There was always some reason not to, some excuse. When she was a child, it was because her mother wouldn't permit her. When she was older, money and her busy social life became the obstacles. Then there was Steve, and he had always opposed such a trip. But now she was free, and determined to leave the shackles of her past behind. Surprisingly, she wasn't conflicted over her break-up with Steve. Her most dominant feeling was a sense of relief. The guy had been fun, a whirlwind to help her transition from living under her mother's roof to being on her own. But the thrill passed and she grew while he devolved, if it's possible for a human being to do such a thing. Truth be told, she was looking for a reason to end it. Oddly enough, the same could be said of her relationship with her family. She'd been leaving them for years, especially her mother. The sale—correction, the theft—of her pendant gave her an excuse to make the final break. She would not regret expelling them from her life, of that she was sure. The only thing she would truly miss was her pendant. It was about an inch and a half in diameter and featured two splinters of wood shaped like a cross. The wood was encased in blue glass. A lace of gold and silver enclosed the glass and bore emeralds and rubies of various shapes. She called it a

19

pendant, but it was actually a talisman. It had fascinated her since she first beheld it. "This was your dad's," her mother told her. From that point forward, it became her only connection to a man she wished she had known.

The plane touched down without incident and pulled Josie from her thoughts. It taxied to its terminal. Josie remained in her seat as other travelers prepared to disembark. Her only piece of luggage was a plastic bag that held her passport and dead cell phone. She thought again about her peculiar predicament. She had run away from everything she knew on an angry whim, with money stolen from her mother. She'd been out of the United States only once before when Heidi took the family on a working vacation to Tahiti five years earlier. Now she was in Germany, and she had no idea what to expect. But she knew one thing for certain: she couldn't go back to her life in Tucson, not after what her mother had done, not after what happened with Steve.

Wearing a confident expression while walking through the airport of Cologne, Germany, she tried to keep pace with hustling people. Signs were in German and no one spoke English. The airport was not large by international standards, but the glass and iron of its construction made it intimidating to a novice traveler.

"Josie," said a voice with a German accent.

She turned to see Konrad, a tall but slouching man with thick gray hair. Wrinkles marked his face and he could do with a tan, but to Josie, he was a pleasant sight.

"Hi, Grandpa," she said, trying to hide how relieved she was to see him.

The old man didn't know how he should welcome her. They'd never met before, and the last picture he'd seen of her was when she was seven years old. As a result, their greeting became an awkward hybrid of a hug and a hand shake.

"Aye...uh...you look like Michael," Konrad said. "That is how I knew you. And with this." He handed her the photo he was carrying.

"Huh. I remember sending that," Josie said. "I can't believe you still have it."

"I keep all things you send."

I wish I still had everything, she said to herself.

***

The ride from the airport to Konrad's house was largely spent in silence. The newly acquainted grandfather and granddaughter had no

20

idea how to break the ice. By the time Konrad parked the Volkswagen in his driveway, they'd been together for nearly an hour and learned nothing new about each other.

"Where are your clothes bags?" Konrad asked as they got out of the car and walked toward the front door of the house. "Did the airplane lose them?"

"I didn't pack anything."

Konrad waited for her to say more, but she didn't. He unlocked the door and guided her into the house like a gentleman.

Josie was struck by the simplicity of his clutter-free home. There was a television, a couch, a recliner, and a bookcase with framed photos on it. A painting hung directly above the case, which depicted a man and a boy playing soccer. A six-year-old tabby cat trotted out from the dining room.

"Franzie," Konrad said with obvious joy. He reached for the cat, but it had already moved to inspect Josie. "I hope you are not allergenic" he told her.

"Allergenic?" she repeated with a chuckle at his misuse of English. "Uh, no."

"Well...be comfortable," he instructed. "It was a long journey from America. Did you eat enough?"

"A little at the airport, but...yeah, I'm hungry."

"I can prepare blutwurst and sauerkraut," he told her.

She nodded and let her eyes wander about the room. The man and boy painting caught her attention first. Who were those people, she wondered. Were they her grandfather and her father? She imagined them laughing and playing. It was a youth she never had. She looked at the framed photos displayed on the bookcase. The most prominent picture was of a boy in a school uniform who looked like she did when she was younger. It was obviously her father.

"Your meal is cooked," her grandfather announced.

Josie made a move toward the kitchen but stopped when she saw a photo of her grandfather shaking hands with President Bill Clinton. In another picture, he stood beside the Pope. Not the current pontiff, but the most famous one: John Paul II.

She entered the kitchen while wondering about the photographs. Did her grandfather Photoshop himself into pictures of famous people? He didn't seem the type to do that. Was he an entourage guy, someone who follows celebrities? That didn't make much sense either. She decided that he must be famous. That was a better explanation. She took her seat with a new-found appreciation of the man serving her meal, but the food itself didn't seem too appetizing. It looked to be boiled lettuce and sausage. She cut into the meat and asked, "Are you famous?"

She took a bite of sausage and tasted a strange, metallic flavor. Konrad was wondering how to answer her question, when she added, "What am I eating?"

"It is my favorite," he replied. "Blutwurst...blood sausage."

"Blood? This is blood?" she asked. "Gross."

"Gross? What do you mean?" Konrad inquired.

Josie set her fork down and said, "I'm not hungry."

***

It was late morning and Konrad stood beside Josie at the train station. In the two days they'd been together, they had made little headway in their communication. They took a stroll, went out to eat several times (as Josie didn't care for his cooking), and visited the mall where he bought her clothes. The latter experience was one he had no desire to repeat, as he found it unpleasant and expensive. But it was not Josie that made him shuffle uncomfortably on the train platform. It was the person they were waiting for, the one individual he thought could help him relate to his granddaughter—Henrietta Adelade, his ex-wife.

As Josie watched trains come and go and men in uniform herd people like cattle, she wondered why her grandfather had taken her there. Her question was answered when Konrad gave a spry seventy-three year old woman an awkward hug and greeting in German. The woman turned to Josie and spoke with a French accent. "You are Josie?"

Josie nodded. The woman set her bags down and grabbed her by the shoulders. "*Ah oui* (Ah yes)," she said. "You very much resemble my Michael."

"She is Henrietta, your grandmother," Konrad explained.

"You are *très*...you are a beautiful girl," Henrietta said. "Why are you here?"

"Uh...I...uh...I wanted to meet my family."

"Alone?" Henrietta asked. "At eighteen years of age?"

"I'm twenty-one," Josie corrected.

The older woman eyed her granddaughter with a scrutiny that Josie found uncomfortable. She liked her grandfather's more casual approach better.

"Well," Konrad interjected. "I am no admirer of this depot. I thought we might play tourist for the day. Would that be agreeable?"

***

The murky Rhine River reflected lavender back to the sky from which it originated. As the sun yielded to the night, Josie stood beside Henrietta on the upper deck of a two-story ship. They watched a three-piece band play an upbeat tune as passengers mingled and chatted. Konrad made his way through the crowd to join his granddaughter and ex-wife.

"I cannot believe our luck," he said. "Tonight is the rehearsal for the Kölner Lichter, the firecracker spectacle and boat parade."

"The Kölner Lichter is in July," Henrietta replied.

"Yes, of course," answered Konrad. "But they prepare for it months before."

"They're gonna shoot fireworks?" asked Josie. "Like the Fourth of July?"

"Oh, it is much more than that," Konrad replied enthusiastically.

The boat pulled away from shore, and Josie saw for the first time that land on each side of the Rhine was ablaze with sparklers and multi-colored lights. Other vessels, both large and small, contributed their own music and revelry to turn the river into a festival.

"I admit," said Henrietta. "I have wanted to see this celebration since it began."

Konrad nodded. "You moved two years before the first festival."

"You live in France?" Josie asked.

"*Mais oui*," Henrietta replied. "I live in Chartres near the Great Cathedral."

"Why do you live there?"

Henrietta and Konrad exchanged glances. "Uh...we separated..." Konrad began.

"The year I was born," Josie interrupted. "I remember. You told me in a letter."

"Yes, well...did you not know that I was born in France?" Henrietta asked.

"I met her there," Konrad added. "After the war. I was twelve years old."

"You've known each other since you were twelve?"

"Yes," answered Konrad.

"I was eleven years of age," said Henrietta.

"Is that when you started dating?" Josie asked.

"No," Henrietta laughed.

"In my mind, we dated," Konrad corrected.

"For eight years, he wrote me," explained Henrietta. "Then we married."

It was clear that they still had affection for one another, and Josie couldn't imagine why they would have divorced. A new aroma promptly pulled her mind from her thoughts.

"Oh, I forget how wonderful that smells," said Henrietta.

"What is it?" Josie asked.

"*Schokolade*," answered Konrad. "Chocolate from the world famous Imhoff-Stollwerck Factory and Museum."

On shore, the factory sat on a concrete structure that resembled a post-modern ship. It was attached to a tower that looked like it had come from a medieval castle. Josie saw men release fireworks from the tower, and they burst in a blossoming bouquet that brought flashes of red, green, and white to the darkening sky.

Five acoustic irradiation towers suddenly shot music and beams of colorful light over the river. Structures on the other side of the Rhine did the same. The effect was a music and light spectacular that could rival any rock concert.

"In the July show, this begins at eleven thirty," Konrad revealed.

Henrietta was mesmerized.

"This is amazing," Josie said. Every beat of music coursed through her body, and she looked at the entranced faces of her grandparents as they moved closer to one another. For the first time in...well, for the first time ever, she felt like she was celebrating a holiday with loved ones, the way normal families did. A warm flush washed over her, and her eyes became clouded by a sentimental fog.

"And this is only the rehearsal," Konrad enthusiastically declared.

The fireworks ended in an orgy of colors, sparkles, pops, cracks, and explosions. Observers from every apparent direction cheered in unison. The music faded and the lights dimmed as the performance came to an end, but the revelry continued. Ships, which were scattered about the river, pitted their on-board musicians against one another. Passengers danced and sang. It seemed that the entire Rhine was in on the festivities.

Josie watched the celebration. It was better than any block party she'd ever seen. The night seemed to be perfect.

"Oh no! No!" Konrad shouted.

Josie and Henrietta looked at him in alarm. They saw that he was gazing at the shore where drunken people climbed an equestrian statue. One man stood by the horse's right leg and mooned boats on the river. Josie laughed.

"Call the police," Konrad ordered Henrietta.

"I am not..."

"Oh, thank the Lord," Konrad said as he heard police whistles and much shouting coming from the statue's vicinity.

He, Josie, and Henrietta watched as officers descended upon the offenders as if they were hardened criminals. The police had the statue cleared within minutes.

"They cannot be allowed to disrespect the Kaiser's monument," Konrad declared.

Josie looked at the statue again. It would normally have been hidden by the dark of night, but police lights and those of countless revelers made it visible. The figure was of a military man on a horse. The animal's left front leg was raised.

"Do you know who Kaiser Wilhelm the Second was?" Konrad asked Josie.

"No."

"*Et*...and she does not need to," Henrietta interjected.

Ignoring his ex-wife, Konrad said, "He is one of our greatest heroes. You are familiar with the Third Reich?"

"She should not hear these notions," insisted Henrietta.

"A Reich is an empire," Konrad continued. "A German empire. Kaiser Wilhelm led the Second Reich. See, his horse's left leg is raised in a gesture of superiority."

> 1) Henrietta knew that Konrad was not merely giving a history lesson. She lost one child to that mistaken ideology and she'd be damned if she'd lose another. "Enough," she said. Switching to French, she added, "*Vous ne ferez pas circuler ces idées tordues. Pas encore* (You shall not pass on these twisted ideas. Not again)!"

Konrad defended himself in the same language, and their exchange erupted into an argument. Josie watched her grandparents lash at one another with words she couldn't understand. Any notion she had that they were a good match evaporated with their bickering. She wondered if her father had been raised in such an environment.

Their dispute lasted the remainder of the cruise. By the time the ship docked, Konrad and Henrietta could barely stand to be in the presence of one another.

When they set foot on land, Henrietta pulled Josie aside and announced that she wouldn't be continuing her visit. She added, "You must come with me to Chartres."

"I don't want to go to France," Josie replied.

"Then you must go back to America," said Henrietta. "You do not belong here."

"I was invited," Josie answered defensively.

"Who invited you?"

"Grandpa," replied Josie. "He wrote me letters."

"Your grandfather has bizarre friends and dangerous ideas," Henrietta confided. "I thought he had let them go, but...his world is not right for a naïve girl."

Naïve? That simple word turned their conversation from merely uncomfortable to outright insulting. Josie pulled away from the woman.

Henrietta implored, "Please. What I say, I say from experience. I gave this advice to your father many years ago. And now he is dead."

"My father died in a car crash," Josie snapped.

"I am not convinced of that," replied Henrietta.

CHAPTER THREE

As Konrad's Volkswagen pulled into the cemetery, Josie felt flush. This was her first visit to a graveyard, and she almost regretted having asked her grandfather to take her there. She told herself to relax. She was merely going to see a stone. But there were so many to choose from: angels, crosses, statues of Mary and Jesus. She and Konrad navigated between markers to find a white slab that stood as high as Josie's knee. The words *Michael Ersman* were engraved on the marble, along with some German text and the dates of his birth and death. Wasn't there anything else to memorialize him?

"What does it say?" she asked.

"It says 'beloved son, friend and patriot,'" Konrad translated.

"Is that all?" she asked.

"Yes."

"Not father?"

"You were not known to us, or him, at the time of his passing," Konrad explained. "We could have the word added if you would prefer."

She shook her head. "Tell me how he died."

***

Josie's mind wandered back in time as the Volkswagen carried her forward. The story Konrad related about her father's demise was the same one she heard from her mother. As the story went, Michael was driving his Jeep over a mountain pass in Colorado. It was the dead of winter, and the snow was deep. They found him at the bottom of a ravine, in a smashed up vehicle, with a broken neck. By all appearances, he died instantly. There was nothing suspicious about it. Why did her grandmother have doubts? Her grandfather didn't. Neither did her mother, who was dating him at the time.

Josie imagined what her life would have been like if her father hadn't died. Her mother might have become a stay-at-home mom or had a respectable career. Her father would have been an important man, maybe a city leader. She wouldn't have had all those annoying half or step-siblings. It would have been an ideal life. But it was not to be. She looked at her grandfather and realized that he was the only family member she was willing to acknowledge.

"Thanks for taking me in," she said.

Konrad smiled. She was running from something, and he thought it would be best to let her reveal it to him at her own pace. As he pulled into his driveway, he had the sense that something else was wrong, something in the neighborhood. The sidewalks were empty, and he didn't recognize any of the vehicles he saw. When he and Josie climbed out of the car, a policeman approached them. Others followed, and Josie watched the officers pepper her grandfather with questions.

"Grandpa?" she asked.

"They are confused," Konrad told her.

An officer spun Konrad around and slammed him against the car. Other policemen pulled their weapons and shouted at Josie in German.

***

The plastic straps securing Josie's wrists grew tighter the more she tried to get out of them. She sat at a metal table in an interrogation room. A female officer with a stocky build faced her, along with a thin male interpreter who said, "You are a thief. No?"

"What? No."

The policewoman checked her notes and spoke. The translator replied, "You are on record in America, Tucson in Arizona. You stole four thousand five hundred and twenty-six dollars from a Steven Cousins."

"Steve?" Josie nearly sprang from her chair. "I didn't take it from him."

The female cop spoke again, and the translator said, "But you admit that you took it? And then you came here to Köln? Why Köln?"

Josie realized that her mother and Steve were conspiring. She could only imagine how that arrangement came to be. "Aren't I supposed to get a lawyer?" she asked.

The interpreter told the officer what she said. The policewoman responded angrily and he translated, "You are a foreigner and a thief. You do not get a lawyer. Now tell us why you are here."

A door slammed somewhere outside the room, and Josie jumped in her seat. "I...uh...I came here to visit my grandfather."

After interpretation, the officer spoke again. The translator said, "You brought stolen money to your grandfather? Was he your accomplice?"

"I didn't steal it," Josie insisted.

Her words were resaid in German, and the reply was, "But you have the money?"

Josie came to the understanding that silence might be her best option. More questions followed, but she didn't respond.

The interpreter finally said, "If you insist on telling us nothing, then a night in General Population might change your mind."

The policewoman grabbed Josie by the arms and jerked her from her seat.

***

Josie entered General Population wearing the same light blue uniform as everyone else. She could feel her heart racing but tried to appear calm. The door slammed and locked behind her. She found herself in a large room painted white with four rectangular windows along the top of one wall. Her cell mates were female and ranged from junkies and prostitutes to middle-aged thieves and juvenile pickpockets.

"Keep cool," Josie whispered to herself. "Keep it together."

Despite such words of encouragement, her mouth went dry and her hands shook. She backed against a wall and prayed for anonymity. Unfortunately, the ability to go unnoticed was not something she possessed. Two husky, tattooed girls in their twenties approached her. The first girl came close enough for Josie to see pierced holes covering the length of each ear and several on her lips, nose, and eyebrows. The jewelry to accompany those holes had been taken by the police. She spoke German, and Josie had no idea what she said. Because she didn't reply to the first girl, the second smacked her across the face. The blow shocked and stung Josie, bringing water to her eyes.

Instinct took over, and Josie struck her attacker with a smack as forceful as the one she received. The first girl hurled punches and cuffs in retaliation. Her partner joined in, and Josie fell to the floor with blows coming at her from every angle. The cell erupted with yelling, scrambling women. The two girls kicked, and each strike sent pain reeling through Josie's body. She deflected one blow from her throat, but it belted her face and sent flashes of light across her field of vision. High-pitched whistles overwhelmed the sounds of excited prisoners. An army of officers swarmed into the cell and hauled the husky girls back. Bloody and in pain, Josie curled up in the fetal position.

***

It took Josie several hours to realize that solitary confinement was meant to be a punishment. To her, it was an initial relief. She was free of her attackers and other potential assailants, and she was alone with her thoughts. But the passage of time on a concrete floor in total darkness gradually wore on her. She heard a nonstop concert of yelling people and slamming doors. Her body ached, and she knew her face was swelling. As she considered her situation, she asked herself why she decided to come to Germany. Of all the places in the world, why that country? Did she want to meet her grandfather or her grandmother? Was it to see her dad's grave? Maybe it was a combination of all three. Perhaps it was none at all. The only thing she knew for certain was that she was in a lot of trouble, and she had no one to help her. She began to worry that she would be left in a dark cell forever.

***

By the time the door finally opened, Josie had been alone, in pitch black, without food, water, or medical care for eighteen hours. The light which flooded into the cell burned her eyes and caused her brain to ache. She heard a familiar voice with a German accent say, "Come, Josie. We can go. This was a mistake."

She peeled her hands away from her eyes and saw her grandfather. He was tall, a towering figure, and he was reaching for her.

***

After careful inspection, the prison doctor determined that Josie was merely bruised and scraped. He gave her ointments and provided her with a warm shower. She drank juice and devoured a hearty breakfast. To her surprise, she was also treated kindly. Dressed again in civilian clothes, she followed her grandfather into the main area of the police station where she was met by more pleasant people.

"What's wrong with them?" she whispered. But Konrad didn't hear her.

She looked around the station and saw a host of friendly faces. It was as if every officer had been reprogrammed to forget the past twenty hours and treat Konrad and Josie as if they were visiting dignitaries. The policewoman who sent Josie to General Population the day before stumbled up to her.

"I…uh, I say sorry you," she stammered in heavily accented German. "Okay?"

"Um…okay," Josie answered.

Relieved, the woman glanced at a glass-encased office and scurried away. Josie followed the officer's eyes and momentarily lost her breath. Walking out of the office, in her direction, was a man who was at least six feet tall with an athletic build, dark hair, dark eyes, and tanned skin. He was dressed in a charcoal-gray tailor-made suit and looked to be in his late twenties. He was, without a doubt, the most handsome man she had ever seen. Was he an illusion created by the maddening hours she spent in solitary? Before she could answer that question, he stopped before her and flashed a perfect smile.

"Josie," he said with a British accent. "It's so nice to meet you." He took her hand between both of his and added, "I'm Derek Schroeder. Shall we go?"

Josie was speechless. She felt flustered and looked at Konrad, who smiled. Her eyes returned to Derek. It seemed impossible for her to even look away from him.

Just outside the police station, a finely-polished black Bentley waited for its passengers. Derek opened the back door for Josie, but she stopped before entering.

"Who is he?" she whispered to her grandfather.

"He is my boss," Konrad replied.

A cab pulled into the back of the parking lot. Henrietta climbed out. She handed the driver money, then saw her granddaughter and ex-husband get into the Bentley. She looked back at the police who watched but did nothing about the departing former prisoners. An expression of stunned surprise fixed itself upon her face.

***

It was a comfortable, spring day as a Mercedes bus stopped outside the marketplace of Aachen. The westernmost city of Germany, Aachen neighbored both Belgium and the Netherlands. It boasted a population of more than two hundred and fifty thousand people and an area of over sixty-one square miles. It was a medieval city and a modern urban center.

Josie and Konrad followed the flow of people exiting the bus. Most of the travelers were students who listened to iPods and carried backpacks. They said farewell to one another by raising their fists with their pinkie fingers extended.

31

"Why do they do this?" Josie asked while raising her own fist and pinkie.

"Aachen is a city unlike any other in the world," Konrad replied.

That didn't answer her question, but Josie had something else on her mind. She was tortured by a powerful cramp in her lower abdomen, though her period wasn't due for quite a while. Her legs also ached with a gnawing pain. She wondered if she was feeling residual effects from her prison beating but decided to ignore the discomfort and follow her grandfather into the market area. Triangular in shape, the market was bordered by cobblestone streets where buses and bikes outnumbered cars. Umbrellas and food stands filled the area, and people milled about to haggle prices with vendors. A fountain with a statue at its peak stood at the end of the market. A massive, Gothic building towered behind it.

"Charlemagne," Konrad said as he gazed up at the statue.

"What?"

"Charles the Great, Charlemagne," he repeated. "The first Holy Roman Emperor. He is the father of this city, The Father of Europe."

He directed Josie to look at the statue. It was a bronze likeness of a standing man. He wore knee-high boots, leggings, and a short cloak with a sword hanging from his waist. He had a beard and wore a crown with a cross upon it. His hands held an orb and scepter. He appeared nothing like what Josie imagined royalty to look like.

"He was a Roman emperor?" she asked.

"Not exactly," answered Konrad. "He was Germanic, but he was crowned by the Pope in Rome to be the Defender of the Christian Faith, God's Holy Roman Emperor. He created the First Reich. Do you remember what a Reich is?"

"It's a...uh...empire or something."

"Yes. A German Empire," he replied. "This city was his capital. We are standing where the King's Hall once was, his Aula Reglia."

Looking around, Josie said, "It must have been a big place."

"It was said to have been greater than the Vatican itself," he answered. "Shall I show you the Rathaus?"

"The what?" she asked.

"City Hall," he answered. "Where The Agency...uh, the company I work for, is located."

Josie tried to ignore her cramps and hoped that she could walk out the ache in her legs. She gazed at the Gothic style Rathaus in front of her. It was charcoal gray with two grand towers on its east and west ends. She followed Konrad up two exterior flights of stairs and saw that statues of kings were affixed in pairs to the side of the building. A bronze door at the top of the stairs welcomed visitors by standing in an opened position. She and Konrad joined a dozen tourists as they entered the ancient Rathaus.

Expecting to find an interior as impressive as the exterior, Josie was slightly disappointed when she walked into the City Hall's foyer. It was large, but aside from vaulted ceilings, it was relatively plain. The walls were egg-shell white, and the floors were made of tile. Crowds of people stood before two giant portraits which dominated the side walls. More tourists viewed a nearby television that played a brief movie.

"What you see in this room are the repairs made after heavy damage from bombing raids in the Second World War," Konrad said.

Josie followed Konrad into a side room and found her disappointment in the building's interior quickly mollified.

"This is the Red Hall," her grandfather announced.

The "hall," which was actually a room, was outfitted with one of the strangest collections of color Josie had ever seen. The lower halves of each wall were red and green with base borders that resembled the design on an oriental rug. Portraits of men from the seventeen hundreds and paintings of scenes from Greek mythology bore gilded frames over the red and green of the walls. The ceiling and upper half of the walls were ivory white and light green with more portraits and gold leaf.

"You work here?" Josie asked.

"No," he answered.

"Does Derek?" she added.

"At times," he replied.

She wondered if this was one of those times but didn't want to be too obvious in her interest. She simply let the conversation trail off with the hope that she'd run into Derek sometime in the course of their tour.

Returning to the foyer, Josie was able to see one of the giant portraits. It depicted a king with long hair, a beard, and a serious expression. The king wore a bejeweled crown with a cross upon it and held a sword in one gloved hand and an orb in the other.

"The Emperor Charlemagne," Konrad told her. "This is a copy of the famous painting by Albrecht Durer that hangs in the German National Museum in Nuremberg."

"I thought the statue was Charlemagne," she said.

"It is."

"This doesn't look anything like the statue," she declared.

"There are many depictions of Charles the Great in this city," he informed her. "And none of them are the same."

"Why? Doesn't anybody know what he looked like?"

"Not really," he answered. "He died in 814 before they had cameras."

Josie looked at him with a frown. Of course they didn't have cameras back then!

"Would you care to see our office?" Konrad asked.

Judging by the rest of the building, Josie thought his office would be truly impressive. She half expected the President of the United States to be waiting there for them. Speaking of presidents, she now understood why he had pictures of himself with President Clinton. She was anxious to see his office and find out what he did for a living.

As Konrad led Josie down a flight of stairs, he wondered what she was thinking. How much could he tell her about The Agency? After meeting Derek and experiencing his influence first hand, she had asked about his business. When those answers only piqued her curiosity, she insisted that he show her their offices. He was, however, aware of the danger of revealing too much to her. In the very least, Henrietta had reminded him of that. He decided to show Josie the visible side of The Agency. What they did in private was changing the world, but it was not for public viewing. Those duties were performed in private places throughout Europe, and their main offices were on the upper floors of the Rathaus.

The "visible side" of The Agency was on the basement level of the Rathaus, and it was nothing like what Josie expected. It resembled what she thought the business end of the Barnum and Bailey Circus might look like. The office was brightly lit with large glass windows and decorated with colorful banners and posters. Painting on the front window identified the office as the *Internationaler Karlspreis zu Aachen*. The front door was open and fourteen people moved hastily about the chamber.

"What does that say?" Josie asked as she pointed to the writing on the window.

"The International Charlemagne Award for the City of Aachen," Konrad translated.

"You give out awards?" she asked with disappointment. His career didn't sound very important.

34

Konrad led her into the office. "Each year we give the Charlemagne Award to someone who has made the greatest strides in bringing the people and cultures of Europe together. The Award is one of the most prestigious prizes in the world. Look here."

He directed her to a wall which was adorned with the pictures of over fifty award recipients. Josie saw that some of the faces looked vaguely familiar. One was a king, another was a queen. There was also a pope, and President Clinton. Each wore a gold medal with an engraving of Charlemagne around their neck.

"Perhaps you have heard of some of them," Konrad told her. "Winston Churchill, George Marshall, Henry Kissinger, Tony Blair, Angela Merkel."

"Konrad..." said a voice in the hall. He was a distinguished-looking man with silver hair and a protruding waistline. He wore a neatly-tailored navy blue suit coat over a white-collared shirt and seemed to have a permanent smile affixed to his face.

"Are you on your way to Oktoberfest, Helmut?" Konrad asked with a smirk.

"My poor friend," said the man in mock sympathy. "Has age confused you that much? October is many months away. This suit is Zeiler. I bought it for the ceremony."

Konrad responded in German and the man named Helmut replied in kind. Soon, they were engrossed in conversation, laughing and joking. After several moments, Konrad turned to Josie and said, "Let me introduce you to the Lord Mayor of Aachen."

***

People greeted the Lord Mayor as he exited the Rathaus with Konrad and Josie. Ever the politician, he returned their sentiments with smiles and handshakes of his own.

"Have you tried *printe*, Josie?" he asked.

"What's that?"

Helmut smirked mischievously, as if he had a great secret to reveal. "*Printe* is what we are known for the world over. It is delicious."

"It is hardened sweet bread, baked in large, flat loaves," Konrad explained.

"We make a softer version for visitors," Helmut added. "But the original recipe is best. Mmmm. I know a little bakery. Best *printe* in Aachen."

"Sounds better than blood sausage," she said with a glance at her grandfather.

Walking along a cobblestone street, she noticed that there were more people in the market area than when she had arrived only a short while before. She watched workers unfurl a large blue and white banner with yet another image of Charlemagne and the words "*Internationaler Karlspreis zu Aachen*" printed upon it.

"This year's ceremony will be even better than the last," Helmut told Konrad.

"That will be your legacy, my friend," replied Konrad. "Every celebration greater than the one before it."

"I wish I could take credit, but the Karlspries staff does the work while I expand my waist with generous helpings of *printe*," laughed the Lord Mayor.

Technicians climbed out of a van with a satellite dish on its roof. They carried cables, cameras, and microphones. In addition to television crews and more onlookers, Josie noticed that there was a growing police presence.

"What are they doing this for?" Josie asked.

"Tomorrow is Ascension Day," answered Helmut. To Konrad, he said, "You did not tell her about Ascension Day?"

"I thought it best to let her see for herself," replied Konrad.

The Lord Mayor shook his head and told Josie, "Ascension Day is when we award the Karlspreis. As you can see, it is an international event."

"Are we gonna be able to see it?" Josie asked.

"I thought I might take you," Konrad answered.

"You will have the best seats in the room," Helmut said with a wink.

Konrad studied the faces of people in the crowd and asked Helmut, "Have there been any believable threats this year?"

Josie fell behind as the crowd enveloped her, and she lost sight of her grandfather and the Lord Mayor. "Excuse me," she said. "Excuse me."

Engrossed in conversation, Konrad and the Lord Mayor also worked their way through the mob. "The threats have not been out of the ordinary, but there have been more of them," Helmut admitted. "That is why you will find greater security this year."

Nervousness gave way to outright anger as Josie lost two steps for every one she gained. "Let me through!" she yelled. "Grandpa! Grandpa!"

Suddenly, two powerful arms pulled her backward. She screamed. A fist struck her cheek with enough force to fill her head with darkness and make her body go limp.

Pushing against the tide, Konrad and Helmut were ignorant to the fact that two men carried Josie across the street, up a flight of stairs, and into a mauve building.

"Hurry up," said the first man to his partner.

They brought Josie up another flight of steps. With a change of direction, they ascended a third staircase. "She won't be out long," declared the first man.

"I didn't think she'd be this heavy," replied his partner.

At the top of the stairs, they kicked open a door which was already ajar. The second man stumbled and dropped Josie's legs, causing the first man to drag her on his own.

As Josie's head hit the arm of a couch, her eyes fluttered open. She saw images move across her field of vision and startled as she recognized Steve's sweaty face.

"Ahh! Get away from me!" she yelled.

"That sounds familiar, huh buddy boy?" said his partner Todd.

Steve glanced at Todd, and Josie took the opportunity to kick him away from her. She pulled her legs up to her chest and looked back and forth at her abductors.

"What are you doing here?" she demanded.

"I called them," Henrietta said as she emerged from the kitchen with a bag of ice. She handed the plastic sack to Josie and gestured for her to press it to her cheek. "I called the police too, but that didn't seem to work."

"That was you?" Josie asked while applying ice to her face. "Why?"

"Because you do not belong here," she answered.

"That's right," Steve added. "Everyone's been worried 'bout ya. Me…and your ma…"

"My mom?" Josie snapped. "You're hangin' out with my mom now?"

"No," replied Steve. "That ain't what I meant."

Josie climbed over the arm of the couch to confront the three of them from a standing position. She winced from a sharp pain in her abdomen but quickly recovered. She looked for a way out. To her dismay, Todd and Steve stood before the door.

"It's time for you to come home," said Steve. "We all want that."

"Listen to him," Henrietta implored. "Your grandfather is *tres*...uh, he is a good man, but his ideas and his associates are not. You are most safe with your family in America."

"What do you know about my family?" Josie snapped. "You never tried to contact me. If you did, you'd know that my mother's a whore, my brothers are punks, and my sisters are brats." Pointing at Steve, she added, "And he's no longer my boyfriend."

"It don't end that easily," said Todd.

"I got this, man," Steve told his friend. "Three an' a half years, Josie, and you're gonna throw it away on one bad night?"

Josie had moved near the windows as she was talking and could see the street below. She was forty feet up, but the height was made shorter by a slow passing bus.

"It was about three hundred bad nights," she replied. "Probably more."

"Bullshit," said Steve. "We got it good."

"*You* had it good. I had a deadbeat boyfriend who stopped being interesting six months into the relationship."

"My ears are meltin'," declared Todd. "Let's go, Josie. We got a plane to catch."

He moved toward Josie, and she realized that it was now or never. To the surprise of everyone, she leaped through one of the windows, shattering the glass and frame.

People outside whipped their heads around to see the screaming young woman and pieces of glass sail down to the street below. Two of those witnesses were Konrad and Helmut. A third was Derek Schroeder, who sat in the parked Bentley less than sixty feet away. He had a passenger in his back seat, a man by the name of Dr. Clement Herzog. Together, they watched Josie hit the top of the bus with enough force to shatter its windows and dent its roof. Everyone was amazed to see her slowly rise to a standing position.

Steve, Todd, and Henrietta looked down at Josie with stunned expressions.

"I'm not going back," she declared. She used the frames of broken bus windows as steps to climb down to the street.

CHAPTER FOUR

Voices in another room woke Josie from her slumber, but she hadn't enjoyed much of a sleep anyway. The pain from her cramps increased, likely attributable to her leap from the building. She desperately wanted a heating pad to curl around. She heard Konrad speaking German. The voice with the British accent belonged to Derek.

"You know I prefer English," said Derek.

"Yes. I forget," Konrad replied. "I have never asked for a favor..."

"Until now," Derek corrected. "We don't do this. You know that."

"I know that we are the most powerful organization in Europe, probably in the world," answered Konrad. "We have saved the lives of millions of people we do not even know. Yet we cannot help one of our own?"

"Your granddaughter is not one of our own," Derek told him. "She's an American, a thief, and the daughter of a stripper. She poses too many risks."

Josie grimaced. Who was he to judge her? She had no idea what they were talking about, but she didn't like Derek's assessment of her.

"She took money from her mother," replied Konrad. "That does not make her a thief."

"I won't argue points with you," Derek answered. "You know the vetting process. It takes months of checks, monitoring, and interviews to qualify. Then we'll only consider the person for a job."

"I will go to Dr. Herzog directly," threatened Konrad.

"Is that so?" asked Derek. "How do you think you'll be received? You're second level. I'm on the Executive Council."

"So was my son," snapped Konrad.

"He was," agreed Derek. "And for that you're afforded access that is beyond your rank. But if you ignore the chain of command and petition the Chief Director himself, all such access will cease."

There was a pause between the speakers, leaving Josie curious about what would be said next. Derek finally broke the silence by saying, "I share your concern, especially knowing her lineage. But I cannot break protocol and hire her simply to give her legal status in this country."

"I am not asking for legal status," Konrad corrected. "I am asking for protection."

"I'm sorry, Konrad."

Josie heard the front door to the hotel suite open, then close. She lingered in bed for several long moments, considering the exchange she'd overheard.

***

Josie wore a burgundy dress that had been a gift from her grandfather. Her dark chestnut hair floated past her shoulders. Make-up hid the bruise and scratches her recent activities had caused and made her look like a magazine model. In short, she was stunning. Konrad felt uncomfortable in his three-piece suit. Though he had attended many ceremonies, he had always considered himself to be a blue-collar man.

Music, singing, and cheering filled the air outside the hotel, letting everyone know that the festivities for the Charlemagne Award Ceremony had begun. As they entered the elevator, Konrad told Josie, "We should have no worries today. Henrietta was sent back to Chartres and your...that young man and his friend are locked up, waiting to be deported."

Josie nodded.

"I am so sorry I lost sight of you," Konrad explained. "I will not do that again."

The elevator reached the lobby and opened its doors to a chorus of music and revelry. Konrad stopped Josie before she could join the excitement. "Are you feeling well?" he asked. "You took a terrible fall yesterday."

"It wasn't a fall," Josie replied. "It was a jump. And I'm fine."

Grandfather and granddaughter left the hotel and found themselves in the midst of the celebration. Entertainers with painted faces amused children while adults enjoyed various beverages. Musicians performed, and people rode bicycles through the crowd. Determined not to lose her again, Konrad took Josie's hand and led her into the mass of humanity.

With banners flying, music playing, and the party in full swing, Josie wondered if she was overdressed. She was about to ask Konrad about it when she saw angry people shouting and waving protest signs. One English poster exclaimed, "Hitler had a Charlemagne award too!"

"Who are they?" she asked.

"Attention seekers. That is all," he answered with a dismissive frown. "We must hurry if we want to make the ceremony."

He stepped up the pace, but it seemed to Josie that he was charting a course away from the protesters. She looked back to see that the police were directing camera crews to focus on happy revelers rather than the malcontents.

Security was tight at the Rathaus, causing Konrad and Josie to take their places in line behind other well-dressed people. They watched guards turn many individuals away.

"Are we gonna be able to get in?" Josie asked.

"I know a few people," Konrad reassured her with a smile.

After careful scrutiny of their documents, the guards let them in. Josie looked back at the throngs of people in the marketplace and guessed that they all wanted to be where she was. It was nice to be the VIP for once.

They passed through two more check points and ascended a staircase at the end of the foyer. Josie avoided the boredom of passing in a slow-moving line by looking out the windows at Aachen Cathedral. She could feel excitement building around her as she reached the top of the stairs and followed the crowd to Coronation Hall. Gowns more beautiful than any she'd ever seen hugged the forms of women bedecked in sparkling jewels. The men who accompanied these ladies wore suits made by Europe's finest tailors. Upbeat music and pleasant conversation filled the air. Despite the extravagance, Josie couldn't take her eyes off an iron symbol hanging above the hall's entrance.

"Charles the Great's monogram," Konrad said in anticipation of her question.

"You mean his initials?" she asked while looking at the *K, R, S* and possible *I* (she couldn't quite tell if it was an *I* or a *T*) presented in the design.

"Most reports say the Great King was illiterate," Konrad told her. "Or in the least, unable to write. So he stamped a monogram on papers in place of his signature."

Following people into the grand hall, Josie asked, "How could he be great if he couldn't even write his own name?"

Coronation Hall was a magnificent setting for the International Charlemagne Award Ceremony. The vaults of its arched ceiling were white with flower and vine designs. Its support beams extended to massive pillars which ran along the walls and were spread intermittently throughout the room. Five ancient frescoes adorned bays between the pillars. A statue of Charlemagne identical to the one topping the outside fountain stood in one corner. Along another wall, the glimmering gold crown and royal accouterments of Charles the Great beamed in a glass case. People settled on cloth-dressed chairs which surrounded circular tables. The tables were decorated with linens, sparkling silverware, porcelain tableware, and floral centerpieces with burning candles. Black and white dressed servers with white gloves attended to the guests' needs. A bay beneath one of the frescoes provided a location for the band, and a podium and head table featuring spots for eight guests sat atop a raised platform along the front wall.

"Come this way," Konrad said as he guided Josie toward the royal treasures.

With much of their surroundings obscured by shadows, the King's relics gleamed like gilded beacons in their glass case. There was a gold and jeweled cross, an orb, three swords, two scepters, part of a lance, a gilded book, and a gold and silver purse which was spotted by precious stones. The most impressive item, however, was the imperial crown. It was octagonal in shape with eight hinged plates studded with pearls and gems.

"In German, we call these the *Reichskleinodien*," declared Konrad with obvious pride. "The Imperial Jewels. These are the treasures of Charlemagne."

"He actually wore this crown?" Josie asked.

"Uh...well, no. Not this exact one," he confessed. "These are copies of the originals which reside in the Imperial Palace of Vienna, Austria."

"But you said this was where his palace was. Why would his jewels be in another country if this was where he lived?"

As Konrad considered how best to answer that, Josie saw Derek standing on the other side of the room. Her eyes narrowed on the pompous bastard. He was hidden in the darkened recesses behind the Charlemagne statue. He held papers and appeared to be involved in a conversation with a man who was largely obscured by the shadows.

"In 1794," Konrad said. "Napoleon invaded Aachen. Fearing that he would steal the treasures, the leaders of the city sent them to the Emperor of Austria with a note that said, 'keep these jewels safe.' But the Emperor misread the note and thought it said, 'keep these jewels in your safe.' That is where they remain today."

Josie laughed. "That can't be true."

"Probably not, but we maintain that the treasures will be returned to us when there is again a Holy Roman Emperor of the German Nation. Let me show you the frescoes."

He directed her to the first of five ancient-looking murals. It was black and white and depicted a bizarre scene—five people, one of whom was a king, kneeling before another king who was seated with an opened book, orb, and scepter on his lap. The seated monarch was wearing the imperial crown Josie had just seen.

"Why is one king bowing to the other?" Josie asked.

"That is the Emperor Otto III," Konrad told her. "He is paying respects to Charlemagne's corpse."

"He's dead?" Josie looked more closely at the fresco. "Why is he sitting up?"

"According to legend, that is how Otto III found him when he entered the Great King's tomb two hundred years after his death," Konrad replied. "The only decomposition of the body was that the end of his nose had fallen off."

A sudden urgency gripped Konrad as he saw The Lord Mayor conversing with Dr. Clement Herzog, the most influential man in the room.

"I can show you the rest later," he told Josie. "Let us go to our seats."

Josie followed her grandfather to the Lord Mayor and another man she didn't know. The stranger talking to Helmut was in his mid-sixties. His gray hair had receded to give him a large forehead. He had few wrinkles, his skin was tanned, and he looked to be in good shape. He was dressed in a bluish silver suit that Josie guessed must have cost a great deal of money. Nearby women waited for him to give them his attention.

"This is Dr. Herzog," Konrad told his granddaughter.

The man he and Derek had been talking about, Josie realized.

Dr. Herzog stared at the young woman before him. Remarkable, he thought. The resemblance was extraordinary. She could have passed for the love of his life so completely one would have thought they were

43

twins or that this young woman was her clone! The only difference, of course, was that they had over forty years between them. Marguerite, his long lost love, was truly lost—deceased for over three decades. Yet there she was, standing before him in the full beauty of her youth. He felt himself traveling back over the years to once again be in his lover's presence, but he shook himself from the memory and returned to the present. Taking Josie by the hand, he said, "I don't know whether to kiss your hand or fear the power of your grip. I saw you jump from that building. How did you not get hurt?"

"Uh...lucky, I guess."

"It was more than that," he corrected. "Tell me...is that a habit of yours?"

"A habit?" Josie asked. "No. I don't usually jump out of buildings."

"That's a relief," he laughed. "We have enough daredevils in this world."

Noticing that Dr. Herzog and Josie were sharing a laugh with Konrad as the Lord Mayor looked on, Derek hastened toward them.

"She is my granddaughter," Konrad told the doctor with obvious pride.

"Yes, I know," answered Dr. Herzog. To Josie, he said, "Your father was an exceptional man and a good friend."

"I've retrieved your notes, Doctor," announced Derek, as he offered the papers in his hand. "Perhaps you would like to peruse them before commencement?"

Dr. Herzog smiled. "No need, Derek." With a conspiratorial look at the growing group of people waiting to speak to him, he leaned closer to Josie and Konrad and confessed, "He has instructions to extract me from lingering encounters."

Josie laughed. Konrad smiled but felt a slight annoyance as he remembered times when aides kept the doctor from talking to him.

As the band in the back of the room silenced their instruments, people got the cue to take their seats. Five guests of honor sat on the platform.

"Doctor, we must sit," Derek said.

Dr. Herzog ignored him and asked Josie, "Is this your first banquet?"

"Yes."

"I hope it will not be your last," he said.

"It might be," she replied with a glance at Derek. "If I don't get a job, I may have to go back to America."

"Is that so?" Dr. Herzog asked. "We are always in need of energetic young people." To Derek, he said, "Igraine could use an assistant. Could she not?"

"Uh, I suppose so," Derek replied, but Dr. Herzog had already walked away. He shook hands with the guests of honor on the platform and took his seat amongst them. Derek glanced at Konrad, who was now beaming. His gaze shifted to Josie, and she smirked, glad to throw the rejection he gave her grandfather back in his arrogant face.

***

The outside celebrations were as lively on the back side of the Rathaus as they were everywhere else. One man, however, was not there for the amusements. He was Jean-Paul Renbleau, and he was a member of the National Sovereignty Movement (NSM), the protest group Josie saw earlier. While his associates were waving signs, he was taking steps to ensure that no one would forget the NSM's opposition to this event.

Early that morning, they had put their attention-getting device in its desired place, but Jean-Paul was nervous about its placement. They had but one shot at this, and he wanted it to be done right. With a stein in hand, he stumbled up to some bushes. He unzipped his trousers and swayed like a drunk trying to relieve himself. He was taking a terrible risk. He could be caught. More than that, the timer was coming to the end of its cycle, and if he was nearby when that final second passed...

"*Achtung* (Attention)," a man behind Jean-Paul yelled. He was an overweight policeman. "*Das ist keine Toilette* (That is not a toilet)."

Jean-Paul ignored him, which was the wrong approach because it compelled the officer to come closer. "*Wenn ich einen tropfen Pisse sehe, werde ich dich verhaften* (If I see a drop of piss, I will arrest you)."

The device's timer was not visible, but Jean-Paul knew that the countdown was nearly concluded. The guard kept threatening him, and he was coming closer. With no other alternative, Jean-Paul kicked the device toward the building, turned, and sent a full stream of urine all over the man. The guard yelled and leaped back. Jean-Paul charged, lowered his shoulder, and knocked the larger man flat onto his back. Stumbling after the collision, he continued his retreat to disappear into the crowd.

***

In the Coronation Hall, Dr. Herzog stood at the podium and waited for the applause to end. Derek, the Lord Mayor and five honorees sat at the table behind him.

Josie and Konrad sat near the platform. As she stared at Derek, Josie wondered what he had against her. She saw him check his watch and look at Dr. Herzog.

Silence overcame the room, and Dr. Herzog opened his lips to utter the first line of his address. Suddenly, a massive explosion rocked the building and shattered the windows behind the dignitaries. Fortunately, the glass had been covered by a black film which caught most of the flying debris. The sheer force of the detonation sent the film and shards flying toward the ceiling as pieces of stone and rolling waves of dust surged into the chamber.

The thunderous explosion heaved Josie and her grandfather to the floor. The noise and screams in the chamber sounded muted to Josie, and she heard high-pitched ringing in her ears. When she opened her eyes, the first thing she saw was Derek lying on top of Dr. Herzog like a protective secret service agent. The doctor, however, didn't appear surprised or scared. His face bore the hardened look of great rage.

**

Two days later, Josie found herself traversing the cavity the Ascension Day blast created in the Rathaus. She followed her grandfather up a stone staircase, nearly half of which was missing or rendered useless by the bomb. The abdominal cramps and ache in her legs remained, though to a lesser degree. Perhaps she was getting better, she rationalized. Looking through the building's gaping wound, she saw men working tirelessly to repair the damage. They stood upon a scaffold and applied jacks, drills, hammers, and other tools to the structure.

"Don't let the attack fool you," Konrad told Josie. "You will be safe here. The Agency is one of the most respected organizations in Europe."

"I can see that," Josie replied. "Is that its name? The Agency?"

"Its complete name is The Charlemagne Award Agency, typically known as The Agency. The award itself is known as the *Karlspreis*...or Charlemagne Award."

"So is that all we do?" she asked. "Give out awards?"

"No. There is more," he told her. "But I will let others explain that. Just keep in mind that you are very fortunate. Many people work for The Agency their entire lives without ever seeing the Executive Offices. And you are starting there."

As they reached the top floor, Konrad stepped aside. "Do not be nervous," he said. "You are a brilliant girl, and they will love you, as I do."

Josie couldn't remember a time when she heard her mother say she loved her, except when she was in an altered state. To have it come so readily from her grandfather brought a flush to her face. She pursed her lips together and nodded, unable to say anything in return. She walked through the open door as he went back down the stairs.

The main offices on the upper floors of the Rathaus were more lavish than their counterparts in the basement. People walked on polished hardwood, and the walls were coated with an ivory white plaster that bore three-dimensional scenes of chubby cherubs at play. Half walls with panes of glass on top of them formed dividers between cubicles.

Josie entered the reception area to see secretaries laboring at their desks. Their work spaces were adorned with computers and piles of folders. A man with a stack of papers passed, prompting Josie to say, "I'm looking for someone named Igraine."

"*Ich spreche kein Englisch* (I don't speak English)," he replied.

Similar inquiries to other employees garnered Josie the same essential response. One woman, however, did say, "*Das Grashaus.*"

Josie considered taking a seat and waiting for Igraine to come to her, but she knew that she had to be proactive. She'd been given a great opportunity and she couldn't let a lack of initiative ruin it. She decided that the *Grashaus* was probably a place like the Rathaus, and she would have to find it in order to locate Igraine.

***

To Josie's relief, it took little research to learn that the Grashaus was a medieval structure located near the market. It was constructed in 1267 and was the city hall before the Rathaus was built. It currently held the municipal archives, but at one time it had been a jail with its own criminal court and yard for executions. As she approached the building, Josie decided that it really did look like a prison. The doors were black iron gates, and the stones that made up the structure were several different shades of gray. Statues of kings were attached to the side of the building and stared back at her.

"Creepy," she mumbled. She imagined the hapless prisoners who were executed on that very spot and shuttered.

"Ve are not open to tourists today," said a female voice with a German accent. "Who are you?"

Josie turned to see a blond woman in her early forties standing on the second story veranda. She had a stocky build, giving the appearance that she lifted weights. Her arms were wrapped around half a dozen rolled up maps and charts.

"My name is Josie Ersman. I'm looking for Igraine."

The woman eyed her suspiciously, and asked, "*Sprechen Sie Deutsch* (Do you speak German)?"

Having no idea what she said, Josie didn't respond. The woman's displeasure became evident in the frown she gave. "Who hired you?"

"Dr. Herzog," Josie answered.

"*Ja*," the woman replied. "But you vill vork for me! And I can fire you."

***

Igraine Medhausen displayed the leadership qualities that most employees despised. She was arrogant, condescending, inflexible, and demanding. She made Josie rush repeatedly from one end of the complex to the other and offered no praise in return. After a brief lunch break, she ordered Josie to carry banners to a storage room. "Put zem in category by zeir date of printing," she demanded.

With an ache in her muscles and a sour look on her face, Josie carried her load up a staircase. She dropped it at the top of the steps and leaned forward, panting for breath. "Let her lug this crap," she said. "It's hot as hell in here."

To her right, she heard the hum of an air conditioner, but the store room she was supposed to go to was across the hall and filled with hot stagnant air. Josie decided to pay a visit to the cooled chamber before returning to her duties in the suffocating heat.

She entered document storage room four through a door that was unlocked. The cool air produced by a small air conditioner coated her skin like a soothing balm. Dust floated in a haze, meaning that someone else had recently been there. The rest of what she saw reminded her of a scene from a whodunit movie. A lone window allowed sunlight to pierce the fog of dust. Crates sat atop one another and were covered by faded tapestries. Bronze statues and globes so ancient they lacked known land masses were also scattered about the chamber. Cases were overstuffed with old books, but the most prevalent items were maps and documents which were stacked on oak tables.

Her grandfather would love this, she realized, but he would probably never get the chance to see it. She decided to look it over for herself and tell him about it later. As she thumbed through the stack of papers closest to her, she saw old maps and the manifests of ships—nothing of interest.

"This is weird," she said as she noticed a picture that was a foot and a half by three foot representation of a stained glass window. It was printed on canvas, but its colors remained vibrant and eye-catching. It depicted a king with a gold crown, red tunic, and bright blue skin.

She placed the print on the top of the stack, stirring up more dust. The more she looked at the image, the more she realized how violent it was. The great king was riding into battle atop a white horse while plunging a white sword into the neck of a man with a gold, cone-shaped hat. He was surrounded by knights wearing coats-of-mail, and carrying long, pointed shields. They were doing battle with people with round shields, one of whom had a battle-ax poised to strike at the great king. Printed at the bottom of the canvas was, *KAROLUS MAGNUS JERUSALEM 1099*.

"Karolus Magnus?" she asked.

She knew what Jerusalem was, and 1099 was probably a year. But what was Karolus Magnus? As she lifted the illustration to return it to the middle of the pile, she noticed another word printed on the back of it: *CHARTRES*. Chartres was where her grandmother lived. Chartres, France. What a coincidence, she thought.

"Vat are you doing in here?" Igraine yelled from the door.

Josie's startled hands jerked and ripped the canvas in her grip.

"Ahh!" Igraine yelled. She charged into the room and pushed Josie aside. Looking down, she saw that the girl had torn the Chartres Document. Of all the pages to rip, of all the documents to discover, why did it have to be that one? It had been Igraine's task to keep it hidden, not destroyed. That would be pointless. The original stained glass was still displayed in Chartres. There, it was simply seen as a piece of medieval art, but in Aachen, that very same picture was a significant step on the road to revelation, a clue to a mystery that must not be solved.

"You have disobeyed me on zee first day!" Igraine yelled. "And you damaged a valuable artifact! You are irresponsible! You are fired! *Auf Wiedersehen!*"

Josie's eyes went wide as she heard what her boss said.

GUY COTE

CHAPTER FIVE

It was odd how sadness could leave a person feeling drained. Why did it require energy to be depressed? Yet that was how Josie felt. All she wanted to do was lie in bed in her grandfather's guest room. Unfortunately, she couldn't do that for long. She had to tell him that she lost what he considered to be the job of a lifetime. Would he allow her to stay with him after that? She could only hope so because she wasn't ready to get her own apartment, not without a job. Reluctantly, she climbed out of bed and opened the door to find him. She shuffled into the living room and her stomach suddenly dropped. She saw Igraine sitting on the couch beside her grandfather. Derek occupied the room's recliner and Franz purred in his lap. He stroked the cat as if he was Marlon Brando in *The Godfather*.

"I was going to tell you," she said to Konrad.

With a glance at Derek, Igraine replied, "You are not fired."

Josie's head perked up like a forest animal that heard a suspicious sound.

"It vas an honest mistake," Igraine continued. "I vas under stress, and I took it out on you. Vill you come back to vork for me?"

Skeptical, Josie searched the faces before her. She finally nodded.

Konrad was relieved, but Igraine looked like someone who had been forced to consume a heaping helping of humble pie. Derek set the cat on the floor and stood.

"Everyone has been nervous since the attack," he said. He shook Konrad's hand. Then he asked Josie, "We'll see you tomorrow?"

"I guess so."

***

Josie returned to work determined to stay out of her boss's hair. The woman hated her and she didn't know why. Derek was an even greater mystery to her. She'd been sure that he disliked her. After all, he was against hiring her. She also knew that he forced Igraine to take her back. So what was he up to?

She tried to concentrate on newly assigned tasks that made her a courier of documents, but she was hit with another severe case of abdominal cramps. They brought with them a pelvic pain and deep-tissue soreness in her lower back. The maladies resembled those which accompanied her monthly "visitor," but they were much worse. The cell phone that her grandfather bought her the day before emitted a ring from her pocket.

"Hello?" she answered.

It was Konrad. Their conversation was brief. He was just checking up on her. She wished she could tell him about her pains but knew she couldn't. He was a man, after all.

The rest of her second day on the job was largely uneventful. She left the office intending to use money her grandfather gave her to pay for a bus ride home, but a red-headed woman stopped her at the top of the stairs. She appeared to be in her mid to late twenties, was nearly the same height as Josie, and had high cheekbones and a slender nose which gave her a very pretty look.

"Are you an American?" the woman asked with an Irish accent.

"Yeah."

"I thought so," said the woman. "I heard you talking. Where are you from?"

"Arizona," Josie answered.

"I've never been there," the woman replied. "But I've been to New York."

Josie wondered where this was going but was glad to meet an English speaker.

"My name is Abby," the woman continued. "Abby Ellis. I work in the Community Health and Development Department."

"Health and Development?" asked Josie. "I thought there were just errand boys and secretaries up here."

Abby laughed. "There's a lot more to The Agency than what you see."

"Yeah," Josie agreed. "So I'm told."

"Would you like a ride home?" Abby asked.

Josie wasn't in the habit of accepting rides from strangers. Then again, she never ran off to Germany either. She decided to take another risk and said, "Sure. Why not?"

***

With the top lowered on her convertible BMW, a cool mix of German hip hop and techno music playing over the speakers, and the car cruising at an impressive speed on the highway, Abby put her American passenger at ease.

"This is a nice car," Josie observed.

"Someday I'll show you what it can really do," Abby promised.

"Why not now?" suggested Josie.

Abby shifted gears and buried the gas pedal. The engine roared and the car surged forward. Josie was elated as the BMW hit high speeds.

Abby asked, "So how do you like working for The Agency?"

"I don't know," said Josie. "I was fired on the first day."

"No."

"Oh, yeah," Josie confirmed. "But Derek got me re-hired."

"Derek?"

"The good-looking guy with the nice car," Josie explained.

"Derek Schroeder," Abby said knowingly.

"I guess that's his name," replied Josie. "What's his deal anyway?"

"His deal?" asked Abby. "Uh...I can tell you that's not his car. It belongs to Dr. Herzog. Derek is his...how to say it? His right hand man?"

"So he's an assistant? Like I am to Igraine?"

"Not exactly. He's on the Executive Council," Abby explained. "But he's only there because Dr. Herzog wants him there."

"What's the Executive Council?"

"I'm probably not the one to explain that to you," said Abby.

"Somebody's got to," said Josie. "And my boss hates me."

"Igraine hates everybody," added Abby. "I can't understand why she was made Dr. Herzog's personal secretary."

"I didn't know she was his personal secretary," exclaimed Josie. "Where does that leave Mr. Perfect?"

"Mr. Perfect?"

"Derek," said Josie.

Turning off the main road, Abby guided the vehicle at a slower pace through a residential neighborhood. "He is Igraine's boss and she's yours," she explained.

"And Dr. Herzog is everybody's boss?" asked Josie. "Including you?"

"Including me," Abby confirmed.

"What does The Agency do?" Josie asked.

"Everything," Abby answered as she stopped the car before Konrad's house.

Josie climbed out of the vehicle, but she had more questions to ask. How did Abby know where she was staying? Why wouldn't anyone give her a straight answer about The Agency? All she managed to say, however, was, "Thanks."

***

Josie's next three days at work consisted of more menial chores that she was less than thrilled to perform, but she refused to let it show. She hadn't seen Derek at all and had only seen Abby twice, but that was from a distance. The third day, however, brought a surprise. She was eating lunch by the Charlemagne fountain when she saw Abby, Derek, and another man walking toward her.

"Josie," said Abby. "What are you doing here by yourself?"

Josie's "surprise" was to find Abby and Derek together. She kept that to herself and simply replied, "I'm eating lunch."

"That's what we're going to do," Abby replied. "Why don't you join us?"

"I only get twenty minutes," explained Josie.

"Says who? Igraine?" asked Derek. "Don't worry about her."

***

The food that was served to Josie in an outside dining area tasted better than the lunch she'd made for herself. Abby and Derek carried on like old friends, but it was with the other man that Abby was affectionate. His name was Leif Christenson. He was Norwegian, in his early thirties with blond hair and blue eyes.

"So am I to understand that your superior has been a bit gruff?" Leif asked Josie.

She hesitated, not sure what to say. Then the other three burst out laughing.

"I told 'em," Abby confessed.

"Don't worry," Leif said. "She's a rite of passage. We've all worked for her." Then he glanced at Derek and added, "Well, not all of us."

"No. Not all of us," Derek agreed.

Josie wanted to say that she thought the woman was a total bitch, but decided that she didn't know any of them well enough to say that. Changing the subject, she asked, "How come I never see Dr. Herzog anywhere?"

"He usually works out of his home," Derek replied.

"What does he do?" Josie persisted.

With a smile, Derek answered, "Whatever he wants."

"I have an idea," Leif declared. "It's our anniversary. Five years."

"Five years?" questioned Josie. She wanted to ask Abby and Leif why they weren't married but decided that it really wasn't any of her business.

As if reading her thoughts, Abby rubbed her unadorned ring finger, glanced at Leif, and said, "Yes. It's been five years."

"We've rented a hot air balloon," Leif continued. "You two should join us."

Josie was taken aback. She glanced at Derek, who had a similar reaction. Abby, however, was not at all surprised by his invitation. She was used to him asking people to join in their excursions.

"Have you ever been up in a balloon?" Leif persisted.

Josie shook her head.

"Then it's settled," he said. "Saturday it is."

***

Leif fired a blast of burning propane into the envelope of the inflatable bag. It sounded like a cross between a grumbling bear and an intense wind, but the noise did nothing to diminish the tranquility of the balloon's trek through the sky.

"It's your anniversary," said Derek. "I've got this."

He took over the operation of the balloon so Leif was free to embrace Abby. To their left, Josie held the rim of their wicker basket, but not because she was nervous. She needed the support, as her period had started and it was all she could do not to curl herself in a fetal position.

Floating twelve hundred feet above the earth, they saw soft rays of light feature certain areas of the countryside while banishing others to the shadows. The vast and verdant landscape was spotted with patches of forest, rivers, ponds, and small towns.

"What do you think?" Abby asked Josie.

"It's incredible," she answered.

"Gives you a different idea of Germany, doesn't it?" Leif added.

"Yeah," Josie said. "All I saw before were government buildings, museums..."

"Jail," Derek added.

Josie looked at him as if she'd been insulted.

"I can't believe how you handled yourself in there," he continued. "Did you know that one of the girls who jumped you was found dead in the Rhine last week? She was killed by the other girl that attacked you."

Josie was more than a bit surprised, and it showed.

Turning to Leif, Derek said, "They were quite dangerous. And she beat them bloody."

Josie didn't win that fight, but it was okay with her if he thought otherwise.

"Didn't you also jump out of a building?" Leif asked. "I heard about that."

Derek laughed. "You're a lethal combination, Josie. Remind me not to get on your bad side."

"I've been trying to figure out if you're on my side at all," Josie said.

Now it was Derek's turn to be caught off guard. Josie actually surprised herself with that comment, though she was careful not to show it.

"Oh, I'm definitely on your side," Derek said with a smile.

"How much?"

Abby and Leif exchanged glances. This was getting interesting.

"I don't know," Derek replied. "How much do you want me to be?"

"Well that depends on what you can do," Josie said.

"I think you'll find that I can do a lot of things," Derek told her.

"Yes. But would I like them? Or can you just blow hot air?"

Leif laughed, breaking the banter between Josie and Derek.

***

Derek brought the balloon to a gentle landing in an open field. Though Josie was impressed by his skills, she winced from the pain the touch down caused her cramped insides. Abby noticed, but the men did not. She tried to keep it that way by turning their attention to the Bentley which was parked nearby. "When did you drop off the car?"

"Last night," Leif replied. He exited the basket and helped the girls get out.

"Let's set up the picnic, shall we?" Abby asked Josie.

The girls carried several bags from the basket to a nearby tree. As they laid out the mid-day meal, Derek and Leif decompressed the balloon.

Abby put fruits and cheeses on a napkin and asked Josie, "Are you all right?"

Fearing that Abby might think she went too far in her flirtation with Derek, Josie replied, "Yeah. Fine. Why do you ask?"

"You should eat bananas and nuts. They're rich in vitamin B and zinc."

"Okay," Josie responded with a perplexed look. "Why would I need to do that?"

"They're natural remedies for menstrual cramping," Abby answered. "And you should walk as much as you can."

"Oh. Is it that obvious?"

"Only to me," explained Abby. "I'm sure the guys didn't notice."

"Good," said Josie. She continued to help prepare the picnic. After several moments, she confessed, "I think something might be wrong with me. I've had really bad cramps and aches for a couple weeks. Has that ever happened to you?"

"For a couple weeks? No," Abby answered. "Not that long."

"I've always had bad periods," Josie admitted. "But they just seem worse now. And they last longer."

"Have you had any premenstrual spotting?" Abby asked. "Fevers? Headaches? Depression?"

"You sound like a doctor," Josie observed.

"I am. So is Leif. You should come into my clinic. I can run tests and..."

"Okay," said Josie as she saw the men coming toward them. "I will. Just don't say anything to them."

"Of course not," Abby replied. "By the way, you and Derek up in the balloon...that was hot."

Josie threw her a look of surprise.

***

The four of them sat on a blanket with Derek and Josie separated by a bottle of Chardonnay. Cheeses, crackers, deli meats, fruit, and *printe* were spread out like a mini-smorgasbord. Wine lubricated their palates and lightened their heads.

"I grew up in the skies," Derek admitted. "My father was a balloonist."

"I didn't know that," said Abby.

"Well, I don't tell people everything," Derek replied.

"You told me your ma was a punk rocker," added Leif.

"What?" Josie asked.

"We looked it up," explained Abby. "It's true. She had a hit in the eighties."

"A one hit wonder," agreed Derek as he took a long drink of wine.

"Your dad raced balloons and your mom rocked out?" Josie asked. "I thought my family was out there."

"His parents were 'out there' and up there," said Leif. "How did they meet?"

"How do any parents meet?" Derek asked. "They were at a cricket tournament."

Leif, Abby, and Josie laughed.

"Oh, yes," said Leif. "That's how my ma and da met."

"Mine got together at the International Curling Games in Rwanda," Abby joked.

Josie laughed, though she'd never heard of curling and had only a vague idea where Rwanda was. She wondered how her own parents met. No one had ever told her.

"Curling in Rwanda?" Leif asked. "I had no idea it was so cold there."

With a nudge to Josie, Abby said, "I'll bet there's a lot these blokes don't know."

Josie fixed her gaze on Derek and replied, "I agree."

"You agree?" Derek repeated.

"Yes."

"What makes you say that?" he probed.

"You told me you can do a lot," she said. "But all I've seen is that you can drive a fancy car, talk big, and play with fire in a basket. I'm still waiting to be impressed."

Derek smiled in a mischievous way. "What does it take to impress you?"

"I like a guy who can take charge," Josie said.

"So you like a man who is forceful and firm?" asked Derek.

"Sometimes," Josie answered. "I also like nice guys."

And that was true. Steve may have turned out to be a shit, but he started out as a great guy. She drank deeply from her glass of wine while

Derek smiled at her. It was obvious to Abby and Leif that something was developing between their two companions.

She's trouble, Derek thought. He knew her biography, but he found himself moving toward her anyway. She responded in kind, and their kiss seemed inevitable…right there, with Abby and Leif watching.

Suddenly, an old school telephone ring sucked the romance out of the air. Derek removed his cell from his pocket, looked at the number on the screen and answered, "*Hallo. Das ist* Derek." He listened to the caller's voice and rose to his feet. "*Ja*," he said. To Abby and Leif, he whispered, "It was an NSM bomb." He walked away from the picnic to continue the call.

"Well, now we know for sure," Leif replied.

"We know what for sure?" Josie probed.

"We know who set off the explosion at the *Karlspreis* ceremony," Leif answered. "The NSM."

Josie's expression revealed that she had no idea what the NSM was.

"National Sovereignty Movement," Leif explained. "In Germany you might hear it called The Movement, or *Bewegung*. But everywhere else, it's called the NSM."

"Are they terrorists?" Josie asked.

"Yes," said Abby. "They're radicals who get more violent with every protest. It won't be long before they kill somebody."

"I saw them," Josie exclaimed. "They were waving signs and shouting. Right?"

"Probably," Leif answered. "They do that every year."

"But this year they set off a bomb," said Abby. "What's next?"

"What are they pissed off about?" Josie asked.

"The EU mostly," answered Leif.

"The EU?" Josie asked.

"European Union," Leif told her. "The NSM doesn't want European countries to be unified. They want it to be like it was, with independent sovereign nations."

Josie had never been interested in politics until it exploded in front of her. Now she was curious. "What's their beef with the Charlemagne Award Ceremony?"

"Each year we give the prize to whoever did the most to bring Europe together as it once was under Charlemagne," Leif explained. "And they're against that."

"They want Europe to be like it was after Charlemagne's kingdom split apart," Abby added. "Separate countries competing and fighting against each other."

"Actually, they're targeting us because they think we're turning the EU into another German empire," Derek explained as he returned to the picnic. "We need to go."

***

It was past midnight when the Bentley pulled into Konrad's driveway. Derek shut the headlights but let the engine idle. He had dropped Abby and Leif off earlier, so he and Josie were finally alone. There was silence, and the mood was right. All the flirtation from earlier was but a prelude to the moment when his lips would touch hers.

Josie was simply gorgeous with dark hair flowing past her shoulders, mesmerizing eyes made exotic by light touches of mascara, and full lips glistening with burgundy lipstick. Derek leaned toward her as if somehow pulled.

Her eyes went from his, to his mouth, and back to his eyes. Her lips parted.

His eyes closed, as did hers. Their lips tingled in anticipation of what was about to come.

Trouble, that alarming word, suddenly popped into Derek's brain. That's what Josie was, *Trouble*. He opened his eyes.

As their bodies continued the momentum of their attraction, Derek turned their would-be kiss into a hug. He tried to make it a worthwhile embrace by putting emotion into it. "You're truly terrific," he said.

Josie didn't know how to react. She half-heartedly returned the hug.

"I almost forgot," Derek added. He opened the car's glove box, extracted an envelope, and gave it to her. "Your first paycheck."

Still mystified, she looked down at the paper he put in her hand.

***

Konrad entered the kitchen as the morning sun crept through the windows. He was followed by Franz, who demanded his breakfast with a high-pitched whine. Grandfather and cat found Josie sitting at the kitchen table, staring at her paycheck.

"Is something wrong?" Konrad asked.

"Can you cash this for me?" she asked. "I don't have a bank account."

"Of course," he replied.

Josie nodded her thanks. Before he could ask her about her date, she stood and said, "I'd like to make breakfast. If you pay for it, I'll get it and cook it."

***

Josie walked over the sidewalk on her way to the market as a Toyota Camry followed far behind her. She was oblivious to the car but thankful for the opportunity to figure out the mystery that had perplexed her all night. Was Derek into her, or wasn't he? He seemed to be, but he didn't kiss her when he had the chance. Was he gay? That would be her luck. All the good guys seemed to prefer other guys. For the first time since leaving America, she thought of her mother in less than negative terms. How would Heidi Seek handle this? She was so confused by Derek that she actually considered calling her for advice. She touched the phone in her pocket but pulled back and said, "What am I thinking?"

The Camry's engine roared into action. Josie turned to see the car come to a skidding halt beside her. Before she could run, the front passenger door flew open and Todd sprang out of the vehicle. He grabbed Josie. The back door opened and he shoved her into the car, slamming the door shut. Tires screeched as the Camry raced down the road.

"What are you doing? Let me out of here!" Josie screamed.

Steve drove while Todd sat in the front. Heidi was in the back near Josie.

"Put your seatbelt on," said Heidi.

"You can't do this!" Josie yelled. "I thought you...how'd you get back here? You were deported!"

"I got connections," snapped Steve. "You know that."

"And you," Josie said to her mother. "You...are you with him? Oh my God, that's gross! Eww!"

"Don't be ridiculous," replied Heidi. "We're here to talk some sense into you and bring you home."

Cars blasted their horns and swerved as the Camry pulled onto the main road.

Josie squirmed to get enough leverage to kick the glass out of her window.

"No you don't!" yelled Heidi. "Todd!"

Todd climbed over the back of his seat to pull Josie back into a proper sitting position. He and Heidi jerked the seatbelt across her body and clamped it into its buckle.

"Keep her still," Steve ordered while looking over his shoulder. The car swerved.

"We got it," Heidi responded. "Just drive!"

Josie discreetly extracted her phone from her pocket.

***

Konrad heard the musical ring tone of the cell charging in his bedroom. It was a phone he used primarily for work, so he ignored the irritating melody and continued setting the breakfast table for his granddaughter's return.

***

Keeping her phone hidden, Josie saw that her call went to voice mail. "You won't get away with this," she threatened her abductors. "I work for powerful people."

"I know," answered Heidi. "That's why we're here. What the hell were you thinking? You can't run off to another country!"

"I'm an adult," Josie replied.

"It's dangerous here," Heidi said. "You belong in Tucson."

"Where my mother lies and steals from me? Where my boyfriend...correction, ex-boyfriend, does nothing all day but get drunk and shoot out TVs? No, thank you."

"Nothin' wrong with a little target practice," Todd teased Steve.

Steve wasn't in a joking mood. "You think you're all that 'cause you serve slop at a half-assed restaurant?"

"No," said Josie. "I just think you're not all that."

"Least he ain't never stole his mother's money," Todd said with a wink at Heidi.

Seeing the wink and Heidi's acknowledgement of it, Josie's eyes grew narrow. "I knew it had to be one of them," she said to her mother. Then she added, "That money was payback for my pendant."

"I don't care about the money," Heidi replied. "You belong with your family where you're safe."

"Safe from what? The three of you are the only danger I face."

"Your grandmother said she warned you, but you didn't listen," said Heidi.

"Oh, so she's behind this? Like the last time?" asked Josie. She could see by the light and words displayed on her phone, that Konrad was calling her back. Without Heidi noticing, she pressed the button to answer the call. "What do you know about keeping me safe, Mom!" she yelled. "You kidnapped me! Where are we going? To the airport?"

***

Konrad's eyes flashed wide as he heard what came from Josie's end of the line. Keeping the call open, he picked up his house phone and dialed the one person he knew with enough clout to affect an immediate rescue—Dr. Herzog. It was a number he had long had but never used...until now.

***

A helicopter raced through the sky as the Camry below eluded three police cars with blaring sirens and flashing lights. The high-speed chase cut off innocent drivers.

In the car, Steve clutched the steering wheel and pulled it left, then right. "How the hell did they find us?" he yelled. "You got a GPS chip on you or something?"

"Yeah," answered Josie. "I'm a dog. They stuck a chip in my collar. Dumb ass!"

"They don't need a chip," Todd announced as he grabbed the phone Josie was hiding by her leg. "Not when they got this."

"Son of a bitch!" Steve exclaimed. "Throw it out the window!"

Todd did as instructed.

Josie laughed. "Oh, that's good. They'll lose us now!" To Heidi she said, "See why I left his stupid ass?"

Brake lights appeared up ahead. The police had erected a roadblock. Cologne Airport, the Camry's destination, loomed in the distance, but it was beyond the block.

"You can't make it," Josie said. "Let me go and they might take it easy on you."

Still traveling at a high rate of speed, Steve jerked the steering wheel to merge into the far right lane. He clipped the bumper of a truck, causing it to fishtail as the Camry swayed. Steve buried the gas pedal. The car surged toward the exit and rammed a motorcycle, sending the bike into a rail and the rider to his death.

"Oh, my God!" Josie yelled as she watched the demise of the cyclist.

Steve drove the car to the exit ramp, but the left front corner of the Camry hit a concrete barrier, causing it to snag. Momentum carried the right side of the car forward, and it spun. The Camry toppled left over right and over again, rolling down the ramp.

Police in the helicopter watched the Camry tumble down the ramp, turning it into a crushed box. With a glance at his partner, the pilot said, "*Niemand kann das überleben* (No one can survive that)."

CHAPTER SIX

Josie's eyes fluttered open to see her grandfather sitting beside her bed with his head hung low. "Where am I?" she asked.

Konrad looked up and relief instantly washed across his haggard features. "Thank God," he exclaimed. "You are in the infirmary, dear."

She had gauze pads on her forehead and scrapes on her face. She wore a thick, white neck brace, and one arm was bandaged. She was attached to an intravenous drip.

"I'm so sore," she said.

"I can't imagine why," Abby responded while entering the room. She was dressed in a white doctor's overcoat and carried a medical chart. "I'm amazed you're alive."

"I feel like I've been beaten up," Josie replied.

"You were," agreed Abby. "But I ran a battery of tests on you. I tested everything." Those last words were meant to have particular significance to Josie. "You don't have internal bleeding or a single broken bone," she continued. "It's a miracle."

Josie understood that Abby was trying to tell her that she had also tested for the cause of her cramps. She wanted to know what the doctor learned, but that was a conversation for them to have without the presence of her grandfather.

"When can I get out of here?" Josie asked.

"Probably tomorrow," said Abby. She headed to the door, then turned and looked back. "It's a good thing you were wearing that seatbelt. It saved your life."

It took a few moments for Josie to remember why she had her seatbelt on. Then it dawned on her. "Where's my mother?" she asked Konrad.

"She is in the hospital," Konrad answered. "Along with the driver. His friend died on impact."

"Todd is dead?"

Her grandfather nodded.

"What about Mom and Steve?" probed Josie. "Are they in bad shape?"

"From what I have heard, she is worse than him," Konrad told her. "They are both being intensively cared for."

"Intensively cared for?" Josie repeated. "Are they here?"

Konrad shook his head. "Dr. Herzog had you brought to The Agency's infirmary. It is the best in Germany. They are at University Hospital in Köln, uh Cologne. It is a good place."

Josie considered what "intensively cared for" meant. Her lips pressed tightly together and her face became flush as she realized that they were in the ICU.

"There she is," announced Derek. "Supergirl."

He entered Josie's room with a dozen long stem pink roses arranged with white budded spray in a crystal vase.

Josie quickly wiped any mist from her eyes. "Don't you forget it," she teased.

"You're like a cat with nine lives," Derek observed. He set the flowers on a table by the window and pulled a chair closer to the bed. "How are you feeling?" he asked.

"I'm okay," she answered.

Sensing that they wanted to be alone, Konrad stood and kissed his granddaughter on the cheek. "I will be back later," he said and left the room.

"Abby says you'll be out of here tomorrow," Derek said. "Is that a good idea?"

"I'll be fine," she told him. "I'm just sore and a little stiff."

"Why don't I take you to Bad Aachen then?" he offered. "It would make you feel better."

"Bad Aachen? What's that?" Josie asked. "The ghetto?"

Derek laughed. "Yes. After all this, would you like to see the slums of our city?"

"No," she answered. "Not really."

***

If there was a ghetto in Aachen, Josie realized that she was nowhere near it. The buildings she passed as she sat in the Bentley were so quaint it was as if they had come from a Grimm's fairytale. She half expected to see Hansel and Gretel skipping across the cobblestone street. Despite the luxury of the car, she was still uncomfortable. Her muscles ached and every movement brought a degree of pain. Oddly enough, her abdominal area was cramp free.

A half hour of driving brought them to the spa section of the city. Derek parked outside the central building of a massive facility. The exterior of the main structure was modern-looking and made mostly of dark glass. Brick and stucco buildings were also part of the complex. A white roof stretched over the primary entrance and was supported by tall, concrete pillars. A sign outside the building read, *Carolus Thermen Bad Aachen.*

There was that word again, Josie thought. Carolus. When she saw it on the picture that got her fired, it began with a K. "What does that mean?" she asked Derek.

"Bad Aachen is not the ghetto," he teased. "It means Aachen Spa."

"What about the other words?" she added.

"Thermen means thermal, or hot springs," he translated. "Carolus is Latin for Charles...Charlemagne. He built this city around its thermal baths."

"Does Carolus also begin with a K?" she asked.

"Yes. Sometimes," he answered. "Why?"

So the picture that made Igraine so upset was of Charlemagne in Jerusalem, Josie realized. What was the big deal about that? Aachen was full of Charlemagne stuff. She noticed that Derek was awaiting her answer.

"Oh, it's nothing," she said. "I just read it somewhere."

"Ah. Well," began Derek. "Before we go in, I have a surprise for you." He opened the glove box and extracted a wrapped present. He gave it to her with a smile.

She opened the gift and was stunned to see a two-tone Datejust Rolex ladies watch with twenty-two flawless diamonds on its bezel and mother-of-pearl face.

"Wow," she said. "It's...I don't know what to say."

"Try it on," he instructed.

She slipped it over her wrist and closed the clasp. It was a stunning watch that added weight to her arm, not so much a heaviness as a worthiness. After just one date, it had been given to her by...

"Dr. Herzog wanted to give it to you himself," Derek explained. "But he will be away for two more days. I told him you would want it now to, uh, boost your spirits."

Josie was disappointed that he wasn't the gift giver, but she tried not to show it.

"Was I right?" he asked.

"Yeah," she said with a smile. "I love it."

"Well, you've had a difficult time here in Germany," he added. "And we thought you should have it. I bought you this." He handed her a bag with a box in it.

Josie removed the present from the sack and opened it to find a black two-piece Brazilian bikini. The bottom was a Rio cut that tied together at the sides, and the top presented a full cut triangular design. It was an eye-catching and suggestive choice, but not lewd or offensive. She looked at him and raised her eyebrows.

***

When Josie shaved that morning, she'd been discomforted every time the razor passed over sore areas, but as she fit the bikini to her body and ran cream over her skin, she was glad that she took the time to groom. She was pleased to be free of her monthly "visitor" and its accompanying pain. She applied cover-up to her scratches and bruises, then looked at herself in the mirror and nodded with satisfaction.

She proceeded into the great bathing hall of Carolus Thermen. It was constructed in the Roman style with eighteen marble columns tracing the central terrace pool. There was a large whirlpool at one end, a mini-pool at the other, and a C-shaped Jacuzzi in the middle of the bathing area. Josie searched the faces and bodies of patrons to find the man with whom she arrived. When she saw him, she stopped and stared.

He wore black trunks that extended to his knees. His tan skin accentuated the form of his muscles and the leanness of his hard body. His abdomen appeared to be perpetually flexed even when he was at rest, and he had just the right amount of hair on his firm chest.

Derek smiled broadly at the sight of Josie. The curves of her legs led to the dark v-shape of her bikini bottom. The suit tapered into strips which were tied in bows on her bare hips. Her flat stomach gave way to the muscles over her ribs, and the fabric of her top extended over half of each bulbous breast. Her flowing hair swept her shoulders, and her dark eyes combined with the black fabric of the bikini to give her a beguiling look that would stop most men in their tracks.

He approached her by the edge of the pool. "It looks like I picked the right bikini."

"How did you know my size?"

"I guessed," he replied. Gesturing to the water, he asked, "Shall we try it out?"

Josie descended concrete steps into the pool. Temperature-wise, the water was about what she expected—eighty degrees Fahrenheit. Its texture, however, was a surprise. The liquid felt unlike any she had encountered before. It was salty, but there seemed to be something more to it than just sodium.

When the water level reached her chest, she turned to face Derek and pushed away from the steps. She floated, and her muscles began to relax. The water coated her skin like a film around her body. "This water feels weird," she said.

"It comes from a thermal spring," Derek answered. "It's mineral water."

He took her hand and led her to the center of the pool where the C-shaped Jacuzzi percolated. "Where are you most sore?" he asked as he guided her into the bubbling pool within a pool.

"Here," she answered, gesturing to the middle of her back.

He turned her slowly in the effervescent water and lifted her into his muscular arms. He exposed her most sensitive area to the massaging bubbles. She closed her eyes as the Jacuzzi worked its magic on her tender flesh. It seemed natural to surrender herself to Derek, as if she were a long-suffering maiden who had found her rescuer.

Derek couldn't help but trail his gaze up and down her perfect anatomy. Her chest seemed to dance with the bubbles which simmered beneath it. His thoughts were of nothing but the desire his body was feeling. That dreaded word *trouble* shot through his brain again. He jerked his head back as if he'd been slapped, but he didn't let her go. Was she really that dangerous? He'd been told to keep her away from The Agency, but he failed. He was then ordered to keep her close, but not too close. What did that mean exactly?

Josie opened her eyes to see him looking like he did when he turned their would-be kiss into a hug, and she knew that she was losing him again. "Where do we go for privacy?" she asked. "For warmer water? The heat would be good for me."

Derek led her to a private pool. It was a grotto, surrounded by faux rock face. A cascade flowed from a gap in the simulated stone to the pool below while mist hovered over water with a temperature of one hundred degrees Fahrenheit. Water caressed Josie's legs as she entered the pool. She allowed herself to melt into the soothing liquid. As she dove under and her backside rose to the surface, she presented a perfectly shaped inverted heart to Derek's trailing eyes. He forgot his orders and followed her into the pool.

Josie rose beneath the waterfall and the torrent flowed over her as she raised her arms over her head. She stepped forward so water would fall more directly on her shoulders. She wiped the salty fluid from her eyes. Before she could open them, Derek rose up from beneath the water and touched his lips to hers. It was a long-desired contact, and she offered no resistance, only acceptance. She let her arms fall onto him, then slide around his neck. He placed a hand behind her head and the other on her hip. His fingers explored her thick, wet hair. Her upper arms felt the heat of his shoulders.

Their salty kiss developed into a passionate release. Lips and bodies melded together, their tongues swaying over one another as if in a sensual dance. The mineral water washed upon them and mist hovered like a fog that enveloped them in its embrace.

***

Josie returned to work with the feeling that she was floating on a euphoric cloud. She couldn't wait to see Derek again and expected to run into him every time she turned a corner or passed a doorway. When that didn't happen, she slowly sank back to earth. Igraine resumed her dictatorial manner by sending Josie on errands throughout the city. Abby and Leif were nowhere in sight. Her phone, which had been replaced again, didn't ring except for check-up calls from her grandfather.

Josie's fourth day back to work finally brought her into contact with Abby. "Josie," the doctor said. "I've been looking for you. Do you have a moment?"

They entered Abby's office and Josie could see that it wasn't typical for a doctor. There were no framed degrees on the wall or posters about health. No medical tools were present, but there were plenty of population charts, graphs, and cabinets.

"Aside from soreness and stiffness from your accident," began Abby, "how have you been feeling? Have you had any more cramps or pain in your pelvis or legs?"

"How did you know I had those pains?" Josie asked. "I never told you."

"Because the tests came in and I know what's wrong with you."

Josie sat in a chair by the desk. "What is it?"

"You have endometriosis," said Abby.

"What does that mean?"

"It means that cells outside of your uterus are behaving like those inside your endometrium," Abby explained.

"Endometrium?"

"The lining of your uterus," said Abby. "The cells are implanting themselves on your ovaries, bowel, rectum, bladder, and the lining of your pelvis. And they are responding to your hormones…causing pain, bleeding, and eventual infertility."

Josie stared at her in disbelief. "What's gonna happen to me?"

"There are four stages of endometriosis," said Abby. "You're in the second stage. If left untreated, your condition will worsen, and you could experience an increase in pain and bleeding. Lesions and extensive adhesions will develop in your pelvic area. The pain could become so great that you might have to be bedridden for days at a time."

"How…how do we treat it?" Josie stammered.

"There's no cure for endometriosis," Abby replied. "But you could get a hysterectomy and that usually prevents the symptoms of the disease from ever returning."

"A hysterectomy?" Josie repeated. "You mean taking out my ovaries?"

"It's an option that you might have to explore very soon," said Abby.

"I'm not even twenty-two years old," declared Josie. "I want kids someday."

***

Josie left Abby's office with a sinking feeling, a red face, and water-logged eyes. Either ignoring or not noticing her emotional anguish, Igraine sent her off on another errand to return a file to the upper floor records office.

Josie entered the documents room to find a clerk behind a desk and rows of bookcases and filing cabinets. She saw four research computers, but none of that mattered to her. She moved like the living dead. The thought that she would never have children stole her spirit. Though she despised her siblings and fled her family, she always hoped that someday she would have children of her own and a loving husband. Now she faced the wicked reality that her dreams would likely never come true.

The room's sensor made a gurgling sound as she passed it. The clerk looked up from a computer but said nothing. Josie proceeded into the room, searching for the cabinet which would receive her document. The file she was to return had a name, *Aufteilung in Bereiche*, and docket number 1056691 printed on its folder. Typically, Josie would match the given words with those on the cabinet drawers to find a document's destination, but she couldn't find a pairing for this particular file.

After a half hour of searching, she remembered her phone. It wasn't as nice as the one Todd threw away, but it had the applications she needed. She used it to access the Internet and find a German to English translation site. She learned that the words on the file meant "allocation in areas." She didn't know what that was, but she thought she'd find other words on the cabinets that were similar to it. Her search led her to such translations as *property deeds, litigation, infrastructure, regional assimilation*, and *personnel/staff*. The last label was affixed to numerous drawers.

"I wonder if I'm in here," she whispered to no one but herself.

She thought of her grandfather. He must have a file. She was curious about what he did for The Agency. Come to think of it, she wasn't quite sure what Derek did either. He probably had a file too. Would there also be one for her father?

The clerk had paid her no mind since she first entered the room, so she was confident that she had plenty of time to peruse the files. Little did she know, hidden cameras recorded her every movement, and the clerk was monitoring her from his computer.

She leafed through files while applying her Internet translator to words she found. Then she found a folder which made all the others seem insignificant. The name on the label was *Ersman, Michael G.* There it was! Her father's folder. Everything she wanted to know about his time with The Agency, and perhaps more. Before she reached for the precious packet, she looked up. What she saw startled her even more than the folder. It was the clerk, and he was coming her way.

If Igraine fired her for looking at something as common as a picture of Charlemagne, what would happen if she was caught analyzing personnel records? Making a snap decision, she pulled her father's file and closed the drawer. She inserted the folder into the one she had arrived with and pretended to be lost. Reading her original packet, she said, "I can't find Aft Lung in Barish anywhere."

The clerk eyed her skeptically and peered at the words on her file. He was about to correct her pronunciation when she added, "I guess I'll just bring it back."

With a German accent, he said, "Leave it vis me."

"No. Thank you," she said. "I'm supposed to handle it."

She hurried away from the clerk, feeling his gaze upon her. Without delay, she passed the sensor and didn't wait to see if it went off.

The clerk watched Josie rush out the door and disappear down the hall. Returning to his desk, he checked the computer to see that her departure was being tracked and the file she took was identified. He picked up a phone to inform his superiors.

That wasn't so bad, Josie thought. No alarm and no guards. The tricky part, however, was yet to come. She had to go back to the office and work the remainder of her shift without Igraine or anybody else finding the "borrowed" file.

"Vat is zis?" Igraine suddenly demanded.

Josie turned to see the woman strutting toward her at a determined pace. She looked frantically for a place to hide the file, but there was nowhere to put it.

A college-aged staffer emerged from the office with a guard and three police men. He pointed in Josie's direction and said, "*Da ist sie* (There she is)!"

Josie was trapped. She was holding the stolen item and was caught between her boss and the police. Visions of prison returned to her mind.

"I zay again, vat is zis?" exclaimed Igraine. She reached for the file, but Josie held it tight. Astonished at the girl's resistance, she tugged. Josie pulled back.

The police descended upon them and Josie realized all was lost. She couldn't run. She couldn't resist. She let go of the packet, but the officers pushed her aside and swarmed Igraine. They threw her against the wall and jerked her arms behind her back.

Josie was stunned as she watched the police apprehend Igraine less than five feet away from her. Looking down, she saw stumbling feet kick the file. The packet opened to her father's folder. She gasped.

In the midst of her struggle, Igraine saw the document and immediately realized what it was. She turned sharply to Josie but didn't have time to accuse her. The police pulled her away from the wall and marched her down the corridor.

Igraine proclaimed her innocence in a screaming voice as she was escorted to the stairs. A crowd of people gathered to watch the arrest, and Josie scrambled to collect scattered, torn file pages before anyone noticed them.

***

The door was locked and Josie was alone in the guest room of her grandfather's house. She had her father's file spread out on the mattress before her, but she couldn't concentrate. Was Igraine arrested in her place? She disliked the woman but didn't want her to take the fall for what she had done. It wouldn't be long, she realized, before the police learned who really took the folder. She wondered if she should run away, but to where? She was finally starting to make a home for herself in Germany. She considered going to her mother in the hospital but realized that was the last person she wanted to see, and Heidi could do nothing to protect her from the authorities anyway.

"I better get as much out of this as I can before the shit hits the fan," she said.

With the help of an Internet translator, she learned that the file ended incompletely. There was no mention of her father's romance with her mother. In fact, there was no account of him even being in the United States. The manuscript concluded with Michael visiting a French basilica called Saint-Denis. Searching other Internet sites, she learned that Saint-Denis traced its history back to Roman times. It was the burial site of many French monarchs and was particularly important to Charlemagne and his predecessors. It was where Charlemagne and his brother Carloman were crowned co-rulers upon the death of their father in the year 768.

"More Charlemagne stuff?" she mumbled.

Studying the remainder of the file, she received a synopsis of her father's life. He was born and raised in Cologne, Germany. He had traveled extensively in his youth but returned home to attend the University of Cologne where he majored in German history. He was mentored by a Dr. Karl Vanderhoff. There were extensive citations attached to Vanderhoff's name, all of which referred the reader to other files.

After graduation, he took an entry level position at The Agency. He worked up the ranks and was the youngest person on the twelve-member Executive Council. His official title was Chief Historian and Propagandist.

"An historian on the Executive Council?" Josie asked. "Is history really that important?" She found the definition for propagandist and said, "He was a spin doctor?"

***

Josie didn't want to return to work but knew her absence would be an admission of guilt. She entered The Agency's offices prepared for the worst but hoping for the best. To her surprise, she learned that her fears were unfounded. The police weren't looking for her. They wanted the NSM's mole, someone who assisted in the Ascension Day attack by diverting security away from the Rathaus so the bomber could sneak materials past check points. That someone turned out to be Igraine.

Investigators and policemen interviewed staffers and searched for evidence. Josie was waiting for her turn to be questioned when Derek emerged from the stairwell. He was met by detectives and security but brushed them aside to approach Josie.

"Are you all right?" he asked.

The stolen file and what happened to Igraine became insignificant to Josie when she considered how Derek might react to her inability to have children. She wanted him to wrap his arms around her and tell her that infertility didn't make her any less of a woman in his eyes. They were not in the place or point in their relationship for that to happen, so she simply asked, "Do you think Igraine worked for the NSM?"

"I don't know." He pulled her away from others and said, "This isn't the right place for you."

"Are you kidding?" she asked. "It's gonna be great. She won't be here to boss me around anymore."

"That's not what I mean," he replied, but he didn't get a chance to elaborate.

A buzz filled the office as Dr. Herzog entered and beckoned Derek over.

Unfortunately for Josie, Derek left the office with detectives and she didn't see him again for the rest of the day. Dr. Herzog, however, stayed to hold court with investigators and employees in a room she had never before seen anyone enter.

Josie was answering an officer's poorly pronounced questions when the records clerk walked by. He stared at her as if he knew what she had done. Her eyes nervously followed him as he entered Dr. Herzog's private chamber. Twenty minutes later, he left the room. Passing Josie for the second time, he said, "He vould like to see you now."

Josie entered Dr. Herzog's personal office with more than a bit of anxiety. The room was not as lavishly appointed as she expected. There was a mahogany desk and a hardwood floor partially covered by a thick oriental rug. Each wall was lined with cases of books, and three unique paintings occupied space not utilized by the cases. It was before one of these paintings that Dr. Herzog stood.

Without looking at Josie, he said, "I despise violence, especially the senseless, cowardly violence of terrorists. And it hurts me terribly to think that my personal secretary was involved in the Ascension Day attack. Did you see anything that might have tipped us off to this?"

"No," Josie answered. "I mean she was...she wasn't very nice. She was pushy, and really rude, but I didn't see anything else."

Dr. Herzog turned to her and said, "I'm going to Brussels next week and no longer have a secretary. Would you be interested in temporarily filling that position?"

Josie was shocked. "I've never been a secretary."

"Is that a no?" he asked.

"No."

Dr. Herzog waited. Was she saying no to the first question or the second?

"Y...yes," she stammered. "I'd be happy to fill that position."

"Good," he said with a smile. He walked around his desk and sat in an upholstered leather chair. Josie realized that was her cue to leave, but before she reached the door, he added, "I would appreciate it if you'd return that file."

Josie stopped dead in her tracks.

CHAPTER SEVEN

The train ride into Belgium had been a lesson in contrasts for Josie. On the one hand, she traveled in the luxury of a first class cabin in close proximity to Derek, who she stole glances at and touched whenever she had the chance. But the air was polluted by Dr. Herzog's anger at learning that Igraine had somehow escaped custody.

By the time they transferred to a limousine for their trek through Brussels, Dr. Herzog had regained his composure and was anticipating his first business meeting.

Their car stopped outside a bizarre-looking complex. It was blue-green, had fifteen floors, and had three side structures. Two of the buildings were connected by a strange facade that looked like a giant net made of steel and glass.

"Welcome to the Charlemagne Building," Dr. Herzog announced. "Home of the European Commission."

"The Charlemagne Building?" Josie repeated.

"Named after The Father of Europe," Dr. Herzog explained.

"Of course," Josie said.

Protocol demanded that Derek and Josie walk behind Dr. Herzog and carry his belongings. They entered the lobby where Josie counted five armed guards and an attendant who was sitting behind a desk. They sprang to attention when they saw Dr. Herzog.

"He gets some respect, doesn't he?" Josie whispered.

"You could say that," Derek agreed.

They watched as Dr. Herzog took time to greet each of the guards by name. Derek leaned over to whisper to Josie. Anticipating a kiss, she moved her cheek to his lips. "We need some time alone," he said. "After dinner?"

***

Dr. Herzog's meeting with directors of the European Commission was largely uninteresting to Josie. She took notes as he instructed and used a digital recorder to capture everything that was said. Her eyes repeatedly drifted to Derek, and she watched him attend to his boss while simultaneously placating the directors. He was a skilled multi-tasker, she observed, but her thoughts frequently turned to their after dinner plans. Would they take a stroll together in the moonlight? Would they kiss? Would it lead to anything more? She could feel her anticipation growing as the meeting dragged on, but she was also conflicted. These were the same feelings she had when she first met Steve, and that attraction ended with a gunshot, a high-speed chase and a crash...then two abduction attempts and another crash, the last one fatal.

As night finally settled upon the city and the workday ended, Dr. Herzog treated Derek and Josie to a meal at one of the finest restaurants in Brussels. After dinner, he excused himself to make a phone call while Derek and Josie had their alone time on a patio which overlooked an indoor brook. Derek leaned against a railing as Josie watched the water beneath them.

Before she could initiate the conversation, Derek said, "I like you a lot."

"Yeah, I got that vibe when we were in the spa," she teased.

He smirked and assumed a more serious tone. "But I really think..."

His no nonsense demeanor put her on alert. Did he know about her endometriosis? He clearly knew about her crazy ex-boyfriend. Before he could say or do something she would regret, she attempted to redirect the discussion. "If you're worried about my ex, don't be," she interrupted. "He's more stupid than he is psycho, and he won't be back."

"I'm not concerned about him," Derek replied.

"My mother's harmless too. Trust me."

"I know," Derek lied. Any woman he ever knew who used her body to make a living was unpredictable at best, and unpredictability got people killed. "I need to talk to you about something else," he said. "I don't want you to work for The Agency anymore."

"What?" she asked in complete surprise. "Why not?"

"What you see here is an illusion," he said. "The bombing. The protests. They are only going to increase. I can't go into detail, but..."

"But what?" she asked. "This job's just getting good and you want me to quit?"

"Quit what?" asked Dr. Herzog as he stepped onto the patio.

Derek grunted at the interruption and whispered, "You've got this all wrong. Meet me for lunch tomorrow, and I'll tell you the rest." With Dr. Herzog only a few feet away, he added, "Don't say anything about this to him."

"I was telling her that she had to quit her job as file runner to be your secretary," Derek told Dr. Herzog. "It's a different pay grade and a different classification."

Dr. Herzog laughed. "You're always thinking like an administrator, Derek. I guess that's what makes you so good."

"Thank you, Doctor," replied Derek. "I try."

"I want you to understand," Dr. Herzog said to Josie. "At this point, yours is a temporary position. But I don't think Igraine will come back to her job anytime soon."

Josie and Derek laughed, though each remained uncomfortable over the conversation they had been having.

"Well, if I'm going to continue to be a good administrator," said Derek. "I had better organize my notes for tomorrow. Good night." He gave Josie a nod and walked away.

"He's a hard working boy," Dr. Herzog said. "He reminds me of your father."

"Um...yeah," Josie replied. She watched Derek depart. Turning her attention to Dr. Herzog, she said, "I'm sorry about the file. I just...I never knew my dad. Nobody ever told me much about him, so I thought I could get some answers by reading his file. I was gonna return it."

"I know you were," Dr. Herzog told her. "But I need to be able to trust the people who work for me. You've already seen what happens when I can't."

Josie nodded, and her eyes lowered to her Rolex. "Thank you for the watch, by the way."

"You're welcome," he replied. "It was actually Derek's idea."

"It was?"

"I paid for it, but...huh, it's hard to miss the spark between you two," he said.

Josie began to feel uncomfortable again, though for a different reason than before. Was he going to try to put the brakes on their match-up?

"And I think it's great," he declared. "It reminds me of a relationship I once had. I'm not as handsome as Derek, even when I was young, but...you. You are the spitting image of my Marguerite. She was very beautiful. And so are you."

"Thank you."

"She never had the advantages that I would be able to give her now," he said. "Hmm...I don't think there is any limit to what she could have achieved if someone in my position had entered her life back then."

Dr. Herzog's ramblings touched a sensitive nerve for Josie, especially in light of her conversation with Derek. She wondered if Derek was about to break it off with her when Dr. Herzog interrupted them. The thought of his rejection filled her with anger and made her feel defiant. Giving her attention back to Dr. Herzog, she said, "Maybe she needed to succeed on her own, without anyone's help."

"I agree," he replied. "I never valued anything I didn't earn for myself."

She waited for him to reveal more about Marguerite, but he said, "If you want to know about your father or anybody else in The Agency, all you have to do is ask me."

"Was he murdered?"

"You're as direct as Marguerite was too," Dr. Herzog said with a sad smile. "The American investigation said it was an accident, but I suspect the NSM. Unfortunately, I have no evidence to back my suspicion."

Questions swirled in Josie's mind, but she didn't know how to state them, or even which ones were pertinent and appropriate. Before she could get a handle on any of them, Dr. Herzog cut the evening short.

"Tomorrow will be a long day," he said. "Like Derek, I should prepare for it. Please excuse me."

***

The next day was, in fact, a hectic one. Dr. Herzog, Derek and Josie met with bureaucrats and politicians. They discussed strategies, trade regulations, and the setting of monetary exchange rates. Derek departed before noon to attend to his own duties, but he reminded Josie of their lunch date—one o'clock at a restaurant called Brasserie Horta in the Belgian Comic Strip Center.

A taxi driver delivered Josie to the restaurant twenty-five minutes before she was supposed to meet with Derek. She had some time to wander about the Comic Strip Center and found sharp colors and exaggerated depictions of comic book art everywhere she looked. A checkered, red-and-white rocket and statues of characters such as Tintin brought the cartoons to life. For a moment, she considered how much her youngest brother would enjoy what she saw. But thoughts of her family gave way to shock when she spotted Igraine through the window of a comic album shop. The woman wore a knitted hat and a gray sweater, but Josie had no doubt that it was her former boss-turned fugitive. She took out her phone to call Dr. Herzog…but stopped. As she moved closer to the window, she saw that Igraine was talking to someone. It was Derek!

Josie fled the Comic Strip Center with rage fueling her every step. She couldn't understand why Derek and Igraine were secretly meeting. For a moment, she imagined that he had something going with Igraine, but quickly ruled that out. Igraine was an old, bitter, and ugly woman. The only explanation was that Derek was conspiring with a fugitive terrorist of the NSM, the same group that might have killed her father.

She knew that she should tell Dr. Herzog, but if she did, there would be no going back. Whatever she and Derek might have had would be gone. Derek would be gone. She couldn't take that risk, so she decided to figure it out herself before informing others.

***

The return trip from Belgium was agonizing for Josie. Not only did she have to lie to Derek about why she missed their lunch date, but she couldn't ask him about his meeting with Igraine because Dr. Herzog was always with them. It was a supreme test of her ability to be secretive, and she must have passed because they dropped her off at her grandfather's house with smiles and plans to see her back at work on Monday. Nothing was out of the ordinary, except in her mind.

***

Josie's thoughts were still on that return trip from Belgium when she and Konrad walked down a corridor at University Hospital in Cologne.

"Would you like me to go in there with you?" Konrad asked.

"Huh? Uh...no," she answered. "I can go. Where did you say Steve was?"

"Are you sure you did not experience some memory loss with the accident?" Konrad asked. "This is the fourth time I have told you that he remains in intensive care. Room 336. Should we go see him first?"

"No," she said. "I don't want to see him. And my head is fine. I'm just thinking about a lot right now." They stopped before a private room with a policewoman sitting by the door. "This must be it."

81

Konrad showed the officer court papers signed by a judge.

"I will be waiting out here," he reassured his granddaughter.

Josie entered the room to find her mother watching a German talk-show on television. The bruises on her face, arms, and upper chest had faded to a light purple and gold color. She had stitches on her forehead, numerous scratches, and her right leg was in a cast. She wore a neck brace, and the side of her face still appeared swollen. Her left wrist was attached to intravenous tubes and was handcuffed to the rail of the hospital bed.

"Hello, Mom," Josie said.

"You took your sweet time getting over here, didn't ya?" Heidi asked bitterly.

Josie ignored her mother's antagonism and said, "Grandpa says you'll be all right."

"I broke my leg in four places," Heidi replied. "You know what kind of scars I probably have under this cast?"

"At least you'll be able to walk," Josie said.

"I'm not worried about walking," Heidi told her. "How many guys do you know who'll pay to see a dancer with scars and a limp?"

Josie walked to the window. Gazing at the city below, she said, "They agreed to let you and Steve go back home if you sign papers saying you'll never come back to Germany."

Heidi took in a deep breath and let out a long exhale. "Is that what you really want?" she asked her daughter.

"Yeah."

"You think your grandfather can take care of you?"

"I can take care of myself," Josie corrected. "I'm twenty-two..."

"Not 'til tomorrow," snapped Heidi.

"Will you sign the papers or not?"

"I did the best I could with you," said Heidi. "You didn't come with a manual, y'know. I wasn't even eighteen when you were born, pregnant from a one night stand, and the man that did it was gone..."

"Whoa, whoa...what?" Josie interrupted. "A one night stand? You told me you and my dad were in love...been dating almost a year."

"You're not a kid anymore," Heidi responded. "So I can stop lying. The truth is that I ran away from home kinda like you are now."

"I'm not running away, dammit! I moved. Why can't anybody see that?"

"Running away or moving, there's no difference when you can barely support yourself," said Heidi. "I ended up in Colorado and took a job as a dancer 'cause that's all I could do. A few weeks later, your dad came into the club. He was lonely and depressed and drinking a lot...you wanna hear the rest of this?"

Josie nodded.

"He was the first guy to spend a lot of money on me," Heidi continued. "I was young and stupid. And out of my mind. We partied all night at his hotel, and he took off the next morning. That was it."

Josie looked at the floor, thinking about what she had heard.

"I'm sorry, Josie," Heidi said. "But that's what happened, and you gotta hear it 'cause you're making the same mistakes I made."

"How'd you find out about his accident?" Josie asked.

"Cops came to the club," Heidi answered. "They said they found matches with our logo in his pocket."

"What about my pendant?" Josie asked. "How'd you get that?"

"He gave it to me after he broke it," Heidi replied.

"It wasn't broken," said Josie.

"Why do you care so much about that thing anyway?" Heidi asked. "He said it was worthless. Or worthless to him, I guess. He broke an emerald off it when he tripped and hit a table."

"Oh, I remember the hole on the side of it," Josie recalled. "That must be where the emerald went. Why didn't you just glue it back on?"

"I don't remember," Heidi answered. "I think he put it in his pocket or something. Again, why do you care?"

"Because that's all I ever had from him," Josie snapped. "And you sold it!"

"I think you've gotten me back for that," Heidi said.

"I don't think so."

"No? Let me see," Heidi responded. "You stole the money I was gonna use to feed the family. You made us come half way around the world to get you...twice! You put your boyfriend in the ICU..."

"Ex-boyfriend!"

"You broke my leg and ruined my career. And...oh, yes...Todd is dead! Am I missing anything?"

Josie's expression went cold as she stared at Heidi. She finally said, "I'll have you and Steve put away for a long time if you don't sign those papers."

She walked out of the room and slammed the door behind her.

***

Josie spent the twenty-second anniversary of her birth pondering her immediate future. She'd taken a risk in that hospital room. Her mother never responded well to threats, especially when they came from her kids. But they weren't in America anymore, they were in Germany. Konrad assured her that he could have her mother and Steve locked up for years. The Agency had a lot of pull with law enforcement.

Josie gave little thought to a birthday celebration and was surprised when Konrad announced that he would be taking her out. The restaurant he chose was quintessentially German—an Aachen pub called Am Knipp. As they entered the pub, Josie was relieved to be alone with her grandfather. It would be the two of them...and Abby and Leif? She was stunned to see the pair sitting at a table and sampling one another's beer.

"I thought your new friends might like to celebrate with us," Konrad told her.

"Did you invite Derek?" she asked.

"I tried, but I could not locate him," he admitted.

As they approached the table, Leif, who was already feeling the effects of several drinks, sang, "*Hoch soll sie leben, hoch soll sie leben, dreimal hoch!*" Josie clearly didn't understand what was said, so he added, "Happy Birthday!"

Other patrons shouted, "Happy Birthday!" Josie smiled, let go of the thoughts that had plagued her all day, and sat with Abby and Leif as Konrad joined them.

The party atmosphere of the pub seemed to be as intoxicating as Josie's bottomless glass of wine. She and her companions ordered food, but almost as an afterthought. Jokes and conversation became their reason-to-be, and they shared both freely with the people who ate and drank around them.

"What kind of wine is this?" Josie asked as she consumed her third glass.

"*Riesling Halbtrocken,*" the waiter said. He set a sirloin steak before Konrad, served Abby vegetarian *flammkuchen*, gave roast beef to Leif, and put a roasted turkey strip meal in front of Josie.

"It means a half-dry Riesling," Abby translated.

"I love this place," said Konrad. To Josie, he added, "Your father felt the same. That is why I brought you here tonight. Perhaps in some way, he is with us."

His comment brought Josie's mind back to what her mother told her about her father and their "hook-up." She had no desire to return to those thoughts on her birthday, so she declared, "I think I'd like to do a shot."

"With your meal?" Abby asked.

"I'm not hungry," Josie said as she pushed her plate aside.

"*Jägermeister, vier Shots* (Jägermeister, four shots)!" Leif yelled to the waiter. "*Und bring die Flasche* (And bring the bottle)!"

Nearby people cheered and chanted, "Jager! Jager! Jager!"

The waiter returned with a tray upon which sat four shots of liquor and a bottle of Jägermeister. As he dispensed the beverages, Leif raised a toast and shouted, "Happy birthday!"

Other patrons shouted the same, or "*Alles Gute zum Geburtstag!*"

Leif, Abby, Konrad, and Josie drank their shots, with the latter three squeezing their eyes shut and scrunching their faces. Leif immediately poured another round.

After several shot-sized servings of Jägermeister, Josie felt energy she didn't know she had and a numbness of her faculties. Her speech became slurred, and she developed a distorted, almost blurred view of her surroundings.

"Derek," Abby said as she saw him enter the establishment. To Leif, she added, "I told you he'd make it."

Josie spun in her seat to see Derek. Her view was blurry, but she had no difficulty recognizing him. He was casually dressed in slacks and a blue, button-down shirt. He carried a present, and there was a woman beside him. She was less identifiable, but she had blond hair and a stocky build. She looked to be in her forties.

"He wouldn't," Josie said. The more she stared, however, the more the woman looked like Igraine. Derek spoke to her, and she smiled. Igraine never smiled!

"He would not what?" Konrad asked her.

Josie ignored the question. He had a lot of nerve to show up at her celebration, she decided. To arrive with the woman who hated her, tormented her, and probably had a hand in killing her father, though, was too much. "Son of a bitch!" Josie exclaimed. She downed another shot and sprang to her feet. She staggered to the entrance.

"Happy Birth...," Derek began to say, but Josie struck him across the face as hard and as fast as she could. Then she jumped the woman.

Formally jovial patrons leaped from their seats, surrounded the combatants, and cheered to shake the rafters. Konrad swam through the crowd to get to Josie.

***

Josie went to work the next day with a piercing headache and pangs of guilt. The woman she attacked wasn't Igraine but a hostess who recently started at the pub after a painful divorce. Derek left after the fight, saying nothing more to her.

She wasn't surprised, therefore, when an assistant told her that Dr. Herzog was in his office and waiting to speak with her. The last time she entered his office, she expected to be fired, and this visit was no different. When she saw that Abby, Leif, Konrad, and the Lord Mayor of Aachen were also there, she felt even more anxious. She worried that her behavior had landed them all in hot water and knew that she wouldn't be able to forgive herself if she caused her grandfather to be fired.

"Ah, Josie. Sit down," Dr. Herzog said as he rose from the chair behind his desk. "We have something very important to discuss with you."

Josie searched the faces in the room for a sign of reassurance but found nothing.

"This is a crucial time for our organization," Dr. Herzog began. "On the one hand, we have had tremendous successes. The most notable being the adoption of one currency for all of Europe."

"The euro," Leif said while nodding his head. Abby frowned and poked him with her elbow for interrupting the Doctor with a statement of the obvious.

"We have also experienced setbacks," Dr. Herzog continued. "Terrorism and financial strain are causing many to question our effectiveness. We're losing support."

Josie wondered what this had to do with her bar fight. She thought again about Derek and wondered why he wasn't there.

"Has it been made clear to you what The Agency's mission is?" Dr. Herzog asked.

"Uh, I was told you wanted to bring Europe together as one big state," Josie answered. "Like Texas."

Dr. Herzog laughed. "What we are trying to do is similar to your America. Separate states and people united by a common government, currency, and culture." He could see that Josie had questions, so he elaborated. "The Charlemagne Award Agency was created in 1951, the brainchild of Kurt Fowler. Our mission has expanded from his initial goal of honoring individuals who best served humanity and world peace."

"I'm sorry, Doctor," Josie interrupted. "But does this have anything to do with what happened last night?"

"Your fight?" asked Dr. Herzog. "No. Though I would insist that if you agree to what I am proposing today, you will cease such activities."

Konrad, Abby, and Leif laughed. Josie was relieved, but even more confused.

"We were the prime architects of The Paris Treaty of 1951," Dr. Herzog continued. "The 1957 Rome Treaty, the Schengen Agreement of 1985 and the Maastricht Treaty of 1992."

Seeing how perplexed his granddaughter was, Konrad explained, "Those were all steps toward the creation of the twenty-seven member European Union we enjoy today."

"What I'm saying," Dr. Herzog added, "is that The Agency, which you are now a part of, has been the primary force in bringing the splintered states of Europe together as they once existed under Charlemagne."

"I get it," Josie replied.

"Good," answered Dr. Herzog. "Because I want you to understand that we cannot truly enjoy the peace, unity, and prosperity of Charles the Great's empire without the Emperor himself." He paused for effect and said, "That is why we are going to clone Charlemagne, and we want you to give birth to his clone."

Josie stared at the doctor, wondering whether or not she heard him correctly. Did he say they were going to clone Charlemagne? Was that even possible? She didn't know what to say and looked at Abby. After a considerable pause, she finally said, "I...uh...I can't have kids."

"On the contrary," Dr. Herzog replied. "You must have a child."

"He's right, Josie," confirmed Abby. "What I didn't tell you before was that there are two things that usually retard the effects of endometriosis. The first is a hysterectomy. The second is a pregnancy."

***

Abby explained the cloning process to Josie as she and Konrad walked her out of the Rathaus. Josie didn't seem to be listening. She was just happy to escape the office without giving Dr. Herzog an answer to his proposition. Abby departed when they reached the open air of the courtyard, but Konrad remained. "I know you have your doubts," he said. "But I do not."

Josie turned abruptly to face him. "You don't? Really?"

"No," he replied. "I have worked for The Agency nearly my entire life. So did your father. Dr. Herzog is offering you this honor largely because of our family's devotion to The Agency."

"What does that mean?" Josie asked. "They want me to give birth to their experiment as a reward for my father dying when he worked for them?"

"Oh, no," said Konrad. "I am not speaking properly. What I mean to say is this honor has been earned by us: me, Michael, and you."

"You keep calling it an honor," responded Josie. "But it just sounds crazy to me."

"I promise you; it is not," Konrad answered. "It is the completion of a dream that has been decades in the making. And of all the women who might have been selected…"

"Don't say it," Josie snapped. "Don't tell me I won the lottery here. I'm twenty-two years old and they want me to give birth to the clone of a king who has been dead for a thousand years. I can't begin to tell you how ridiculous it is."

"Yes," acknowledged Konrad. "Of course, Josie. You are right."

She eyed Konrad suspiciously, and wondered if he really thought she was right.

"You are young," he continued. "With a wonderful future ahead of you. If this is not your purpose, then no one, not even me, should push it on you."

"I'm not saying it's not my…what'd you call it? Purpose?" asked Josie. "It's just…this is…I gotta figure this out."

"I know," said Konrad. "And I am sorry. It is only that…this is the greatest of honors. To be the mother of the clone of Charlemagne, the future leader of all of Europe…I let my excitement get the better of me. It is you who must decide."

Josie nodded, thanking him for understanding. It was obvious that she wanted to get away from him, the Rathaus, and everything associated with the proposition.

Before he let her go, Konrad added, "I only ask that you consider this carefully. Such an opportunity will never come our way again."

He returned to the Rathaus, and Josie was left to wander the streets of Aachen alone. As her legs moved, she thought about what her grandfather said, "Such an opportunity will never come our way again." So to add more weight to her decision, she had to consider this an opportunity for her, him, her dead father, and the entire Ersman legacy. "As if I don't have enough to deal with already," she said aloud.

There was also the twist of fate Abby had revealed to her. This pregnancy might stop the effects of her disease. That was an opposite remedy to the one the doctor had suggested earlier. Her choice, therefore, was to get pregnant or have a hysterectomy. It was an impossible decision to have to make.

Then there was the issue of the impregnation itself. It was preposterous to think that they could clone someone who'd been dead for over a thousand years...wasn't it? And where would they get the stuff to make the clone from anyway? In the very least, she highly doubted that clone babies were born like real babies.

Several of those issues had been explained by Abby when she walked her out of the office. It was complicated, she told her, but they thought they now had the ability to achieve their goal. They would extract cells from Charlemagne's bones which have been on display in Aachen Cathedral for over a thousand years. Then they would remove the DNA from one of his cells. They also needed to remove the DNA from an egg taken from her ovary. The next step would be to fuse Charlemagne's DNA with her hollowed-out egg and introduce an electric current which would stimulate the cloned embryo to begin development. In the case of long-dormant DNA like Charlemagne's, an additional step was required to bring it back to life. It was a task which had long been impossible to achieve, but The Agency recently developed the technology to make it happen. Once that was done, it would be a matter of in vitro fertilization to complete the process.

Ethical questions swirled through Josie's mind as she aimlessly explored the cobblestone streets. If they could clone Charlemagne, they could also clone a psycho like Hitler. Did she really want to participate in something like that? Then there was the matter of necessity. Was our world so messed up that we needed to bring back someone from the Middle Ages to fix it?

Josie's wanderings took her to Aachen Cathedral, perhaps the only tourist spot in the city she hadn't visited.

***

The English language pamphlet Josie grabbed after paying her admission said Charlemagne built the Cathedral in 796 and had it dedicated to God's Earthly Mother, the Virgin Mary. "It's nice to know he respects mothers," Josie said, but she tried to shake the thought. Was she really considering their offer, she asked herself.

She watched as some tourists listened to guides while others meandered about the Cathedral. She wandered further into the building, and saw an expanse of space above her. Her gaze slowly lifted to behold an octagonal dome which seemed to stretch endlessly over her head. A thick cable extended from the dome's center to dangle a massive chandelier so close to Josie she thought she could jump up and touch it. The walls of the octagon consisted of two floors which rose to the base of the dome.

As Josie ventured into the next chamber, she remained ignorant of the man who entered the church behind her. He was Jean-Paul Renbleau, the NSM agent who set off the Ascension Day bomb, and he had been following her since she first left the Rathaus.

A glance at the pamphlet told Josie that she was entering the Glass Chapel, and the reason for its name was obvious. Thirteen huge stained-glass windows allowed colored light to filter into the room. A gilded orb that looked like the sun with the Virgin Mary in its center hung from the ceiling between two glass-encased gold reliquaries. The boxes resembled large dollhouses, but they didn't contain toys. They held human remains. According to the pamphlet, one of them housed the bones of Charlemagne himself.

"There they are," she mumbled. "In that little house are the bones they'll use to make the clone." She looked up at the golden orb and saw that its depiction of Mary had her holding the baby Jesus. The irony was unmistakable to Josie—the Madonna and child hovering over the remains that could potentially turn her into a mother.

She didn't have time to linger on those thoughts. A gun barrel poked her back, and a man with a French accent said, "Act normal and don't speak."

Josie gasped. She turned to face the man, but he spun her back around and said, "I told you to act normal."

Josie affected a rigid pose. "What do you want?" she asked.

"I want you to come with me," he replied.

"Who are you?"

"All you need to know is that I'll shoot you if I have to," he answered. "But..."

Josie didn't wait to hear the rest of what he had to say. She ran as fast as her legs could take her, weaving around tourists and objects.

"*Merde* (Shit)!" Jean-Paul exclaimed. "*Arrêtez-vous* (Stop)!"

Josie sprinted into the room with the dome. Over thirty tourists were gazing up in awe, and she squirmed into their midst. Her heart racing, she watched her would-be abductor run into the chamber and stop when he could no longer see her.

As a guide spoke to his group in Norwegian, Josie looked about. The crowd she was hiding within moved toward the Glass Chapel. She searched for an escape, then saw a roped off flight of marble stairs. She bolted toward it.

The sudden movement caught Jean-Paul's attention, and he sprinted after her. He collided with a young man who was already upset because his girlfriend was making him go to the Cathedral instead of the pub. The man cursed in Italian and pushed him. The shove sent an already off-balance Jean-Paul skidding across the floor.

Josie used a stone railing as a pivot point and ascended another set of stairs as rapidly as she had the first. She emerged in the second story gallery, which was an open area without much room to hide. She saw a simple-looking chair made of marble slabs held together by bronze L-shaped brackets sitting upon a perch. It had six steps leading up to it and an altar with a wooden door in its base attached to the back of it.

Jean-Paul scrambled to his feet as the Italian challenged him to a fight. The man's girlfriend tried to calm him down, but her efforts were wasted. Yelling in his native tongue, the man stalked toward Jean-Paul, who wanted no part of this distraction. He saw two security guards making a rapid approach.

"*Benehmt euch* (Behave yourselves)," the first guard said. "*Dies ist eine Kirche* (This is a church)."

Jean-Paul realized that it would be better to appease security than to provoke them. He apologized and offered a handshake to the Italian. The man's girlfriend convinced him to accept the offer, and the two men made their peace before security.

The best hiding place available to Josie was inside the altar. She stepped over a chain which cordoned off the chair structure and tried to open the altar's wooden door, but it was stuck. She strained. She pulled. It would be moments before the man with the gun arrived and she was desperate! A surge of adrenaline hit her, and she tugged with every ounce of her strength. The door opened with a crack that echoed through the chamber. Relieved, she crawled into the dark interior of the altar and closed the door.

With an eye on the guards, Jean-Paul pretended to study the massive chandelier. More tourists came his way, and he looked back at the guards. All clear. He stepped over the velvet rope which barred entrance to the stairs and charged ahead.

Kneeling in the dark, musty altar enclosure, Josie tried to stay quiet. A stack of metal rods pressed painfully into her shins. She wondered who her attacker was. Had he been hired by her mother and Steve or by her grandmother? Whoever it was, they had hit a new low. Abducting her was bad enough, but using a gun to do it was unforgivable.

Jean-Paul knew that he had little time to nab his prey before the guards caught up with him. Charlemagne's throne was a highlight of the Cathedral and was constantly monitored by cameras. Where was the girl, he wondered.

The rods which pushed against Josie's legs caused her considerable discomfort, but she couldn't see them in the darkness and had no idea what they were. She pulled the phone from her pocket and used its light to view her surroundings. She was in a storage space for religious items. Candelabras, vestments, booklets, crucifixes, jars of holy water and oil, even wafer hosts accompanied the rods which were used to support the items.

A quick but thorough inspection of the area yielded nothing for Jean-Paul. He heard voices speaking German and looked over a rail to see guards passing under the chandelier on the first floor. They were approaching the stairs he had recently ascended. He glanced back toward the throne and saw broken wood by the altar's door.

Josie heard someone taking cautious steps on the marble floor. They got louder as the person came closer. It would be mere moments before he found her. She was trapped, a sitting duck, but she had no intention of staying that way. She threw the door open and sprang out of the altar. She clutched a pointed rod in her right hand and held her phone, which was set to camera, in her left. Her thumb rested on the flash button. She looked like a modern version of a medieval knight who had traded a sword for a religious rod and a shield for a camera phone. She would startle him with the flash and stab him with the rod. She looked around, but the man was nowhere in sight.

Suddenly, two hands grabbed her from behind and threw her violently to the left. The rod in her grip struck the side of the chair with an impact that rattled her teeth and broke off a piece of the ancient marble. The camera flash went off inches from the chair's fresh wound. She lost the element of surprise to her attacker.

Jean-Paul struck her forearm, forcing her to drop the rod. He wrapped his arms around her in a bear hug, but Josie threw her head back hard and fast, striking him in the nose and breaking it on impact. He screamed and released his hold. Josie ran.

Like a bowling ball striking pins, Josie collided with five guards who were running up the steps. One nearly fell over the railing. Three others hit the wall. Josie barreled over the fifth and stumbled down the remainder of the staircase.

She sprinted out of the church, still clutching her phone.

Outside the Cathedral, Josie ran directly into a very surprised Derek, who was on his way into the building. They each fell back a step and stared at one another. It took a moment for Josie's expression to change from the manic look of someone fleeing to one of genuine bewilderment. Derek appeared equally confused. His gaze moved beyond Josie to see Jean-Paul hobbling out of the church with his hands over his bloody nose.

"Grab her, Derek," yelled Jean-Paul. "Grab her!"

Josie looked back and saw three guards suddenly descend upon the Frenchman. She turned to Derek with the realization that he was partnered with her would-be abductor. The look that crossed her face begged a single question...why? But Derek had no intention of answering that question. A deranged look filled his eyes, and he grabbed her by the shoulders. Josie screamed, clutched the flesh of his groin and squeezed with all her strength. Derek yelled. In the mayhem of the moment, she was sure that she felt something pop or burst in her hand. Derek released her and fell to the ground clutching the wounded part of his anatomy.

Josie fled frantically into the street. She looked back to see that Derek wasn't pursuing her and, in so doing, collided with a fast-moving motor scooter. The impact was sudden and powerful, hurling Josie into the air. She hit the cobblestone street head first. Her forehead split, and darkness engulfed her as her blood soaked the stones.

***

Josie awoke with no knowledge of where she was or how long she'd been there. She had to guess that it was a fairly long time because she could feel ample razor stubble beneath her arms. Her head was bandaged, she was in a hospital gown, and once again, she was attached to an intravenous tube. More tubes stretched into her nostrils, and she was connected to a heart monitor. To her surprise, she didn't have any pain and felt relatively clear headed.

One of her monitors must have sent out an alert because Abby, Dr. Herzog, Leif, and a woman Josie didn't know came charging into her room. Relief washed over their faces when they saw that she was awake and apparently coherent.

"Let me guess," Josie said. "I'm back in the infirmary."

Smiles lit up the faces of her visitors.

"You gave us a terrible scare," replied Dr. Herzog.

"Where's my grandfather?" she asked.

"I sent him home to get some rest," said Dr. Herzog. "He's been here day and night for the past two weeks."

"I've been here for two weeks?" Josie asked. "Ah...a...am I all right?"

Stepping forward, Abby said, "Yes, Josie. You are."

The woman Josie didn't recognize introduced herself as Madeline. She was in her fifties with streaks of gray in her dark hair. She spoke with a German accent. "We have kept you in an induced sleep while monitoring the swelling in your head," explained Madeline. "You do not appear to have any brain damage, but we were concerned."

Josie took a few moments to process the woman's statement. Then she smiled. "Well, that's good to know," she said. With a glance at Dr. Herzog, she added, "But I think I've seen enough of hospitals and doctors for a while. I'm sorry, but I'm gonna have to pass on your offer to become Charlemagne's mother."

The smile on Dr. Herzog's face disappeared as Abby and Leif exchanged uncomfortable glances.

CHAPTER EIGHT

Abby guided her sports car into the parking area of the Aachen Arkaden Shopping Center. Josie sat in the passenger seat, watching people enter the three-story mall. Her head was no longer bandaged, though stitches were visible just below her hairline.

"I can't figure out why he did it," said Josie. "Can you?"

"I don't know him too well," Abby replied. "Derek's a bit of a loner."

"But…" Josie cut herself short of explaining that she saw him with Igraine in Belgium. "What about that other guy," she asked. "I've never seen him before." She remembered her phone and took it out of her pocket. "Maybe you know him. I think I took a picture of him in the cathedral."

As Abby parked in a vacant spot, Josie searched her phone for the only picture she had taken. Her brows crinkled in confusion as she viewed the image that appeared.

"What the hell is this?" she asked.

She peered more closely at the picture. It was a close-up of a stone with a word carved into it. She enlarged the picture and saw that the word was *REGENSBURG*, and the carving looked to be very old.

Abby glanced at the phone, and asked, "What's that?"

Then it occurred to Josie. She accidentally took the photo when her would-be abductor threw her against the marble throne. The writing was apparently hidden under the piece that broke off when the rod in her hand hit the stone.

"Pretty weak marble," she said.

"What?"

"Huh? Uh, nothing," Josie lied. "I guess I didn't get a picture of him after all."

"I'm sure Dr. Herzog will find out who Derek was working with," said Abby. "And why they attacked you."

"Yeah," Josie replied, though her mind was still on the word *REGENSBURG*.

After several moments of silence, Abby finally slapped her thighs and said, "Well, are you up for some shopping? It's time to get your mind on something fun."

***

Abby and Josie followed shoppers through the mall's glass doors, and a vast expanse of retail opened up before them. Stores Josie didn't recognize, many with names she couldn't pronounce, employed a variety of looks to entice customers. What truly struck Josie was the art-deco feel of the place. Equestrian statues of assorted colors shared space with oversized porcelain masks, sharply pointed plants, and yellow and tan marble boxes that stood three feet high. The walls between the stores were neon green and displayed a variety of abstract expressionist prints.

"Is this a mall or a museum?" Josie asked.

"It's a little bit of both, I think," answered Abby. Like a moth to a flame, she approached the first designer shop she saw.

Josie didn't share Abby's tastes, so she said, "I'm gonna check this place out. I'll meet you back here in ten minutes."

Abby didn't hear her, and Josie didn't bother to look back. She gazed at the open space above her and saw a glass dome which allowed sunlight to rain down upon the three shopping levels. Staircases and escalators took patrons where they wanted to go. The mall was impressive, but Josie's mind kept returning to the image on her phone.

She took the device from her pocket and did an Internet search for Regensburg. It yielded over twelve thousand entries. Walking and reading the first few entries, she learned that Regensburg was a city in Southeastern Germany that dated back to the Stone Age. It currently had over a hundred and thirty thousand residents, and Pope Benedict XVI had once been a professor at The University of Regensburg.

"What does that have to do with anything?" she asked.

It occurred to her to look up the throne the word was carved upon. She learned that the ancient chair in Aachen Cathedral had belonged to Charlemagne.

"Oh, yes," she said sarcastically. "Who else?"

Putting two and two together, she searched for the words Charlemagne and Regensburg as a pair. It didn't take long for her to find a site that told of a plot that was hatched at Regensburg by Pippin the Hunchback. It was a conspiracy to murder Charlemagne, his wife, and his male heirs.

"Interesting," said Josie. "Now who was Pippin the Hunchback?"

Before she could answer the question, she ran directly into the large barrel chest of an olive-skinned man with a goatee and dark, penetrating eyes.

"Oh, uh, sorry," she said.

The man didn't respond, but something about his expression told Josie that he was uncomfortable with their encounter. He walked away from her, and Josie watched as he met up with a burly man with reddish blond hair and a full beard.

"You need to see this top," said Abby as she approached from the opposite direction with a box in a bag. "It's fantastic…what?"

Josie gazed at her friend with a curious expression on her face. "Nothing. I…" She looked back to see the men disappear behind a display. Turning to Abby, she said, "I can't wait to see what you bought."

"After we eat," said Abby with a smile. "My treat."

***

Josie and Abby ascended an escalator with other shoppers. As Abby imagined wearing her new purchase, Josie thought about the man she encountered. Something about the look on his face said that he knew her. Was she just being paranoid?

"Y'know, I could really go for Mickey D's," she joked, fully convinced that she wouldn't find one in a German mall.

"Mickey D's?" Abby asked.

"McDon…" Josie froze as the olive-skinned man with the penetrating eyes stepped onto the escalator. He was with his bearded friend, and they were staring back at her.

"McDonald's," said Abby as she stepped off the moving staircase and saw the restaurant with the famous golden arches standing before her.

"Let's go," Josie ordered as she led her by the hand into the eatery.

The two women charged into the packed restaurant, and Josie made a bee-line for the counter. She kept a constant lookout for the two men and missed seeing a tall, dark-haired man cut in front of several people to get in line behind her.

"You must be hungry," observed Abby.

"Yeah," Josie replied. She saw the front door open, and the two men she feared walked in. Their eyes immediately went to her.

Josie's heart sank. "Abby, I think we're..."

"You are American. Yes?" the dark-haired man in line said with a Scottish accent.

"Excuse me?" asked Josie.

"American. You look and sound like an American," he replied.

"Uh, yeah. So?" Josie said, still distracted. She looked back at the men and saw that they took their place in line ten people behind her. With a glance at Abby, she confided, "Those guys at the end of the line are..."

"I like America," the dark-haired man added. "The New York Yankees and...Ronald McDonald. What sandwich do you recommend?"

"Look guy, I don't mean to be rude, but..." It dawned on Josie that the man she was talking to was tall and muscular. He might be able to help, she thought. Her demeanor changed as she shared with him the merits of a Big Mac.

Abby watched with amused surprise as Josie told her new companion what to order and invited him to join them for the meal. The three of them set their food and drinks on a table and the dark-haired man took a seat. Still standing beside Josie, Abby whispered, "Don't make it too easy for the lad."

Josie directed her attention to the two men, who now seemed agitated and looked repeatedly back at her. "Do you know them?" she asked.

"No," said Abby. "But they must know you."

"They followed me in here," Josie said as she grabbed her drink from her tray.

The dark-haired man quickly moved his hands across the table and opened his sandwich wrapper. He watched Josie sip her soda while looking at two tough men.

"What do you think I should do?" Josie asked Abby.

"I don't know," Abby confessed. "But they definitely have their eyes on you."

Josie nodded and drank more soda. She thought for a moment that it tasted odd, but found herself wanting more of it.

"I think we should get security," Abby said.

"And say what?" Josie asked. "Two guys are staring at us?"

"Are you going to sit?" the dark-haired man asked.

Josie turned to look at him and found her eyes suddenly playing tricks on her. He seemed to swell to illogical proportions, then shrink back down to his normal size. She looked back at the two men and her vision shifted to a blurry haze. Through her distorted view, she could see that they were charging toward her! She reached for Abby but felt like she was moving in slow motion. "Run!" she yelled.

The last thing Josie saw was Abby's horrified face. She heard screams and gunshots as everything collapsed into black. She felt herself falling into a pit of darkness.

***

Josie awoke in a recliner. She had a bandage on her left arm, and her right wrist was handcuffed to a radiator. More disturbing than that was the fact that eleven people stood around her. Derek was one of those people, and Igraine was another.

"I'm so sorry, Josie," Derek began. "This is not how I wanted it to happen."

Josie glared at him.

"You were in serious danger," he continued. "We had to rescue you."

With a glance at her handcuffs, she asked, "This is your idea of a rescue?"

"We'll let you out of them when we know you won't run away," Derek told her.

"I'm supposed to believe that?" she asked. "You and a guy jumped me with a gun. And now this? How did I get here?"

An attractive, thirty-year-old brunette stepped in front of Derek, and said, "You...uh...you were given chloral hydrate...."

"You slipped me a Mickey?"

"It was a mistake," the woman said. "And the person who did it has been reprimanded."

"Reprimanded? How?" Josie asked. "Did you slap his wrists? He drugged and kidnapped me, and all you can say is that he was reprimanded?"

"He was severely disciplined, Josie," said Derek. "But we have something more important to talk to you about."

Josie stared at him, impatiently waiting for him to say more.

Derek hesitated, glancing at others around the room. Then he said, "I hate to tell you this, but...you're pregnant."

Josie did not expect to hear that, and her hard expression turned to one of bewilderment.

"Blood tests don't lie," said the brunette. "And we ran three of them. You're definitely pregnant."

"Considering I haven't had sex in months..." Josie began, but a new thought popped into her mind. Her breaths turned heavier and her eyes became narrow. "Didn't you say I was given a date rape drug?"

People around the room exchanged nervous glances.

***

Josie was moved into a white-walled bedroom with a tiny bathroom. There were no windows and only a bed and a dresser. For twelve hours, she remained locked in this prison with the computer print-out of her blood tests to read and re-read. Was she really pregnant? She didn't actually think she had been raped when she was unconscious. Besides, she wouldn't have become pregnant that quickly even if something was done to her. Their tests had to be wrong, she decided. Or they gave her someone else's tests.

***

By the time two armed men led her out of her room, Josie had calmed down enough to listen to her captors. Her escorts brought her back into the living room where she found the same crowd as before. The men compelled her to sit in the recliner and cuffed her again to the radiator.

"Josie, you may not trust us," Derek began. "But..."

"May not?" she mocked and rattled her handcuffs on the radiator.

"I don't know how else to say this except to come right out with it," he replied. "You refused to become the mother of their clone, but they did it to you anyway."

"How do you know I refused them?" she demanded. "How'd you know they even asked me?"

"I was Dr. Herzog's assistant for years," Derek explained. "I knew what they were planning, how it was progressing, and when it would happen. I knew they were targeting you from the moment Dr. Herzog saw you jump out of that window."

"Vat's done is done," observed Igraine. "Tell her vat she really needs to know."

"They lied to you," Derek said. "This was never about cloning Charlemagne."

"What are you talking about?" asked Josie. "There's either a clone, or there isn't. What am I saying? I can't possibly be pregnant."

"There is a clone," the brunette said. "It's just not of Charlemagne."

"Who are you?" Josie asked with annoyance.

"My name is Pamela," the woman replied. "I was Leif Christensen's partner before he fell under the sway of Dr. Herzog. I helped him develop the technology to stimulate dormant cells."

"Do what?"

"She worked with Leif in a cloning program," Derek explained. "Nobody ever told you Leif was the Chief of Cellular Transference and Manipulation?"

Josie shook her head and looked away, causing the others to exchange glances.

"Ah, she doesn't care about zat," interjected Igraine. "Josie, listen to me. Josie! You are pregnant vis zee clone of Charlemagne's son, Pippin zee Hunchback."

Josie snapped her head around. "What the...let me outta here! You're a bunch of frickin' nut jobs."

"It's true," Derek confirmed. "The Agency never cloned Charlemagne. They cloned his son instead. In January of the year 814, Charlemagne faked his death and buried his already dead son in his place. The bones The Agency used to make a clone were not Charlemagne's, they were Pippin's."

Josie frowned and arched her eyebrows, showing her obvious impatience.

"I know it sounds fanciful," he continued.

"Fanciful?" Josie asked. "More like ridiculous. Tell me, Mr. Know-It-All, how did I get pregnant if I didn't have sex or have in vitro? It doesn't happen from sitting on toilet seats."

"Are you aware of everything that happened to you in the past month?" Derek inquired.

"Are you saying they knocked me up when I was ..." She didn't finish the sentence and everyone around her saw recognition sweep across her facial features. "They couldn't have," she said.

"They did," replied Derek. "You were in an induced coma for four weeks, plenty of time for them to extract one of your eggs, remove its nucleus, replace it with the nucleus of one of Pippin's cells, stimulate the dormant DNA, then implant it as an embryo inside of you. In vitro fertilization."

"They told me I was out for two weeks," Josie said rather meekly.

"Actually, it was closer to five," Derek corrected.

"How...uh...how do you know this?" Josie asked.

"Let's just say I'm still very much in touch with what goes on over there."

Josie appeared morose and didn't speak for several long moments. Finally, she said, "If you're so in touch, why didn't you stop it from happening?"

"I didn't learn about it until after it was done," Derek replied. "Why didn't you quit The Agency when I told you to?"

Josie's face became instantly hardened with anger. "You're crazy, every one of you. This is all bullshit! Are you gonna let me go now?"

***

The Agency's ultra-secret, underground complex was a hive of buzzing people. Everyone seemed to be concentrated on the objective of finding and retrieving Josie alive. The facility's command center featured computers, maps, charts, and a touch-screen monitor mounted to the wall. Dr. Herzog, the Lord Mayor, Leif, and Abby joined an inconsolable Konrad before the monitor which displayed a map of Southern France.

Abby gasped as she saw two men enter the room. They were the burly individuals who followed Josie in the mall. The olive-skinned man was named Petra and his beard-wearing partner was Hans.

"The man who took her was NSM," said Petra with an Italian accent.

"We know that much," replied Dr. Herzog. "And they took her to Southern France. The tracking device she carried was silenced along Autoroute du Soleil, an hour outside of Nimes. Beyond that, we know little."

"I ask again, why are the authorities not involved?" Konrad demanded.

"They are," assured Dr. Herzog. "I have local, national, and international investigators working on it. It's a top priority. We'll find her, I promise you."

"I do not doubt that," replied Konrad. "But will it be too late when we do?"

***

It came as no surprise to Josie that her defiance landed her back in the locked bedroom. She found herself with more time to contemplate what her captors told her. It sounded preposterous, but she wasn't sure if she refused to believe it because it was so ridiculous or because she was angry at the people who told it to her. She wondered who they really were. The NSM? If so, they probably killed her father, and she knew she couldn't trust them.

It was late at night or early in the morning, Josie wasn't sure which, when the door opened and Derek entered.

"Josie?" he asked as he turned on the light. "How are you?"

She sat up in bed and gave him a cold look.

"That was a stupid question," he admitted.

"You think?"

"I'm sorry," he repeated. "I truly am."

"Save it."

"I can't erase what was done," he said. "But we really had the best of intentions."

"Did you?" asked Josie. "Honestly? You couldn't have just told me all that stuff? You had to attack me at gunpoint, then drug and kidnap me? What happened to Abby? Did your guys shoot her?"

"My guys?" he repeated. "We only had the one who drugged you—Bernard. The other two work for Dr. Herzog."

"I'm supposed to believe that?"

"Of course," he replied and moved closer to her. He sat on the bed and set his hand on her arm, but she jerked away from him. Ignoring her response, he asked, "Do you really think Dr. Herzog would let you wander the mall or anywhere else without security?"

Josie shrugged.

"You're carrying the clone that he spent years—and millions of euro—developing," Derek added.

The expression she wore told him that she didn't believe him.

"Whether you accept it or not, you're pregnant," he said. "And The Agency will never let you go. You need to stay here. We're the only ones who can protect you."

"This is your idea of protection?" she snapped. "Locking me up in a tiny room and handcuffing me to a radiator? I can't believe I ever trusted you. Did you also sell the watch you stole off my wrist?"

"We took it because there was a tracking device in it."

"And our trip to the spa?" she asked. "Was that a set-up too? The kiss? Your feelings? Did you really have any feelings for me, or were you using me?"

"I...my...what happened at the spa was genuine," Derek replied. "But that's a lifetime ago now. You're in serious danger, and that's what we need to focus on."

Josie sat in silent contemplation for several lingering moments. Then she asked, "Aren't you the one who gave me the watch with the tracking device?"

***

Over the next two days, Josie was visited by Pamela, Igraine, and other NSM members—but not Derek. Her visitors tried to be pleasant and, for the most part, were. Josie found it entertaining to witness Igraine's tortured attempts to be polite. The woman stumbled over her innately rude nature nearly every time she opened her mouth. One memorable exchange occurred when she brought Josie a pasta dish with a glass of milk.

"You must drink your milk," Igraine said. "Very good. Did I tell you I vunce had a cow viz your name? Josephine. Ve called her Josie. She vas a great milker."

"You're comparing me to a cow?" Josie asked.

"No," exclaimed Igraine. "You do not look..."

"You say I'm pregnant," said Josie. "I'll be making milk soon, so that must mean you think I'm a cow!"

"I did not...oh bah! You are a miserable girl," declared Igraine as she stormed out of the room and slammed the door.

Josie chuckled, but that was one of her few enjoyments. She filled the rest of her time with an analysis of what was true and what wasn't. Though she refused to admit it, she actually wished Derek would come to see her again.

When her captors felt that enough of Josie's rage had passed, they took her out of the house for some fresh air. Her escort was Pamela, and three armed men guarded them. Josie wondered where she was as she walked over narrow streets bordered by white and pink stucco buildings.

***

"Saint-Guilhem le Desert," Hans said with a Swedish accent. When people looked at him, he added, "That's where they took her. It has to be."

"Why do you say that?" asked Dr. Herzog.

Pointing at the map on the monitor, Hans replied, "They were traveling south along Autoroute du Soleil when we lost them."

"Yes," declared Konrad. "We know that already."

"One reason we couldn't identify their vehicle as it escaped Aachen Arkaden is because it lacked plates," Hans continued. "I received a report that an elderly man in Montpellier complained of nearly being run over by a black utility vehicle seventy-six hours ago. He was particularly upset because the vehicle had no identifying plates on it."

"Yes. Of course," exclaimed Dr. Herzog. "Montpellier is what? Forty-five kilometers from Saint-Guilhem? We have suspected Saint-Guilhem of having Bewegung sympathies for some time now. It would make sense for them to go there."

"That's an eleven-hour drive from Aachen," observed the Lord Mayor.

"All the more reason for us to leave now," replied Petra.

"Who are these men?" Abby whispered to Leif.

***

Josie still denied her captors' claims but felt a bit more relaxed as the sun beat down and a cool breeze washed over her. With her armed escorts lingering a dozen steps behind, she strolled with Pamela over a cobblestone street.

"This is a peaceful village," said Pamela.

"It's nice," agreed Josie. "And I'm glad to be out of that room you locked me in."

"I hope we can stop doing that."

"That's up to you," Josie observed.

"You don't believe what we said?" asked Pamela.

"That I'm pregnant? Or that I'm carrying the clone of a hunchback?" Josie asked.

"Both."

"I can believe the first a lot more than I can buy the second," said Josie.

"You don't think it's possible that someone other than Charlemagne was buried in his tomb?" Pamela asked.

"What does it matter?" inquired Josie. "They couldn't really have cloned him. And who cares if it's a dead king or his dead son?"

"Sheep, monkeys, rats, wolves…they've all been cloned," answered Pamela. "As we speak, scientists are close to cloning a woolly mammoth that's been extinct for ten thousand years. I promise you, they can and they did clone whoever was buried in Charlemagne's tomb. And you ask why it matters. Well, one was a kind, just king, and the other was a murderous traitor."

"Okay," replied Josie. "You said that Charlemagne faked his death and buried his dead son in his place, right?"

"Right."

"Why?"

"In January of 814, the Emperor Charlemagne was very sick and weak. He'd been on his deathbed for seventy-two days," explained Pamela. "In that time, his enemies were attacking his kingdom on several fronts."

"Yeah…" said Josie.

"He was too frail to command, but, as long as he lived, his son and successor Louis the Pious had no real authority," continued Pamela. "His empire was vulnerable, and his enemies took advantage. He was in jeopardy of losing the empire he had worked his entire life to create."

"Why didn't he just retire and tell everyone his son was in charge?" Josie asked.

"He tried, but he was the only king anyone had ever known for almost fifty years," Pamela answered. "No one was going to follow Louis as long as Charlemagne was still alive. And that meant that the empire would be defenseless."

"If he was already dying," said Josie. "Why didn't he just kill himself?"

"He was a deeply religious man," Pamela replied. "He believed that suicide dooms your soul to hell. He had to wait until The Lord took him naturally."

"But he didn't die, and he didn't get better?" asked Josie.

"That's right," said Pamela. "So his advisors staged his death and buried Pippin the Hunchback, who died three years earlier, in his place. That way Charlemagne could die a natural death and Louis could assume control of the kingdom."

Josie walked in silence long enough for Pamela to think she had won her over. Finally, she said, "That's a great story, but I don't believe it. Sorry."

***

Once again, her refusal to accept what her captors said landed Josie back in her room. "So much for not wanting to lock me up," she mumbled.

Pamela's explanation had too many holes in it to be believable. Such an elaborate hoax couldn't have been pulled off in front of so many people. Someone would have noticed that the person being buried wasn't

Charlemagne. And with the amount of conspirators needed to do the job, surely someone would have said something. There was also the substitute body to think about. Pippin had been dead and buried three years before they exhumed him for this charade. His corpse would have begun to decompose. In the very least, its stench would have been horrendous.

Although she was convinced that Pamela's story was wrong, Josie couldn't understand why Regensburg was carved on Charlemagne's throne. Regensburg was the place where Pippin the Hunchback plotted rebellion against his father. Why would someone have carved that reference on Charlemagne's throne?

After her thoughts had tortured her to the point that she was sure she couldn't take any more of it, the door opened and Derek entered the room. He carried Josie's watch, phone, and a phone charger. He set them on the bed and said, "You're free to go."

"What?"

"We're not going to hold you anymore," he added. "We tried to convince you of the truth, but...it would be foolish to lock you up until you believed us."

"Foolish?" Josie asked. "That's what you call this? Foolish?"

"We didn't want you to go until you heard what we had to say," he explained. "Now you have. I hope you forgive us."

He exited, leaving Josie with a brow crinkled in confusion. "Where are you going?" she demanded. "Come back!" To herself, she added, "Damn! He's an ass!"

***

The main route to the abbey church could only accommodate three pedestrians walking abreast, but that didn't deter people from lining both sides of the walkway. Others leaned out of windows and perched themselves atop walls. NSM members mixed with the crowd, which stretched for a quarter of a mile. Everyone wanted to see the upcoming procession. Derek and Pamela stood side by side, close to where they had been keeping Josie.

"Do you think she'll give away our location?" asked Pamela.

"No," Derek answered. "I think she'll join us."

Josie descended the slope of another narrow passageway. For the first time in days, she was free and wearing clean clothes. Pamela provided her with jeans and a tan sweater to keep her warm in the cool October weather. As she walked, she played with the applications on her phone and admired her watch. She kept the charger in her pocket. Voices and singing interrupted her activities, and she looked up to see hundreds of people. Unaware of why they were assembled, she joined the crowd. Then she spotted Derek with Pamela, and a flash of jealousy shot through her.

"I am told you are free to go," Igraine said from behind Josie.

"Uh, yeah," answered Josie.

"Ven vill you leave?" Igraine asked.

"As soon as I figure out where I am and how to get out of here," Josie answered. Her eyes returned to Derek and Pamela.

"Touring buses pass through zis village every day," Igraine told her. "And viz tomorrow being Halloveen..."

"What's the deal with them?" Josie asked while gesturing to Derek and Pamela.

Igraine frowned in irritation. She had something more important on her mind. "You vill not tell Zee Agency vhere ve are?"

Josie knew better than to tell Igraine that she would send police after them the minute she was free. Instead, she lied, "I might not go back to them at all."

"You vill," Igraine said. "But make me vun promise before you go to zem. Look up zee Saint-Denis Manuscript. Promise me. Saint. Denis."

Josie found the normally intense woman to be even more emphatic. The forcefulness of her stare compelled Josie to answer, "Okay. I promise."

Igraine nodded and walked away.

Strange woman, Josie told herself. She looked back at Derek and Pamela, who seemed to be getting closer to one another. *Speaking of women...*

Josie surprised Pamela by appearing between her and Derek. Derek, on the other hand, took her arrival in stride.

"What's going on?" Josie asked.

"It's a procession," Derek replied. "Priests from the abbey are about to carry the reliquary of the True Cross down this walkway."

"It usually happens on May third," said Pamela. "The Feast Day of Saint Guilhem. But this year, Monsignor wants the procession to take place before Halloween as well. He hopes the True Cross of Christ will lessen the impact of Satan's Holiday."

Ignoring Pamela, Josie asked Derek, "What's the reliquary of the True Cross?"

"It's made of gold and jewels," he answered. "And has pieces of the cross in it."

"What cross?" probed Josie. "*The* cross?"

"Yes. The actual cross of Jesus," he replied. "If you believe the legends. The pieces were a gift from Charlemagne, who had others fashioned into a talisman, which he wore at all times. They say he was even buried with it."

"Charlemagne again? Is there any place around here he hasn't been?" Josie asked.

"This abbey was founded by Guilhem, his favorite cousin," said Pamela.

A chorus of cheers and chants erupted farther down the walkway. Josie peered at the procession and saw spectators kneel before passing priests. Then the golden reliquary came into view. It was carried by two priests and was shaped like a cross with precious stones adorning nearly every inch of it.

"Where are the pieces from the cross of Jesus?" Josie asked.

"Inside the reliquary," Derek told her.

"Son of a bitch!" Josie exclaimed. She saw the dark-haired man who drugged her standing on the other side of the walkway. His arms stretched to the sky as he recited a prayer.

Seeing Bernard, Derek turned to Pamela. "I told you to send him away."

"I did," she replied. "He must have come back for the procession."

Derek set his hands on Josie's shoulders in an attempt to reassure her, but she ignored him.

Priests passed Bernard, and he lowered his large body to kneel. As he did, a blast like that of a powerful firecracker cut through the melody of prayers and the back of Bernard's head exploded in a spray of bone, blood, and brain matter.

People screamed. Some ran while others froze in shock. Bernard fell against a wall and streaked the stones with blood as he slid to the pavement.

"Holy shit!" Josie yelled.

Frantic people scattered and collided with priests from the procession. The golden reliquary fell to the ground. A holy man dove to protect it. But the shooter didn't want the reliquary. It was Petra, and he came for just two things—revenge for his failure in the mall and Josie.

He carried a .44 Magnum and was accompanied by armed police. Hans and more officers marched up the other end of the street toward Petra.

"Run!" Derek yelled to Pamela. She took off in a sprint, but Petra ended her escape with a single gunshot to the chest. She crashed to the ground and tumbled down the walkway.

Josie screamed. Derek kicked in a nearby door and dragged her through it. Once inside, they collided with a teenage boy. A middle-aged woman sprang from her seat at the kitchen table and yelled at them in French.

"Up the stairs!" Derek ordered as he pushed Josie toward a flight of steps.

She did as instructed until she noticed that he wasn't following her. She looked back and saw him shut the door, prop a chair under its handle, and push a table against it. He ordered the woman and boy into another room and pulled a pistol from the back of his pants, prepared to make his stand.

"No!" Josie yelled.

"Go Josie," he commanded. "Climb out the back window and into the next house. They'll never catch you."

"I'm not gonna let you..."

"I said go!" he hollered. "Don't let them get you!"

Outside, Petra and Hans ordered officers to surround the building while other police maintained the crowd. Konrad emerged from the midst of the mob.

"You cannot charge in there!" he yelled. "He will kill her!"

"Move away, old man," Petra ordered. "This is our mission."

To everyone's surprise, Josie leaned out a window and yelled, "Hey! Back away from the house."

"Josie!" hollered Konrad.

"I'm fine, Grandpa. Tell them to back up. I'll come out if they promise not to hurt anyone else."

Inside the building, on the first story, Derek heard Josie. He listened as Konrad told the police to do what she said.

As Josie descended the staircase, Derek asked, "What are you doing?"

"I'm saving your ass," she said. "They won't hurt me, but they'll kill you."

"I'll pay that price," he told her. "You can't let them get you."

"Go out through the window like you told me to do," she instructed.

As she approached the door, he grabbed her arm. "Don't do this," he pleaded. "I didn't tell you this before, but Pippin the Hunchback was evil. Pure evil. All the accounts agree on that. If his clone is allowed to be born..."

Josie cupped his face in her hands and pressed her lips against his for a lingering kiss. She leaned back and told him, "I don't believe a word you've said."

Outside, the crowd watched as the door opened. Josie walked out alone. Anyone who was looking closely could see Derek run up the staircase behind her.

***

While a manhunt for Derek and other NSM members scoured the village, Josie endured hours of inspection by authorities and doting by her grandfather. She spoke by phone with Dr. Herzog but revealed none of what Derek and the NSM told her.

When it was time to begin their trek back to Germany, Josie joined Konrad, Hans, and Petra in a luxury van. She didn't trust the two men Konrad said The Agency appointed to be her guards. In fact, she wasn't entirely sure whether or not she still had faith in her grandfather.

Eleven hours was a long time to spend in a vehicle, even if it was built for comfort. To pass the time, Josie read about pregnancies and cloning on the Internet. Then she remembered her promise to Igraine. What did she ask her to look up? The Saint-Denis Manuscript?

With Hans driving, Petra in the front, and Konrad asleep beside her, Josie searched for the words *Saint*, *Denis*, and *Manuscript*. Over three hundred thousand entries popped up, but she knew that only the first few dozen really mattered. After more than an hour and a half, she found a reference to an article in an old archeology magazine. She couldn't locate the article itself, but the citation told her of the discovery of a previously unknown text written by Einhard, the biographer of Charlemagne. Conjecture claimed that the manuscript was unearthed at the Basilica of Saint-Denis in the tomb of Bertrada of Laon, Charlemagne's mother.

"Great," Josie muttered. "She wants me to look up more stuff on Charlemagne. Will they ever let it go?"

As Konrad stirred beside her, Josie located other sources which claimed that the manuscript in question didn't even exist. The last person to have supposedly seen it was an American professor named Dr. Karl Vanderhoff, but he denied ever having heard of it.

Josie was sure she'd seen Dr. Vanderhoff's name before, but she couldn't recall where. She definitely knew the next name she saw, however. It belonged to the man who was said to have found the manuscript in Saint-Denis and brought it to Dr. Karl Vanderhoff's attention. That man was Michael Ersman. Josie was stunned. Her father found the Saint-Denis manuscript? Was that why he went to America, she wondered. She had no idea, but she knew one thing. She would have to find out.

CHAPTER NINE

When Hans pulled into a gas station, Josie excused herself to use the facilities. She snatched a pregnancy test on the way into the bathroom and administered it in private. She had to find out for herself if...if...it took only a minute to see the results.

Josie exited the gas station more determined than ever to escape. The day was ending, darkness was approaching, and Hans and Petra were pre-occupied. She would never get a better chance to make her move, so she bolted across the street and into a depot filled with rail cars and storage containers. Quickly realizing what was happening, Konrad ran after her.

"Josie! Wait," yelled Konrad. "Josie!"

She looked back to see her grandfather hobbling after her. Oh no, she thought. The old fool! She was about to tell him to go back when she saw the van tearing after them. Its back end slid across gravel, sending a spray of dirt and rocks.

Petra chased the escapees on foot. He fired his pistol and hit a rock near Konrad.

Inside the vehicle, Hans clutched the steering wheel. His eyes were glued on his targets. The older one was expendable, but the girl was not.

Konrad stumbled as a second gunshot grazed his arm. "Ahh!" he yelled.

"Grandpa!" exclaimed Josie. She went back and pulled him toward a gully.

Jerking the wheel hard to the left, Hans kept up the pursuit. His vehicle kicked up more gravel as it surged after the runners.

Josie and Konrad landed in the mud-strewn gully. A mass of earth suddenly toppled toward them as if it was a crashing wave. The van roared up behind it like a mythological monster with two burning eyes.

113

Konrad yelled. The vehicle's silver underbelly and spinning tires thundered upon him, making his death by crushing imminent. To his surprise, the heavy machine suddenly crashed onto a huge boulder and dropped no further.

"Hurry, Grandpa!" Josie ordered as she dragged him up a mound.

From seemingly nowhere, Petra tackled Konrad. The two men rolled down the opposite side of the mound, wrestling and striking at one another.

Hans jumped out of the van and grabbed Josie's leg. "You're not going anywhere," he declared.

She kicked him in the face with her free leg, causing him to release his grip and fall backward. She saw a train moving on the other side of the mound and used the exaggerated steps of a man on the moon to wade down the dirt pile toward it.

The rolling, wrestling men came to a stop when Konrad slammed Petra's spine against a boulder. Petra's face registered shock as air escaped from his lungs. Before he could recover, Konrad punched him in the nose. Blood splattered like the insides of a crushed tomato.

"Let's go!" Josie yelled.

Konrad and Josie lumbered after the train as it made its way out of the yard.

"We're gonna miss it!" Josie hollered. "Run! Run!"

The caboose was their last chance to catch the train. Konrad stretched for the ladder on the back of it. He was almost there. He reached. He strained. A step behind, Josie grabbed for a rung of metal, but a bullet ricocheted near her. She stumbled back. Looking over her shoulder, she saw Petra aim his gun for a second shot.

Konrad snatched the ladder, but Josie tripped on a rock. She staggered, about to fall. Konrad threw his wounded arm around her and pulled her close to him. Another bullet from Petra barely missed its mark. The train pulled Konrad off-balance, dragging him and Josie behind it. He could feel the muscles in his arms and back tear, but he held his grip. Josie fought through the pain of her legs scraping against crushed rocks and railroad ties as she grabbed the ladder and haul herself onto the caboose. She helped her grandfather onto the ladder as a third shot missed him by an inch. Together, they climbed the rusty rungs, and collapsed onto the roof of the car. Josie looked back to see Petra and Hans with the last rays of sunlight disappearing behind them.

***

Josie finally had to accept the fact that she was pregnant. The test she took in the bathroom confirmed it, as did the three the NSM administered. She was furious and felt betrayed in the worst way, but the larger question was whether or not her grandfather had anything to do with it. She wasn't sure how the conversation with him would go when she started it out by saying, "I'm pregnant and your precious Agency made me that way when they put me in a coma." She expected him to deny any involvement, which he did, and she thought he would be angry, which he was, but she never anticipated his depression. He slipped into such a melancholy state that she realized he really didn't have anything to do with it. It wasn't until she showed him what she learned about Michael Ersman and the Saint-Denis Manuscript that he showed any signs of life.

Over the next few days, he secured transportation across France, accessed funds, and created false documents with a vigor she'd never seen him display. He purchased two tickets on a flight bound for Denver, Colorado, where Dr. Karl Vanderhoff resided.

As they flew over the Atlantic Ocean, Konrad explained that his years with The Agency taught him many things about covert activities.

"How long did you work for them?" she asked.

"I started as one of Dr. Fowler's young assistants," he revealed.

"Dr. Fowler?"

"The man who founded The Agency in 1951," said Konrad.

"You've been with The Agency since the beginning?"

"I was young then," answered Konrad. "But yes, you could say that."

His revelation raised more questions in Josie's mind, but she was tired. She managed to ask, "How come you weren't a director or someone higher up?"

"I believe it is because I traded my influence to see my son ascend the ranks more easily than I could," he told her.

"Why couldn't you be promoted?"

"I have a past that is...uh, unpopular and embarrassing to The Agency."

Josie struggled to keep her eyes open, but asked, "What did you do?"

"I was in the *Deutches Jungvolk*, a branch of the Hitler Youth that was for the very young. I joined at the age of eight, though my parents had to lie and say I was ten."

"What's the Hitler Youth?" she inquired.

He was about to answer the question when he saw that his granddaughter had drifted off to sleep. Perhaps it was best that she didn't hear the rest of what he had to say. The Agency's past was undeniable, but unmentionable, as was his own. He gave himself fully to The Agency because it was founded by former Nazis who sought to keep Hitler's greatest dream alive—a vision of Europe unified under one remarkable leader. They were so close. In a mere nine months they would achieve...then he recalled the duplicity with which they impregnated his granddaughter. It was the last straw, he told himself. First Michael...now Josie. The question he refused to ask, however, was whether or not it was his fault.

***

Dr. Karl Vanderhoff collected the last of his unread term papers and prepared to leave his office, thankful for another brief day. He was a tall man, about six and a half feet, with broad, but slouching shoulders. His stomach was slightly larger than it should have been, and his hair and trimmed beard were almost exclusively white. His face looked worn and wrinkled, and he had a noticeable scar on his forehead. As he reached for the door, a knock sounded on the opposite side. Great, he thought, another kid who doesn't know the difference between Bede and Becket. Opening the door, he came face to face with Josie. Konrad stood behind her.

Aside from his height, Josie found Dr. Vanderhoff to be what she expected. He was an elderly man who likely spent his life in a library. Konrad, however, was struck by the professor's familiarity. He'd seen him before but couldn't recall where.

"Dr. Vanderhoff?" asked Josie.

"Yes."

"My name is Josie. This is my grandfather. Can we have a few minutes of your time?"

Dr. Vanderhoff welcomed them into his office. It was well-kept with three cases of books, leather bound chairs, and a wooden desk etched with leaf and vine designs. A laptop sat on the desk with term papers stacked neatly beside it.

Josie thought the room was unremarkable except for a sword hanging from the wall behind the desk. It was sheathed in a golden scabbard. Its pommel was crafted of gold and silver and was decorated with mirror images of a fleur-de-lis. What most caught Josie's attention was the inch of blade that was exposed because the scabbard was not in its usual position. The steel changed colors from lavender to light green before her eyes.

"I don't write letters of recommendation for applicants I don't know," Vanderhoff began. "If that's why you're here."

"No. That's not why we're here," Josie said. "We wanted to ask you about the Saint-Denis Manuscript."

"Saint-Denis?" asked the professor. "It's been a while since I've had a visit from you people."

Josie looked at Konrad, who was still curious about how he knew Vanderhoff.

"I'd say it's been at least twenty years," the professor added. "But as I told your colleagues back then, I can't help you."

"I don't...we don't have colleagues," Josie said.

"You're reporters for a conspiracy publication, aren't you?" Vanderhoff asked. "Or writers of some sort. Either way, it's like I said. I can't discuss what doesn't exist."

"Are you sure it doesn't exist?" Josie persisted. "We might not be talking about the same book."

"You're asking about a mysterious manuscript that was supposed to have been written by Charlemagne's biographer and buried in the grave of Bertrada of Laon," Vanderhoff said. "Are you not?"

"Okay," Josie replied. "We are talking about the same book."

"Yes. Well. Like I said, I can't help you." The professor returned to the door and opened it as a means of showing his visitors out.

"Then why would they say it was brought to you?" Josie asked.

"Who said that?" Vanderhoff asked.

"I don't know," she confessed. "I saw it on the Internet."

"On the Internet," he mocked. "Well if it's written there, it must be true. I'm sorry, but you've wasted your time. I hope you didn't travel far to get here."

"Actually, we traveled quite far," said Konrad. "We are from Köln."

They came from France, Josie thought, not Köln, or Cologne.

Konrad, however, was talking about something else. He remembered where he had last seen Dr. Vanderhoff. "This is Michael's daughter," he said.

Dr. Vanderhoff stared at Konrad, then closed the door, walked back to his desk and sat behind it. "I didn't think you recognized me," he said.

With a look at Josie, he added, "Your father was one of my best students."

Josie was perplexed until she realized, "You're the guy mentioned in the folder...my father's counselor."

"Mentor," Vanderhoff amended.

"Advisor," Konrad corrected. "Michael was in no need of a mentor." To Josie, he added, "This man was your father's academic advisor at university."

"The University of Cologne?" Josie asked. "Did my father come to see you about the Saint-Denis Manuscript?"

"Sit," Vanderhoff said while gesturing to the chairs in front of his desk. Josie did as instructed, and so did Konrad, albeit reluctantly.

"I evaluate people according to four criteria," Vanderhoff explained. "Common sense, mental acuity, and physical and intellectual bravery. Most rate high in one or perhaps two of those aptitudes, but few have all four in equal measure. Experience has shown me that the ones who possess all four in equal parts affect the greatest change in this world. Michael Ersman was one such person. I was deeply saddened when the path he chose led to an early end."

"The path he chose?" Konrad repeated.

"The one you led him to," Vanderhoff specified.

Konrad stood, but did so slowly and with great pain from his torn back muscles. "My son was realizing his destiny," Konrad declared. "It was a course he chose, as I told you once before." To Josie, he said, "Come. This man has nothing we need."

He stormed out of the office, but Josie didn't follow him. She gazed at the professor and said, "I guess you two have a history."

"Not really," Vanderhoff admitted. "I only met him once when I tried to talk your father out of joining The Agency. I would also offer that advice to you if that is what you're considering."

***

The rest of Josie's encounter with the professor was cordial but not as productive as she had hoped. No more mention was made of The Agency. All she learned was that her father visited him days before dying in a Colorado ravine. The purpose of the visit was not elaborated upon except to say that Michael was nervous and that he thought the authorities were after him because he defaced a monument.

"Defaced a monument?" Josie asked. "Was it Bertrada's tomb?"

"Charlemagne's throne in the Aachen Cathedral," Vanderhoff corrected. "He said he covered the engraving with plaster."

"What engraving?"

"Actually, he said he re-covered it, whatever that means," Vanderhoff added. "I told him that what he did was stupid. That throne is a national treasure."

"What engraving?" Josie repeated.

"He didn't say," Vanderhoff answered. "But of course he was referring to the Nine Men's Morris board that is etched into the side of it."

"The what?"

"Nine Men's Morris board," he repeated. "It's an ancient game, like chess. No one knows why it's on The Emperor's throne. I think it was carved by Einhard. He was the only person at court who could challenge Charlemagne's supremacy at the game."

"Einhard, his biographer?" Josie asked.

With a nod, Vanderhoff said, "The two men spent hours matching skills and wits with one another. Just the two of them."

***

The only sounds during the ride back to the Denver airport came from the dispatch CB in the front of the cab. Josie was lost in thought while her grandfather remained irritated. For him, the Vanderhoff encounter brought back unpleasant emotions. More than thirty years earlier, the professor rebuked him for encouraging Michael to join The Agency. The fact that Michael died before ever achieving greatness in The Agency as Konrad envisioned only made it more difficult to see Vanderhoff again.

Josie's thoughts also concentrated on Dr. Vanderhoff. She liked the old guy. He clearly knew what he was talking about when it came to The Agency. But why did he mention a Nine Men's Morris etching? Did her father cover it or re-cover it with plaster? Did the authorities really follow him from one continent to another because of it? Then it suddenly hit her! Her father didn't cover a game board. He plastered over *REGENSBURG*, the word she accidentally photographed. Dr. Vanderhoff said Einhard carved the Nine Men's Morris board on the throne, but he must have also carved *REGENSBURG*. The Emperor's biographer was saying that the man who was emperor was the one who hatched the plot at Regensburg—Pippin.

119

Josie had no sooner reached that conclusion when she realized that she was overthinking it. Pippin died before becoming emperor, and dead men don't sit on thrones. *REGENSBURG* must have been carved on the throne for a different reason. A smile crept up her face as she decided that Derek was wrong about Pippin taking Charlemagne's place in burial. Then she remembered the painting she saw in the Rathaus' Coronation Hall. It depicted the two hundred year old corpse of Charlemagne in its tomb, sitting on a throne.

***

As Konrad used cash and their false identifications to buy plane tickets back to Germany, Josie used her phone's Internet to search for the painting she had seen in the Rathaus. After several minutes, she found the black and white image.

"Two thousand seven hundred and twenty-one American dollars," Konrad said as he approached Josie with their tickets in hand. "A last minute purchase penalty."

"Did this really happen?" Josie asked while pointing to the picture on her phone.

Konrad sat beside her and looked at the painting he had seen many times—Alfred Rethel's depiction of Otto III discovering the corpse of Charlemagne. It featured Charles the Great sitting upon a throne even though he was dead. He wore his crown, a veil over his face, and held an orb and scepter in his hands with an opened book on his lap. The Emperor Otto III and four other men knelt before the deceased Charlemagne.

"That is what the men testified and The Emperor confirmed," Konrad replied. "In those days, an emperor's word was law, so yes. I suppose it did happen."

"What emperor?" Josie asked.

"Otto III."

"When did they go into the tomb?" she probed.

"In the year 1000," Konrad answered.

"And Charlemagne died in 814?"

"Yes."

Josie looked back at the image. The corpse of Charlemagne seemed to be in perfect condition with no noticeable deterioration. "There's no way," she concluded. "What did you say? Only the end of his nose had fallen off?"

"Yes, I think. You can read the testimony yourself," he told her. "I am sure it must be on the Internet somewhere."

That sent Josie back on her search. She was a woman on a quest. The only thing that disturbed the pace of her investigation was the seemingly endless cycle of her having to visit the water fountain to rinse out her over-salivating mouth and to go to the bathroom to address a constant urge to urinate.

Twenty minutes before boarding, she found three intriguing items on the Internet. They were accounts of the visitation of Charlemagne's tomb in the millennial year. The first was by a bishop named Thietmar. The second was by Count Otto of Lomello, who was the count of Otto III's palace. The third chronicler was a man named Ademar de Chabannes, who was not an actual eyewitness to the event.

The bishop named Thietmar revealed very little except to say that Otto III did, in fact, locate Charlemagne's tomb. Count Otto of Lomello gave the most detailed account. Josie read what was written to her grandfather, "'He was sitting upon a throne, just as a living person might. None of the parts of his body had, however, decayed in the slightest, even though a little bit off the end of his nose was missing; this the Emperor ordered restored with a piece of gold.'"

"So it is as I said," Konrad replied. "They will call us to board soon, so..."

"It's this third guy, though," Josie interrupted. "Listen to this. 'His head, linked by a golden chain, was proudly erect. A piece of the True Cross was deposited within the diadem.' What's a diadem?"

"It is a crown," her grandfather told her.

"A crown? They put a piece from the cross of Jesus in Charlemagne's crown?" Josie asked. "Why would they do that?"

"Maybe it was sacred to Charlemagne," Konrad said. He heard an airline employee make a boarding call for their flight. "That is our plane."

"That's right!" Josie declared. "Derek said Charlemagne carried splinters of the Cross with him in an amulet. Do you think they put the pieces in his crown?"

"Possibly," Konrad replied, but he was more concerned with not missing their flight. He urged Josie toward the line of passengers boarding the aircraft.

Josie felt like she was a sleuth unraveling a mystery. What did Charlemagne's True Cross amulet look like? She was surprised that she hadn't considered that question before. As she followed passengers approaching the plane, she realized a glaring coincidence. Charlemagne and her father both had amulets with bits of wood in them. Was there a connection between the two? She wanted to believe that the similarity between the two pieces of jewelry was more than just happenstance.

***

Clumsy passengers bumped Konrad as they made their way down the aisle of the plane. He sat beside Josie, who had the window seat. Her attention remained fixed on her Internet connection, oblivious to her grandfather's inconveniences.

She re-read the third account of the enthroned corpse of Charlemagne by Ademar de Chabannes, hoping for clues about the fragments of the True Cross. Aside from their obvious religious importance, why did the writer specifically mention them when describing the condition of the body? As she sought to answer that question, another mystery begged for her attention—the deterioration of the corpse, or lack thereof.

"Ahh," groaned an exasperated Josie. "Every time I look for an answer, another question pops up. I can't understand why Charlemagne's body didn't rot in the hundred and eighty-six years between when he died and when they entered his tomb."

"I will give you something else to consider," said Konrad. "Look for an Italian man who visited Aachen in 1300."

"Why?" she asked.

"Look on your phone," he replied. "It will tell you better than I can."

Josie did as he suggested but found nothing. Her frustration grew until she came across Tolomeo da Lucca. He was Italian and he wrote about a visit he made to Aachen in 1300. As she read the man's account, she became even more confused.

"You have to turn your phone off," the steward told Josie.

"All right," she said, but instead of complying, she returned to the screen. She read aloud, "'Tolomeo da Lucca saw the body of Charlemagne sitting on a chair above his tomb. And he said it was a man-made image.'"

"Turn the phone off now," the steward insisted. "Please."

"Okay," Josie snapped. She looked again at the screen but could feel the weight of the man's eyes upon her. She frowned and made a show of pressing the off button.

"Thank you," the steward said in a less-than-pleasant manner.

Josie shook her head at the annoyance and turned her attention to her grandfather. "What does that mean?" she asked. "A man-made image?"

"It was a funerary effigy," Konrad told her.

"A what?"

Konrad began to explain what he meant by "a funerary effigy," but the loud hiss of energized engines drowned him out. The plane pushed forward, picking up speed. Josie glanced out the window as it surged over the blacktop and leaped into the air.

Once her ears popped and the plane settled on a steady altitude, Josie turned her attention back to her grandfather. "There's something else that's bothering me about that," she said. "The Italian guy went to Aachen in 1300? Almost five hundred years after Charlemagne's death. But he said he saw the body of The Emperor sitting on a chair. Five hundred years later and his corpse was still in good shape?"

"Perhaps I should finish what I was saying about a funerary effigy," Konrad replied. "The bodies of prominent citizens have been displayed in sitting positions dating back to the Ancient Greeks and Romans," he explained.

"So a dead body sitting on a chair is a funerary effigy?" Josie asked.

"An effigy is an image or a likeness of a person," he told her. "Sometimes it is the real body. Other times, it is not."

"I don't get it."

"The corpses of important people would have been on display for months," Konrad explained. "And, of course, they deteriorated in the open air. So artisans encased them in wax to preserve them. That is a funerary effigy."

"A dead body covered with wax?" Josie asked.

"The wax was shaped and colored and painted," Konrad elaborated. "It was meant to cover decomposition and make it appear that the person was still alive."

As the flight progressed, Josie learned that many cultures, including modern ones, created wax effigies of important people. A large number of these images had part or all of the deceased person's body encased within them.

A half hour into their journey, Josie felt the familiar call of her bladder. She made her way to the plane's lavatory but felt a sharp abdominal cramp as she entered the confined space. The pain was so intense that she dropped onto the toilet and hunched over. Her discomfort eventually subsided and she was able to return to her seat, but she was determined not to tell her grandfather what happened.

For the remainder of their flight, Josie and Konrad continued to pose theories concerning the treatment and condition of Charlemagne's corpse. Their flight neared German airspace, and Josie raised another issue. Was it possible that Charlemagne could have faked his death and buried Pippin the Hunchback in his place? Before Konrad could give his opinion, she felt the proverbial light bulb go on above her head. Could it be that expert artists used wax to transform the body of Charlemagne's son, dead and buried for three years, into a convincing effigy of his father? Did Derek and the NSM tell her the truth after all? The very real possibility that she was pregnant with the clone of Pippin the Hunchback rather than Charles the Great gave her a sinking feeling.

***

Once again back at Cologne's airport, Josie felt as if her unplanned pregnancy had put her in an emotional tug of war. She couldn't believe she was pregnant and was irate over the way it happened. She was also horrified that it might be the clone of an evil, hunchbacked prince. She followed her grandfather through the terminal with her mind obsessing over her predicament.

The flow of traffic carried Josie and Konrad past a bar which was illuminated by yellow lighting. One of the patrons sipping a beverage was Hans. He watched them pass and typed a quick text to his partner.

Further down the concourse, Petra received the message. He was glad of the confession he extracted from the man who made Konrad and Josie's traveling papers a week before. After that, they were easy to find.

"Are you sure we should be doing this?" Josie asked as she and her grandfather unknowingly passed Petra. "We'd be safer back in America."

"We would not," Konrad replied. "You are a considered a thief in the States."

"I don't know," she said. "This doesn't seem like a good idea now that we're back in Germany."

"Do you want to run from The Agency for the rest of your life?" he asked. "Better to go to them now when you have leverage in your womb. Demand everything you want. Then you can leave under your own terms. It is the only way to be free."

At Petra's direction, two disguised policemen began trailing Josie and Konrad.

"I'm still not sure, but I know one thing," said Josie. "If I'm pregnant with Pippin's clone instead of Charlemagne's, we can't tell Dr. Herzog."

"I do not think you are," Konrad said. "But if so, he would know that already."

Josie stopped abruptly to look at her grandfather. "Why would he do that on purpose? Why would anyone clone an evil guy with a deformity?"

"Yet another reason why I do not believe that is the case," Konrad replied as they resumed their trek.

Josie suddenly buckled over as she felt daggers stab her from the inside out.

"Josie! What is it?" demanded her grandfather.

She groaned and clutched her lower abdomen. Through her squinting eyes, she saw two suspicious-looking men behind her, and she saw Petra. She may have considered going back to Dr. Herzog, but she couldn't let Petra bring her in. He already tried to kill her and her grandfather once. Forcing herself to stand upright, she said, "We gotta run."

Konrad also saw Petra and grabbed his granddaughter's arm to guide her past shops and customers. The plain-clothed officers hurried after them.

"There," Konrad said. "That way!"

Josie could see that he was pointing toward a railing with glass panes attached to the front of it. A nearby staircase descended to a lower level, and three huge banners stretched from the ceiling to the ground floor in the open space beyond the railing.

Konrad saw that Petra was getting close, and he ordered Josie to take the stairs. "Run," he shouted, as he threw himself at Petra.

Ignoring her pain and fueled by adrenaline, Josie scrambled down the stairs.

One of the policemen joined Petra as he fought Konrad. The three wrestling men hit the railing with enough momentum to carry them over it. Petra was the first to topple over, and he pulled Konrad with him. The policeman was able to brace himself against the thick glass of the railing and prevent his descent.

With the other officer racing behind her, Josie had no chance to see Konrad and Petra sail over the railing, grab its crossbeam, and dangle above the ground floor.

As Konrad held the beam for dear life, Petra gripped it with one hand and struck at him with the other. The officer joined Petra's efforts and Konrad felt himself rapidly losing his hold on the beam. With wide eyes, he looked down and saw that a fall would likely be fatal. His grip was slipping…slipping. He yelled as he fell backward, his limbs flailing. His right arm brushed a banner and he grabbed it. He threw his left hand over and snagged the streamer with both hands and all of his strength.

Though she was in pain, Josie beat her pursuer to the first floor and its crowds of people. She saw her grandfather and the banner that was ripping. "Grandpa!" she yelled.

The longer the tear in the banner became, the faster it grew, and Konrad descended at a rapid rate. He landed back first on a table that was covered by food and surrounded by people. Drinks splashed into the air, and the diners sprang from their seats.

"Oh, God…are you all right?" Josie asked as she rushed to his aid.

"My back," he answered. "I…" He saw the officer help Petra climb over the railing above them. "The train station," he said. "That is our best chance to escape."

Together, grandfather and granddaughter pushed their injured bodies to carry them as fast as they could toward the exit. Security guards charged into the atrium from assorted directions as Petra and the officer who helped him raced down the stairs.

"*Ich bin die Polizei! Haltet sie! Haltet sie* (I am the police. Stop them! Stop them)!" shouted Petra in German.

Surprised travelers got out of Josie and Konrad's way and moved back as policemen ran past them.

Josie and Konrad entered the circulation of a rotating door. Through the glass that surrounded them, they saw taxis, buses, and the roof of the train station. Suddenly, the door locked in place. They pushed, but it wouldn't budge. A policeman held the rotating door with his foot and drew a pistol from his holster. They were trapped like fish in a barrel.

"Push the door toward him," Konrad ordered. "Hurry!"

They shoved the rotating door toward the policeman. He wasn't prepared for that maneuver and stumbled back as the door crashed into him. His gun fired, and people screamed. With their passageway now free, Josie and Konrad escaped into the street.

***

A canopy of glass and interlaced metal made the rail station appear as impersonal as the airport, but Konrad and Josie had no time to waste on such sentiments. They joined the flow of travelers descending a staircase to meet idling trains. Handing Josie his wallet, Konrad said, "We are not safe yet. Buy us tickets to any place far from here."

"What are you going to do?" she asked.

"Delay any danger," he replied. "Now go. Hurry."

Josie scurried down the remainder of the steps. She opened the wallet to extract money and turned to look back at her grandfather. Horror flashed across her face as she saw Hans appear at the top of the stairs with a pistol in his hand. "Grandpa!" she yelled.

Before Konrad knew what was happening, Hans shot him in the back. Konrad hit the wall, slid along the staircase railing, and toppled down the steps.

"No!" Josie screamed.

Hans charged after Josie, taking two steps at a time.

She ran away from him and saw passengers enter a waiting train. The doors began to close, leaving her one last chance. She dove into the train, and the doors closed behind her.

Josie was met by a chorus of complaints from the people she collided with, but she ignored them all. She climbed slowly and painfully to her feet. The train surged forward and she stumbled back. When she was able to regain her balance, she looked out the window and saw Hans standing on the boarding platform with a gun in his grip. Konrad lay lifeless behind him, blood seeping from a hole in his back.

GUY COTÉ

CHAPTER TEN

Josie felt nauseous, but it wasn't because she was sitting on a vibrating seat in a moving train. She was sickened by the thought of her grandfather's murder. She opened his wallet, and found her third grade school picture. The photo was worn and faded. He must have been carrying it for years. Her eyes swelled with tears as she imagined what the image must have meant to him. Now, many years after that picture was taken, she was only beginning to know him, and he was stolen away from her.

The train arrived at its Parisian destination, and Josie disembarked with the pace and appearance of an old lady. The pain in her abdomen grew with every step she took, and her mental anguish only accentuated her physical condition. She had no idea what she should do or where she should go until she saw a map on the wall that showed train routes entering and exiting Paris. One of the lines went to Chartres. Did she dare to go there? Her grandmother had orchestrated two of her abductions, one of which landed her mother and Steve in intensive care and got Todd killed. On the other hand, Henrietta had been right about her grandfather's associates in The Agency. Another piercing stab from the invisible dagger within her forced her to make up her mind. She knew that she had no other alternative but to go to her grandmother.

***

As another train took her to Chartres, Josie searched the Internet to find her grandmother's address. When she arrived in the city, she selected the cabdriver who had the kindest looking eyes and handed him a paper with Henrietta's address written on it. She was too weak, tired, and tortured to take notice of a grand cathedral standing atop a hill in the center of the city. In fact, she could barely keep her eyes open.

Night settled upon Chartres as the taxi pulled into the driveway of a hundred-year-old house with wooden clapboards and vines covering most of its front. Josie paid the driver and made her way slowly up a crushed stone pathway to the door.

"Well, this is it," she told herself.

She knocked on the wooden door but received no response. She repeated the action and got the same reply. Too weary to do anything else, she lowered herself to a sitting position against the door.

"I'll just wait here," she told herself.

That's how Henrietta found her three and a half hours later. Josie was delirious, shivering and sweating in the cold night air.

***

Josie awoke to hear people speaking French. The fog in her head cleared quickly, and she realized that she was in a hospital. She yanked an oxygen tube out of her nose and reached for the intravenous one that was attached to her wrist. A doctor, a male nurse, and Henrietta charged into the room.

"No, Josie. Stop," said her grandmother.

"What did they do to me?" Josie asked. "Why did you bring me here?"

"Tu...uh, you were out of your mind," Henrietta said. "And you had a fever."

"Let me go," Josie ordered while squirming in the bed. The doctor and nurse strapped her wrists to the metal rails and reapplied the tube she had disconnected.

"Josie, dear," Henrietta said in a voice as soothing as she could make it. "They did not do anything to you but run tests. You are with child."

"I know," Josie exclaimed. "Now get me out of here."

It took a half hour for Josie to calm down enough to talk rationally with Henrietta and the doctor, but she didn't reveal why she was afraid of being hospitalized. How could she tell them that the last time she was in a hospital she was artificially inseminated against her will? She was also afraid that the hospital would log her into a database that could be accessed by the people she was running from.

She was in the process of deciding what she could and could not tell her grandmother when the doctor spoke. His French words were interpreted by Henrietta. "You have what is called a corpus luteum cyst," she said.

Josie's head perked up.

"He says that such cysts are not uncommon," Henrietta continued. "One in ten pregnant women get them."

"Is it cancerous?" Josie asked.

"Oh, *pas du tout*," the doctor said.

"Not at all," Henrietta translated.

As the conversation continued, Josie learned that the corpus luteum was a body of cells that formed in all women after ovulation. For pregnant women, it nourished and supported the new pregnancy until the placenta could take over. Thereafter, it shrank. In one in ten pregnancies, however, the corpus luteum developed into a cyst. Usually, the cyst posed no problem, but in certain cases it grew in size, twisted the ovary or ruptured.

"That may happen to you," Henrietta said. "Your cyst is ten centimeters and *le plus grand*...the largest he has seen. He fears it may rupture or damage your *ovaire*."

The doctor departed to give the patient and her grandmother a chance to discuss the situation, but they had more to talk about than just that.

"*Qui est le père du bébé*...who is the baby's father?" asked Henrietta.

Josie took a breath, paused before exhaling, and said, "It's a long story."

Henrietta waited for further explanation, but Josie wouldn't provide it. After a few moments of silence, she asked Henrietta, "So what does he want to do? Operate?"

"Yes," Henrietta replied. "He said your cyst must be removed. He told me you are in terrific pain."

"Terrific? No, I wouldn't say it was terrific," Josie said. "What would the operation do to my pregnancy?"

"He asked me how long you have been pregnant," Henrietta answered. "*Mais, je ne savais pas*...I did not know."

"Me either," Josie replied. "Maybe nine or ten weeks."

"How could you not know?" Henrietta snapped. She took a moment to collect herself, and said, "There should be no menace...ah, what is the word...threat. There should be no threat if you are ten weeks pregnant."

The two women continued their discussion but kept it on a medical level. They brought the doctor back in, and he helped them decide upon a laparoscopic procedure in which a telescope would be inserted through

Josie's navel and small surgical instruments would remove the cyst, or, if need be, the entire ovary.

"I don't want my ovary removed," Josie declared in a panic.

Through Henrietta's translation, the doctor explained that if the cyst strangled the ovary there would be no other alternative. The twisted ovary would have to be taken out or the pain she would endure and the potential hazards to her pregnancy would be unacceptable. He added that they wouldn't know for sure if damage had been done to the ovary until the scope had been inserted.

**

As she waited to be wheeled into surgery, Josie's mind revisited all the horrific things that had happened to her since she first fled to Germany. She wondered if she should ask the doctor to terminate her pregnancy while he was in there. It was all too much for Josie to take, and she began shaking in her bed. Tears streamed down her face from water-swollen eyes.

"What did I do to deserve this?" she wept. "What?"

Henrietta rushed to her granddaughter's side and wrapped her arms around her. "It will be all right," she said.

Through her tears, Josie said, "I miss Grandpa."

**

The surgery took less than two hours. Josie's ovary was saved, and since she couldn't bring herself to discuss termination with the doctor, the pregnancy was unaffected. The cyst was peeled away from the ovary, the fluid within it was drained, and the remainder of the cyst was removed through the laparoscopy incision.

Before the doctor left Josie and Henrietta alone, he asked one more question. "Did you use fertility drugs?" Henrietta interpreted.

"What?" Josie asked in surprise. "No. Why do you ask?"

Henrietta translated for the doctor, and listened to his reply. "He does not think it is possible for a cyst to grow as large as yours without such medications," she explained.

Josie, of course, had no idea if she'd been given fertility drugs or not. After everything else that transpired, she wouldn't be surprised if she had.

**

Josie left the hospital in a wheelchair pushed by an orderly. She waited for Henrietta to bring her car around while thinking of ways to explain her pregnancy.

A police car pulled into a space fifty feet away, and Hans, Petra, and a French officer climbed out. They walked toward the hospital but stopped abruptly when they saw Josie climb into Henrietta's compact car.

Driving out of the hospital area, Henrietta thought of little but the questions she intended to ask her granddaughter. "Where is Konrad?" she demanded.

Josie gazed out the window and saw a field that would bear flowers in the spring, but it was winter and everything seemed lifeless. "He's dead," she said. "Shot in the back as we tried to escape."

Henrietta startled as if shocked by an electrode. The steering wheel jerked in her hands. "*Il est mort?* He is dead?" she asked in disbelief. "How...uh, who did it?"

"Two guys..." Josie began, but the whine of a siren interrupted her.

"*Merde* (shit)!" Henrietta exclaimed. She looked in her mirror and saw a speeding police car with flashing lights and a screaming siren. She brought her car to a stop on the side of the road, and said, "Of all the times to be stopped..."

Josie became immediately nervous as she realized that the police would arrest her and hand her over to Dr. Herzog's killers if they found out who she was.

An officer approached the car, and Henrietta lowered her window. She tried to explain away her erratic driving, but he ordered her to step out of the vehicle.

Looking in her side view mirror, Josie was horrified to see Petra climbing out of the police car. "Get out of here, Grandma!" she screamed. "Get out!"

"Huh?" Henrietta asked.

"They killed Grandpa!" Josie yelled. "It's the guys that killed Grandpa!"

Henrietta applied her foot to the brake, shifted into drive, and buried the gas pedal. The car's tires spit tiny rocks at the policeman, and the vehicle sped down the road.

Petra cursed in Italian. Speaking French, he ordered the officer, "*Dans la voiture* (Get in the car)!"

"The police killed Konrad?" Henrietta asked while clutching the steering wheel with one hand and raising the driver's side window with the other.

"That guy works for The Agency," Josie said. "He and his partner have been chasing us for weeks."

It suddenly all made sense to Henrietta. The Agency killed her husband just like they murdered her son. "*Pourquoi*...uh, why do they want you?" she asked Josie.

"I have something they want very badly," Josie replied.

"What?" asked Henrietta.

Josie couldn't say. Not yet.

The policeman drove with his eyes intently fixed on Henrietta's car. Petra called Hans back at the hospital and gave him their coordinates. He didn't have to issue his partner any instructions; Hans already knew what to do.

Henrietta was familiar with the Chartres area, but she wondered where they could hide. The Agency had a far reach, so she decided that their best bet was the center of town with its shops and bistros. She pushed her four-cylinder vehicle for all it had.

The straight-away stretch of the road provided an advantage for the police car. It pulled alongside Henrietta's compact. Petra lowered his window and flashed his gun.

"Ram them," Josie ordered.

"*Etes-vous folle*...are you crazy?" Henrietta demanded.

Josie saw that Petra was about to shoot them and pushed the steering wheel sharply to the left.

Metal scraped and crunched as the two cars collided. Petra was knocked off balance. His right arm swung, but he held the gun firmly.

Henrietta tried to pull away from the police car, but found that she couldn't. The vehicles were locked where they had crunched together. "*Oh mon Dieu* (Oh my God)!" she exclaimed. "We're stuck."

The police driver maneuvered to the right, trying to push them off the road. Henrietta steered to the left, and more metal crunched as the machines pressed together.

"Look out!" Josie screamed as a bus sped toward them from the other direction.

Petra fired his gun and the bullet shattered Henrietta's side window. It sank into the dash in front of Josie and deployed an airbag which pounded the air from her lungs.

The bus blasted its horn while approaching the interlocked vehicles. It was unable to pull to the side as the road's shoulder formed a slope that would tip it over.

The cars were racing toward an imminent collision with the bus. Suddenly, Henrietta's hood flew up and obscured her view. She slammed her foot on the brake pedal. As rubber streaked behind jamming tires, the police car continued its forward surge. With a loud pop, the two locked vehicles broke their bond.

Henrietta's compact skidded to a halt and momentum forced its hood to slam back into place. She saw the police car swerve at the last second to avoid the bus. It sped over the shoulder, but the slope was too great. It rolled to the side, then onto its roof.

Josie was still fighting with the airbag as the bus drove by. Henrietta hit the accelerator. The road was narrow and winding, causing her to make a half dozen sharp turns. Josie swayed beneath the press of the airbag and the restraint of her seatbelt. Feeling nauseous, she asked, "Where are we going?"

"The best place to hide is among the *foule*...uh, crowd," Henrietta declared.

She stopped the car in the middle of a narrow street. She hurried out of the vehicle and rushed to the other side to help Josie get out.

They were surrounded by stone buildings which were packed side to side without any gap between them. The street ran perpendicular to a brick paved area, over which passed cars, a man on a bicycle, and pedestrians dressed in winter wear.

"Are we leaving the car?" Josie asked.

"Do you have pain?" Henrietta replied. "Can you walk?"

"I can run if I have to," Josie responded.

"Let us hope you won't have to," said Henrietta.

Henrietta and Josie entered a brick-paved area. As sirens blared throughout the city, locals wondered what was happening, and Henrietta realized that they could not hide among the people. Her eyes drifted to the majestic Chartres Cathedral. "I changed my mind," she said. "We need asile (refuge), not the crowd."

She directed Josie's gaze to the great church. The Gothic structure had two spires—one with a pyramid shape and the other of a more flamboyant design. The contrasting steeples towered over a pale green roof and were surrounded by flying buttresses. Colorful, stained glass stretched above each of three entrances, and a huge rose window of circular shape and floral designs stood like a Cyclopean eye overlooking the town.

Henrietta and Josie walked quickly toward the church. They saw people watch as another screaming police car passed. The entire town seemed to be an emergency zone.

"What do you have that they want so badly?" Henrietta asked.

"Me."

"I don't understand," Henrietta replied.

"Oh, here they come," Josie said as two policemen approached them from the other side of the street.

"*Pardon, mesdames* (Excuse me)," said one of the officers. "*Pardon... uh, comment vous appelez-vous et où allez-vous* (what are your names and where are you going)?"

Josie didn't understand what was said, but her grandmother did. Henrietta gave the young policemen fictitious names and an explanation that made each of them smirk. The officers chuckled and let the women continue on their way.

When they reached the entrance of the church, Josie asked, "What did you say?"

"I told them you were a sinner," replied Henrietta, "and you needed to repent."

Josie frowned.

Henrietta followed people into the grand cathedral. Josie trailed her and glanced back as she heard another wailing siren. In the not-so-great distance, she spotted Hans. He was conversing with a half-dozen police, two of whom were the men who had just stopped Henrietta and herself. She ran into the church.

"I think they know where we are," Josie told her grandmother.

Henrietta put a finger to her lips. "The best way to draw attention to yourself in a holy place is to talk loudly," she whispered. "Come. The cathedral is *très*...very large."

The cathedral's size (nearly one and a half football fields) and its thick stone construction banished the wailing sirens and all other sounds of the outside world. As Josie walked alongside Henrietta in the great church's darkened shadows, she had the sense that she was but a bit player in an epic play. The centuries-old cathedral offered a glimpse of the vast expanse of eternity which seemed to minimize the fears and concerns that had been tormenting her.

As Henrietta led her granddaughter deeper into the cathedral, Hans and four policemen entered behind them. A priest rushed up to the lawmen and was promptly informed of the reason for their visit.

"Uh oh," said Henrietta. "La police."

She directed Josie's attention to the officers, who were asking people if they had seen the fugitives. Josie's pulse quickened as she saw Hans talking to the priest.

"We gotta run," said Josie.

"No," corrected Henrietta. "We need to walk...quickly."

They disappeared behind one of the many stone pillars that supported the cathedral. The column reminded Josie of ones she saw in the Coronation Hall of Aachen's Rathaus, but there was no time to think about that. They kept moving.

Careful not to look back, Josie could feel eyes upon her. It was as if they burned her skin with a glaring heat. She prayed that she and Henrietta hadn't been noticed.

Henrietta saw university students moving as a pack from one stained-glass window to another. Some of them carried notebooks while others held portable computers or phones. They followed a middle-aged professor.

Henrietta directed Josie to the group, and they joined the students before a tall window that was shaped somewhat like an obelisk. It had twenty-four multi-chrome panes, but the principal color was blue. The professor spoke with a Scottish accent as his students took notes in various ways.

"The subject of the upper half of this window is the '*Chanson de Roland,' the 'Song of Roland,'*" explained the professor. "It is a straightforward recitation of events described in the story."

Josie ignored the professor and watched a policeman approach a young couple.

"Panes two through seven, however, have confounded scholars for centuries," continued the professor. "They depict Charlemagne's crusade to Jerusalem."

Charlemagne? Josie turned and looked at the window.

"In the second pane, Charlemagne appears in a dream to the Emperor of the Eastern Empire, Constantine V," said the professor. "In pane three, he receives a letter from Constantine, urging him to rid the Holy Land of the Saracens. The interesting thing, of course, is that Charlemagne never actually went to Jerusalem."

Josie studied the parts of the window described by the professor but also looked to see that the police were still unaware of the whereabouts of her or Henrietta.

The teacher continued, "In the next scene, we see Charlemagne and his loyal knight Roland being greeted in the city of Constantinople by Emperor Constantine."

One of the students, a girl with short, blonde hair and a Scottish accent, asked, "You said Charlemagne never went to Jerusalem. Is that also true of Constantinople?"

"Yes, Keiran," replied the professor. "The most southeast he is known to have traveled is Capua in Southern Italy."

"Then why would this window depict him in Constantinople and Jerusalem?" asked a chubby male student with a Scottish accent.

"'Why' is an interesting question, Sean," replied the professor. "But it would be more appropriate to ask 'when.'"

A palpable sense of mystery spread among the students, and Josie felt it too.

"If we look at the fifth image," continued the teacher. "We see Charlemagne and two of his knights battling the Saracens. And Charles, who is wearing the crown, is in the process of cutting off the head of the Saracen emir."

As Josie looked at the pane the professor was referencing, she realized that she had seen it before. She just couldn't remember where.

"There are several problems with this depiction," said the professor. "The first is that Charlemagne went to great lengths to maintain good relations with the Muslim caliphs who controlled the Holy Land. For a good Christian king like Charles would have been most concerned with the safety of his subjects making their pilgrimage."

"So it would make no sense for Charlemagne to sack Jerusalem and cut off the emir's head?" asked the student named Keiran.

"That's right," said the professor. "To further make my point, let me direct you to the appearance of the combatants in panel five."

The students looked back at the stained glass, as did Josie. Then it hit her! She'd seen the image in the Grashaus in Aachen. It was what caused Igraine to fire her.

"The long, pointed shields of the Christians," said the professor, "and their manner of dress, as well as that of the Saracens, is not from the late seven hundreds."

Henrietta saw one policeman approach another and gesture in their direction.

"The Christians and Saracens in this pane are wearing battle gear and brandishing weapons of the First Crusade," added the professor.

"When was that?" Josie asked in spite of her desire to be anonymous.

Henrietta was shocked that Josie spoke. The students were surprised, and a few of them giggled. Josie immediately realized her mistake and smiled awkwardly.

The professor was so carried away by his lesson that he didn't seem to know who asked the question. "The First Crusade began in 1095, and the Christians took Jerusalem four years later."

Josie thought, 1095? Four years later? 1099! Just as the picture in Aachen said. Why would the stained glass show Charlemagne fighting in a place he had never been, two hundred and eighty-five years after he was supposed to have died?

Unfortunately, Josie couldn't stay to find out. The policemen who had gestured in their direction began walking toward them. Henrietta gave her granddaughter's arm a tug and led her away from the crowd and into the shadows.

"We'll go to the ambulatory," said Henrietta. "There are three chapels there and niches to hide in."

As Josie followed her grandmother and stayed close to the wall, she heard the professor say, "Now the sixth pane shows Constantine honoring Charlemagne's victory with a gift of three reliquaries, the first of which contained a piece of the True Cross..."

Josie looked back at the professor and saw Hans. He joined the two policemen in their brisk approach of the professor and his group.

"We gotta move faster," she told Henrietta as she took the lead.

Henrietta and Josie did such a good job of keeping to the shadows that visitors to the cathedral didn't notice them until they were almost close enough to touch them.

Josie glanced back at Hans and saw students tell him which way she and Henrietta had gone. He walked hastily in that direction.

"Excuse me," Josie said to people she passed. She saw Hans draw a pistol from inside his coat. "Run," she told Henrietta.

Seeing the man with the gun, Henrietta said, "He would not dare! Not in the House of the Lord."

"He killed Grandpa in a crowded train station," Josie revealed. "I don't think he cares if this is the House of the Lord."

"We need to run," Henrietta agreed.

Hans and the two policemen were also running. People hurried out of their way. Another cop who saw Josie and Henrietta yelled for them to stop and charged after them.

The pair had been plainly seen by nearly everyone. They raced toward a door in the back of the cathedral. If it didn't open, Josie knew that they were as good as captured...and possibly dead.

Fifteen feet to go to the door. Ten. Five. They suddenly heard the click of a hammer being cocked on a pistol. As if in slow motion, a lone hand rose up from the shadows before them with a gun in its grip. The weapon was aimed at Josie's forehead.

The man with the pistol stepped forward. It was Derek! "Get down, Josie!" he ordered.

She dropped to the floor, and Derek fired at the pursuing police. Sounds of the shot echoed through the church. People screamed and fled in every direction.

Derek jerked Josie to her feet and kicked the wooden door open.

CHAPTER ELEVEN

The warm water felt like a soothing balm on Josie's battered body. As she ran soap over her chest, she felt tenderness and swelling. In the moist fog created by her shower, she could see that blue lines were developing on her breasts where they had never been before. The areolae around her nipples were darker, and her belly was thicker.

She turned off the water and gently ran a towel over her body while inspecting her new features. She stepped out of the shower and wiped the moisture from the mirror to gaze at her reflection. What she saw was not the sexy girl who accompanied Derek to a spa in Aachen. Instead, the mirror gave her a young woman with stitches from a surgery and the body of someone who appeared to have traded exercise for visits to a pastry shop.

In the apartment they occupied in Saint-Denis, sex was the furthest thing from Derek's mind. He had spent the past several hours organizing a meeting by way of secret, coded messages. The people were assembled, and the summit was about to begin.

Dressed in loose jeans and a maroon sweatshirt with her hair still damp, Josie entered the living room to find a dozen people, only three of whom she recognized. She took her seat in a recliner. "Are you gonna handcuff me again?" she asked Derek.

Henrietta, who sat nearby, looked sharply at her granddaughter.

"No," Derek replied. "You're free to go at any time."

Josie looked at the assembled people with her eyes settling briefly on Igraine. "Am I here for another history lesson?" she inquired.

"In a manner of speaking, yes," Derek confessed.

"Vat did you find ven you looked for zee Saint-Denis Manuscript?" Igraine asked.

141

"Nothing," Josie replied. "It doesn't exist. It's an urban legend or something."

"How did you come to zat conclusion?" Igraine probed.

"I went to Colorado to talk to a guy named Dr. Vanderhoff," Josie told her.

The professor's name caused people to exchange glances.

"Vat did he say?" continued Igraine.

"He told me my father came to see him before he died," Josie said. "That's all."

Henrietta looked quickly at Josie. "*Qu'est-ce* ...what?" she asked. "Michael?"

"I'll tell you about it later," Josie said to her grandmother.

"No," insisted Henrietta. "Tell me now."

"Why did you send me after something that doesn't exist?" Josie asked Igraine.

"It does exist," said Derek. "Or at least it did. Your father found it here in Saint-Denis twenty-three years ago."

"Who has it now?" asked Josie. "Bigfoot?"

"What do you know of my Michael?" Henrietta demanded of Derek.

"Very little, I'm afraid," confessed Derek. "I know that he opened Betrada's tomb and found one of the clues left by Einhard."

"Who?" asked Henrietta. To Josie, she said, "What is he talking about?"

"Did you tell your grandmother anything?" Derek asked Josie.

"She told me enough," Henrietta snapped. "You should be ashamed!"

That caught everyone by surprise, especially Derek. People whispered.

"What does she mean?" a Frenchman named Philippe asked Derek.

"I don't know," Derek replied. To Henrietta, he added, "What are you saying?"

Correctly sensing that she had revealed something damaging to Derek, Henrietta laid it on heavier. "This pervert a *séduit et*...uh, seduced and impregnated my granddaughter. Then he sent her across borders, running for her life. And he shot his gun at her in the holy Cathedrale Notre-Dame!"

Her accusations elicited more muttered comments from the assembled group.

"Uh, Grandma," Josie began.

"Is this true, Derek?" asked Philippe.

"Of course not," Derek declared. "I haven't a clue why she's saying this, but...she's not...I'm not...that is not my child!"

Josie saw several people converse in whispered voices. Derek looked desperate.

"Whose babe are you carrying?" Philippe asked Josie.

"I just told you," Henrietta blurted. "*Le perverti*, the pervert!"

"I asked the girl," Philippe insisted and looked to Josie for an answer.

Josie could feel the weight of other eyes upon her. She looked at Derek, who pleaded with her to tell the truth.

"Well," said Josie. "It could be his."

"I knew it!" exclaimed Henrietta.

"What?" asked an astonished Derek. "I never had intercourse with her. Bloody hell."

The group was abuzz and beyond mollifying. A forty-something Irishman escorted Josie and Henrietta to a back bedroom, closed the door, and locked them inside.

"I guess we're no longer 'free to go at any time,'" said Josie.

Henrietta sat on the bed. "It's time for you to explain things," she said. "I want you to begin with what you said about Michael."

***

Almost two hours later, Josie concluded her tale by saying, "So obviously Derek is not the father of my baby, though you made a pretty good guess."

She told Henrietta everything, from the start of her odyssey to their rescue in Chartres Cathedral. Henrietta asked few questions, with the exception of one notable inquiry—whether or not Dr. Vanderhoff was involved in her son's murder.

That was something Josie hadn't considered. She was still unsure if her father had even been murdered. She hoped to someday learn the truth, but until then, all she could say was, "Anything is possible."

The two women heard the rattle and click of the unlocking door. Just in time, Josie thought. She was ravenously hungry.

Igraine stood in the open doorway and said, "Vat vere you zinking?"

"What?" Josie replied.

"Do you realize vat your lies have done?" asked Igraine.

"How do you know I'm lying?" said Josie.

Igraine shook her head. "Foolish girl," she said. "Your game cost you zee support of zee only people who could keep you safe." She left the room and without looking back, added, "Zee door is open. Go."

It took another ten minutes for Josie and Henrietta to walk out the open door. They had decided upon a course of action that involved leaving France altogether. They would find some place beyond the reach of The Agency... perhaps Asia. As they passed through the living room, they saw Derek and a thin, black man with white, curly hair. Josie stopped before them. They were studying an ancient document which was encased in a plastic sleeve. Derek's gun sat on the table before them.

"Josie," said Henrietta. "We need to get to the Metro."

"How'd you know we were in Chartres Cathedral?" Josie asked Derek.

"Zachary," Derek replied with a gesture to the man sitting beside him.

"I sold you a ticket in the Paris depot," said Zachary with a French accent.

"I guessed where you'd be after that," added Derek. "You're lucky I was right."

Josie didn't remember Zachary, but she was pretty much out of it at that time anyway. "How long have you been tracking me?" she asked Derek.

"I've been looking for you since you left Saint-Guilhem," he told her.

Josie was glad that he'd searched so hard for her. Perhaps it was a sign of how he felt about her. Ignoring her impatient grandmother, she sat back down on the recliner.

"What's that?" she asked in reference to the extremely old document.

"It's the history lesson I intended to give you earlier," Derek answered. "The one I hoped would convince you and the executive directors of the NSM."

"Executive directors?" Henrietta asked.

To Josie, Derek said, "You didn't think the little explosion on Ascension Day or that sad resistance at Saint-Guilhem was all the NSM had to offer, did you? We're a multi-national organization with thirty-six chapters. We're almost as big as The Agency, which we've vowed to destroy."

"I have not dealt with The Agency for many years," Henrietta replied. "But I remember it having twice the chapters that you now boast of having."

"Well, it hardly matters anyway," said Derek. "This clone project will be their greatest achievement, and the world's worst nightmare."

"I think you're over-reacting," Josie told him.

"Let's hope I am," answered Derek, "because I'm powerless to stop it. You don't believe me. And thanks to you, neither does the NSM."

"We could stop her now," Zachary said with a glance at the pistol on the table.

"Yes, we could," Derek agreed. "If we were murderers, which we're not." To Josie, he added, "Can your Agency say the same?"

"We must get to the Metro before dark," Henrietta told Josie. "It is *le plus dangereux*...uh, most dangerous after dark."

"Yes. Danger is something you should avoid," said Derek. "Good luck doing that without the help of the NSM."

***

A train sped out of the station as Josie sat beneath a sign which read, *Basilique de Saint-Denis.* Henrietta checked the Metro map in her hands while standing nearby.

"We will have to go into Paris to find the transportation we need," Henrietta decided. "But it should not take long."

Josie looked around the station. It was clean and modern, with digital photos of Saint-Denis sights alternating like a slide show on pillars. People who waited to crowd onto the next train seemed impersonal to her, and some appeared outright menacing. She glanced at the travel papers her grandfather had secured for her weeks earlier. If they could lead Derek to her, they could certainly let Dr. Herzog's men know where she was. To her horror, she saw that a camera was mounted on the ceiling and pointing directly at her. "Damn," she said and covered her face. "I'm going back to Derek."

"*Quoi*, what?" asked Henrietta. "No."

"You didn't tell me there were cameras in here," Josie scolded. She hurried to the stairs and ascended them as rapidly as possible.

Henrietta looked at the ceiling camera and hurried after her granddaughter.

Josie's fear was not misplaced. Two more cameras recorded the pair's departure from the train station.

***

145

Josie met Derek in the stairwell of the apartment as he and Zachary were leaving.

"Did you also use surveillance cameras to find me?" she asked.

Henrietta hurried up the stairs after her granddaughter.

"Uh…yes. Somewhat," admitted Derek. "When I could access them."

"I'll bet Dr. Herzog's goons have no trouble accessing them," Josie replied. She pushed past him and entered the apartment. Derek and Zachary followed her, as did Henrietta.

"Lock the door," Josie said as she paced the living room. "I can't go anywhere. They've got cameras all over the place."

"It's an Orwellian nightmare," Derek agreed.

"What am I supposed to do?" Josie asked.

"Come with me. We should not be having this discussion in their presence," Henrietta declared with a gesture to Derek and Zachary.

"I wish I had Grandpa," Josie said. She turned around, turned back, and spun around again, indecisive. She sat in the recliner and buried her face in her hands.

Derek gestured for Zachary to sit on the couch where he, himself, took a seat.

"We need to get you away from these people," Henrietta insisted.

Josie shook her head, her face still buried. "I can't trust anyone," she said. Looking at Derek with moist eyes, she added, "You tell me Dr. Herzog tricked me. His killers are after me, so I begin to think you're right. But your story is crazy. I don't want to believe it. I can't believe it. And you tried to kidnap me three times!"

"That's why you need to trust me," Henrietta told her. "Family is all we have."

"Family? You and my family also kidnapped me," Josie accused. "And you had me thrown in jail where I was beaten up and almost killed!"

"I know you don't want to believe me," Derek said. "But they made you pregnant, and your baby is the clone of Pippin the Hunchback. You have to deal with it."

"I know I'm pregnant, dammit!" Josie exclaimed. "But…I don't…How? How can it be Pippin's clone? I know about the wax effigy and the word carved on the throne. But that doesn't prove anything."

Derek instructed Zachary to get the document they'd been looking at. Zachary returned to them moments later, carrying the delicate paper encased in a plastic sleeve.

"Twenty-three years ago, your father opened the tomb of Queen Bertrada to find a manuscript written by Einhard," Derek explained.

"Which doesn't exist," Henrietta said.

"Which can't be located," he corrected. "But he didn't think to open the tomb of Charlemagne's father, which was beside the Queen's. We did. And what we found with the dusty remains of Pippin the Short was this."

Zachary handed the ancient paper to Josie. "Be gentle," he said. "It's nearly twelve hundred years old."

"What is it?" Josie asked.

"It's a papyrus letter written by Einhard in May 818," Derek explained.

Josie studied the brittle, yellowish-brown paper. The text upon it was faint but legible in a language she couldn't understand and with some letters she didn't recognize.

"Scholars call it a capitulary," Derek revealed. "It's a royal order."

"What do you mean by 'royal order'?" Josie asked. "You said it was written by Einhard. Was he a king?"

"No. He was a scholar and courtier," Derek explained. "He wrote it at the behest of his king. The king we're talking about is Charlemagne."

"When was this written again?" Josie asked.

"It's dated May of 818," Derek added. "But Charlemagne was supposed to have died four years earlier, in January of 814."

"It's obviously an order from a different king," interrupted Henrietta.

"No," Derek objected. "If you read it, you'll see that it instructs Abbot Waldo of Saint-Denis to prepare the abbey's hospital and mortuary for a royal visit within the month. It stresses that the abbot must keep this visit in his confidence on pain of death."

"Again," added Henrietta. "Why could it not be another king?"

"The word that is used is 'imperator,'" Derek answered. "Emperor...not king. In 818, the only official emperor was Louis the Pious, Charlemagne's son and successor. At that time, he was on campaign in Brittany and in no need of a mortuary."

"So you're saying that Charlemagne got sick in 813, faked his death in 814, and stayed sick four more years until they brought him here in 818?" Josie asked.

"That's precisely what I'm saying," Derek replied. "The letter in your hand proves it. While still lingering on his death bed, Charlemagne ordered Einhard to take him to the place where his parents were buried."

"Where he would be buried?" Josie added.

"Where he is buried," answered Derek.

***

Josie was extraordinarily tired. Then again, it was two o'clock in the morning. The cold night air caused her breath to form a cloud that vanished as soon as it appeared. That fog was replaced by the respiration of Derek, Zachary, Igraine, and Henrietta.

The only sound that could be heard was the frozen ground as it crunched under the feet of the women. Derek drew a crowbar from the inside of his coat, and Zachary clutched a rubber mallet.

"What are you doing?" asked Josie. To Igraine, she added, "You said it was open."

"I said it vas accessible," Igraine corrected. "Do you zink zee Basilica vould be open at zis hour?"

"Then how is it accessible?" Josie asked.

"Zee perimeter alarm has been disabled," Igraine told her.

"No," proclaimed Henrietta. "*Ce n'est pas vrai* (This is not right)!"

Derek inserted the crowbar between the jamb and the door, and Zachary struck it with the mallet. They repeated their efforts until the door of the Basilica opened with the crack of broken wood. With great hesitation, Josie followed them into the building.

Henrietta grabbed her granddaughter from behind. "*C'est un péché terrible*," she declared. "*Un péché terrible!*"

"English, Grandma."

"This is a terrible sin," Henrietta translated.

"I know," Josie agreed, but she proceeded into the Basilica of Saint-Denis. She felt unsteady on her feet and wasn't sure why. Was it guilt? Or fear?

The Basilica was the first Gothic church of France, and it was a jaw-dropping creation. It was the size of one and a half football fields and seemed to be constructed entirely of stone, marble, and stained glass. Elaborate statues of kings, queens, saints, and cherubs occupied nearly every niche, while monolithic columns supported the ribbed vaults of the ceiling. The vaults rested on pointed arches which allowed the walls to be opened up with large windows. The moon and stars cast muted light through the glass and distributed long, eerie shadows throughout the Basilica. The effect was unnerving, not unlike a haunted house. Derek bumped a pillar with the iron bar in his hand, causing a reverberation that was loud enough to startle the dead. That seemed to be an appropriate analogy, for there were countless marble sarcophagi situated throughout the Basilica.

"Be careful," Igraine scolded. "Zere could be custodians or even priests in here."

As Josie looked around, it seemed that tombs rested wherever her eyes fell. Some of the sarcophagi were fenced off while others were slightly elevated. Many more could be easily touched by anyone who passed them by. They all shared one trait, however—the lid of each marble box boasted an elaborate statue of the person to whom the grave was dedicated, and every one of them was in the position of a dead body.

"These are the kings and queens of France?" Josie asked. "How many are there?"

"Zey are not all kings and queens," Igraine answered. "Royal families are here too. Saint-Denis has more zan seventy funerary statues."

"We should leave them alone," Henrietta said.

"I need to see Charlemagne's real grave," Josie answered. "If it's here."

"Then we should come back when we are permitted," replied Henrietta.

Josie didn't reply. She was distracted by fog and black speckling spots which fluttered about her field of vision. She thought gnats were encircling her and tried to bat them away. When she realized that they didn't exist, she leaned against a nearby pillar.

"Here they are," said Derek. "Pippin the Short and Bertha of the Big Foot." He turned to Josie and could see that she didn't look right. "What's wrong?" he asked.

"Nothing," she lied. Walking forward, she asked, "Bertha Big Foot?"

"Yes," Derek chuckled. "That's what they called Charlemagne's mother."

"His father was 'The Short' and his mother was 'The Big Foot'?" Josie asked. "No wonder he had a hunchback for a son."

She stood near Derek, but still felt uneasy, as if her head was somehow detached from her body. Forcing herself to focus, she looked at the coffins. They were lying side by side among several other sarcophagi, near a black iron gate. Each statue held a scepter and wore a crown, but the tombs seemed to be shallow.

"They're really buried in there?" she asked.

"Yes. Or what's left of them," Derek replied. "Most of the others are empty."

"Empty?" repeated Josie.

Henrietta joined them as Igraine and Zachary pulled small flashlights from their pockets and searched the other sarcophagi.

"It happened during the French Revolution," said Derek, "when there was a backlash against religion and royalty. Revolutionary officials ordered their workers to dump the royal bodies of Saint-Denis into pits filled with lime."

"That's terrible," declared Josie. "They left these two alone? Why?"

"Because they weren't monarchs of France," Derek answered.

"That's an area of debate," Henrietta interjected.

"Yes," he admitted. "It is today. But at the time of the Revolution, the French traced the birth of their nation to Charles the Bald."

"What's with these nicknames?" asked Josie.

"He was the grandson of Charlemagne," Derek replied. "France as we know it did not exist under Charlemagne, his son Louis, or anyone who lived before them. It was part of a larger Frankish empire. Louis divided the empire and gave what is now France to his son Charles the Bald. That's when the French say their country was born."

"I disagree," said Henrietta.

Near the front of the Basilica, a silver-haired priest seeking quiet communion with The Lord was surprised to hear voices carry across the cathedral. He knew the building was supposed to be empty at that late hour. He had to investigate.

"You can disagree all you want," Derek told Henrietta. "But I am right. When Revolutionaries decided to eradicate the French monarchy, they started with their first true king, Charles the Bald, and they continued through to Louis XVI."

"They left the ones before Charles the Bald alone?" Josie asked.

"Yes," Derek answered.

"That's how my father was able to find a book in her coffin?" she asked with a gesture to Queen Bertrada's stone effigy.

150

"And why we found the capitulary in his," Derek said in reference to Pippin the Short's tomb.

The priest, whose name was Marcel, crept forward in the darkest shadows. He watched the beams of flashlights search the funerary statues. These visitors were not the faithful who had simply overstayed their welcome, he realized.

"I found it," exclaimed Zachary.

Derek, Josie, and Henrietta rushed over to join Zachary and Igraine beside four sarcophagi. Tan markers leaning against the base of one of the tombs identified them as belonging to Carloman, Ermentrude, Philippe, and Constance de Castille.

"Where is it?" Josie asked.

"There," Derek declared while pointing at a tomb with a statue of a king on it.

Josie looked at the grave to which he was pointing, read the plaque, and gazed again at the tomb. "It says Carloman," she replied.

"Carloman was Charlemagne's brother and co-ruler until he died suddenly at the age of twenty," Derek told her.

"Great," said Josie. "Where's Charlemagne?"

"There," Derek repeated. "That is Charlemagne's tomb. He died here at Saint-Denis, in secret. Einhard and Abbot Waldo buried him in a vault alongside his parents, but they marked the grave for Carloman, his brother, because they had already 'buried'..." He used his fingers to make quotation marks. "...Charlemagne in Aachen."

"That is not a vault, *et*...and his parents are over there," said Henrietta as she pointed at the tombs of Pippin the Short and Bertha of the Big Foot.

"They moved the graves and made the statues you see in the 1100's," Derek explained, "but, I assure you, that is Charlemagne."

"How are we supposed to know that?" asked Josie.

The priest named Marcel found a hiding spot a short distance from the intruders. He thought they were grave robbers, but he was unaware of the assault on Pippin the Short's tomb eight months earlier. It had been covered up by the powers that be. If he had known of the break-in, he would have realized that these people were more than thieves. They were enemies of the state, labeled as such by the European Union.

"The capitulary," answered Zachary.

"Yes," agreed Derek. "I didn't bring it with me, but at the bottom of it, in post script, is a reference to the remains of Carloman."

He could see that Josie remained unconvinced. Blowing out an exasperated breath, he said, "In case you haven't noticed yet, the names of sons had political significance in Charlemagne's world."

Josie nodded.

"Pippin the Short, Pippin the Hunchback, Charles the Great, Charles the Bald...."

"I get it," said Josie.

Derek continued, "A male heir had no right to his inheritance if he did not bear the name of a ruling ancestor."

"Yes," snapped Josie. "You explained that." She was becoming impatient.

"Charlemagne named his second son by his third wife, Carloman, after the child's dead uncle," explained Derek. "But four years later, he changed it to Pippin. In doing that, he disinherited his first born son, Pippin the Hunchback."

"So that made Pippin the Hunchback become a traitor?" Josie asked.

"Exactly," Derek replied.

"You still didn't explain why that is Charlemagne's tomb," declared Henrietta.

"Oh zis is taking too long," Igraine announced. "Show zem."

Hiding in the shadows, Marcel wished he had a cell phone. The nearest land line was in the chaplain's quarters.

Derek gestured for Igraine to be patient. "Einhard was leaving another clue," he told them. "The people who paid attention to these things back then, priests and scholars, knew that Charlemagne's brother Carloman was buried in Reims."

The ache in Josie's head grew. It felt as if knives were slicing across her cranium—from the front to the back, from the inside and the outside. She heard ringing in her ears and felt pressure behind her eyes. Was Derek's history lesson causing this?

"Yet Einhard marked this grave as Carloman's because that's the name that was used to steal the identity of the person who was really buried in Charlemagne's tomb in Aachen," Derek revealed. "Pippin the Hunchback."

"Oh, for God's sake," declared Igraine. "Open zee tomb and show zem!"

Marcel didn't understand much English, but he knew what it meant when the intruders raised tools and moved closer to a coffin. He also saw the gun tucked in the belt of the man carrying the crowbar, prompting him to scurry to the chaplain's quarters.

"You can't open it," declared Josie.

"Oh, *mon Dieu*...my God!" exclaimed Henrietta.

"You von't believe us," Igraine accused. "You vant proof. Zis is proof."

"How's it gonna prove anything?" asked Josie. "You'll show me a skeleton and some bones. I'll have no way of knowing if it's Charlemagne or his brother."

"And it's wrong," added Henrietta. "*C'est sacrilège* (It's a sacrilege)!"

"The post script on the capitulary directed us to Carloman's remains," Derek explained. "Not his tomb. There must be some identifying mark. Otherwise, why would Einhard send us here? Remember, Charlemagne was quite a bit larger than Carloman. He also lived nearly sixty years longer, so their bones would be very different."

Igraine took the crowbar from Derek's hand and gave it to Zachary. He placed the tip of the bar beneath the lid of Carloman's coffin and struck it with his mallet. He hit it several more times and lifted it, then moved to another spot and resumed the procedure.

Even though the mallet was rubber, the banging noise and the breaking of marble sounded like explosions in Josie's ears. The faint amount of light that shone through nearby windows burned like spotlights on her eyes. She felt nausea rising in her throat.

"We should not be here," Henrietta told her granddaughter.

As Zachary struggled to break the bond between the lid and the main body of the coffin, Derek and Igraine tried to help him by lifting the lid.

"Come, Josie," said Henrietta. "Now is our chance to..."

Josie was in obvious pain, bent over with her hands covering her ears.

"Are you having cramps?" asked Henrietta. "Are you *constipe*...uh, constipated?"

Marcel hung up the phone in the chaplain's chamber. He had called the authorities, but he didn't feel any better. He could still hear the sounds of the vandals.

It took a considerable strain from Derek and Igraine and ten minutes of relentless hammering by Zachary to finally break the seal between the lid and the coffin. Dust and jagged pieces of stone were scattered about the floor. Zachary set his tools down.

The clang of the crowbar on marble tile reverberated in Josie's head and caused her to belch the contents of her stomach onto the floor before her.

Outside the giant Basilica, five police cars with flashing lights but no sirens raced down a slightly curved road to come to screeching stops. Officers scrambled out of the vehicles and were met by Marcel at the second of three front entrances.

With red faces, veins bulging from their necks and wrenching muscles, Derek, Zachary, and Igraine removed the lid from the coffin.

"Set it down," instructed Derek. "Carefully. Carefully."

The weight was too great and the ancient piece crashed to the floor.

"No!" exclaimed Derek. "Bloody hell!"

Zachary and Igraine looked inside the sarcophagus. Igraine turned to Josie. "Here is your proof," she said.

Josie summoned all of her strength to stand upright and walk toward the coffin. Henrietta tried to assist her. Derek watched the women approach. What's wrong with her, he wondered. He noticed the puddle of vomit on the floor behind them.

The police quietly entered the church with their guns drawn.

Josie stopped before the marble box. It was a considerable effort for her to keep her eyes open, but she had to see what was inside.

"Charlemagne," pronounced Derek.

"Now do you believe us?" asked Igraine.

Though the inside of the box was mostly dark, its contents were visible. There was a lot of dust, no fabric of any kind, and a skeleton that was incomplete. Almost half of the skull had turned to dust, but six teeth remained. There was no flesh and no hair. There was, however, a piece of jewelry. Josie peered closely into the coffin.

"She is about to be sick again," declared Henrietta. "This is too much for her."

Josie brushed her grandmother's concerns away with the bat of her hand. As her eyes focused through their pain, she said, "Oh, my God."

Lying on what should have been the chest of the deceased was a gilded pendant on a chain of gold. It was encircled with a lace of gold and silver that bore emeralds and rubies of various sizes. It had been severed at the top and opened to resemble the shape of the letter *U*. The contents that would have made up its middle were missing, but Josie knew what belonged there because she was looking at a duplicate of the pendant her mother sold so many months before—her father's necklace.

"Charlemagne's talisman," Derek said. "The one he wore at all times. The one he was buried with."

Josie reached for it. She wanted to hold it in her hands, but she stopped herself. "It's broken," she told Derek. "Why is it broken? Where are the pieces of the Cross?"

"I don't know," Derek said. "Maybe it happened during the French Revolution."

Josie looked back at the corpse and the pendant. She had so many questions, but her pain only allowed her to ask one. "Does Dr. Herzog know Charlemagne is here?"

"He knows," replied Derek.

"Then why would he clone Pippin the Hunchback?" she asked.

"Zee issue is not vhy he did it," said Igraine. "It is zat he did it. And now zat you have accepted zee truz...you cannot allow zee clone to be born. You must abort it."

Josie shot her a surprised look.

"What did you say?" demanded Henrietta. "How dare you speak such words in the House of God!"

Four policemen suddenly popped out from behind statues, sarcophagi, and pillars. They trained their guns on the intruders as one of them yelled in French.

The others raised their hands, but Derek pulled out his gun and shot the speaking policeman in the shoulder. He sprang on top of Josie, and she crumpled under his weight. The pair fell behind the sarcophagus of Carloman/Charlemagne.

Igraine and Zachary made their moves as well. They hid behind the tombs of Philippe and Constance de Castille. Igraine fired her pistol at the police, who were shooting at them.

Gunshots struck pillars and statues, stone railings, and the floor. Debris and dust kicked up from many directions. Henrietta scurried to the far side of a marble staircase.

A cop dragged his comrade with the shoulder wound out of harm's way as his fellow officers traded shots with Derek and Igraine. It was a standoff with flying bullets.

In the back of the church, Marcel watched in horror as the sacred temple of The Lord was assaulted by gunfire.

Josie was in great pain, causing Derek to say, "I have to get her out of here!"

Igraine nodded and scrambled toward the wall while shooting repeatedly.

"Give me the gun!" Zachary yelled to Derek. "I'll take their fire!"

Derek tossed his pistol to Zachary. Catching the weapon, Zachary ordered, "Go!"

"Come on, Josie," commanded Derek.

"I can't!" she exclaimed.

Zachary started shooting as Derek pulled Josie to the back of the Cathedral.

Every step for Josie was unimaginably painful, and each gunshot felt like a detonation in her head. She tried to look where she was running, but her eyes burned and threatened to pop out of their sockets like corks from champagne bottles.

An officer ordered two policemen to pursue Derek and Josie.

Six rounds from two different guns suddenly assailed Zachary's body and sprayed his blood over the grave of King Philippe. He collapsed onto the monarch's stone effigy.

Henrietta watched Derek pull Josie toward the rear of the Church. She saw two policemen chasing after them and charged forward to crash into them. The collision knocked them to the floor and intertwined Henrietta's body with those of the policemen.

Igraine continued to draw fire as she shot at the police. Her weapon clicked. She squeezed the trigger again. Click. Click. She looked back to see Derek and Josie exit the Cathedral. Satisfied, she threw her gun at the police and raised her hands.

CHAPTER TWELVE

Kristina Troy was an American who lived in Paris. She was in her late twenties, with a clear, slightly rosy complexion, long blond hair and blue eyes. Her natural beauty, elegance, and charm enabled her to become the personal nurse of the patriarch of the Frontenac family, one of France's wealthiest clans.

Kristina closed the bedroom door behind her and stepped into the living room of her apartment to meet Derek.

"She's having a migraine," Kristina told him.

"A migraine?" asked Derek. "Is that all?"

"You've clearly never had one," said Kristina.

"No," he confessed.

"It's horrible," she added. "If this is your first one, like it is for her, it's even worse. You don't know what to expect. You feel like you're going to die."

"How can she get rid of it?" asked Derek.

"She can't do much," Kristina answered. "She needs to rest and get plenty of fluids. Normally, people take medications when they feel it coming on, but she can't."

"Why not?" he asked.

"Didn't she tell you she was pregnant?" replied Kristina.

"Oh...yeah," he answered. "We discussed that."

***

Josie passed the night and much of the next day in a deep slumber. When she finally awoke, she was disoriented and wondered where she was. The bedroom door slowly opened, and she saw a pretty blond peering back at her.

"There's no point in asking how you feel," said Kristina as she entered the room. "I know. It's like you've been hit by a ten-ton truck."

"Where am I?" Josie asked.

"My apartment," replied Kristina.

"Who are you?"

"We met last night," said Kristina. "I can see why you don't remember, though."

"She's a, uh, friend of mine," answered Derek as he followed Kristina into the room. He had showered, shaved, and dressed in a button-down shirt beneath a navy blue sweater with khaki pants. He held sheets of paper in his hand.

Josie's gaze traveled back and forth between the two. "I should have figured," she said. "Where's my grandmother?"

"Probably in prison," Derek answered. "She risked herself to help me get you out. Do you remember that?"

Josie shook her head ever so slightly.

"Can you give us a moment?" Derek asked Kristina.

"Of course," she replied, and added, "Stay here as long as you need to."

Josie smiled, though the effort was clearly forced. When Kristina left the room and closed the door behind her, she asked, "How do you know her?"

"We're friends, like I said," Derek answered. "I've known her for a long time."

Josie wasn't buying his answer, and it showed.

Derek removed a decorative doll from a cushion chair, dragged the chair closer to Josie, and asked, "Do you remember what we discussed at Charlemagne's tomb?"

"We discussed a lot."

"You asked me why Dr. Herzog would make a clone from the remains in Aachen if he knew Charlemagne was buried in Saint-Denis," he continued. "This is why."

He gave her the papers in his hand. She felt the urge to intertwine her fingers with his and draw him closer to her, but she resisted. So much had passed between them—the abductions, deception, double-dealing, the violence, not to mention the pregnancy. And what guy would want to be with a girl who was pregnant with someone...or something...else's child?

She returned her attention to the papers and saw that they formed a family tree which began with Pippin the Hunchback and continued through hundreds of descendants and their spouses. One particular family line was highlighted.

"It's a genealogy starting with Pippin the Hunchback," Derek explained.

Josie nodded.

"I marked the line of descent that you need to follow," he added.

Her eyes trailed the colored line through pages two, three, four and five. On the sixth sheet, the highlighted progression came to an end with one name—Clement Herzog.

"Where'd you get this?" Josie asked.

"Most of the information came from Dr. Herzog himself, without him even knowing it," Derek admitted. "It took four years to assemble all the research."

"You didn't have it with you last night," Josie observed.

"It's been in my email file for weeks," explained Derek. "I printed it this morning."

Josie eyed him skeptically.

"Look at it," he directed. "Dr. Herzog is a direct descendant of Pippin the Hunchback! What better reason could he have for cloning him?"

"I can think of a lot of family members I wouldn't want to clone," replied Josie.

She studied the papers but really wanted to ask him about Kristina. She was a gorgeous, single woman who was not pregnant, and he was being vague about how he knew her. But rather than say anything, she just stared at the genealogy line.

Derek returned to the living room while considering his frustrations with Josie. She put up a gruff exterior. She had been cold toward him since Chartres, but when she looked at him, it was with an expression worn by most of the women he had romanced. And something happened in that bedroom. He wasn't sure what, but he felt energy, or a kind of sexual tension. The question for him, however, was how did he feel about her? More specifically, how did he feel about the trouble that surrounded her? She had been his assignment, and she still was. But it was becoming far more complicated than that. It was one thing to rescue her, to assist her, to even save her. It was quite another to fall for her, and Josie was not the kind of woman with whom he could have a passing fling.

Kristina emerged from the kitchen with two glasses of wine and a plate of cheese, grapes, and sliced French bread. Derek took one of the glasses.

"Ahh, just what I need," he said.

She set the food on a table and sat. "What will you do about it?" she asked.

"About what?" he replied while spreading cheese on a slice of bread.

"Your baby," Kristina answered. "It is your baby, isn't it?"

Derek stopped before taking a bite of food. "Why do you assume that?" he asked.

Kristina smiled. "It's not my business anymore."

Derek shook his head and ate his cheese and bread.

"Still," she continued. "It's a little suspicious. I haven't seen you in...what? Seven months? And you show up at five in the morning with a pregnant girl."

"I'm not trying to make you jealous," said Derek.

"Oh, I didn't think that," she laughed.

Derek washed his food down with wine and sat back. "I'm helping out a friend."

Kristina nodded and sipped her wine, but she obviously didn't believe him.

Josie decided that it was time to get out of bed. She checked her appearance in the dresser mirror and scrunched her nose. "Ugh, I'm a mess," she said. Though it hurt her head, she applied one of Kristina's brushes to her tangled hair. She walked out of the bathroom but stopped when she heard Kristina ask, "How long have you known her?"

"Why would you want to know that?" Derek replied. "You don't really think I got her pregnant, do you?"

Oh, here we go, Josie thought as she continued to eavesdrop.

"She's a beautiful girl," Kristina admitted. "Very cute."

"And smart," Derek added. "But it didn't happen."

"Ever the gentleman?" Kristina asked. "You haven't always acted that way."

Derek chuckled and drank more wine. "And you're not always a lady."

Josie listened for another twenty minutes, but they made no more revealing comments. Nevertheless, she'd heard enough. She returned to bed and sulked over Derek's past with Kristina and disinterest in her, romantically speaking. The fact that she was also holding back from him didn't register in her thinking.

***

Three hours later, Josie's hunger brought her into the dining area and before a delicious eggplant soufflé. It was unlike anything she had ever tasted. She ate so much that she feared she might appear gluttonous, but she couldn't help herself. Kristina was a great cook, and she was simply starving.

After the meal, the women left Derek to clean up while they searched for a new ensemble for Josie. She was hesitant to disrobe before the beautiful woman she viewed as her competition and was embarrassed by her waistline, her visible blue veins and the stitches which sealed her surgery scars.

"Let me see them," Kristina said.

Reluctantly, Josie revealed her scars.

"The stitches need to come out," said Kristina. "I can do it now, if you want."

Josie considered her options and realized that it was in her best interest to have a nurse do the job. She lay on the bed and presented her surgical wounds to Kristina.

"Be sure to put Vitamin E or cocoa butter on your scars," Kristina instructed. "It should help to fade them. Cocoa butter also works on stretch marks."

"Stretch marks?" asked Josie. "I didn't even think about that. Will I get 'em?"

"Most pregnant women do," replied Kristina. The thought of getting stretch marks really seemed to bother Josie, so she added, "They shouldn't be too bad."

"It's not that," Josie confessed. "It's...he tricked me, and now I'm pregnant!"

Who is she talking about? Kristina wondered. *Derek?*

"Do you know anybody that's had an abortion?" Josie asked.

"Uh...yes," she said, surprised by the question. "But I really think that's something you should discuss with the father of the child."

"The father of the child," Josie laughed. "Have you ever heard of Charlemagne?"

Kristina was now thoroughly perplexed. "Charlemagne?" she asked.

"That's who Derek's company is named after, isn't it?"

161

Derek didn't tell her that he left The Agency? Maybe he and Kristina weren't as close as Josie originally thought.

"He's a king from the 1400's," Kristina continued.

"Forget it," Josie said. "I was only joking."

Kristina removed the last stitch and said, "Let me find some cocoa butter."

Josie watched her enter the bathroom, which adjoined the bedroom. As objects rattled about the cabinet, she thought about Kristina's response to her comment. A king from the 1400's, she had said. The 1400's?

"I found some," Kristina announced as she returned to the bedroom.

Josie accepted the cocoa butter with a smile and a nod, and said, "It doesn't matter, but Charlemagne was a king in the 800's, not the 1400's."

"Okay," replied Kristina.

Josie opened the jar, scooped some cream out and smoothed it over her scars.

"There must have been two Charlemagnes then," added Kristina.

Josie looked at her with a curious expression.

"The people I work for have a manor house with a tapestry that I see at least a dozen times a day," Kristina continued. "It shows a parade and a king leading a queen to Notre Dame. I'm pretty sure the bottom of it says 'Charlemagne, 1492.'"

***

Kristina's Mercedes epitomized luxury travel, but its passengers were too preoccupied to consider its soft leather seats, mahogany veneer, and tranquil ride.

"I don't think you realize how bloody reckless this is," Derek told Josie.

"I gotta check it out," she replied.

"What if they recognize you?" he asked. "Or me?"

Kristina listened but continued to drive in silence.

They were going to the Frontenac's manor house, which was a scenic, forty-minute drive from Paris. It was a route Kristina was familiar with—partially on highway, mostly over country roads. Icicles hung from the branches of trees they passed, and there was a slight brush of snow on the ground, a sure sign that the harshest part of winter was just around the corner.

Josie searched the Internet as she had all that morning and much of the night before. There had to be an explanation for why the tapestry Kristina claimed to have seen placed Charlemagne in Paris in 1492. It was as baffling to her as the Chartres window had been. Ten minutes from their destination, she found an entry that caught her attention.

"Listen to this," she said. "According to Jean Nicolai...this site says he was a theologian, whatever that means."

"It means he studied religion," Derek explained.

"Okay," she said. "Well, there are a lot of people named Jean Nicolai, but this one was around in the 1600's. He wrote...I'll just read it....'And the representative Charlemagne was about one lance high and had a girth to match his height, holding in his right hand a naked sword and in the other hand the golden globe topped by the cross. This said personage wore a real crown, and on the crown was a golden cross. This said king, mounted on a horse with a blanket decorated with fleurs-de-lis, saluted Anne of Brittany and made her a beautiful speech for her happy arrival; and in this state he traveled in front of the noble lady all the way to Notre Dame of Paris. And the date of this was the ninth day of February, fourteen hundred and ninety-two.'"

She looked up from her phone, expecting Derek or even Kristina to comment.

"What do you think?" she asked. "Charlemagne in Paris in 1492."

"I don't think anything," Derek answered. "That was written by someone who was well over a hundred years removed from the supposed event. He must have been composing a piece of fiction."

"No," Josie corrected him. "Because later on he says...and I'm reading it here...'That said event was a true occurrence I know by means of the Chroniques de Notre-Dame and The Valois Tapestry.'"

"It's pronounced Val-wa," corrected Derek. "The Royal House of France."

"Oh, yes," said Kristina. "That's the tapestry I was talking about. Monsieur Frontenac said it was a gift to his family from the King of France a long time ago."

"See," said Josie.

"I don't understand what you're looking for," said Derek. "You saw the remains. You know Charlemagne is dead...he'd have to be. He lived twelve hundred years ago."

Josie sat for a moment in silence, contemplating his comment. Then it hit her. Charlemagne was an old man in 814—the year history claimed that he died. Was she seriously thinking that he was still alive in 1492? Almost seven hundred years later?

"You're right," she admitted, while exiting the Internet. "Even if those weren't his bones in Saint-Denis, he would have died in the early 800's."

"It was him in Saint-Denis," said Derek. "You know it was."

Josie nodded.

To Kristina, Derek added, "There's no point in going on. Take us back to Paris."

"Uh, no," replied Kristina. "We're here. That's the manor house in front of us."

Josie leaned forward to see a country estate with a frozen pond, vast grounds, a circular driveway, and expensive cars parked before the main house. The central building was three stories tall with six gables on its roof, four chimneys, and fenced off balconies.

"Wow," said Josie.

"We can still turn around," Derek told Kristina.

"No," declared Josie. "We've come all this way. Let's at least go in."

"It's okay, Derek," informed Kristina. "The Frontenacs are nice people. You have nothing to worry about with them."

Derek frowned, but he was outvoted. He said nothing more as Kristina parked behind a silver Maybach 62, a car that was twice as expensive as Dr. Herzog's Bentley.

Kristina led her guests to the front door, which was engraved and made of solid oak. The entrance opened before she could even reach for the knocker. Marie Frontenac, a brunette girl of eighteen, rushed out and nearly collided with the newcomers. She was followed by two female friends of the same age.

"*Merde*, Kristina (Holy shit, Kristina)!" exclaimed Marie. *"Tu m'as surprise* (You surprised me)!"

Kristina laughed and introduced Derek and Josie. Before she could tell the girl their real names, Derek extended his hand to Miss Frontenac and said, *"Je m'appelle François. C'est ma sœur, Jasmine* (My name is François. This is my sister Jasmine)."

Kristina was taken aback by his lie, but she didn't correct him. She and Marie conversed like close confidants, then concluded their exchange with hugs and kisses on the cheek. Kristina led Josie and Derek into the manor house where they were treated to a glimpse of country living, billionaire style.

In the center of the foyer, an oak staircase stretched to the second floor. The walls on each side of it were lined with valuable art work and exotic taxidermy. Persian rugs and antique furniture filled the room. A tray with tumblers and a variety of liquors sat upon a glass table, and a cabinet housed china and figurines that were hundreds of years old.

The item which most interested Josie hung from the wall at the top of the stairs. It was a tapestry that was faded and very old. "Is that it?" she asked Kristina.

"Yes," began Kristina. "But..."

"*No me dijeron que podia llevar invitados* (I was not told you would bring guests)," said a Spaniard named Enrique. He was middle-aged with little hair, a rotund belly, and skin that looked permanently tanned.

"Ahh, Enrique," said Kristina. "*Habla Francés* (Speak French)," she instructed.

He repeated himself in French, and Kristina responded in the same language.

Josie didn't understand what they said, but she could tell that Enrique was upset. He was the butler and seemed to be particular about who entered the house. Kristina silenced him by dropping Marie Frontenac's name. With a scowl on his face, he walked away.

Turning to Josie and Derek, Kristina asked, "Shall we view the tapestry?"

The tapestry was six feet wide by nine feet tall. A golden border that bore green fleurs-de-lis and meandering, leafy vines surrounded the main picture. The primary image depicted a multitude of people following a king, who sat upon a tall horse. The monarch had long, gray hair and a flowing, white beard. He wore a crown with a cross upon it. He held a sword in his right hand and a golden orb in his left. Between himself and his horse was a blanket decorated with fleurs-de-lis. A much younger and demure-looking queen, Anne of Brittany, rode behind the king on a smaller horse. She and the procession followed the king to Notre Dame Cathedral, a grand church which stood in the foreground. *CHARLEMAGNE 1492* was embroidered into the bottom of the image.

"This thing must be ancient," Josie mumbled, but she was mostly interested in the parts of the tapestry that she found to be familiar. The crown worn by the king and the orb which sat in his left hand resembled the imperial treasures she'd seen in the Coronation Hall of Aachen's

Rathaus. The monarch's face looked much like that of Charlemagne as presented in the portrait which hung in the foyer of the same Rathaus.

"What's that?" she asked while gesturing to the horse blanket in the image.

"It's the fleur-de-lis," Kristina answered. "It means lily flower."

"It's the symbol of French kings, dating back before Charlemagne," said Derek.

"You said Charlemagne wasn't a French king," Josie observed.

"The symbol actually goes back to the Frankish kings," Derek corrected.

What held Josie's attention was the sword brandished by the king on the tapestry. The weapon's blade appeared to be multi-colored with strands of pink, light green, and lavender. She knew she'd seen it before; she just couldn't remember where…or when.

A plump woman in her fifties named Eloise descended a staircase from the third floor to the second. "Kristina?" she asked. *"Pourquoi es-tu venue?* (Why are you here?)"

"Eloise," Kristina replied. "Monsieur Frontenac's other nurse."

The two nurses spoke. After a few moments, Kristina turned to Derek and Josie and said, "Monsieur Frontenac will be offended if I don't pay him a visit. Do you mind?"

Neither of them objected, and she followed Eloise to the third floor. Derek and Josie glanced at each other. They were left alone.

"Kristina's a nice girl," commented Josie. "Isn't she?"

"Yes," agreed Derek. "Very nice."

Josie wanted to ask if he'd ever slept with her, but she thought better of it. She looked at the tapestry and said, "There's a window in Chartres with Charlemagne on it."

"I'm sure there is," answered Derek. "They honor him throughout Europe."

"This one showed him in Jerusalem two hundred and eighty-five years after he was supposed to have died," she added.

While tending to his affairs, Enrique kept an eye on Kristina's friends. He was sure he had seen them before, especially the girl.

"Why do you think that is?" Josie asked Derek. "And why does this tapestry put Charlemagne in Paris in 1492?"

"I don't know," Derek admitted. "They were probably trying to connect their ages with the age of Charlemagne. Like today's Americans do with George Washington."

It suddenly occurred to Enrique where he had last seen the girl. It was on the news. She was also featured in an email addressed to Monsieur Frontenac (he usually read the old man his messages). The email had been sent to all Agency administrators, both active and retired. The girl was wanted by authorities and by The Agency. He promptly called the police. He also dialed a number which had been given to him by the man Monsieur Frontenac admired above all others, Dr. Clement Herzog.

Derek wanted to leave the estate as soon as possible, but he and Josie were at the mercy of Kristina. They could do little but return to the sitting room and wait for her.

As Josie surveyed the taxidermy and tried to decide if it was morbid or merely bizarre, Enrique approached them with a smile and an offer of a beverage. They each declined, so he suggested some cheese. A maple beignet? Perhaps an éclair?

"He knows who we are," Derek whispered to Josie.

"What makes you say that?" she asked with obvious concern.

"Don't you find his sudden hospitality to be a bit odd?" Derek asked rhetorically.

Enrique returned from the kitchen with two steaming cups. "Cafe?" he offered.

"Merci, mais sortons (Thank you, but we'll go outside)," Derek told the butler.

Enrique started to object, but realized he was overplaying it and backed off.

Derek led Josie to the door.

"Where are you going?" asked Kristina as she passed the tapestry.

"Thank God," muttered Derek. To Kristina, he announced, "We're ready to go."

"Don't you want to see the rest of the house?" she asked.

"No," Derek and Josie replied in unison.

Kristina couldn't leave immediately. She had to order prescriptions for Monsieur Frontenac, take an inventory of medicines, and notify Enrique of her schedule for the upcoming week. Taking care of an elderly, bed-ridden patient required planning.

Fifteen minutes later, Kristina led her visitors out the front door. "I'm sorry I took so long," she told them. "Enrique must have asked me a hundred questions."

Josie and Derek exchanged worried glances.

167

As they approached Kristina's Mercedes, they saw eight vehicles, six of which were police cars, racing toward the house. Their lights didn't flash and their sirens were silent, but Derek and Josie knew why they had come.

"Run!" Derek ordered.

"Where?" asked Josie.

"Anywhere!" he exclaimed as led her into the snow.

Kristina panicked as her friends ran and police cars sped down the driveway. Enrique opened the door and shouted to the authorities while pointing at Derek and Josie.

Josie outpaced Derek. She glanced back, but he shouted, "Keep running!"

Derek knew the police came to make arrests. As long as they made one, then perhaps they wouldn't try hard for a second. At least that was what he hoped as he walked toward them with his hands in the air. When Hans and Petra rushed out of one of the unmarked cars, he realized that any chance for a favorable outcome was gone. He stopped abruptly, spun around, and raced after Josie.

As luck would have it, Hans and Petra were meeting with the Prefect of Police for the city of Paris when Enrique's call came through. They were heading out the door when Dr. Herzog phoned them with orders to retrieve Josie at all costs or to die trying.

That was precisely what they intended to do as they raced after the fugitives. Derek was close, but Josie was the prize. Unfortunately, she was about two hundred yards ahead of them. It would be hard to catch her, unless they were resourceful. Petra stopped running, took aim with his pistol, and fired.

The bullet sailed through Derek's leg, and he collapsed to the ground with an agonizing scream.

Josie stopped abruptly, turned, and saw Derek flailing in the snow with Kristina running toward him. Police emptied out of their vehicles, and Josie gave up all pretense of flight to rush to Derek's aid.

With the man lying in crimson snow and two girls racing toward him, Hans and Petra knew that they were about to make amends for their failures. And they were delighted to do so.

CHAPTER THIRTEEN

Josie stood in a dark room before a one-sided window. She could see out, but the people she watched couldn't see in. The cells before her were made of concrete, and their front walls were constructed of unbreakable Plexiglas. Derek and Kristina were in one confine, and Igraine and Henrietta were in another. Derek was clammy with sweat and shivering on the cold floor. His pant leg had been torn away and used as a tourniquet. Blood and puss oozed from his leg wound, and Kristina tried in vain to care for him.

It was torture for Josie to watch Derek suffer while Kristina tried to help him. She looked into the other cell where Henrietta and Igraine wore bruises on their faces.

The door behind her opened. Dr. Herzog entered and closed the door.

"You had us worried, Josie," he said.

"He needs a doctor," she replied. "Get that bullet out of his leg."

"That depends on you," Dr. Herzog replied.

"Me?" she asked. "Okay. Then I order you to get him a doctor."

Dr. Herzog laughed. "No," he said. "That's not what I meant."

"What then?" Josie demanded. "What do you want?"

"I want you to stop running from us," he told her.

"You lied to me!" she screamed. "You must have broken about a hundred laws with what you did to me. And it's not even Charlemagne's clone that I'm carrying."

"They've gotten into your head," he replied calmly.

"No," Josie corrected. "What's gotten into my head is the murder of my grandfather by a guy you hired."

"It would be pointless for me to try to explain anything while you're in an agitated state," Dr. Herzog responded. "So I'll leave you with this

169

kernel of truth. The welfare of those four people depends on you. All I care about is the healthy birth of that child."

He opened the door and departed, returning Josie to the solitary darkness of the prison observation room.

***

Josie's "prison" was a spacious suite of a half dozen rooms in The Agency's subterranean compound. She had a fully stocked kitchen with state-of-the-art appliances, a changing room with Victorian style furnishings, and a bathroom that featured a multi-jet shower, a bidet, and a toilet. Her bedroom was a combination of the elegant and the modern. It could easily fit two king-sized beds, though she only had one, and provided a closet with shelves and more hanging space than most small boutiques. The library was furnished with wall-to-wall bookshelves which were fully stocked with a variety of titles. Plush leather furniture gave the room a leisurely feel, and two computers connected it to the outside world.

After wandering about her new home, Josie settled upon a sofa in the entertainment room and stared at a blank television screen. A pool table, jukebox, and three pinball machines became nothing more than dust collectors to her. She thought of the deception that grew in her womb and realized that there was nothing she could do about it as long as she was held by The Agency.

Abby Ellis entered the room with Madeline, Josie's former doctor. Madeline carried a bag filled with medical materials.

"Josie," said Abby. "I'm so glad you're safe. You look great."

"Hi, Abby," Josie replied flatly.

"How are you feeling?" asked Abby.

"Like a prisoner," answered Josie. "Were you in on it too?"

Abby glanced at Madeline, who opened her bag. "I'm pretty sure I have no idea what you're talking about," said Abby. "We're here to examine you."

"Of course you are," Josie responded.

There was no point in resisting. Josie knew that guards were nearby, so she removed her clothes for the two women. She allowed them to touch her, prod her, and lift her flesh. She spread her legs for Madeline while Abby inspected her surgical scars.

With a slight German accent, Madeline told Abby, "We'll need to run tests in the lab...urine, stool, hemoglobin, ultrasound. I must also measure the height of the fundus."

Abby nodded in agreement. To Josie, she asked, "How did you get these scars?"

"I had a cyst, but they removed it," Josie answered.

Abby and Madeline looked concerned. "What kind of cyst?" Abby asked.

"Corpus luteum," guessed Madeline.

"Yeah," Josie answered. "The doctor thought I got it from using fertility drugs, but I never took any...that I know of."

"Where was the surgery performed?" asked Madeline.

"Why don't you ask Dr. Herzog's hit men," quipped Josie. "They found me there after they killed my grandfather."

There was a silent pause. Then Abby said, "I'm sorry, Josie."

"Why?" asked Josie. "Did you have something to do with it?"

"What?" Abby snapped. "No. How could you think that?"

Josie didn't reply. She just stared at Abby for what seemed like an eternity. Abby finally turned and followed Madeline to the door.

"I suppose you're gonna let Derek bleed to death!" Josie shouted at her.

"I already took care of him," Abby replied.

***

The next day, guards brought Josie into a laboratory. The room was white, sterile, and filled with machines, monitors, medical tools, and a host of beakers holding chemicals. A single bed with stirrups occupied a place of distinction, and Josie was brought to it. As she hiked up her gown, climbed onto the bed, and put her legs in the stirrups, she sent her mind on a distant vacation. Voices and medical personnel swirled around her, but she blocked most of them out. Only occasional comments made it over the wall she deliberately constructed.

"My best guess is seventeen weeks," Madeline said.

Other voices with different accents mentioned words like "chorionic villus," "amniocentesis," "maternal serum," and "magnetic resonance."

Josie's mental escape abruptly ended when a metal speculum was inserted into her vagina. Her eyes shot open as pressure was put on her vaginal walls. It was a painful and uncomfortable experience, made more so by the presence of Dr. Herzog. When he peered between her legs, she felt complete humiliation. That feeling combined with sentiments of defeat, subjugation, and downright dirtiness.

Dr. Herzog turned to Madeline and asked, "What has the ultrasound revealed?"

"We haven't administered it yet," Madeline replied.

Dr. Herzog nodded, turned, and walked out of the laboratory.

Abby wheeled a monitor and a computer closer to Josie but was careful not to make eye-contact with her. As Madeline put a thin plastic sheath on a transvaginal probe, a technician removed the speculum.

"We are performing an ultrasound," Madeline told Josie. "Try to relax."

That's easy for you to say, Josie thought. She stared at the ceiling as the probe entered her and moved within her vaginal cavity.

"There he is," proclaimed Abby. She turned the monitor to face Josie. "See?"

Josie wanted to look, but her anger at The Agency prevented her. She eventually gave in to her curiosity and turned to see a moving image of her developing baby. Its large head and small body made it look like a cute alien. Its hand covered its eyes as if it was playing hide and seek with the probe. For the first time, she was able to see that an actual human being was growing inside her, and she smiled faintly.

***

Unfortunately for Josie, the reality of her captivity gradually extinguished any pleasure she derived from seeing an image of her child. Guards and cameras monitored her movements, and her cell phone had no reception. Her only connection to the outside world was the computer in the library. As she accessed the Internet, however, she realized that a block had been put on certain sites and emails were not permitted.

She was about to log off when it occurred to her that she knew very little about the man whose clone she was creating—Pippin the Hunchback. The Internet told her that he was born around 769. He was the first child of Charlemagne and Himiltrude. Most sources claimed that his mother was not Charlemagne's legitimate wife, but merely his concubine. Therefore, he was put aside when Charlemagne married and had three legitimate sons named Carloman, Charles the Younger, and Louis the Pious.

By all accounts, Pippin was a well-liked boy, but he had a curvature of the spine which was viewed as a weakness in those days. His deformity coupled with the illegitimacy of his birth ensured that he would not inherit his father's throne. Charlemagne formally disinherited him in 780 by giving his name to his oldest legitimate son, Carloman. That was the turning point for Pippin. He became a defiant, conniving young man. In 792, he joined with discontented nobles to hatch a plot which would kill Charlemagne, his wife, and their three sons. Once the murders were complete, Pippin intended to assume power. The plot, however, was exposed and Charlemagne put the conspirators on trial in the town of Regensburg, where the scheme originated. The nobles were found guilty and executed, but the King showed clemency toward his son and banished him to the monastery at Prüm, where he lived out his life as an obscure monk.

Such was the official history of Pippin the Hunchback, but Josie wasn't satisfied. "There must be some good things written about him," she said.

She soon realized that there were not. The only other fact she learned about Pippin the Hunchback was that the wives of two of his brothers accused him of being involved in their husbands' premature deaths.

"I can't read any more of this," she said.

With a single keystroke, she exited out of the website and returned to one which featured a sketch drawing of what Pippin might have looked like. With a large nose, curved back, long fingers, and dark eyes, he looked positively diabolical.

The door to the library opened, and Abby entered carrying a single picture in her hand. "Dr. Herzog wanted me to give you this," she explained.

Somewhat skeptical, Josie accepted the offering. She looked at it and felt her stomach drop. Energy drained from her limbs. The picture was a printout of her sonogram, and it showed a lovable, innocent creature. Moisture filled Josie's eyes, and she cried into her hands, dampening the picture with her tears.

"It's all right, Josie," Abby said. "Your baby is fine. He'll be a beautiful boy."

"No, he won't!" cried Josie. She pointed at the computer screen which displayed the grotesque depiction of Pippin. "That's my baby!"

***

Abby and Josie remained in the library, talking into the early morning hours. Josie was still furious about being impregnated against her will, and she knew that Abby had a hand in it. Abby didn't deny her involvement but said, "They were going to do it with or without me. I thought I should stay and look out for you as best I could."

Josie thought it was a lame excuse, but she needed a friend at that moment, so she overlooked it. She told Abby how she knew they cloned

Pippin instead of Charlemagne and shared her confusion over the Chartres window, which placed Charlemagne in Jerusalem in 1099, and the Valois tapestry, which depicted him in Paris in 1492.

Far from finding Josie's claims ridiculous, Abby shared some confusion of her own. She admitted that she thought the arm bone from which they drew cells used for cloning was shorter than it should have been for a man of Charlemagne's rumored height. She also thought it lacked the frailties typically found in the bones of older people. What she didn't tell Josie was that she discovered a puzzling article about Charlemagne years earlier. It didn't mean much to her then, but Josie's findings suddenly gave it weight.

As the women concluded their night of sharing, each had the feeling that they had made strides toward rekindling their friendship, but issues of distrust remained. Josie thought Abby was too closely aligned with The Agency, and Abby found Josie to be unpredictable and a bit of a mystery.

***

Josie didn't see Abby for the next several days. The absence added to her insecurities about the Irish doctor, so she decided to focus on the welfare of the four prisoners. It took a special dispensation from Dr. Herzog and the escort of two tough men, but Josie was allowed to visit with the captives. A guard stood on each end of the corridor as she sat outside the Plexiglas wall of their confines.

Each of the prisoners had been tortured and asked questions about the NSM and their knowledge of Josie's pregnancy. Josie felt the urge to both cry and lash out as she listened to their accounts. She despised Dr. Herzog for what he was doing, but all she could offer the prisoners was, "I'm so sorry. This is my fault."

"Yes, it is," agreed Igraine. "Now vat vill you do about it?"

Josie looked back and forth between the cells, unsure how to respond.

With a bitter tone, Henrietta added, "I warned you of this. These people are *mechant*...uh, wicked. Now do you believe me?"

"Yes," Josie admitted.

"Zen do somezing," Igraine prodded.

"What do you want me to do?" Josie asked. "I'm a prisoner, just like you."

"You're not like us," replied Derek. "You're free to roam about this place. And you have something they want very badly. Use it."

174

***

Josie realized that Derek was saying what her grandfather had said in the airport. "You have leverage in your womb," observed Konrad. "Use it," advised Derek. But how, she wondered. She didn't know how to manipulate people. She wasn't her mother.

A gentle knock on the bedroom door interrupted Josie's thoughts and put her on edge. "It's Abby, Josie. Can I come in?"

She was tempted to say no but replied, "Yes."

Abby entered tentatively with a thick manila folder and closed the door.

With a glance at the document, Josie asked, "Is it time for more tests?"

"Yes," Abby replied while shaking her head no. It was a mixed signal reply that raised Josie's curiosity. "Just the routine heart rate and blood pressure." She came within whispering distance of Josie and asked, "Is there a radio in here?"

Perplexed, but with sense enough not to say anything, Josie opened a cabinet to reveal a sound system with satellite technology. She selected a hip hop channel that played songs without interruption. The music blared from speakers set in the ceiling.

Abby waited for the song to reach its most frenzied point and said, "You never know who might be listening." She opened the folder and added, "I talked it over with Leif, and we decided that you should see this."

"What is it?" Josie asked while glancing at the papers.

"It's a political manifesto written in 1306," she answered.

"Why are you showing it to me?"

"Because it mentions Charlemagne," said Abby. "It might have something to do with what you were telling me."

"What does it say?" asked Josie.

"It's written in French," answered Abby. "But...here. I highlighted it."

Josie couldn't understand the featured words, but read them nonetheless. "Charlemagne," she read. *"Don't le règne avait duré cent vingt-cinq ans."*

"Charlemagne," Abby translated. "Whose reign had lasted one hundred twenty-five years."

"How long?" asked Josie.

"A hundred and twenty-five years," Abby repeated. "Which is impossible, even if he assumed the throne as a baby. And, of course, he didn't."

"No. He didn't," replied Josie. "Who wrote this?"

"Pierre Dubois," Abby replied. "He was a lawyer who worked for the King of France in the late twelve, early thirteen hundreds."

"It doesn't make sense," Josie said. "This guy thought Charlemagne ruled for a hundred and twenty-five years. A stained glass window put Charlemagne in Jerusalem two hundred and eighty-five years after his death. An old tapestry showed him in Paris in 1492...almost seven hundred years after he was supposed to have died."

"You're right," agreed Abby. "It's very strange."

"How did you get this?" Josie probed.

"I found it in The Agency's archives," Abby told her.

"In Aachen?" inquired Josie. "How'd you get it out?"

"I checked it out," Abby answered. "With about thirty other folders. Then I copied it and returned the original. It wasn't that hard."

Josie knew from experience that The Agency kept a close watch on its records. If Abby had copied the folder, Dr. Herzog probably knew about it. He either told Abby to bring her the folder, or he didn't consider the discovery to be very important.

"You said Leif read it too?" asked Josie. "What did he think?"

"We both thought it was bizarre," Abby replied. "But we're scientists. We signed on to the cloning project because it was our field's equivalent of going to the moon. We didn't care about history, so we put the folder away and forgot about it."

Josie eyed her with a healthy dose of skepticism, and it showed.

"When you put everything together..." said Abby. "This folder, the stained glass window, the tapestry, Derek joining the NSM..."

"You making me pregnant without my permission," Josie added.

"That too," Abby agreed. "Let's just say things don't seem right around here. Don't get me wrong...I still believe we cloned Charlemagne. But I'd like to help you figure out the rest of it."

"Even if it gets you into trouble?" asked Josie. "What about Leif?"

"He was ready to quit when Derek left."

***

Josie spent several days plotting her next course of action. She still wasn't sure if she could trust Abby, but she was left with few options.

Somehow, she had to get word to the outside. There had to be someone out there who could help her...her mother!

"Are you kidding?" she asked aloud. Did she really think her mother would do it? The woman was underhanded and deceitful. She used everyone, even her kids, to get what she wanted. Josie had to admit, however, that she knew how to work a pregnancy to her advantage. And that was the one thing Josie had that The Agency wanted.

Without explaining too much, Josie asked Abby to get a message to her mother, who in turn, would contact Steve. If they knew what happened to her, they'd come for sure. At least she hoped that was the case.

***

While she waited for Abby to get back to her, she endured whatever tests The Agency put her through, requested little, and complained even less. She hoped that she and her mother could conspire together with Abby as the go-between. There was no telling what kind of deviant trick her mother might devise to thwart The Agency.

She also thought about what she'd do when she was free, and in every scenario she imagined, one key thing was missing—her pregnancy. She didn't like the sound of it, but she felt that an abortion would be the only responsible thing for her to do. The child within her was the clone of a deformed, evil man, and it had no business being brought back into the world.

Josie's head ached with the weight of her thoughts, so she retreated to the facility's Olympic-sized swimming pool for relaxation. She wore a one-piece suit that hugged her extended belly and swollen breasts. After only a short time in the water, she saw Abby and climbed out of the pool to approach her.

Abby wrapped a towel around her and whispered, "They won't help us."

Josie stepped back to look at her. She wasn't prepared to hear that.

"I'm sorry," Abby continued. "Your mother and your ex want nothing to do with you."

Josie's eyes remained fixed on her. She was all too aware of her mother's shortcomings, and Steve had faults to spare, but she thought they still cared for her. After all, that's why they tried to abduct her. Right? Well, not really. She asked herself if they would refuse to help her even after they heard what happened. The sad truth was that she didn't know.

As she considered what Abby said, she saw Hans replace a departing guard. He took a drink of soda and stared back at her. The ceiling lights reflected off the ring he wore on his left hand. It was gold with a light-green emerald. There was something strange about the stone and the setting, as if they didn't belong together.

Josie returned her gaze to Abby. "I'm sure you did your best," she said.

"I did," Abby reassured her.

Josie walked toward the exit, putting on a tough exterior for Abby and the killer who stood in her path. Hans murdered her grandfather, and she trembled with a hatred that increased with every step she took in his direction. When she was less than a foot away from him, she glanced at his left hand that wore the ring and held the soda. "I'm surprised you can hold that can with so much blood on your hands," she said.

CHAPTER FOURTEEN

The emerald ring slowly tapped against the pistol which Hans held in his left hand. He squeezed the trigger, and a bullet ripped through Konrad. An instant later, the hand that wore the ring struck Derek's cheek and split his flesh. He fell into the arms of Kristina, whose eyes were swollen and bruised. Coated with blood and strips of skin, the ring remained on the hand as it swung a baton into Henrietta's jaw. Igraine charged forward only to have the baton thrust into her solar plexus. The ring-wearing hand grabbed her throat, and Igraine's face went from red to purple. Everything became a blur except the light-green emerald that gleamed through the blood that coated it. Suddenly, the pendant that had belonged to Josie's father appeared in close view. It had a hole where an emerald had once been: the stone Michael Ersman had in his pocket the day he died.

Josie's eyes shot open in the dark of night. She turned on a light and sat up in bed, her thoughts fixed on her disturbing vision. Was the emerald in Hans' ring the same stone that had been in her father's possession when he died? If so, she knew the answer to the most important question she could ever ask. It went deeper than that, though. If Hans killed her father, then he had been ordered to do so by Dr. Herzog.

Her bedroom door shuddered with the force of a heavy thud. Josie startled. She heard a man and a woman whispering. The door handle rattled. Josie searched for a weapon but found only a lamp and a clock.

The door flew open, and Leif and Abby scrambled into the room. A large guard lay unconscious behind them. Leif wore a gun on his belt while holding a rag and a bottle of clear liquid. Abby clutched a pistol.

"Get dressed, Josie," Leif instructed. "Hurry."

Josie didn't move, still unsure of what was happening.

179

"You wanted to escape," added Abby. "Now is your chance."

Josie sprang from the bed half naked, adrenaline coursing through her veins.

***

Leif led a cautious trek down the corridor while Josie and Abby followed. Josie wore sneakers with a loose-fitting skirt and a yellow and black striped top. It was an ensemble she didn't care for, but it was all she could grab in a hurry.

"Don't I get a gun?" Josie asked.

Leif handed her the liquid and rag. "You're in charge of the chloroform," he said. "I'd rather anesthetize the guards than kill them."

Josie wondered if a pregnant woman should handle chloroform but said nothing.

"The west entrance is probably our best route," Abby announced.

"We can't go that way," Josie said.

"Why not?" asked Abby.

"Because the prisoners are on the other side of the compound," Josie answered.

"We're not freeing the prisoners," Leif said. "Only you."

"Then I'm not going," Josie replied.

"What?" Leif asked in astonishment.

"They'll kill them if I escape," she told him. "Dr. Herzog warned me."

Leif stopped in the middle of the corridor, causing the other two to do the same. He knew Josie was right, and so did Abby. Finally, he said, "Oh hell!"

***

Two guards manned the detention center control room at night. The first lay unconscious on the floor as Leif stood over him with a bottle and a rag in his hand. The second convulsed in a corner while blood oozed from a gunshot wound in his chest.

"I shot him," Abby said as she held the pistol. "I can't believe I shot him."

"It was him or us," Leif told her while rushing to the control panel.

"But I'm a doctor," Abby replied. "I don't kill people. I save them."

"That's why I should have the gun," said Josie.

Abby looked at the pistol and handed it to Josie.

"Finally," Josie declared.

After several failed attempts, Leif unlocked the prison cells. A monitor showed prison doors opening and the inmates awakening.

Leif, Josie, and Abby charged into the cell ward and reunited with the prisoners.

"Leif," said an astonished Derek. "I didn't know you cared."

"Yeah, well...not as much as she does," he said with a gesture to Josie.

Derek and Josie held each other's gaze until Henrietta charged out of her cell and grabbed her granddaughter by the shoulders.

"You're a good girl," Henrietta declared. *"Très bon travail* (Very good job)! I knew you would come back for us." To Igraine, she added, "I told you she was a good girl!"

"Yes. Vonderful," Igraine replied. "Now vat is your plan to get us out of here?"

"The first thing she needs to do is give me this," Derek said while taking the pistol from Josie's hand.

"Hey," Josie began, but realized it was futile to protest.

"I think there's a hallway that runs perpendicular to this one," Derek told Leif.

"There is," Leif replied. "With a stairwell at the end of it."

Without further discussion, Derek led Leif and the women into the narrow hallway that bordered the prison wing.

"Thanks for coming to get us," Kristina said to Josie.

Josie nodded.

The escapees encountered no resistance in that passageway or two others. Each destination was well-lit but devoid of guards.

"Quickly," Derek instructed, while keeping his followers close to the wall.

As they walked in silence, Josie glanced at Abby and wondered why she was risking her life like this. She'd been sure the woman was hiding something and doubted that she had even contacted her mother. She finally decided to press the issue. "What did my mother say when you told her where I was?" she inquired.

"What?" Abby asked in surprise.

Josie repeated the question.

"I spoke to your ex-boyfriend."

Josie wondered how she reached him when the number she gave was supposed to ring her mother. Rather than make that inquiry, however, she asked, "What did he say?"

"He said they were too busy to come," Abby answered. "Why are you asking me this now?"

Steve might have said a lot of things, Josie thought, but that wasn't likely to be one of them.

"Bloody hell," Derek exclaimed as he spotted a camera in an upper corner of the corridor. He asked Leif, "Do you have a silencer?"

Leif nodded, took careful aim and shattered the camera with a muffled shot.

"No talking unless you absolutely have to," Derek told the women.

The escapees continued their trek down the hallway. They were on the third level beneath the earth's surface. Somehow, they needed to ascend three floors without being noticed. With their hearts racing and their eyes in search of danger, they passed an idle elevator on their way to a stairwell at the end of the corridor.

Derek halted the group in front of the stairs. A heavy steel door with a window built into it stood before him. He peered through the glass, took a deep breath, and jerked the handle. It was locked. He tried again. It didn't budge.

"I'll get it," Leif declared while aiming his pistol and silencer.

"Why don't we take the elevator?" Kristina asked.

"It's too confining," Derek replied. "They could trap us."

"I haven't seen anybody in any of the halls," Kristina protested. "Maybe they..."

"The door!" Josie exclaimed.

Derek saw the door handle turn slowly. Before he could warn others, the door opened swiftly inward and a hail of bullets flew from the stairwell.

Kristina screamed and Abby hollered.

Three guards wearing helmets, vests, and battle gear climbed the steps while shooting automatic weapons into the doorway.

Leif charged at the women with open arms. "Go back," he commanded. "Go!"

The women turned. Igraine, who had been in the rear, was now in the front. She prevented the group from moving forward as she saw five more guards stalking down the corridor toward them. They wore gas masks and held weapons. "Back!" she shouted.

Derek, Kristina, and Josie fretted over the men in the stairwell while Abby, Henrietta, Leif, and Igraine watched more guards approach them from the other end of the hall. They were trapped between two forces.

Looking behind her, Josie saw Hans emerge from the midst of the five stalking men. He was the only one without a gas mask.

"Give me a gun," she yelled. "Leif! Derek!"

An Uzi-toting gunman stepped out of the stairwell, his face visible behind the mask of his helmet. It was Petra. "Give up," he commanded. "Or we'll kill all of you!"

Josie was horrified as she looked back and forth between the two groups of armed men. Somehow, she mustered the wits and bravery to yell back, "Dr. Herzog will be pissed if you do! I've got his clone! Or don't you remember?"

Realizing the truth in Josie's statement, Petra ordered his men to hold their fire.

"Get them to the elevator," Derek told Leif. "Quickly!"

"But we'll be trapped," Kristina observed.

"Now," Derek ordered and fired several rounds at Petra.

Petra stumbled into the safety of the stairwell, and the gunfight resumed.

"Run!" Leif ordered the women. "To the elevator!"

Igraine led the race toward the elevator, and everyone followed except Derek.

An indiscernible shout from Hans compelled his guards to fire smoking canisters at the group. One of the cans hit Igraine in the face and knocked her into Henrietta. The canisters spewed gray smoke, which quickly filled the hallway. The escapees coughed, were blinded, and quickly became confused.

One of the guards handed Hans a gas mask, which he fit over his face.

"*Je suis aveugle* (I'm blind)!" shouted Henrietta.

Leif fired repeated shots at the approaching guards, but the smoke engulfed him and he could no longer see. "Go...to...the elevator!" he ordered between coughs.

"Where is it?" Abby screamed.

"Josie!" yelled Henrietta. "Josie! *Où es-tu* (Where are you)?"

Derek saw smoke envelop the escapees and roll toward him as he crouched outside the door frame. Bullets flew from the stairwell, and he knew that it was only a matter of time before they would be caught or killed. They had a better chance in the stairwell than in a smoke-filled corridor, so he yelled, "Josie, Leif, Kristina...this way!"

Derek lay flat on his stomach and rolled into the doorway. His gun cracked with each shot he fired into the stairwell, and several bullets hit their mark.

"Derek, where are you?" Kristina rasped.

"Here!" he replied.

He fired three more shots. One bullet burst through a guard's bicep, and another cracked a mask. The men fell back, bounced, and skidded down the staircase.

As the others blindly felt their way toward Derek, Josie went in the opposite direction. Between coughs, she called, "Grandma! Grandma!"

Henrietta yelled back, "Josie..." She heard sucking, growling breaths like those of an underwater diver rumble behind her. Two powerful hands grabbed her.

All the men in the stairwell had been disposed of except for Petra. He used his Uzi to release a spray of bullets in Derek's direction.

Kristina screamed as a streaking projectile missed her by half an inch.

Lying on the floor, Derek had Petra dead to center. As the Uzi's shots sailed overhead, he took aim for Petra's groin, below his bulletproof vest. With a smirk, he pulled the trigger. The gun clicked. He squeezed the trigger again, and again. Nothing.

Like a sprinter hearing the shot of a starter's pistol, Derek sprang from the floor and crashed into Petra. The Uzi fired wildly, and Petra's back slammed a stair banister.

Abby and Kristina followed Derek into the stairwell. The smoke was much thinner than it was in the corridor. As Derek wrestled with Petra, Leif helped Igraine, Abby, and Kristina up the stairs.

Petra was too encumbered by his weapon to hurt Derek with his fists. When the others had safely ascended the stairs, Derek threw him down the lower staircase. Petra toppled with the pull of gravity, and Derek raced after his friends.

Josie had no idea what was happening around her because she was blind and choking in the smoke. Two mask-wearing guards suddenly seized her and dragged her deeper into the fog. She tried to resist, but couldn't. She heard the "ding" of the elevator's bell. The guards threw her into the tiny compartment where she collided with Henrietta. A man hidden by a mask and holding a pistol entered behind her. The doors closed.

Smoke drifted to the ceiling of the elevator and the man with the gun removed his mask. Josie rubbed the blurriness out of her eyes to see that the man was Hans.

"Why do you insist on running from us?" he asked. "People are always hurt or killed when you run. And we catch you anyway."

"Maybe I don't want to end up like my grandfather," Josie replied.

"That was unfortunate," agreed Hans.

With a glance at his ring, Josie added, "Or my father."

Hans said nothing as he pressed a button on a panel. The elevator began to move.

Henrietta, however, shot her granddaughter a perplexed look.

Josie's heart raced, but her hatred for Hans overcame any fear she had. "Where'd you get that ring?" she asked.

Confused by her question, Hans glanced at his left hand. "It was a gift," he said.

"Where'd you get the emerald?" Josie specified.

Hans shot her a cold glare that told her he knew what she was referring to. It was as close as he would come to admitting guilt. With an unsteady voice, Josie told her grandmother, "The stone in his ring was in my father's pocket the day he died."

It took a moment for Henrietta to understand what Josie was saying, and her eyes flashed wide. "You killed my Michael!" she screamed. "*Salaud* (You son of a bitch)!"

***

Two floors up, Dr. Herzog walked through a lavishly appointed lobby with a Russian named Demetri Pavlov. The Russian wore a pistol in a shoulder holster and carried an Uzi. He was a veteran warrior who fought above and below the law. The men stopped outside a closed elevator and watched the numbered lights click down as the elevator traveled up. It was a floor counting system unique to subterranean buildings.

A bell sounded as light number one flashed. The doors slid open, and Dr. Herzog and Demetri saw Henrietta charge at Hans, who shot her directly in the face. The flesh and bone between her eyes collapsed inward and the back of her head exploded like a popped pimple.

Josie screamed.

Henrietta's lifeless body struck the wall and collapsed to the floor of the elevator.

Dr. Herzog immediately jerked the pistol from Demetri's holster and shot Hans in the head. The bullet exploded the man's brains onto the mirrored wall beside him. A spider web crack spread over the glass, and Hans dropped in a heap.

Josie wailed and looked with wild eyes at the two lifeless bodies. She turned her attention to Dr. Herzog, who lowered his gun.

***

Josie slept in a medically-induced slumber. She was in a bed in the infirmary of The Agency's underground complex, and tubes fed liquid into her veins.

Outside the room, Dr. Herzog and Helmut, the Lord Mayor of Aachen, observed the patient through a window. A nurse logged Josie's medical notes into a computer while conversing with Madeline, Josie's doctor.

"Poor child," Dr. Herzog observed.

"Yes," agreed the Lord Mayor. "To lose both grandparents in such a manner...before her own eyes."

"At least she is free of nightmares," revealed Madeline.

The Lord Mayor gave Dr. Herzog a quizzical look.

"We gave her a low dosage of Prazosin Hydrochloride," Dr. Herzog explained. "It reduces anxiety and nightmares."

Demetri entered the medical wing and approached Dr. Herzog. "We cannot locate Petra," he announced with a Russian accent. "Perhaps he follows the runaways."

Dr. Herzog nodded. To the Lord Mayor, he said, "Excuse me, Helmut."

He took a last glance at Josie and strode toward the exit.

***

Josie came out of her sleep feeling refreshed. Unfortunately, it took only moments for her to remember the ghastly murder of her grandmother. A weight of sadness and a profound sense of guilt fell upon her. Her father's mother died because of her. The same could also be said of her grandfather and Pamela, the NSM woman.

Her thoughts were interrupted by a knock on her door. Dr. Herzog entered with a hot fudge sundae which had small *printe* wafers extending from it. "I thought you might like this," he said with a smile.

"I didn't invite you in here," Josie said coldly.

"It will melt if you don't eat it right away," Dr. Herzog persisted. "I made it myself with pistachio. I read someplace that you liked that flavor."

"Do you plan on keeping me here for the whole pregnancy?" she asked bluntly.

He set the ice cream on a tray, clearly irritated by her refusal to eat it. "As I said before, that depends on you," he replied.

"No," she corrected. "You said what happens to the prisoners depends on me. Are you admitting that I'm a prisoner too?"

Dr. Herzog pulled a chair closer to the bed and sat on it. "The prisoners have escaped," he told her.

"Good."

"Yes," he agreed. "It probably is. I never wanted to be in that business anyway. I was just trying to protect you."

She laughed in mock amusement.

With a glance at the melting dessert, Dr. Herzog said, "You're not going to eat your ice cream, are you?"

"Not if it was made by you," she answered.

The doctor sampled the treat and lingered for several more minutes. He finally stood to leave. "You should know that I had nothing to do with the deaths of your grandparents," he said.

"And you should know that I don't believe you."

***

Josie spent the next four days contemplating her predicament and wondering if Derek and the others made it to safety. Guards were never far from her, and Madeline paid her a professional visit every other day. The Lord Mayor tried to see her, but she rebuffed him with insults.

After granting her ample time and space away from him, Dr. Herzog joined Josie in the library. He found her perusing Internet gossip sites. "Who is the latest starlet to be arrested?" he asked. "Or is the flavor of the week a politician in a sex scandal?"

Josie rolled her eyes and turned away from him.

"I've known my share of morally bankrupt politicians, I can assure you."

She tried to ignore him, but it was obvious that he wasn't going to leave.

With a chuckle to himself, he added, "And they were not always male. Powerful women have some of the most debauched affairs."

"What makes you think I want to talk to you?" she snapped. "Leave me alone."

Dr. Herzog didn't reply, opting to let silence linger between the two of them.

"Where do you get off?" she added. "I really want to know. It wasn't enough for you to ruin my life. You had to murder my family too? What did we do to you?"

"I was told that Hans shot your grandfather while defending you," he replied.

"Who told you that?"

"All the intelligence we had said that Konrad abducted you, gave you a new identity, and took you to America," Dr. Herzog explained. "Is that not what happened?"

"No," she said. "Not really."

"Not really?" Dr. Herzog repeated. "Well, that was all we knew. Your grandfather had terrible money problems. We could only guess that he took you to America to somehow ransom you. When that failed, he brought you back to Germany, where my men found you. You have to see it from our perspective."

"I don't have to do anything," she replied defiantly.

"I'm just trying to explain that we had no idea what Konrad's intentions were when he ran off with you," he told her. "I thought Hans shot him to protect you. But when I saw him kill your grandmother with my own eyes, I did something about it."

Josie had to agree that he certainly "did something about it." It was not in his interest to kill a loyal employee like Hans, so was he telling her the truth? "He murdered my father too," she said. "Did you know that?"

The old man's face registered shock. "Are you sure?"

"Yeah," she answered. "Or he had something to do with it. The emerald in his ring was my father's. He had it on him the day he died."

"I told you before that I suspected foul play in your father's death," he said.

"Suspected or ordered?" she asked.

Dr. Herzog was taken aback by her allegation. "Hans was not working for us at the time," he explained. "Neither was Petra."

"Who were they working for?" she asked skeptically.

"I would have to check the records," he answered. "But I think they were independent contractors. They were usually employed by Dante Caroli."

"Dante Caroli?" Josie repeated in surprise.

Dr. Herzog continued, "He's a mobster who works out of Sicily and..."

"Las Vegas."

"That's right," he replied. "How did you know that?"

"I remember seeing something about him on TV," she lied. The truth was that Dante Caroli was the mobster who employed Steve a long time ago—at least that's what Steve claimed.

"I'm not proud of our association with such thugs," he confessed. "But our enemies are dangerous. It becomes necessary to hire people who are equally dangerous."

Josie listened to him, but her mind was on Dante Caroli.

"If you can prove what you're saying, we can re-open your father's case," he said.

"Okay," she replied. "That's step one. Now how are you gonna make good for getting me pregnant...with the clone of Pippin the Hunchback?"

***

An hour later, Dr. Herzog presented Josie with an ancient-looking manuscript. It was comprised of pages in a Latin text with English translations written beside them.

"I should have given this to you months ago," he admitted and left her without further explanation.

Josie found the Latin to be unreadable. The English wasn't much better, but she gave it her full attention and was eventually able to envision what she read....

The sun glistened off the water of the Aller River, near its confluence with the Wesser. The Saxon village of Verden sat along the water's edge. It was populated by a people King Charles had been trying to Christianize for over a decade. On a beautiful fall day in 782, the King finally lost his patience with the obstinate pagans.

Thrusting scroll upon scroll into the arms of his lieutenants, King Charles commanded, "Bind every man listed here—hand and foot— along the river's shore."

Livestock was scattered, huts were destroyed, Saxons were tortured, fires were lit, and the village was upended in an effort to find the men on the King's lists. Priests implored the pagans to amend their ways. Though many vowed to do so, every Christian there believed, as the King did, that the Saxons spoke words without meaning.

"I have done all I can think to do to end their heathenism," the King complained to his bishops, advisors, and lieutenants. "I destroyed their idols. I burned their sacred tree. For ten years, I have returned with my armies as frequently as a spring thaw."

"You adore the lilies of peace," observed Count Theoderic. "But you do not fear the roses of war. Thus you radiate white and crimson."

The King set a hand upon the Count's broad shoulder, "And for what these Saxons have done to our armies, Kinsman, I shall be more crimson than white."

Theoderic smiled, as did others. None dared to contradict the King, except his first-born son.

Prince Pippin entered the King's tent after having witnessed the arrest of forty-five hundred Saxon nobles and commoners. "What do you mean to do to them?" the Prince asked his father.

He already knew the answer, for the King's wrath was famous, and the manner in which the prisoners were restrained bespoke only one foreseeable outcome.

"I mean to bring a final end to their resistance," King Charles answered.

"These are not the rebels you seek," protested the Prince.

The King breathed an exhaustive sigh. This was not the first time his eldest son had challenged his decision. He dismissed all from his tent but the Prince.

Though the King's advisors left his presence, they did not venture beyond listening distance. Countless others joined them to hear the Monarch correct his son.

"Do not think to dispute me, boy," King Charles commanded.

"My most humble apologies, Father," replied Pippin. "But I fear you are about to issue a command for which you will be forever tormented."

"These godless Saxons slaughtered our armies to a man," the King declared. "Chamberlain Adalgis and Marshal Geilo among them!"

"I am not without regret for their deaths," Prince Pippin told his father. "But they were not following your orders when they attacked the mountain dwelling Saxons. They acted on their own. To win glory for themselves."

"That is not enough to absolve these Saxons of their spilled blood," said the King.

"These are not the same Saxons," insisted the Prince. *"Widukind and his nobles led this massacre, and they have fled to the land of the Danes."*

"I will deal with Widukind when The Lord permits," informed King Charles. *"Until then, I must bring these people into submission."*

"But they are innocent!"

"My son," said the frustrated King. *"I fear your deformity has made you acutely sensitive to the suffering of others. That is an admirable quality for a monk or a woman, but not for a king. Now leave me. I have rebels to punish."*

For the remainder of the day, King Charles made good on his promise to bring crimson to the Saxons. Forty-five hundred men were beheaded in his presence. There was so much blood that the river was said to have run red for days.

The King compelled Prince Pippin to watch the slaughter in the hopes of diminishing the boy's sensitivities. The effort failed in the manner he intended, but it strengthened the young prince's resolve to end his father's tyrannical rule.

Ten years later, Prince Pippin led a revolt against the King. It failed, as did others, but the butchery at Verden was viewed as an act of such cruelty that King Charles feared retribution from his people and his god for the remainder of his days.

GUY COTE

CHAPTER FIFTEEN

For the first time in her captivity, Josie sought out Dr. Herzog. The significance of that fact was not lost on him as he made time in his busy schedule to meet with her. They sat in his office within the subterranean compound. It was a room adorned with expensive furniture, original art works, a Persian rug, and an imposingly large desk.

"I came here to talk about Pippin," Josie said.

"I gathered as much," replied Dr. Herzog. "But before we talk about my ancestor, I'd like to clarify something."

Josie was taken aback by his admission that he was related to Pippin.

"I alone authorized your impregnation," he continued.

"Am I supposed to forgive you because you're man enough to admit it?"

"No," he replied. "It was wrong and you have every right to despise me for it."

"Thanks for giving me permission."

"I only hope that you can understand why I did it," he said. "Your endometriosis was such that you would have needed a hysterectomy within a year. Pregnancy, as you know, was the only real alternative. At that time and moment, we were ready to attempt a clone. Waiting would have only compromised the procedure. And I was convinced that you would accept our offer."

"Why me?" Josie asked. "There must have been hundreds...thousands of women you could have chosen for this."

Dr. Herzog devoted serious thought to her question. Finally, he answered, "Yes. We considered many women, but none of them had the...let me just say that The Charlemagne Award Agency is loyal to its people. The service rendered to us by your father and your grandfather factored heavily into my...our decision making."

"Did my grandfather talk you into it?"

"Not entirely. No," he replied. "Your family was merely part of the equation. As I said before, I also knew that this might be your only chance to have a child, and...hmm, I must make a confession to you...oh, how do I say this? You remind me so completely of my Marguerite. By selecting you, I suppose I thought that, in some small measure...uh...I might be selecting her. It was my way of giving her a bit of the greatness that I could never provide when she was alive."

Josie stared at him for a moment that felt like an eternity. He looked back but then averted his gaze. She didn't know if she should be insulted that he thought of her as someone else or honored that he considered her the reincarnation of the most important person in his life. Ultimately, she decided that his longings for Marguerite were romantic. He must have loved the woman more deeply than Josie could even imagine.

Dr. Herzog didn't know where to go next with their conversation, so he removed a contract and bank book from a desk drawer and gave them to Josie.

"What's this?" she asked, as she took the items.

"You wanted to know how I would...what did you say? 'Make good'?"

She perused the contract, which was filled with legalese she didn't understand. Then she saw a large number with the word euros beside it.

"We put one hundred and fifty thousand euro into an account in your name," he told her. "We'll add another six hundred and fifty thousand to that when you enter the third trimester, and two point two million when the child is born. That's a total of..."

"Three million euro," Josie said.

"Yes," he replied. "And it doesn't stop there. We would like you to help raise and nurture the child, and for that we will provide you with luxurious housing, all expenses paid, and an annual stipend of two million euro. When he reaches the age of ten, The Agency will pay you a bonus of two point five million euro, and five million euro when he turns eighteen."

They were being generous, but Josie was skeptical. Why would The Agency offer her millions to do what they were already forcing her to do for free? She thought deeply about the arrangement and set the book and contract on her lap. "What's so special about Pippin?" she asked.

"What do you mean?" inquired the doctor.

"Cloning Charlemagne made sense," she explained. "He was the best king. You're bringing back his kingdom, so why not bring him back too?"

"We are not bringing anyone back," he corrected. "A clone has no memory of a former life. It won't be exactly like the person it was cloned from because it will have none of that person's upbringing to shape it. It will only have the same DNA."

"I get that," Josie said. "But why Pippin? Of all the people to clone..."

"You've seen that the historical Charlemagne was actually a ruthless tyrant who imposed his will by bathing his empire in blood," Dr. Herzog explained.

"Yes," Josie agreed.

"Pippin was a wise and compassionate soul," added the doctor. "Did you know he was but fifteen when he tried to prevent the massacre at Verden?"

"There have been many wise and compassionate people," Josie countered.

"Charlemagne is celebrated the world over because he was a brilliant king," Dr. Herzog answered. "He promoted learning at a time when most were illiterate. He created a governmental system that linked vastly diverse cultures and became the standard by which governments were measured for more than a thousand years. His innovations in communication, transportation, architecture, and law reform were hundreds of years ahead of their time."

"Charlemagne," Josie specified. "Not Pippin."

"That's correct," he agreed. "But Charlemagne had a lust for blood that his first born son did not have. Pippin had the innate wisdom of his father, but none of his failings. Given the chance, he would have been a far greater king."

"So you want to give him the chance," Josie observed.

"Our European Union will need an incorruptible steward," he explained. "Not a king or a dictator, but a natural born leader who will work within our democratic system to meet the needs of our diverse population." He paused. Then he looked directly at Josie. "I'm an old man. I have no children. But I have an ancestor who could have been the greatest of leaders. I want to help him reach his potential as a father would for a son."

Josie realized that his plan really had little to do with her and much to do with him creating the family he wished he had made with Marguerite. But as crazy as it sounded, it appealed to her idealized concept of a family. If he was going to use her to create his perfect clan, then she could do the same to him and his Agency. For the first time, she began to feel a sense of pride in their strange enterprise.

***

Petra hobbled over snow-coated leaves and dirt with a limp he acquired when Derek threw him down the stairs. There were few structures nearby, but The Agency's subterranean compound stretched like a behemoth beneath him. He stumbled toward a shed made of concrete blocks and picked the lock. He entered to find tools and planks. A table stood along the back wall with two wooden boxes resting upon it and two below it.

Petra closed the door behind him and directed his flashlight beam toward one of the crates. To his surprise, the lid was not nailed down. He lifted the cover and pointed the light inside. He sucked in a quick breath as he saw what stared back at him. The light which trembled in his hand danced over the green and swollen features of Hans. The skull was collapsed, but the body was well-preserved for being nearly a week without life and not embalmed. A frozen February in Germany was to thank for that.

Petra was not a man given to tears, but a liquid gloss filled his eyes as he looked on the lifeless face of the man he had known for more than two decades, the man with whom he had shared his adventures and his bed. He searched his lover's hand for the ring he always wore. It had been a gift from Petra on their fifth anniversary. He removed it from Hans' frozen finger and slipped it onto his own. He would never take it off again.

Petra sat with Hans' remains until tears froze on his cheeks and his body shivered. In that time, he formed a plan. It was born out of pain, rage, and fantasy, but recent events had made it oddly realistic. The first step in his scheme was to steal Hans' body.

***

Derek, Kristina, Abby, and Leif had been fleeing for the better part of a week. They did their best to keep a low profile, but it was difficult. Josie's lie about Derek being the father of her child had caused the NSM to turn its back on them.

Igraine broke from the group shortly after their escape. She didn't tell them why she was leaving, only that she would meet with them six days later in the remains of a bombed-out castle on the banks of the Rhine, nine miles outside of Cologne.

"Are you insane or stupid?" Igraine demanded as she saw the fugitives huddling outside the remains. Her nose was still swollen from its break. "Get in zee castle."

"We thought it would fall in on us," explained Abby. "Look how feeble it is."

Igraine shook her head. "Get in," she ordered. "Before you are seen."

The group entered what was left of the medieval castle. They passed through a rubble-strewn hallway to reach a room that had three and a half stone walls, part of a ceiling and a hearth. Glass littered the floor in addition to spent machine gun rounds.

"Why are we meeting here?" Derek demanded. "Do you have any weapons or supplies? We're starving."

Igraine extracted a cell phone from her pocket and typed out a single text.

Ten minutes later, Derek's questions were answered when eighteen men entered the bombed-out room. They were heavily armed and carried bags of food, clothing, medical supplies, and money. The men were ethnically diverse and rough-looking, with long hair, piercings, beards, and tattoos covering much of their bodies.

Their leader, and someone to whom they all deferred, was Dr. Karl Vanderhoff. He wore jeans, hiking boots, and layers beneath a thin, but warm jacket.

"It's been a while, Derek," Dr. Vanderhoff said while offering his hand.

"Uh, yes sir. It has," Derek replied with the shake of his hand.

Dr. Vanderhoff added, "I see you were unable to prevent the pregnancy."

Derek nodded and looked away in shame.

"I'm sorry," Abby interjected. "But who are you?"

"Excuse me...'scuse...move your ass," a male voice said from behind the crowd. The men grudgingly parted to allow Steve Cousins to push his way up to Dr. Vanderhoff. He reported, "The trucks and the drivers are ready, Mr. Caroli."

***

Josie's reconciliation with Dr. Herzog granted her greater freedom. She was no longer closely followed by guards, and she had access to more Internet sites. She grew content in her underground dwelling, and her disposition improved considerably. She even spent pleasant hours in the company of Dr. Herzog and the Lord Mayor of Aachen. She had been wrong about The Agency, she realized. But what did that say about Derek and the NSM? She tried to think objectively about whom she could trust and whom she couldn't, but the pampering she received in her new home made that difficult.

One thing was for certain, however. She had a new enthusiasm for her pregnancy. She would be the mother of a child, not just any child, but a special person who would grow to become a world leader. She returned to the Internet in search of more tales recounting the greatness of Pippin the Hunchback.

To her dismay, hour after hour passed and she learned nothing new about Pippin. All the sites she encountered told of his treachery at Regensburg and his exile at Prüm. They placed his birth sometime between 767 and 770 and said that he died in either 811 or 812. He was a minor historical player, barely mentioned in reports of his day. Frustrated, Josie looked up the massacre at Verden. She read thirty-nine accounts of that horrible scene and not one of them mentioned an exchange between Charlemagne and Pippin. In fact, she couldn't find a single reference which even placed Pippin at Verden.

Worried that Dr. Herzog might have tricked her again, she searched for Pippin's whereabouts in the fall of 782, when he would have been at Verden. After four more hours of research, she found a reference to the thirteen-year-old Pippin the Hunchback in an 1832 newspaper. The article was a review of Victor Hugo's *The Hunchback of Notre Dame*, and it said that Prince Pippin was the inspiration for the novel. According to the review, Pippin was imprisoned in the bell tower of the church of Thionville in 782. While Charlemagne was in Verden in the fall of that year, his family awaited him in the town of Thionville (in present day France). Young Pippin was upset that his father had disinherited him two years before and relegated him to a religious vocation, which was to begin the next year. So he mocked the assignment by declaring himself the "Pope of Fools" and made his younger siblings behave as if they were his flock. This sacrilege so angered his stepmother, the Queen, that she had him locked in the bell tower of the local church until his father returned to forgive his transgressions.

Josie's heart sank as she realized that Dr. Herzog had lied to her yet again. She had no reason to be excited about her pregnancy. She was carrying the clone of an evil, deformed bastard. She returned to her room and crawled into bed with the hope that sleep would somehow curb the depression she knew would be forthcoming.

***

Josie awoke in a mood so sour she couldn't even tolerate her own company. Everything she saw irritated her, especially her body. Her ankles, feet, hands, and face were swollen. Varicose veins ran like a road map across her outer thighs. Her breasts were heavy with dark areolas and they displayed more blue veins than her legs. Her belly extended so far, she found it difficult to see her own feet. The idea that she was ruining herself to bring a monster into the world made her even more resentful.

She showered, changed into clean clothes, and devoured a hearty breakfast, ignoring everyone in her vicinity. In the process, she focused on what she knew she had to do—get away from The Agency once and for all. She couldn't wait for Derek to rescue her, and she couldn't jeopardize more lives. She had to escape on her own.

Unfortunately, knowing what to do wasn't the same as knowing how to do it. She spent three days considering possible plans, and then she realized that she did need help. She required the assistance of her dead grandparents.

Dr. Herzog was out of the country when Josie cornered the Lord Mayor on the conference level of the compound. She played on his sympathy and explained that she never had a chance to pay respects at her grandparents' graves. Their deaths tormented her night and day, and she needed closure. With the Lord Mayor as a reluctant ally, she pitched the idea to Dr. Herzog via video conference. His response was vague, and he was careful not to alienate Josie with a patently negative answer. He put up every roadblock to an affirmative reply, however. What he failed to reveal was that Josie's grandparents didn't have graves. They had been cremated and their ashes were discarded.

Josie suspected as much and called his bluff. "On my father's tombstone, it said he was a patriot," she told him. "A patriot to The Agency, I guess."

"Yes," Dr. Herzog replied. "I had that word added to his marker myself."

"I thought so," she lied. "My grandfather was with you guys even longer than my father—from the beginning. I'd love to see what you wrote on his grave."

Josie made it clear that a simple picture of Konrad's stone wouldn't suffice, and Dr. Herzog realized that a contented Josie would make for a much safer pregnancy.

***

As Dr. Herzog ordered employees to fashion tombstones for her grandparents, Josie implemented the next phase of her escape plan. She ate a large meal on the day she was to visit their graves and filled her pockets with food. She wore her Rolex and put her phone, charger, and Konrad's wallet with her fake identification papers in a purse that, to her annoyance, didn't match her outfit. In her front pocket, she placed her real I.D. cards and the bank book Dr. Herzog gave her.

Dr. Herzog was not about to send Josie into a hostile world with only the Lord Mayor as her companion. He put three guards and Demetri Pavlov on her security detail. Their assignment was simple—take her to and from the cemetery, limit her interactions with others, and keep her safe.

Josie hadn't expected such an escort. Her mind worked feverishly to modify her escape plan as the men guided her into the back of Dr. Herzog's Bentley and drove toward their destination. Then she saw a branch of Aachen's most popular bank, the same institution that held her hundred and fifty thousand euros.

"Wait," she exclaimed. "You have to take me to the bank first."

"I don't sink so," Demetri responded. "I take you to grave and back."

Josie exhaled in exasperation. She turned to the Lord Mayor, who sat beside her, and said, "I can't go to the cemetery without bringing them something." Her eyes grew misty with tears and she added, "When will I have a chance to go back there again? Please. I just want to get some money to buy them flowers."

The Lord Mayor realized that she was right, but he was supposed to limit her activities. "We'll stop at the flower shop," he told her. "And I'll pay for it."

"Then it will be from you," she replied. "Please. Let me buy my own bouquets with my own money."

Demetri protested, but Helmut outranked him. At the Lord Mayor's insistence, Demetri parked the car in the bank's lot. Helmut further instructed the armed men to wait outside for fear that their weapons might scare people inside the bank.

Josie and Helmut walked through the bank's rotary door to find a lobby with a row of customers, security, and bank personnel. Josie took her place in line, and the Lord Mayor stood beside her. How could she draw a decent amount of money from her account with him standing so close to her? This was her only chance because she knew that The Agency would post her on a worldwide database the minute she escaped. She wouldn't be able to enter any other banks, and she couldn't run without money. Her heart beat rapidly as she approached the teller. To make matters worse, the woman behind the counter recognized the Lord Mayor, and the two conversed in German.

Josie took advantage of the Lord Mayor's distraction by filling out a withdrawal slip. The form was written in both German and English. She waited before recording the amount she wanted to take out of her account. With his conversation concluded, the Lord Mayor turned to Josie, who hid the slip. "Can I have some privacy?" she asked.

Helmut smiled and stepped off to the side, allowing Josie to scratch a figure of fifty thousand euro on the withdrawal form. She slid the slip along with her bank book and identification cards to the teller. The woman's eyes opened wide when she saw the amount Josie requested. She looked at the Lord Mayor. Thinking that Josie was in need of support, Helmut nodded and smiled at the woman behind the counter.

The teller used a computer to access Josie's account. Though the withdrawal was large, it was only a third of the balance of funds. The Lord Mayor was signatory on the account and he nodded his assent. Everything seemed to be in order.

"*Entschuldigen Sie* (Excuse me)," the bank teller said to Josie.

The woman walked to the back of the bank, and Josie realized that she was in trouble. She looked for an escape, but there was none to be found. Her nerves began to work overtime, but, to her surprise, the teller returned with stacks of money. Josie looked quickly at the Lord Mayor and saw that he was busy talking to a female admirer.

Josie hurriedly stuffed the money in her purse and rejoined the Lord Mayor. As they walked toward the rotary door, she heard, "*Ihre Quittung* (Your receipt)." Looking back, they saw the teller waiving a slip of paper.

"I'll get it," Helmut said. Before Josie could protest, he walked to the counter.

If he reads that paper, it's over, Josie thought. She let out a loud gasp and buckled over. Helmut rushed to her side.

"I...I gotta get to a bathroom," Josie announced. "Quickly. Where is it?"

The Lord Mayor, a security guard, and a loan officer, escorted Josie to the woman's restroom in the rear of the bank.

Helmut paced nervously outside the water closet.

"I think there's a problem," Josie announced from inside a stall.

"I'm coming in," Helmut replied and reached for the door handle.

"No," she commanded. "Get me a doctor!"

Helmut looked back and forth between the bathroom door and the front entrance.

"Hurry," she pleaded.

The Lord Mayor finally raced through the bank lobby, out the revolving door, and into the parking lot. As he told Demitri what was happening, people inside the building heard a window shatter in the women's restroom.

Once again, Josie was on the run.

CHAPTER SIXTEEN

The NSM may have doubted Derek's motives but not Dr. Vanderhoff's. He was a founding member of the organization. In fact, he was the only founder still alive. Within the NSM, Dr. Karl Vanderhoff was beyond reproach. Dante Caroli enjoyed an equally unimpeachable standing in his organization. He was the CEO of a syndicate that law enforcement in more than thirty countries considered criminal. His people were gun runners, vigilantes, assassins, and even revolutionaries.

The dual nature of the man known as both Vanderhoff and Caroli was displayed nowhere better than in the safe house he commandeered in the German countryside. More than forty people who would never have associated with one another in any other setting stood side by side in their admiration of Vanderhoff/Caroli.

Derek and Leif joined Somalis to view a map of The Agency's underground complex. "We're not really storming the compound. Are we?" Leif whispered.

Derek shrugged and watched Steve Cousins strut around the multi-ethnic group with an overblown sense of his own importance. Recalling what he knew of Steve's relationship with Josie, he felt a powerful urge to punch the man in the face.

***

Josie wanted to bask in the open air of the world around her, but she knew that The Agency would be looking for her. She traveled by taxi, paid with cash, and avoided public places that were likely to have cameras. She rented a cheap room in an obscure lodging. It was cold and had scratchy, shag carpeting. There was a television with six channels, but the only technology she cared about was her phone and its ability to connect to the Internet.

She fastened each of the door's three locks, lay on the bed and stared at the ceiling. She made it. She was free. She was frightened. Again, she thought of Derek. Was there any way that she could find him? Probably not, she realized, and she needed to implement the rest of her plan on her own anyway.

She returned to the Internet and found that everything was in German. She had been spoiled in The Agency's complex because their system was programmed to access English sites first. She used her phone to translate the German pages she visited, but the process was tedious. She reminded herself that her freedom and the future of Europe depended on her finding what she was looking for. Eventually, her persistence paid off.

***

Dr. Herzog stormed hastily about the compound's command center. Twenty operators monitored phone and Internet traffic while a dozen technicians checked images from cameras within a five hundred mile radius. Local police and Interpol agents came and went with frequency as the Lord Mayor watched with a look of shame on his face.

"You are useless here, Helmut," observed Dr. Herzog. "Go back to the Rathaus."

"*Tut mir sehr leid* (I'm very sorry)," the Lord Mayor said for the twentieth time.

Helmut left the room as Demetri Pavlov entered. The Russian narrowed a hardened gaze on the Lord Mayor, who avoided looking at him.

A twenty-four-year-old computer operator with a Welsh accent called Dr. Herzog over. "I think I found something," he said. "It is an Internet search from a mobile eighty-six kilometers from here." He made several strokes on his keyboard and added, "Each site is translated into English, and they appear to be looking for...no, they are definitely looking for...abortion doctors."

"*Mein Gott* (My God)!" exclaimed Dr. Herzog. "That's her."

***

Josie was uncertain about her decision to abort the clone. She had a longing for family—at least her definition of it—and a desire to do right what her own mother had done wrong. But the clone growing within her wasn't the answer, and she knew it.

The Internet informed her that most countries in Europe, Germany included, allowed abortion on demand in the first trimester only. She, however, was in her fifth month. There were exceptions to the rules, though. Ireland, for example, permitted abortions into the second trimester if the patient was suicidal. Josie realized that she had options, but the window of opportunity for ending her pregnancy was rapidly closing.

She felt alone as she contemplated her decision. She returned again to the principle historical figures in her drama—Pippin the Hunchback and Charlemagne. Perhaps there was something she'd overlooked in their stories that would help her to make up her mind. Unfortunately, the Internet yielded nothing new about Pippin.

Charlemagne, however, was well-documented—almost too well. She scanned the material about him rather half-heartedly, her mind primarily focused on the decision she needed to make. Suddenly, a peculiar image appeared on her phone. It was entitled *The Coronation of Charlemagne in Rome*, and it was dated 1516. It was a fresco that was on permanent display in the Vatican. At first glance, there didn't appear to be anything out of the ordinary about the painting, but the caption beneath it was most irregular. It read, *"François I (1494-1547) as Charlemagne."*

Josie looked more closely at the image and saw that the person in the painting who was supposed to be Charlemagne clearly was not. He was being crowned by the Pope as Charlemagne had been on Christmas day in the year 800, but he had a larger nose than Charlemagne and a different hairstyle with no facial hair. Curious, Josie searched the Internet for pictures of François I, and sure enough, they matched the features of the man being crowned in the painting entitled *The Coronation of Charlemagne in Rome*.

"What is this?" she asked.

It was enough of a mystery to distract her from the abortion issue, at least momentarily. She read more about François I and learned that he was the King of France from 1515 until his death in 1547. He was said to have ambitions of empire but terrible ineptitude in battle. In fact, he was actually captured during one battle and held for a while as a prisoner by his arch nemesis, The Holy Roman Emperor Charles V.

Reading on, Josie learned that François I married his cousin, Claude of France. She was the daughter of his predecessor King Louis XII and Anne of Brittany. "I don't know what's funnier," Josie said. "That he married his cousin or that she was named Claude."

Then it occurred to Josie that she had encountered Anne of Brittany before...but where? Using a search engine, she typed Anne of Brittany and Charlemagne. The Valois tapestry that she, Derek, and Kristina saw in the Frontenac country estate appeared on her screen. It depicted Charlemagne escorting Anne of Brittany to Notre Dame in 1492.

"This is weird," she observed.

She wondered why someone would make a painting of Charlemagne's coronation but replace Charlemagne's face with that of François I. And why was Charlemagne depicted escorting François's mother-in-law into Paris in 1492, seven hundred years after Charlemagne was supposed to have died? She felt a headache coming on, no doubt assisted by the small screen she read from and the translations she had to keep making. She prayed that it wouldn't be another migraine, but she also couldn't stop reading about this latest peculiarity.

As she looked for more information about François I, she ran into repeated references to a mysterious tutor who had been assigned to the young François I by his cousin and predecessor, King Louis XII (husband of Anne of Brittany). The tutor's name was lost to history, but he was said to be old, wise, rather large, and quite cantankerous. In fact, he was so disagreeable, that court gossip claimed that he abruptly abandoned King François I in 1517, only two years into his reign. But that wasn't the end of it. Enemies of François I asserted that the tutor resurfaced four years later in the court of François' greatest foe, Emperor Charles V.

Josie felt pressure between her temples, and her eyes were tired. Her view alternated between blurry and normal. Something told her that what she was doing was important, so she looked up material on Holy Roman Emperor Charles V. What she learned was that he was the most powerful ruler in Europe since Charlemagne, but he was constantly at war with François I. The hostility between the two men was so bad that they kept Europe in a perpetual state of warfare for the first half of the sixteenth century.

Josie tried to learn more about the mysterious tutor who abandoned François I and showed up in Charles V's court, but didn't have much luck until a woodcut etching appeared on her screen. It depicted two figures standing side by side—Karolus I and Karolus V. Karolus I appeared to be a large, burly woodsman. He had a pudgy physique, a crown of reeds, long and somewhat unmanaged hair, and a dirty tunic. He looked as if he had come straight from the wilderness. Karolus V, on the other hand, seemed to be a cross between a king and a merchant. He wore a crown that resembled a beret, a long, fur-lined overcoat, expensive clothes with puffy sleeves, and a bejeweled necklace that hung over his coat. He held a scepter in his right hand.

Josie knew that Karolus was Latin for Charles, and further reading told her that the wood carving was used as the cover illustration for the 1521 printing of Einhard's biography of Charlemagne.

"What the hell?" she asked. "The woodsman is Charlemagne?"

Closer inspection told her that the woodsman in the carving resembled the Charlemagne she had seen in other paintings. The year in which it was placed was 1521; the same year that a nameless tutor left the court of François I and arrived in the palace of Charles V. It was also the year that François and Charles began fighting.

Could Charlemagne be François's tutor, she wondered. Her head hurt too much to give it more thought, so she closed her eyes. Her body surrendered to a much-needed sleep, but her free-roaming mind played with images and numbers for much of the night. A stained glass window pictured Charlemagne in Jerusalem in 1099. A tapestry depicted him in Paris in 1492. A coronation fresco portrayed François I as Charlemagne in 1516. A wood carving showed Charlemagne and Charles V standing side by side in 1521. It was the stuff of illusion, put to great use by Josie's dreams.

***

The fact that Vanderhoff led two secretive organizations independent of one another for so long spoke volumes about his ability to compartmentalize. He was a master at giving his people only that information which he thought they needed. Therefore, his followers had different ideas about why they were traveling in a six-vehicle caravan in the dark of night to attack The Agency's compound.

Derek, Kristina, Abby, and Leif rode in the back of a van with Steve, three men from Bosnia, and two from Poland. In addition to weapons, Steve and the Bosnians possessed liquor, which Steve drank and the others did not.

"You're too sexy to be involved in this business," Steve slurred to Kristina.

"It's as much my fight as it is anyone else's," she replied.

"Actually, it's not," interrupted Derek. "You should be on your way back home."

"Thanks to you and Josie, I doubt I have a home to go back to," said Kristina.

"You know Josie?" asked Steve. "I'm her boyfriend."

Kristina was stunned by the revelation, as were Abby and Leif.

"You're her boyfriend?" asked Abby. "Steve Cousins?"

"Her ex-boyfriend," Derek corrected.

"We're reconcilin'," Steve slurred.

"I doubt she'd say the same thing," replied Derek.

Abby stared at Steve. She had never spoken to him, despite telling Josie otherwise. She felt guilty about lying, but Josie had revealed conspiracies that were nothing short of earth-shattering. Charlemagne faked his death, his evil son was buried in his place, and they cloned the wrong person...it was so much bigger than simply cloning a dead king. If Abby and Leif could keep Josie to themselves, there was no limit to the opportunities that would come their way.

As he watched Steve consume more alcohol, Derek considered his own reasons for joining Vanderhoff's enterprise. Josie was a vital part of Vanderhoff's plan to defeat The Agency, and Derek was responsible for her. But somewhere along the way, he developed feelings for her. Her welfare was becoming more important to him than destroying The Agency.

A crescent moon glistened in the night sky as the caravan parked in a tree-lined area outside The Agency's subterranean compound. As people climbed out of the vehicles, Igraine rushed about with notes in hand.

Phase one began with the Bosnians waving bottles and pretending to be drunken locals. They crossed the road and staggered into a field that was sprinkled with abandoned sheds.

"Wait!" Steve yelled. To Kristina, he added, "Gotta play drunk with my peeps."

Phase two was made up of fifteen men who would follow phase one after the "drunks" had disabled the cameras and secured entrance to the compound. With the help of the second phase, the third would gain entry into a different part of the complex. Their task was to neutralize all security and enable the final extraction team to rescue Josie.

Vanderhoff looked up from his notes to see Steve stumbling after the Bosnians. "No!" he yelled. "Somebody get that fool. He's supposed to stay with the trucks."

***

Beneath the earth, a military-style operation was in its final stages of planning. Dr. Herzog didn't want to leave anything to chance in his reacquisition of Josie. He was issuing last minute instructions to Interpol agents when Demetri rushed up to him.

"Excuse, sir," Demetri said. "But..."

An operator monitoring the compound's cameras interrupted, "*Wir haben Besucher. Betrunkene, denke ich* (We have visitors. Drunks, I think)."

Demetri frowned. The operator had stolen his thunder.

Looking at the monitor, Dr. Herzog saw that the only person who appeared to be drunk was Josie's former boyfriend, Steve. The other two were acting. "It's a rescue mission," he announced. "They think we have Josie."

***

Josie awoke to the sound of knocking on her door. She scrambled out of bed and searched for an escape, but the bathroom window was too small for her to fit through. She hoped that if she remained quiet, her visitor would go away, but the knocking got louder. A voice said, "I know you're there. Please open up, or I'll break down this door."

Josie began searching for a weapon of some sort.

After two minutes, the voice added, "I was hoping to avoid this."

Josie heard the buzz of a chainsaw and saw its blade slice through the door. Frantic, she reached for a lamp, but it was bolted down. She grabbed the clock, tugging its cord from the outlet. She rushed to the side of the door and waited for the intruder.

Completing its cut through to the bottom of the door, the saw disappeared into the hallway and became silent. A leg suddenly burst through the severed door. Josie swung the clock, but the intruder caught it and jerked it out of her hand. He entered the room, and Josie saw that he was the Lord Mayor of Aachen. She stared at him in disbelief.

"They know where you are," the Lord Mayor said. "You need to get out of here."

"Wha...how?" Josie asked. "How did you find me?"

"You have more friends than you know," he replied. "Now go!"

"Where?"

"Someplace safe," the Lord Mayor answered. "And don't hesitate."

***

As Vanderhoff's besiegers prepared their attack, Derek continued his effort to convince Kristina to go home. She remained adamant in her refusal.

"If I learned anything from seeing you almost die in that cell, it's that I want my life to mean something," Kristina explained. "Those people are wicked! What they did to Josie, it's...it's like the experiments Nazi's performed on the Jews."

"What do you mean?" Derek asked.

"I know about the cloning," she replied. "It's like playing God. It's wrong."

"You're right, but we're a little late," answered Derek. "She's already pregnant."

"That can change," said Kristina.

Derek looked surprised, but Igraine approached them before he could say more.

"Dr. Vanderhoff vishes to speak viz you," informed Igraine.

She led Derek to Vanderhoff, who was on his phone.

"*Danke*, Helmut," said Vanderhoff. He pressed a button to end the call and turned to Derek. "Josie already escaped."

"What?" asked Derek. "What are we doing here? Where is she?"

"That's not your concern right now," Vanderhoff explained.

"It most certainly is," declared Derek.

"Not at the moment," Vanderhoff said. "We can get The Agency's leadership."

"Dr. Herzog?" asked Derek.

With a nod, Vanderhoff said, "Decapitate the beast and its claws are useless. But we have to act swiftly. Thanks to that idiot, they probably know who we are."

"We need to find Josie."

"I've taken care of that," Vanderhoff reassured. "I want you to go in with the main assault. You and your friends know that compound. Capture Herzog and bring him to me. Alive, if you can manage it. Dead, if you must."

Derek left Vanderhoff to assemble his team. As much as he didn't like it, Kristina wanted to be involved, and her mind was made up. "All right," he said to her. "You're in. Where are Leif and Abby?"

***

Dr. Herzog saw Abby and Leif on a monitor. They held guns as they ran across the field. They resembled children at play more than soldiers

210

at war, but in his eyes they were traitors like Derek and Igraine. Turning to one of the operators, he asked, "*Konnen wir sehen, woher sie kamen* (Can we see where they came from)?"

"*Ja* (Yes)," the operator replied. He used his keyboard to direct a camera toward a not-so-distant line of trees. Suddenly, static shot across the monitor, and it dissolved to white with dashes of black. The images from two more cameras also went to static.

Dr. Herzog told Demetri, "Take forty men to get whoever is behind the trees."

***

One of the Bosnians used a hand held Wi-Fi signal jammer to scramble the signal of a wireless camera. Steve tried to assist the Bosnians, but he had no purpose because he had no scrambler. As he passed one of the sheds, he saw Abby and Leif, who were preparing to enter the structure. It was a secret passageway into the underground facility.

"Hey! What are you doing?" yelled Steve. "Get back!"

"Delay him," Abby told Leif. "We need to get to Josie before he does."

"Maybe we should wait for the others," Leif replied.

Abby reached for the door, but it flew open before she could touch it. Men with Uzis charged out of the shack, and the first man fired a burst of bullets into Abby's chest.

"Abby!" Leif screamed. He shot at the men, but his bullet hit Abby in the neck.

Other men fired at Leif, and he dove to the ground.

The Bosnians and Steve found cover behind trees and shot at the men who were streaming out of the shed.

"Tell me that wasn't Abby!" exclaimed Derek.

"I think it was," replied Kristina.

Vanderhoff lowered his night vision binoculars. "Rogue attack," he said. "Does anybody have any discipline around here?"

Derek grabbed Kristina by the wrist. "Let's go," he ordered.

The pair ran across the road but away from where Abby was shot.

Six guards traded gunfire with Steve and the Bosnians across a wide distance, and neither side succeeded in hitting the other.

Behind Steve and the Bosnians, the top of what appeared to be a tree stump lifted like a lid and four more men climbed out. Without a word of warning, they fired their Uzis. The Bosnians were immediately shredded by streaking bullets. A projectile grazed Steve's arm, but he escaped further harm by leaping into a nearby bush.

Vanderhoff and his team didn't know that underground tunnels stretched like tentacles beyond the main body of the compound. To their surprise, Demetri and his men surged out of the earth from four locations behind Vanderhoff's encampment. They fired their weapons indiscriminately and bodies gyrated as bullets struck them.

Mayhem followed as people dove behind vehicles and into the shadows. Punctured gas tanks spilled fuel to the ground. Screams and gunfire filled the night.

With an Uzi in one hand and a pistol in the other, Igraine charged up to Vanderhoff. "Zis is a slaughter," she exclaimed. "Ve need to get you out!"

"Give me that," Vanderhoff said as he seized her Uzi. Weapon in hand, he rushed forward to join the artillery exchange.

A van which had been leaking fuel suddenly exploded, killing four nearby men.

Grabbing Vanderhoff's arm, Igraine said, "Please. Ve must go!"

Derek and Kristina ran toward a shack they knew to be an entrance to the compound. Derek held an automatic pistol. He saw Leif stand nearly forty feet away. "What is he doing?" he asked and slowed their run to an eventual stop.

"We can't stay here," Kristina declared.

"Leif!" Derek yelled. "Get down!"

Leif was oblivious to everything but Abby, who was sprawled in maroon colored snow. Her eyes were open and her face was frozen in shock. "Abby," he cried.

Derek moved toward Leif, but Kristina restrained him. Suddenly, bullets from two guns pummeled Leif, stole his life, and heaved him onto Abby's corpse.

"Oh, God!" said Derek.

"C'mon," Kristina exclaimed as she pulled Derek toward the shack.

Moments later, they burst through the door of the shed and found an interior filled with planks, rusty tools, and a floor lined with straw. They heard the muffled sounds of an alarm. Derek moved boards and hay to reveal the rope handle of a secret entrance. He tugged on it, but it was locked. He fired four shots into the door and pulled the rope. The door opened with a crack and revealed a downward leading staircase. He descended the passageway, followed by Kristina. The alarm grew louder with each step they took.

The staircase led to a corridor with a tile floor. As Derek and Kristina stepped cautiously toward it, a female guard sprang before them and fired her gun. Derek shot back, but she fled down the hallway. He hurried after her, jumping down the last steps.

Derek saw that the passageway formed a *T* with another hall that ran perpendicular to it. The female guard turned a corner at the end of the corridor and disappeared. Three more guards passed from the perpendicular hall. In their midst, Derek saw Dr. Herzog. The two men exchanged stares, but before Derek could shoot, Dr. Herzog was gone.

Derek was about to pursue him when he heard the rapid thuds of someone stumbling. He turned to see Kristina collapse down the stairs. Rushing back, he caught her before she hit the floor. Blood seeped from a wound in her stomach.

"Don't let me die," she pleaded.

***

Outside, Demetri and his men converged on Vanderhoff and Igraine. A van suddenly burst through the trees and landed between the two parties. Sitting in the driver's seat, Steve threw the door open.

"Get in," he shouted to Vanderhoff and Igraine.

They scrambled into the vehicle. Steve buried the gas pedal, speeding toward Demetri and his men. With barely a moment to spare, they scurried out of the way.

"Bet you're glad you brought me along. Huh, Mr. Caroli?" exclaimed Steve.

GUY COTE

CHAPTER SEVENTEEN

As she stared out the window of a taxi, Josie felt her pulse quickening. She was approaching a Tucson, Arizona, residence that was all too familiar to her.

"That'll be eighteen seventy-five," the cab driver said.

Josie pulled a euro note from her purse and gave it to him, her mind on what would happen to her next. She wondered if she made the right decision. The Lord Mayor told her to go someplace safe, but did he have her mother's house in mind when he said it?

"What the hell is this?" the driver asked.

"It's euro. I gave you over thirty bucks," Josie explained.

"I don't take foreign money," replied the driver. "I don't take food stamps either."

"Then call the cops," she told him, "'cause it's all I got."

The driver was unhappy but left with few alternatives. "Get out," he said.

Josie had no luggage except for her purse. She'd been wearing the same clothes for a week. She walked toward the house and thought she could hear yelling. As she reached for the front door, she paused. Yelling turned into screaming and shouting. She took a deep breath to fortify her resolve and opened the door.

Josie expected to be hit with mayhem as she entered the house but got silence instead. Did she imagine the noises she heard moments before? She walked through the living room and into the kitchen. The sink was full of dishes. Food littered the counters. It was a surreal experience for her to find the home that had caused her so much angst sitting still. She passed into the back dining area and again thought she heard the sounds of her siblings. She opened the back door, and the first thing she saw was sixteen year old Eric grabbing Rodney by the shirt.

"Give me the keys," Eric commanded.

"I don't have 'em," replied Rodney, who was two years younger than Eric.

Jennifer, their twelve years old sister, dangled a set of keys. "I do," she teased.

"Give 'em to me now," demanded Eric as he stalked toward her.

"Mom said you can drive only when you take her to work and pick her up," lectured Jennifer. "And she's not working today!"

She intended to run when Eric got closer but forgot that plan when she saw Josie step onto the back porch.

Eric sprang forward and grabbed Jennifer. To his surprise, she didn't resist him. He turned to see what she was looking at. Three of Josie's six siblings stared in stunned surprise at their older sister who returned to them with a pregnant belly.

"She went and got herself pregnant," Rodney said to no one in particular.

"Mom!" screamed Jennifer. "Maaaa...mom!"

* * *

The table in the back dining area hosted the summit between Josie and her family. Over iced tea and chocolate chip cookies, she related the events that led to her current predicament. Her younger siblings lost interest midway through the tale and departed, but Eric and Rodney stayed. Heidi hung her head and slowly shook it from side to side.

When Josie finished, Eric observed, "That's messed up."

"You saw your grandparents blown away?" asked Rodney.

Josie nodded.

"You guys...go do something," ordered Heidi.

Reluctantly, Rodney left the table. Before following him, Eric said to Josie, "I got my license if you need me to drive you to doctor appointments and stuff."

Josie was surprised and told Heidi, "Wow. He's changed."

"Not really," her mother replied. "I just never let him drive."

Josie nodded and asked, "Are you still in touch with Steve?"

"Not for a couple of months," Heidi replied. Josie watched her limp as she carried the drink pitcher into the kitchen. She wore shorts, and the scars on her right leg were noticeable.

Heidi suddenly slammed the pitcher on the counter and demanded, "How could you let this happen? You were always my smart one. Well, look around 'cause this is the life you're gonna have from now on."

Josie prepared herself for her mother's attack.

Heidi took a deep breath, and said, "All right. Okay. Let's just be sure you don't make any more of the mistakes I made. We'll start with the father of the child. He's still alive, I hope." That last part was meant as a joke, a reference to Michael Ersman's death.

Josie didn't take it that way. Of course the clone's father is dead, she thought.

"We've got options," Heidi continued. "Especially if that rich kid is the father."

"Derek?" Josie asked. "How do you know about him?"

"Your grandmother told me."

Josie fidgeted. She was clearly irritated.

Heidi continued, "Back to that guy...Derek? If he's the father, you should be able to get some money. How do we get him to pay, though? That's the question."

"I told you how I got pregnant," said Josie. "And it wasn't by having sex!"

"Josie...c'mon," replied Heidi. "I'm trying to help you."

"Then believe me," implored Josie.

"I'm supposed to believe that sci-fi crap?" asked Heidi. "You were impregnated with a clone, but it wasn't the one you were supposed to get. And they did it when you were in a coma?"

Josie began to reply, but stopped herself. She exhaled and closed her eyes. When she opened them again, they were coated with tears. "I knew it was a mistake to come here," she said. She climbed out of her chair and walked to the front door.

Heidi watched her daughter extract her phone from her purse and press redial.

Josie spoke into the phone, "I need a driver...but not Raoul. He was a jerk."

Heidi grabbed the device from Josie's hand and ended the call. "Do you think I'm gonna let you waddle your pregnant ass back out of here?" she asked.

"Give me the phone," Josie said.

"No," her mother replied.

"Give it to me."

"I'm trying to be here for you, Josie. But you gotta be straight with me."

"I am being straight," Josie snapped. "Why would I make this stuff up?"

"I don't know," Heidi replied. "Is there a difference between lying and stealing? That's how this whole thing started, isn't it?"

"Yeah," retorted Josie. "When you stole my pendant!" She stormed out the front door. "Keep the phone!" she yelled over her shoulder.

***

Josie walked down the sidewalk at a rapid pace. She clutched her belly and chastised herself for seeking solace in the care of her family. *It's me against the world*, she reminded herself. She turned to face the traffic and search for a taxi.

Clutching the steering wheel of an old Cadillac, Eric announced, "There she is!"

Heidi sat in the passenger seat. Her hair was tied back, and she no longer wore the shorts which displayed her scars. She saw her pregnant daughter turn toward traffic and attempt to hitchhike. "Brilliant, Josie," she said. "Brilliant."

Josie watched a large white Caddy pull up to her. It had pimped out rims, tinted windows, and a dash that was coated with shag carpeting and figurines standing upright. Heidi lowered the car's passenger side window and said, "They make slasher films that start out with pregnant girls hitchhiking on the side of the road."

"I'm not hitchhiking," replied Josie. "I'm looking for a cab."

"Get in," her mother said. "Please."

Josie didn't want to get in the car, but she knew her mother was right. Alone on the sidewalk, she was a target for a killer. "Take me to the airport," she ordered.

"I thought we'd go to the mall and get you some pregnancy clothes," Heidi said.

Josie desperately wanted new clothes, and she was hungry. With little reluctance, she agreed to Heidi's proposal.

***

After grabbing lunch in the food court, Eric left with a promise to return with the car in two hours. Heidi and Josie proceeded to a store which catered to pregnant women. Bathed in soft colors, it had adorable cartoons of crawling, laughing babies painted on its walls. Josie suddenly stopped and put both hands on her belly. She turned to her mother with wide eyes. "It...it moved," she declared.

Heidi rushed to her daughter's side. She put her hand on Josie's belly. "Ohhh," she gushed. "This is so exciting. You must be what? Eighteen to twenty weeks?"

"I don't really know," Josie confessed. "A little over five months, I guess."

Heidi looked at her daughter's face, and they momentarily forgot their animosity.

Surrounded by cradles and bottles, rattles, diapers, and formula, Josie realized that the child moving inside her wasn't a monster or even a clone. It was her baby, and it was up to her to keep him safe. She resolved to never consider the "A" option again.

Mother and daughter proceeded to a carousel which displayed stylish tops. Heidi found a pretty, pale blue shirt and showed it to Josie. "What do you think?" she asked.

Josie liked it and said so with a smile and a nod.

"I'll get a cart," Heidi announced. She touched her daughter gently on the cheek as she passed. "You'll be the most beautiful girl in Lamaze class," she said.

It had been so long since Heidi and Josie had done anything fun together that each had forgotten how great it felt. Josie watched her mother return with a cart and the blue top folded within it.

"I was thinking," Heidi began. "Your chest is...it's nice to have big boobs, isn't it? Anyway, uh...we should go for the stylish-sexy look that accents your chest. But your baby bump is what we really want to feature."

Mother and daughter spent the next hour and a half comparing styles, trying on clothes, mixing and matching outfits. By the time they were ready to check out, their cart was full. The teller gave them a price of $931.10.

"Uh, do you take euros?" Josie asked.

"What's that?" the teller replied.

"Euro," Josie repeated. "European money."

"No," the girl said.

Heidi laughed and handed the teller her credit card.

***

Half way around the world, a man whose task was to monitor all transactions of Josie and her known associates sat up in his seat. "*Umstandsmode...da ist sie* (Maternity wear...there she is)!" he exclaimed. He sent a prearranged text to Dr. Herzog's phone.

***

Josie sat in the back seat as Eric parked the Caddy in front of the house, near a compact car. Heidi occupied the front passenger seat. The three of them watched David, the youngest boy in the family, chase his half-sister Cheyenne across the yard with a water-spewing hose. A buxom young woman walked out of the house with four-year-old Alexia wailing uncontrollably in her arms.

"Here we go," Heidi sighed. To Josie, she said, "Don't have more than one." She exited the car and limped up to the woman.

"How long has she been walking like that?" Josie asked Eric.

"I don't know," he answered. "Since she got her cast off, I guess."

Feelings of guilt shot through Josie as she remembered that her mother broke her leg while attempting to bring her back home. As Eric and Josie removed shopping bags from the car, Josie heard Heidi say to the woman, "Thanks, Sam. Are you on tonight?"

"You know I am," the woman responded. "Every night."

"Okay," Heidi said while taking Alexia into her arms. "I'm coming in too, so I'll pay ya when I see ya. All right?"

"No problem," the woman replied. As she walked to the compact car, Josie heard her mutter, "Psycho kids."

Josie and Eric carried the bags into the house while Heidi held Alexia and hobbled with obvious pain. Though her own arms were full, Josie held the door for her mother. Inside, she watched Heidi set Alexia on a couch and take several moments to talk the crying child into a calmer state of mind.

When Heidi returned to the dining room, Josie asked, "You're working tonight?"

"Somebody's got to," answered Heidi.

"Is Chuck coming back?"

"I don't think so," Heidi replied. "Not this time."

Heidi went into the kitchen to address another parental matter.

***

Vanderhoff paced the living room of a two-bedroom apartment. It was his latest safe house, situated in an upscale Cologne neighborhood. Igraine concluded a phone call, and Steve sat on a sofa beside a middle-aged couple who were owners of the residence.

Igraine said, "Mikos can have tventy Greeks in Brussels by zee end of zee veek."

"That's not enough," said Vanderhoff. "And we need to be elsewhere."

"Ve have Dutch, Albanian, and French commitments as vell," Igraine added.

"What're ya thinkin', boss?" asked Steve

"I'm thinking that if you had done your job in the first place, we wouldn't be in this position," Vanderhoff replied.

Steve squirmed beneath the weight of Vanderhoff's oppressive stare.

"I can place anozer call to Helmut," Igraine said. "Perhaps…"

"You told me to watch her," Steve blurted out. "How'd that become 'don't let her go to Germany'? I had no way of knowing that."

The man and woman retreated to a back room as Vanderhoff returned a burning glare to Steve. Vanderhoff glanced at Igraine, nodded, and followed the man and woman.

Steve knew he had misspoken, and his eyes drifted to Igraine.

"Your services here vill no longer be required," she said. She, too, departed to the rear of the apartment.

Kristina lay unconscious on a bed in the back room. Her arms were attached to thin plastic tubes, and her abdomen was covered by bandages. Derek washed her face.

"She needs a transfusion," Derek said. "And we can't do that here."

"Yes, we can," replied Vanderhoff. "I have a specialist at my command."

"We don't know her blood type," added Derek.

"She will recover, Derek. Have faith," said Vanderhoff. "In the meantime, you're going to America."

"I'm needed here."

"You're needed in Arizona," Vanderhoff corrected. "The Agency has located Josie, and they're on their way to retrieve her as we speak."

Derek was caught between his fidelity to Josie and Kristina. Both needed his help, and neither seemed capable of surviving without him.

***

With a bag draped over her shoulder, Heidi leaned into the white Cadillac and handed Josie twenty dollars. "Take them for ice cream," she said.

"Can I come?" asked Alexia from her car seat in the back. Jennifer sat beside her, and Cheyenne listened to her iPod while watching women enter the Pussycat Pavilion.

"Not tonight, Buggabear," replied Heidi. "Your sister's gonna take care of you."

"Have fun," said Jennifer.

As Josie drove out of the lot, she watched her mother in the rear-view mirror. Heidi limped with visible discomfort and would have to compete in the strip club with women who were younger and more attractive than she was. It was a tough way for a mother to make a living, and Josie could finally see that it was not done out of vanity. Heidi was providing for her family the only way she knew how. Josie touched her belly and wondered if she would be willing to do the same for her child.

They were approaching the Dairy Treat stand and Alexia yelled, "Ice cream!"

"Mom gave you money for our ice cream," Jennifer lectured. "You can't keep it."

"I know," Josie said as she parked before the Dairy Treat. Then she saw a pawn shop. It was the only business of its kind within five miles of the Pussycat Pavilion. "I'm going to the pawn store," she told Jennifer. "Can I trust you to get the ice cream?"

"You can trust me," said Cheyenne as she took the money Josie offered Jennifer.

"No," Jennifer protested. "That was for me."

"I don't care who does it," Josie snapped. "Get the ice cream and meet me after. I'll just be a minute." She turned off the car and walked to the nearby shop.

Two teenage Hispanic males wearing white tank tops, low-hanging jeans and do-rags sat on the hood of a nearby Pontiac. The first male told Josie, "Nice ride."

"Yeah," she said. "And I'm getting a Glock right now, so it better stay that way."

"Why you gotta be like that?" the second male asked.

Josie entered the store as the owner, an overweight six foot six inch man, prepared to lock up for the night. Bells chimed with her arrival.

"I'm closing," the owner said.

"Okay," Josie replied. "But can you answer a couple questions for me?"

"I get paid to answer questions," the owner told her.

Josie glanced out the window to check on her sisters. She turned to the man and said, "About eight months ago, my mother came in here with a pendant."

"So," the man said.

"It was gold," she continued. "With emeralds, rubies and blue glass with two pieces of wood shaped like a cross in the middle. Do you remember it?"

"Do you pay?" he replied.

"C'mon man," exclaimed Josie. "Don't you ever do anything to be nice?"

"You obviously didn't read the sign on the front of my shop," said the owner. "'Bastard Bill's Pawn.' I'm Bastard Bill."

Josie frowned and turned back toward the front door.

"I remember that necklace for three reasons," Bastard Bill added. "The woman who sold it to me was hot as hell. Some old guy offered me twice what I paid. And I found out the French government would have paid even more than the old man did."

"How do you know that?" Josie asked.

"There are only three of them in existence," he said. "That one, another that disappeared and the third that's sitting in a museum in France. Or so the Internet says."

Josie gazed at the large man with a mystified expression.

"Oh, hell," exclaimed Bill. "I got plans to go to the Pavilion tonight, and you're gonna make me late." He walked to the back of his shop and ruffled through folders. After several minutes, he returned with a paper and handed it to Josie.

She gasped as she looked at the page. It was a close-up photo of a pendant that resembled hers in every way except that it wasn't missing an emerald.

"Is that what you're lookin' for?" he asked.

"Yeah," Josie answered. "It says here Reims. That's the French museum?"

"It's the name of the town the museum is in," he said. "So...that's everything."

"What about the guy that bought it?" Josie persisted.

"What about him?" Bill replied. "He was tall, old, and gray. He paid in cash."

GUY COTE

CHAPTER EIGHTEEN

Heidi didn't take it lightly when Josie revealed that she'd be returning to Europe. Any goodwill that developed between them evaporated, and Josie boarded a plane bound for France without a single family member at the airport to see her off.

That's not to say that she was alone. Two men, each with a different agenda, followed her onto the plane. The first was a Russian who wielded enough clout with authorities to be permitted to carry a gun on an international flight. The other wore a convincing disguise, but made no attempt to hide the emerald ring on his left hand.

There were no flights from Tucson to Reims, France, so Josie went to Paris, which was only eighty miles from Reims. It took nearly thirteen and a half hours to fly from Arizona to the French capital, and Josie spent much of that time wondering why there were three pendants. She also wanted to know how her father acquired one of them. And who was the old man who bought the pendant from Bastard Bill? She hoped the answers to her questions would be found in Reims.

Having traveled extensively in recent months, Josie wasn't intimidated by the expansiveness of Paris-Charles de Gaulle Airport. She joined the flow of foot traffic while pulling a small suitcase on rollers behind her. Demetri Pavlov followed her from an inconspicuous distance. Petra also trailed Josie, but he was disguised in a blond beard and wig that made him look like a Nordic fisherman. Unlike Demetri, he was aware of his competition for the pregnant girl and was prepared to eliminate it.

The pursuit continued past shops, kiosks, bathrooms, and bars. Demetri was under orders to bring Josie in safely, and he had airport security ready to make a move as soon as he gave them an order. He sent officers a text and watched them get into position.

Petra saw guards receive their messages and prepare to snatch Josie as she approached an airport exit. He grabbed a cup from a nearby railing and adopted the persona of a jovial traveler. Sloshing ice in the cup and laughing heartily, he approached Demetri. By the time the Russian noticed him, it was too late. Petra collided with him, mumbled, "*Unnskyld* (Sorry)," and drew the pistol from the front of Demetri's pants. He shot two of the guards approaching Josie and fired a slug into Demetri's hip.

Screams, cries, and shouts immediately filled the terminal. People ran and security personnel descended on the area from every direction.

Josie was shocked. "Not again!" she exclaimed and bolted for a set of glass exit doors.

Petra melded into a cluster of manic people while keeping his eyes on Josie.

By sheer will, Demetri fought through the pain of a shattered hip bone to stand and hobble after Josie. Security would get the gunman, but he couldn't let her get away.

Josie burst through the front doors with a host of frightened people. They descended on unsuspecting cabbies and bus drivers like a swarm of locusts. Josie rushed up to the nearest taxi but lost it to a trio of young men. She looked back into the airport and saw Petra staring back at her. She recognized him beneath his disheveled disguise. "Damn!" she exclaimed. "Doesn't he ever give up?"

Blood soiled Demetri's clothing as he dragged his right leg behind him. Looking through the glass, he saw Josie lose another battle for a taxi. Then he spotted the man who shot him. His attacker still held the gun and was about to exit the airport.

Josie tried to get into a bus, but an old man pushed her away and took the last available spot. She stumbled back and fell onto the bag she was dragging behind her.

Petra was almost out of the airport. He was close to capturing Josie when someone grabbed him and dragged him backwards.

Struggling to rise, Josie was accidentally hit by a woman and knocked back to the concrete. Through glass windows, she saw a man with a blood soaked hip wrestle Petra to the ground. Five more police descended upon them.

Josie scrambled to her feet and scurried up to a cab. A horrified man and woman beat her to it, but she shoved them away. "Not this time!"

she yelled. She threw her bag into the back seat and crawled in after it. "Reims," she told the driver.

Josie's cab pulled into traffic as two gunshots erupted from the mass of bodies that had enveloped Petra in the airport. Men fell back, and Petra sprang from the pile as if he had exploded from a cannon. From the back seat of her car, Josie saw Petra fire shots into the window before him and leap through the glass, out of the airport. He landed on the curb amidst a shower of jagged shards. More screams filled the air.

"Oh, my God!" Josie exclaimed. To her driver, she ordered, "Go faster!"

***

It was mid-day when Josie's cab arrived in Reims. The printout she received from Bastard Bill said the pendant she sought was displayed in the Palais du Tau, so she instructed the driver to take her there.

The giant, gray and white stone Palais du Tau was shaped like a *T* (tau, in Greek) and bore numerous windows and a pointed roof with extended chimneys. It was a palace in medieval times but was turned into a world-famous museum in 1972. Josie left the cab and approached the grand building by passing through a well-manicured courtyard. She paid little attention to the Cathedral of Notre-Dame de Reims, which stood nearby.

As Josie entered the Palais du Tau, Petra arrived in a taxi he had hijacked from the airport. He'd been pursuing her by car for over an hour but only recently reacquired her location. Abandoning the vehicle and his disguise, he followed her into the museum.

Josie paid the admission price and stored her suitcase in a bin but held onto her purse and a large amount of money. She took an English-language brochure from a stand and followed visitors into the building's main entrance chamber.

Petra paid his fee and grabbed a brochure to play the part of a tourist. Of course, the gun he concealed beneath his pants didn't contribute much to his ruse.

The brochure proved to have more information than Josie needed. It took her several minutes to realize that the pendant was located on the third floor, along with objects associated with the coronations of kings. She was not yet so pregnant that she found a flight of stairs impossible to climb, but it was difficult for her to proceed all the way to the third floor. She had to stop several times to catch her breath and, on one occasion, to wait for the baby to stop moving within her.

Petra followed her at an inconspicuous distance. A man with a ski cap, winter coat, and week old stubble trailed Petra.

Even in the waning days of winter, the mid-day sun cast its light through the many windows on the third floor. Josie followed visitors into a long, narrow chamber with white walls and arched ceilings. Reliquaries and gold and jewel-encrusted artifacts were displayed beneath glass cases. Interested individuals peered at the pieces. The closeness of the displays and the volume of visitors made it difficult for Josie to navigate the chamber.

"Excuse me," Josie said. "Pregnant lady coming through."

Josie was ignorant of the man with the gun stalking behind her. But where she was unaware of Petra, he didn't know a man was following him. And like him, that man was unopposed to violence as a means of achieving his objective.

Josie made one unsuccessful attempt after another to find the pendant in the display cases. It occurred to her that a piece of such rarity would likely be housed in a secure area. Gazing toward the end of the chamber, she saw a passageway to an inner room with an armed guard standing in its entrance. "That's it," she muttered to herself.

As Josie had expected, the new chamber she visited was protected by alarms and motion sensors. Royal, ermine-lined robes, crowns, scepters, orbs, swords, and gilded, bejeweled pieces sat beneath glass cases and rested upon velvet pillows. Ancient tapestries lined the walls. Josie studied the cases but couldn't find the object of her search.

With fewer tourists and one overweight guard in the chamber, Petra decided to make his move.

Josie spotted a small display located along the wall. It had a green, velvet background and a single golden necklace resting within it. She rushed to the case.

Petra reached for Josie but missed her by inches. Fortunately, he had not yet pulled his gun to reveal his intentions. He saw her stop before a wall display. She was the only person there, so he slid the pistol out from under his belt and stalked toward her.

There it was! Josie's eyes grew moist as she beheld the object she had traveled so far to see. It was a mint-condition twin of her pendant, except this one had the emerald that hers was missing. Hanging from a golden chain, it had gilded filigree that housed emeralds and rubies of various shapes and encircled a blue-tint glass in which was set two splinters of wood in the shape of a cross. It was an ancient and magnificent relic—one of only three. Now she had seen them all and for a time owned one.

Petra reached to pull Josie into his pistol. He was almost upon her. Suddenly, a hand grabbed him by the neck as a gun barrel was shoved into his back, his own maneuver used against him. The man who had been following him whispered into his ear with an English accent, "Make another move and it will be your last."

Josie thought she heard a faint whisper, and part of her felt that people were behind her, but they would have to wait to see the pendant, she decided. Her eyes drifted to the plaque on the base of the display. The following words were written in French, German, English and Spanish: *NINTH CENTURY TALISMAN OF CHARLEMAGNE. Housing pieces of the True Cross, this talisman was believed to confer on the bearer supernatural healing powers in accordance with those possessed by the Savior. It was said to have been worn by Charlemagne and was mysteriously found in his crown when his tomb was opened in 1166.*

"1166?" Josie asked herself. "I thought the tomb was opened in 1000. They opened it again in 1166? Why?"

With one swift movement, Petra rolled to the left and knocked the other man's gun hand aside. The pistol fired, and a bullet struck the pendant's display. The glass cracked but didn't shatter. People in the chamber yelled, and Josie turned to see that Petra and a man whose back was to her were engaged in a struggle. Both men held guns.

"Run, Josie!" shouted the man in the cap. His gun fired again. There were more screams. The combatants turned, and Josie saw that the man fighting Petra was Derek!

The room's only guard wrapped his arm around Petra's neck, enabling Derek to rush to Josie. Petra squeezed the trigger of his gun, and the shot barely missed Josie.

"Let's go!" commanded Derek while tugging Josie toward the exit.

The overweight guard's great bulk caused Petra to stumble and bend over. The security man held tight and lay on Petra's back as he staggered beneath the added weight. The guard's swinging legs knocked over displays. Petra finally flipped him onto the floor and shot him directly in the heart.

Derek pulled Josie down the marble staircase while putting his gun into his coat pocket. "Hurry!" Derek ordered. "Hurry!"

"Don't you think I am?" Josie screamed. Unfortunately, she couldn't move as freely as her companion and scrambling people knocked her from side to side.

Petra entered the upper stairwell and charged down the steps. Gun in hand, he shoved people out of his way.

Patrons swarmed the first floor of the palace, and security tried in vain to stop them. Derek and Josie followed the mob to approach the main exit. Suddenly, an imposing security guard grabbed Josie and shouted at her in French. She struggled to break free, but he pulled her toward other guards. Derek struck the man in the jaw with a solid punch. The blow freed Josie but didn't stop the man. He descended upon Derek.

"Get out of here!" Derek told Josie.

"No!" she yelled. "We can't get separated again!"

Derek was too preoccupied to argue with her, but he got his wish as the flow of the crowd carried Josie through the front doors of the Palais du Tau.

As people ran across the manicured lawns of the palace's court yard, Josie looked through the windows to try to find Derek. Instead, she saw Petra. She scrambled away from the building as fast as she could.

In the museum, Derek fought a losing battle with the large guard and fell against a window. Peering through the glass, he saw Josie reach the road. He turned back to the guard and received a punch that spun him around. Before being hit again, he saw Petra escape through a side exit. Josie was about to face the killer alone!

***

Screaming, flashing police vehicles raced to the Palais du Tau. Josie lowered her head and looked toward Notre Dame as cops sped past her. She had to get off the streets, but where could she go? The Cathedral was too close to the palace. She needed to get farther than that. To make matters worse, she could feel another headache coming on, and her nose was runny. She wiped fluid from her upper lip and noticed that she had a bloody nose. "I'm falling apart," she said.

Petra was also fleeing authorities, but he was the predator as well as the prey. He crept along a side wall of Notre Dame Cathedral, mindful of police. Then he saw Josie.

She scrambled into a parking lot. Her heart was racing, and her vision was getting blurry. To her horror, a hand grabbed her and pulled her between two cars.

She tried to scream, but Derek covered her mouth. "Quiet," he commanded.

He led her through a maze of parked cars as Josie wondered how he escaped the palace. They stopped at the edge of the lot.

"We need to get there," Derek said while gesturing to buildings across the street.

Josie nodded and surged forward, but Derek pulled her back.

Petra stood in the parking lot, only two feet in front of them. He held his gun and looked around. He didn't know exactly where they were, but they were nearby. He could feel it.

Josie trembled, not knowing how much more she could take. Two voices shouted in German, and Petra bolted across the street. Officers ran after him.

"Let's go," Derek said as he pulled Josie toward the street.

"You wanna follow them?" she asked in astonishment.

"No," he replied. "They'll be in the alley. We'll take the tunnels."

***

Derek led Josie through a cold, damp tunnel. Sparsely-placed lights kept complete darkness at bay, but shadows dominated the passage. Distant voices echoed off the walls like the warnings of hovering specters. Josie's body returned to its shivers under the combined effects of fear, chill, and downright eeriness.

Derek wrapped his jacket around her and rubbed his hands up and down her arms to warm her. "We should be safe down here," he said. "There are over a hundred and twenty kilometers of tunnels beneath Reims."

"Really?" Josie asked as her shivers began to subside. "Why?"

"The Romans carved them over two thousand years ago," he answered.

"If we're so safe," said Josie. "Why am I hearing voices?"

"Champagne houses use the tunnels as cellars and conduct daily tours."

Josie slipped her arms through the sleeves of the coat and followed Derek deeper into the tunnel, staying close to the clammy walls. "Where are we going?" she asked.

"I'm not sure," he confessed. He took her by the hand and led her into an empty chamber which had been hewn out of the side of the tunnel. A dim, distant bulb cast faint light into the abandoned vault. "We should wait here until dark, then..."

231

"How'd you find me? Is my watch still bugged?" Josie asked.

"Your mother told me where you were going," Derek admitted.

"My mother?" she exclaimed. "How…how'd you know I was with her?"

"I went to Tucson to protect you from The Agency," he told her. "I'm surprised I got there before them."

"How'd The Agency find me? What about my family?"

"I moved your family to a safe house," he said.

"Oh, thank…how'd you do that?" she asked suspiciously. "I thought the NSM didn't want anything to do with you."

"Your family is under Dr. Vanderhoff's protection," he revealed.

"Vanderhoff?" she asked in confusion.

"He created the NSM, and he's been looking out for you since you were born."

"Dr. Vanderhoff?" she repeated. "The professor? My father's professor?"

"I didn't know he taught your father," Derek replied.

Things began to make sense to Josie. Vanderhoff and her father were close. That's why Michael went to him after discovering the manuscript in Betrada's tomb. The book must have been bad for The Agency, so Michael took it to Vanderhoff, who opposed The Agency. Shortly after that, Dr. Herzog sent Hans to kill Michael.

"The pendant!" Josie exclaimed. "Dr. Vanderhoff was the old man who bought it from Bastard Bill. But why? And how could he have been looking out for me my whole life? I never saw him until a few months ago."

"You'd have to ask him that yourself," he replied. "Are…are you bleeding?"

Once again, a trickle of blood ran from Josie's nostril. She quickly wiped it away.

"How long has this been happening?" he asked.

"It's nothing. I hit it earlier," she lied. "What about my pendant?"

"What pendant?"

"Do you know why I came back here?" she asked.

"Not really," he admitted. "Your mother didn't explain it very well."

Josie summarized what she knew about the three pendants or talismans. She concluded by saying, "The sign in the museum said

Charlemagne's talisman has healing powers that came from The Savior. I'm guessing that means Jesus?"

"That's what the legend says," admitted Derek.

"And Jesus...I wish I'd read the Bible," she said. "Wasn't Jesus able to cure sick people? Didn't He raise someone from the dead...raise himself from the dead?"

"Yes."

She was getting closer to finding an answer to the questions she'd been asking. She could feel it.

"If you're thinking that Charlemagne cured himself or was raised from the dead by his magic talisman, then I'd refer you to the grave we saw with his body in it," said Derek. "And you had the talisman for years. Did it ever prevent you from being sick?"

Thinking back, Josie recalled several times when she put the pendant on to comfort her when she was sick. It made her feel as if her father was there with her. But there were no miracle cures in any instance. Her illnesses simply ran their courses.

"Legends are just entertaining stories," Derek said. "Nothing more."

"What about the weird things I found?" she persisted.

"The stained glass window and the tapestry?" asked Derek.

"And more," she said. "Abby showed me something a guy in the 1300's wrote that said Charlemagne ruled for a hundred and twenty-five years. That's impossible...unless Charlemagne never died after they faked his death in 814."

"Never died," Derek repeated. "Eternal life?"

"You don't believe me? Okay," she said, "what about the year 1521? Charlemagne tutored the King of France, a guy named François. But he left when the king had a painting made of himself taking Charlemagne's place at a coronation."

"I think you're reaching."

"Am I?" she asked. "Five years later, Charlemagne showed up at the court of François' enemy, Charles V. Charles then defeated François and took him prisoner. Oh...and the Anne of Brittany we saw in the tapestry was François' mother-in-law. Tell me again that I'm reaching."

Derek laughed. "You're reciting the famous Legend of the Joyeuse Sword."

"The what?"

"A sword named Joyeuse, Charlemagne's magical sword," Derek replied. "There are countless stories about it. The one you're talking about claims that a special office was created after Charlemagne died, the Office of the Keeper of the Sword. The position passed from generation to generation of Charlemagne's descendants, and each Keeper was responsible for seeing that the sword called Joyeuse was held with honor—never used for evil—and led the coronation procession for every French king."

Josie remembered seeing something about that in her research but didn't understand it at the time.

Derek continued, "The sword was supposed to make the person who wielded it invincible in battle. According to the tale you read, the Keeper in the 1500's, whose name escapes me, used this sword to train King François of France. But the King had no humility and claimed to be 'The New Charlemagne,' even going so far as to commission that painting you mentioned. This angered the Keeper, so he took the sword from François and hid out in the wilderness, plotting to humble the arrogant French king. He resurfaced four years later in the court of Charles V."

"And Charles used the sword to defeat François and take him prisoner?"

"Yes. In the Battle of Pavia," Derek said. "But it doesn't end there. Charles refused to give the sword back, so the Keeper broke his jaw. It never set properly and that's why all the portraits of Charles V show him with an oversized jaw. The truth is that Charles had a genetic disorder where the lower jaw outgrows the upper. It's called Habsburg jaw. Legends are created to give history a dramatic flair, Josie."

"What does the sword look like?" Josie asked.

"*The Song of Roland* says it changed color thirty times a day."

"A sword that changes color?" Josie asked. She knew she'd seen it before, but where? Her eyes suddenly shot wide open. The sword on the wall in Dr. Vanderhoff's office changed colors. Was Vanderhoff the Keeper of the Sword? That might explain his interest in her pendant. Perhaps he was the Keeper of All Things Charlemagne.

***

It took ingenuity for Petra to outrun the police, but minimal effort for him to realize that Josie and Derek escaped into the tunnels. He walked the chilly, darkened passageways in hope of finding some indication of where they went. To his surprise, he heard a female voice ask, "How did Charlemagne get his pieces of the cross?"

A short distance from Petra, Derek replied, "It's a good thing I took a course in medieval legends. Charlemagne received fragments of the

True Cross from a pilgrim named Fredelandus. The pilgrim was on his way back from Jerusalem with a piece of the True Cross which he intended to enshrine in a church he had built."

"But Charlemagne convinced this guy to give it to him instead?" Josie asked.

"Yes, with the King's promise that he'd build another church on that very site."

"Where's the site?" Josie asked.

"Charroux," Derek replied. "In Western France."

Petra gripped his gun as he closed in on his targets.

"Do you know how to get in touch with Dr. Vanderhoff?" Josie asked Derek.

"Yes," he replied.

"Have him meet us in Charroux in two days," she instructed.

"Why?" inquired Derek.

Josie saw Petra creeping along the wall. "Run!" she yelled and took off with her hands supporting her belly. She felt a solid object in the pocket of Derek's coat. His gun!

Derek charged Petra. At the last moment, Petra dipped his shoulder, caught him by the waist and flipped him onto his back. Derek hit the floor with a painful smack.

Josie turned to see Petra point his pistol at Derek, who was on the floor. She fired three shots from Derek's gun. The first two missed, but the third grazed Petra's shoulder.

Derek scrambled to his feet. "Go, Josie!" he yelled as he tackled Petra.

Josie didn't wait to see the results of the struggle. She raced as fast as she could manage. Her left hand clutched her belly while her right held the gun. She rounded a curve in the tunnel, her lungs gasping for breath. Two shots cracked behind her. Who fired the gun, Derek or Petra? Her heavy body seemed to move in slow motion as she feared for Derek's safety. She wanted to go back for him, but they'd been through that before. He insisted that she keep going and not look back.

She followed a tunnel that branched off to the right and felt a chilling breeze slap her face. Her eyes searched the shadows for danger as her legs carried her as fast as they could. Her tunnel came to an abrupt end, forming a *T* with another passageway. Josie took a left and heard voices. It was as if ghosts were mocking her. She could feel her heart beating in her chest. Her breaths became quicker, and her mouth was dry. The walls and ceiling seemed to be caving in on her.

Light formed a haze at the end of the tunnel, and voices waxed and waned in volume. Josie willed her tired, over-stressed body to run toward a staircase at the end of the passageway. She stumbled up the steps and surfaced in a back alley where vehicles passed on the street in front of her. Beyond the road, she saw the setting sun disappear behind a towering church.

***

The best place for Josie to find anonymity and await the onset of darkness was in a church. She entered Saint Remi Basilica with quivering hands and blood trickling from her nose. The Romanesque-style church offered bays where she could hide.

Keeping to the periphery of the basilica, she felt like a tiny speck inhabiting a giant world. Marble columns wider than any tree she had ever seen stretched to vaults which opened overhead. She heard whispered voices and echoing footsteps. She prayed that Derek was safe, but it wasn't a real prayer. She had never developed the skill of truly petitioning heaven. She glanced at a large cross which hung above the altar. A statue of the dying Jesus was affixed to it. *Was he really God? If so, wouldn't that endow His cross, the True Cross, with supernatural powers?* She needed to meet with Dr. Vanderhoff to get some answers.

Her wanderings through the basilica brought her to a curious display. Oval shaped, it was a massive marble shrine with statues of royal and religious figures carved into it. Each white effigy was separated by a column of brownish-red marble. Josie circled the oddity until she saw a plaque that explained what it was. Written in French, German, English, and Spanish, it said that the monument represented the unmarked graves of many archbishops, kings, and princes who had been buried in the monastery. The first name to be listed was King Carloman (751-771), the brother of Charlemagne.

Josie smiled. Derek was right, she realized. Einhard marked the grave in Saint-Denis as belonging to Carloman only as a ruse. Charlemagne had been buried in Saint-Denis, and the final resting place for his brother Carloman was in Reims, as the plaque before her stated. She was about to walk away when she noticed a footnote at the bottom of the plaque. It read, *Note: The remains of King Carloman were exhumed and re-interred in the Basilica of Saint-Denis in the thirteenth century.* Josie stared at the footnote in disbelief. Derek lied. The tomb they opened in Saint-Denis was not Charlemagne's, but his brother Carloman's, just as its marker said.

"That lying bastard!" she exclaimed. "Why would he do that?"

As she stared at the plaque, she realized that there existed an issue far greater than Derek's deceit. Charlemagne's grave had not been found, and it may have never existed.

GUY COTE

CHAPTER NINETEEN

It was mid-morning and Josie had stood among the snow-frosted ruins of Charroux Abbey since just after sunrise. She had no way of knowing if Derek would meet her as they had agreed or if he would bring Dr. Vanderhoff with him. She didn't even know if Derek had survived his bout with Petra.

Hours passed and she received no sign from either man. She settled upon a bench and huddled within the folds of Derek's coat. A hundred and twenty foot tall edifice known as the Charlemagne Tower stood behind her like a majestic guardian. It was the last remaining part of the abbey and was octagonal in shape with tall arches separated by marble columns. It seemed to be the logical spot for Josie to meet Derek and Vanderhoff if they ever arrived.

When the sun finally returned to the horizon, Josie realized that they weren't coming. She was cold, exhausted, and extremely worried, but she needed to find lodging. She stood and took her first steps to leave, but stopped.

Igraine, Kristina, and thirteen weapon-toting men and women walked toward her with Derek and Dr. Vanderhoff in their midst. Relief washed over Josie's weary features. She rushed up to Derek, threw her arms around him, and squeezed so tightly he thought his ribs would crack. She swiftly broke the embrace and punched him in the chest.

"Don't ever lie to me again," she commanded.

"I didn't lie to you," he replied.

Josie turned to Dr. Vanderhoff. His face was wrinkled. His beard was longer than she remembered and the scar on his forehead seemed to be more noticeable.

"I didn't think you'd bring so many people," she told him.

"These are dangerous times," Vanderhoff answered.

"For you or for me?" she asked.

"Let's take a walk," Vanderhoff suggested.

***

A quarter moon spread its muted light through the sky as Vanderhoff's team situated itself in the ruins. Derek, Kristina, and Igraine remained beneath the tower, watching Josie and Dr. Vanderhoff walk and talk amidst snow-covered ancient stones.

"I commend you on your choice of a meeting place," said Vanderhoff.

"Wasn't this where he got the pieces of the True Cross?" she asked.

"Who?" inquired Vanderhoff.

"Charlemagne," she said as she stepped forward to face him.

Igraine fidgeted as she saw Josie and Dr. Vanderhoff square off, but she was under orders not to intervene unless summoned.

"When an emperor entered Charlemagne's tomb in 1000, he found pieces of the cross of Jesus in Charlemagne's crown," said Josie.

Vanderhoff's blank expression revealed none of his thoughts.

She continued, "When they opened his tomb again in 1166, they found the pendant that is now in the museum at Reims. It has two pieces of Jesus' cross in it, and they found it in Charlemagne's crown. Why would a pendant that is supposed to hang around a neck be found in the Emperor's crown?"

"It sounds to me as if you already know the answer," said Vanderhoff.

Pointing to his forehead, she asked, "How'd you get that scar?"

"An old friend gave it to me," Vanderhoff answered.

"How old?"

Following a gesture from Vanderhoff, Igraine came forward with a backpack. She left the sack and returned to her spot beneath the tower.

Vanderhoff unzipped the bag and reached into it. "Months ago," he said. "You came to me looking for something."

Josie watched him extract an ancient leather-bound book from the pack. "The Saint-Denis Manuscript," she exclaimed. "You told me it didn't exist."

"It was composed in Latin," he said. "But I can translate it for you."

"How would I know you weren't lying to me again?" she asked.

"That seems to be an affliction of yours. You can't believe anybody."

"Yeah," she agreed. "But I'm gettin' used to it."

Vanderhoff smirked and said, "This is the last book of Einhard, hidden for over eleven centuries." He turned to the first page and read, *"In crepusculum vitae meae sum."* He translated, "I am upon the twilight of my life." He read ahead, stopped, and interpreted, "And I am conflicted as no man before me. The vows of secrecy I took could not foresee the strife which has befallen the land of my lord and king. Therefore, my conscience compels me to reveal to humanity the secret I keep. For it is a hope…a dream…which shall one day return peace to this land…."

As Vanderhoff continued his translation, Josie got the impression that he wasn't reading so much as he was remembering. He sat on a stone, and she sat beside him.

"Fifteen years before King Charles was to become emperor, he received from a traveler a slice of wood," continued Vanderhoff. "The man declared it to be a true fragment of the tree to which Our Lord was nailed. As the King was a believer in the importance of relics, he divided this sacred wood into pieces for the purpose of bequeathing them to abbeys throughout his kingdom. Aniane, Alet, Charroux, Paunat, Sarlat, Moissac are but some of the abbeys to receive such grants. For himself, the King kept seven splinters in accordance with the divine importance of that number. But when his favorite duke, Guillaume, embraced the monastic life and founded an abbey of his own, the King gifted him one of his pieces."

Josie remembered the True Cross procession she saw in Saint-Guilhem le Desert.

"As my familiar name is Bezaleel…" Vanderhoff stopped and explained, "That means that he was a metal worker and gem-cutter."

Josie nodded.

Vanderhoff continued, "…I was given the task of fashioning two of the splinters into a talisman for the King to wear at all times, and the King himself selected the slivers to be used from the six which remained."

"Einhard made the pendant?" Josie asked. She saw Vanderhoff nod.

"I did not know at the time, though the King surely did, that the fragments he selected were unlike the others," Vanderhoff translated. "For they had been bathed in the blood of The Lord Jesus."

Josie stumbled to her feet. "That's it!" she exclaimed.

"Is it?" he asked.

"Yes," she declared. "The other pieces had no magic because they had no blood. It was only the blood of Jesus, the blood of God, which gave the wood healing powers."

Vanderhoff closed the book that he had not really been reading.

"I know what happened," Josie declared. "I know exactly what happened."

Vanderhoff waited for her to elaborate.

"The King was on his deathbed," she explained. "He'd been there for years. As long as he wore the pendant, he wouldn't die. But he also couldn't be completely cured. So Einhard broke it open, cut him where his crown would've been...on the forehead. Then he put the wood with the blood of Jesus on it inside the cut. With the Holy Blood in him, the King was healed. He would never get sick again, and he would never die."

"I believe the word you're looking for is immortal," said Vanderhoff.

"I'm right. Aren't I?" After a pause, she added, "You're Charlemagne."

Vanderhoff smiled. "Twenty-three years ago, I heard those words from a man I loved like a son," he admitted. "For his own protection, I told him he was wrong."

"But my father was right," she persisted. "Like I am."

He reached beneath his coat and shirt to extract a talisman that dangled from a gold chain around his neck. It was Josie's pendant with the missing emerald. She gasped at the sight of it. "I gave this to him to prove I wasn't what he claimed. If this was magical and I was who he said I was, then I would die as soon as I took it off...right?"

Josie barely heard his question. She desperately wanted to touch the pendant.

"What I didn't tell him was that three talismans were made," said Vanderhoff. "The original with the blood of Jesus, another to be placed on the Hunchback's body, which occupied the Emperor's tomb, and the third to identify the immortal Charlemagne whenever he chose to reveal himself. The latter two were constructed long after the original."

His insistence on referring to Charlemagne in the third person made her question her conclusion. Perhaps he was the Keeper of the Sword, not the Emperor, she thought.

Vanderhoff continued, "Einhard made the Regensburg carving on the throne, wrote this manuscript, added a deceptive post script to the

Saint-Denis capitulary, then buried it with Pippin the Short. He then left the broken talisman in Carloman's tomb and ensured that the false emperor was buried in a sitting position with the True Cross placed in his crown, in order to reveal two things—Charles the Great was alive, and he would return."

Josie listened intently, waiting for him to either confirm or deny her conclusion.

"What he failed to realize," said the old man, "was that I didn't want to return."

There it was! The affirmation Josie sought.

Vanderhoff explained, "For more than a millennium, I let others steer the ship, trying from time to time to be the unseen navigator, usually to disastrous results."

"Like in the 1500's with François and Charles V?" Josie asked.

"Yes," he admitted. "And others. But no age has frightened me more than this one, for a single person, properly placed, now has the capacity to end life on earth."

Josie nodded as she thought of all the crazy leaders who threatened the world.

"I deeply loved all my children," Vanderhoff said. "And I did well by each of them, except the first. Pippin was a sweet child who grew to be an angry man. He was weak-willed and easily used. I could not allow him to be king, and he hated me for it."

He set his large hand on Josie's belly, making the child within her leap.

"I drove him to plot against me, then I condemned him to a life he despised," confessed Vanderhoff. "For that I have carried guilt longer than any man should. Your pregnancy brings me a chance at redemption, and I thank you. But that boy must never be handed the reins of power."

***

Several hundred feet overhead and a mile from Charroux, Capitaine Gerard LeVaine piloted a Tigre HAP helicopter. It was one of three state-of-the-art French military machines to be used for government-sanctioned purposes only. Capitaine LeVaine "borrowed" the helicopter for two simple reasons—allegiance and a desire for revenge. Eleven years earlier, two men who worked for a powerful man thwarted a terrorist attack in Paris that would have killed Gerard, his wife, and their two-year-old daughter. The violence was perpetrated by the NSM for a political goal that cared nothing for the lives of innocent people.

Capitaine LeVaine was a loyal airman, but when one of the men who saved his family came to him with a plan to attack NSM agents who were operating on French soil, there was no doubt that he would do his part. Thus, he found himself flying an elite helicopter to a tiny French village while Petra sat behind him in command of a thirty millimeter gun turret, nineteen rockets, and four air-to-air missiles. Petra wore a bandage on his right shoulder, the result of Josie's shot, which grazed him in the tunnel.

On the ground, Dr. Vanderhoff led Josie back to the tower. Before getting close enough for the others to hear, he said, "In twelve centuries, I have revealed my true identity to precious few. In this age, only you and Igraine know my secret. That must not change under any circumstance. Are you agreed?"

"I can keep a secret," she replied.

"I trust you will," he answered.

As they rejoined Derek, Kristina, and Igraine, Vanderhoff said, "There's a farmer who owes us at least one night's lodging twenty kilometers to the east."

"How do we get this little army over there without being noticed?" asked Kristina.

Derek wanted to know what Josie and Dr. Vanderhoff had spent so much time discussing, but Josie wouldn't meet his gaze directly.

"We'll leave the same way we arrived," answered Vanderhoff.

"You don't think six vehicles converging on a remote farmhouse will raise eyebrows?" asked Kristina.

"I zink zee doctor knows more about zis zan you do," said Igraine.

"Igraine's right," said Josie. "Don't question him."

Both Kristina and Derek were surprised by Josie's comment.

One of Vanderhoff's men alerted them to the sounds of an approaching helicopter.

In the Tigre, Petra searched with night vision binoculars. He knew Josie and Derek would be in the village because he heard them discuss it in the tunnel.

"Is it the police?" asked Derek. "The Agency? Military?"

"The Agency," answered Vanderhoff. "No combat chopper would fly out here under normal circumstances...especially at night." To one of his female guards, he ordered, *"Tirez sur l'hélicoptère* (Shoot the helicopter)!"

Petra saw sparks flash from the end of a gun as bullets struck the door near him.

By the tower, Vanderhoff commanded, *"Dispersez-vous! Rassemblez-vous voitures dans dix minutes!* (Scatter! Meet at the cars in ten minutes!)"

The helicopter's chin-mounted gun turret sprayed rapidly fired artillery across the grounds. Stone and granite dust flew off the tower. Four of Vanderhoff's guards were riddled with bullets, convulsing in place until they fell lifelessly to the ground. The others met the chopper's violence with automatic fire of their own.

Capitaine LeVaine jerked the control stick to the right and back. The Tigre soared over and up in avoidance of gunfire. *"Les missiles!* (The missiles!)" he shouted.

Petra needed no instruction. The squeeze of his finger released a rocket. The resulting explosion sent concrete, soil, and wood from a bench soaring into the air. A hole containing debris and two more dead people was left in its wake.

Derek pulled Josie by the arm as they raced away from the attack zone. He yelled, "The cars are parked just over the..."

Two rockets found the group's vehicles and exploded them in fiery blasts.

Petra considered all targets expendable, but one. *"Cherchez l'enceinte* (Search for the pregnant girl)," he ordered the pilot.

Capitaine LeVaine scanned through night vision goggles, but he saw only enemies firing up at him. The Tigre's gun turret spit bullets back in rapid response.

Igraine tried to steer Vanderhoff to a cluster of trees, but he said, "Don't worry about me. Protect Josie."

Every fiber of Igraine's being told her not to abandon Dr. Vanderhoff, but he gave her an order. Turning to Kristina, she said, "Guard him viz your life!"

The whirling machine continued to trade fire with six opponents while Petra used his binoculars to look for his target. He spotted Igraine running across the ruins.

Igraine saw Josie and Derek fleeing hand in hand and tried to catch up with them.

Maneuvering the Tigre to avoid gunfire, Capitaine LeVaine noticed that two people were holding hands as they ran. One of them was clutching her belly with her free hand. *"La voilà!* (There she is!)" he exclaimed.

Petra moved his binocular view from Igraine to the other two. Sure enough, there was Josie. He saw a man come out from behind a nearby building and rush up to her. He turned his view away from the couple and back to Igraine.

Igraine saw a man come from nowhere to approach Josie. She could tell that he was the incompetent fool she had fired only weeks before. She tried to warn Josie, but a streaking rocket struck the ground only inches from her. The explosion instantly blew her apart, mixing pieces of Igraine with ruins and soil in a fire that lit up the night.

The force of the detonation threw Josie and Derek to the ground.

"Oh my God!" exclaimed Josie. She scrambled to sit up. "Igraine!"

A man suddenly appeared to help her to her feet, and Josie found herself standing before her ex-boyfriend.

"Come with me," said Steve.

Derek rushed to Josie's side. "I've got her," he declared.

Another rocket whistled through the sky and turned a nearby wall to gravel.

"You got her, fine!" exclaimed Steve. "But let's get the hell out of here!"

"Not without Dr. Vanderhoff," Josie declared.

Overhead, the killing machine rained artillery upon its last remaining opponents.

"If you wait for him, you'll be dead," said Steve.

"Come on, Josie," urged Derek.

She saw another projectile explode a grove of trees as the Tigre sprayed bullets across the ruins. Josie grabbed Derek's hand, and they followed Steve into the unknown.

***

In terms of escaping danger, Steve turned out to be quite adept. The helicopter didn't follow them, and they encountered no police or Agency vehicles. In fact, they saw no one at all. Steve, Derek, and Josie seemed to spend an eternity traversing the fields of Western France. As usual, Josie's mind worked like a centrifuge with thoughts and questions spinning within it. Dr. Vanderhoff/Charlemagne had been alive for nearly thirteen hundred years, and nothing could kill him? What if one of those rockets had blown him up like it did Igraine? Then there was Steve.

She couldn't imagine how he ended up in Charroux at the precise moment that she needed to be rescued.

Also curious about Steve, Derek said, "I know Igraine released you, so who are you working for now?"

"Igraine?" Josie said in surprise. "You were working for Igraine?"

"Igraine works—or should I say worked—for Mr. Caroli," replied Steve.

Josie stopped walking and stared at her ex.

"Mr. Caroli and Dr. Vanderhoff are one and the same," Derek explained.

Josie tried to wrap her mind around what she just heard. Dante Caroli, Dr. Vanderhoff, and Charlemagne were the same person?

"I was...uh...let go by Igraine," Steve admitted. "But I didn't think she meant it. I just needed a chance to redeem myself to Mr. Caroli and find my girl."

He tried to embrace Josie, but she moved away from him.

"That doesn't tell us who you're working for now," Derek reminded him.

"Her," Steve replied with a gesture to Josie.

"Me?" she asked.

"I came here to protect you," explained Steve. "Like I said, you're my girl...though there's a lot more to ya now. Mind tellin' me who the father is?"

"You knew she was pregnant," snapped Derek.

"Did not."

"This guy's a bloody moron," Derek told Josie.

Ignoring Derek's observation, Josie asked, "How'd you know where I was?"

"I didn't," he answered. "I followed them, hoping they would bring me to you."

"You followed us to find Josie so you could redeem yourself to Dr. Vanderhoff?" Derek asked. "You have some questionable motives."

Adding everything she learned together, Josie asked, "If Caroli is Vanderhoff and he's been looking out for me my whole life, and you were working for him, what does that make me to you? An assignment?"

Steve gazed at her, momentarily lost for words. He smiled and tried again to embrace her. "Josie, c'mon. You really think that?"

"Yeah. I do." She wouldn't let him touch her.

Derek stepped between them. "You should answer her question."

Steve was caught, and his brain wasn't working fast enough to talk his way out of Josie's accusation. He replied, "I could. I could talk about all the stuff we did that made our relationship real, but that ain't gonna do anything to change how cold it is out here, or that she's probably hungry due to her advanced...uh, condition. An' do I have to remind you that the helicopter's still lookin' for us? Seems to me we should be walkin' and talkin'."

**

Unfortunately, Steve didn't answer any more questions for the rest of their trek, and it wasn't until sunrise that they found lodging. It was a motel that looked to be out of use, but they located a clerk, who rented them two adjoining rooms.

Josie showered beneath a rusty nozzle in her room. She would have preferred to share the space with Derek. They hadn't kissed or touched romantically in months, and she longed for some reassurance that he still found her attractive. But Steve's presence was like an extinguisher sprayed on the flame that burned for her and Derek.

She walked out of the bathroom with her skin damp and her thoughts on Derek but was shocked to find Steve sitting on her bed with a smile on his face.

"You look different from the last time I saw you come out of a shower," he said.

Josie charged back into the bathroom and screamed, "Get out of my room!"

"Why're you so bashful? I've seen you naked hundreds of times."

"Not since we broke up!" she yelled.

"True," he admitted. "We need to talk 'bout that. An' I still wanna know who, uh, knocked you up."

"Get out!"

"All right...okay. We can talk later. I just came in here to leave ya some food."

She waited to hear him open the door. A moment later, she heard it close. She peered back into the room and was relieved to see that he was gone. As promised, he left cheese, apple pieces, and croissants behind for her. She scurried to lock the front door.

A moment later, she heard a loud crash against the wall that separated her room from Derek and Steve's. Derek shouted, "You bastard!" She looked about, unsure and indecisive. Then she heard Derek yell, "Josie, get out of here!"

248

A gunshot exploded from the room next door. Two more shots followed.

"Derek!" she yelled.

She charged the front entrance, fumbled with the lock, and opened the door. She found herself face to face with Petra, who held a pistol. She stumbled back as he walked forward. She heard movement behind her and turned, hoping to see Derek. The door that adjoined the rooms opened, and Steve walked through, holding Derek's gun.

"Put your coat on," said Steve. "It's time to go."

Glancing beyond him, she saw Derek lying motionless in the next room. The carpet around him was soaked in blood. Her body quivered and her voice trembled as she pled, "Derek?"

He didn't respond.

GUY COTE

CHAPTER TWENTY

Dr. Herzog entered The Agency's subterranean command center to find it occupied by a dozen hard-working people. Demetri Pavlov hobbled toward him with the aid of a cane, his left arm in a sling.

"You have been briefed on the Charroux incident, yes?" asked Pavlov.

Dr. Herzog nodded, and Pavlov tapped an operator on the shoulder with his cane.

The operator turned to Dr. Herzog and said, "We recorded two calls from Derek Schroeder's phone. The first was to America...the second to Karl Vanderhoff."

"Play the recordings," Pavlov ordered.

The man pressed a key on his pad. Static emanated from his computer along with the weak and quivering voice of Derek. "...France...I...I...can't...I...ah...try...tried...," said the recording. "Got...got her. I...make it. S...sssave...uh...her!"

A female voice said, "They...ot her! Who?" The connection ended in static.

"Play the other one," commanded Dr. Herzog.

The operator made more keystrokes, and another low quality recording of Derek's voice played. "If...alive...I...ah...failed...sh...shot." The message ended abruptly.

"We think the calls came from a motel outside Confolens," Pavlov said. "It is twenty-six point seven kilometers from Charroux. In the Poitou-Charentes region."

"Of course it's in the Charentes region," Dr. Herzog snapped. He went to a computerized board on the wall and summoned a map of the area. "Why would they go to Confolens which is two and a half times as far as Mauprevoir? They must have been led there, but by whom?" He turned to the operator. "I think I know who the woman in America is, but I want you to find out for sure." With a glance at Pavlov, he added, "It sounds like Derek was dying. Have someone retrieve his body."

That was all the emotion Dr. Herzog had for his former assistant turned traitor. He walked out of the room without saying another word.

***

Heidi sat beside Christopher Wallace on a flight bound for Cologne. Mr. Wallace was a middle-aged husband, father of three, and high-priced attorney from Phoenix. He earned his reputation and his fortune in sensational cases. His wit and influence made him an imposing figure despite his brief height, nearly bald head, and egg shaped body.

"I know we've been through this," Heidi began, "but I'm just not convinced that Germany is where we should be going."

Wallace looked up from the document he was reading. "This isn't my first abduction," he told her. "Or international case."

"But the message I got," Heidi continued, "I could have sworn he said she was taken when they were in France."

"That doesn't matter," replied Wallace. "The Charlemagne Award Agency operates out of Germany, and I have important friends in that country."

"I don't know for sure that it was The Award Agency," she confessed. "Josie never said anything about them."

The attorney returned to his reading and said, "We have enough to get started."

"I hope so," Heidi replied. Trying to spend her nervous energy, she brushed her hands over her chest and down her stomach to straighten her shirt. Wallace watched her through his peripheral vision. Her tight-fitting black jeans barely reached her hip line. Her red fingernails trailed down her thighs on their way to her lower leg. Leaning forward, she adjusted a strap on her stiletto shoe. The lawyer gazed more overtly at her lacy, pastel, thong panties which were now visible to him.

Clearing his throat, he said, "We should discuss the matter of my fee."

"I gave you five thousand dollars already," she said.

"And this trip will eat up most of that," he replied.

"That was all I have," Heidi declared. "I…" She quickly recognized the look in his eyes, and felt relief. His desires placed him in her realm of expertise, and she transformed herself from Heidi Jackson, frightened mother, to Heidi Seek, woman of allure and passion. With a throaty, sensuous voice, she cooed, "I'll bet you do your best work at three thousand feet."

Glancing toward the back of the plane, he replied, "I think I might."

***

Dr. Vanderhoff and Kristina escaped Charroux having lost Igraine and thirteen warriors. The deceased would be sorely missed, especially Igraine. Vanderhoff had known her since she was a child, when her parents were killed in a Cold War skirmish in East Berlin. He took her in, raised her, and she became one of the most dependable assistants he'd ever had. His heart ached from her loss, but his prolonged life had given him so many dearly departed. A single tear escaped his eye as he missed each of them.

The voicemail left by Derek was followed by a clumsily typed text that gave a location. Vanderhoff and Kristina hotwired a car and raced to the given address in time to find Derek unconscious and lying on a blood-soaked carpet. They couldn't move him far, so they situated him on the motel room's bed. He had lost a lot of blood from three wounds: one bullet passed through his right bicep, another shattered his clavicle, and a third pierced his lung. He had internal bleeding, and he was drowning in his own fluids.

"He's lost too much blood," Kristina said. "I don't have instruments to remove the bullet or bone fragments. I can't even drain the fluid from his lung. He needs a hospital."

Dr. Vanderhoff was acutely aware that Derek had only moments to live. "We're less than a kilometer from town," he replied. "Go get supplies, and I'll stay with him."

"But he'll die," she said.

"I know you're a nurse, my dear, but you don't know everything." He handed her money and urged her out the front door where their stolen car sat idling.

She protested, but he said, "Hurry. And do not turn off the car."

Vanderhoff watched Kristina depart the parking lot and drive down the road. Sirens blared in the distance, and he knew that time was limited. He hurried to Derek, knowing what he wanted to do. The young man would die otherwise, and he had already done it a short while before. That's how Kristina had survived her wounds. But he was conflicted then, and he was just as troubled with this decision. Nearly every time he used his miraculous blood to save another, the results had been horrific. Would he ever learn not to intervene in history? Would he ever realize that he can't play God?

His blood had been mingled with that of the Creator of the Universe, and it had given him eternal life. If he shared a few drops with the sick or wounded, it would not be enough to make them immortal like him. Only an injection of the pure blood of Jesus could do that, but it was enough to momentarily cure any ailment, even gunshots.

"Lord above, forgive me," he said as he withdrew a fold-up knife from his pocket. He removed a bandage Kristina had fastened to Derek's clavicle and found blood sitting in the wound like a stagnant pool. He squeezed his hand tightly around his knife blade, and quickly pulled the weapon back. The result was a laceration that bled plentifully. He fed three thick droplets of his blood into Derek's wound. He watched his own cut heal itself, leaving flakes of dried blood in its wake. Using the tip of his knife, he stirred the fluids in Derek's wound as if they were the ingredients of a recipe.

***

Three police cars and two civilian vehicles raced into the motel parking lot. Officers scrambled out of their vehicles and fanned out to search the area while Pavlov led more armed men to motel room doors. Still wearing a sling and using a cane for support, he allowed others to kick in doors and look through the rooms.

A policeman shouted, "*Ici!* (Here!)" and ran into Derek's motel room.

Pavlov and others followed the officer. Inside, they saw the blood-soaked carpet and signs of a struggle. One of the men noticed scrapes on the bottom of the doorjamb and a trail of disrupted gravel in the parking lot.

Pine trees hid Vanderhoff as he dragged an ironing board that Derek was attached to by strips of linen. Disturbed soil left a path behind them. He heard bubbling water and turned to see the free-flowing Vienne River.

As police followed the trail, Vanderhoff dragged Derek and the board into the river. Derek didn't regain consciousness, but his body trembled in the frigid water.

"*Les voici!* (Here they are!)" exclaimed an officer.

Police raced to the river's edge.

From the water, Vanderhoff saw authorities scramble about the river bank. Their leader with the cane shouted orders, and they began shooting. The metal foot stand of the ironing board rang out as a bullet struck it.

Vanderhoff dragged Derek deeper into the river. He was now over his head. A bullet grazed his forearm, and he winced from the pain. Treading water, they drifted into a powerful current, which grabbed them and pulled them down river. They tumbled and rolled as if they were leaves in a gale-storm wind.

Authorities on shore watched the fugitives tumble in the raging waters. Pavlov's face became fixed with anger. Several of his men shot at the escapees, but they were gone, swallowed by a furious river.

***

Kristina sped down the road with bags of supplies on the seat beside her. She feared the worst with Derek but hoped for the best. Perhaps Dr. Vanderhoff was right and her friend was not ready to expire. After all, he had brought her back from the brink of death, and she had no idea how. She heard sirens and looked in her rear view mirror to see police cars racing toward her from Confolens. Her heart leaped in her chest. She pulled to the side of the road and prayed that they'd pass her by. The first car did, but the second parked behind her and two policemen climbed out of the vehicle.

***

Josie's captors had bound her wrists behind her back and blindfolded her on the way to her incarceration. Consequently, she had no idea of her whereabouts. The only thing she knew was that she was once again locked in a bland bedroom, and there was plenty of opportunity to mourn the death of Derek, yet again. This time, however, she knew he was gone. She saw him lying motionless in his own blood. Josie wept, filled with despair. Konrad, Henrietta, Igraine, Pamela, and now Derek had perished because of her.

To make matters worse, it was her birthday. She was twenty-three years old, though her condition and her experiences made her feel like a fat, exhausted, old lady. She heard a key enter a lock. The door opened and Steve brought clothes and a bag of fast food into the room, setting them on the bed beside her.

"Happy birthday," he said.

She fixed a burning glare upon him but said nothing.

Petra entered with a gun in his hand, and Steve departed. Once the door was shut, Petra said, "Eat. I need you to be healthy."

255

"Why didn't you take me to the compound?" she asked. "Where's Dr. Herzog?"

"I don't work for him anymore," he answered. "Neither does your man Steve."

"He isn't my man. He means as much to me as you do!" she exclaimed. "Which is nothing."

"Oh...the Ersman defiance," replied Petra. "I remember it well. Your father had it, at least until I broke his neck. He didn't say much after that."

Josie stared at him with hard, cold eyes. Then she laughed in mockery. "You're too soft to kill my father," she said. "It was the other guy...the one whose brains were splattered all over the elevator wall."

A look of emotional pain flashed across Petra's face before he composed himself and said with a smile, "I ended Michael Ersman's life, and I'd be happy to do the same to his daughter and her unborn child."

***

Studio lights burned upon Heidi, her lawyer, and the young woman who was their interpreter. They sat in leather chairs and occupied a slightly raised stage. The Americans were dressed conservatively: he in an inexpensive three-piece suit and she in a pale, yellow blouse and black, knee-length skirt. The show's host was Johan, who looked years younger than he really was. He was separated from his guests by a sign which hung before curtains and bore the name and logo of the show: *Köln Augesetzt! (Cologne Exposed!)* The red light on the top of a studio camera flashed on, and Johan began speaking German. He asked Heidi a question. The interpreter translated, "Who was this visitor who moved you and your family into hiding?"

"Perhaps a better question, Johan, would be what was this visitor?" interjected Wallace. "You see, he was a member of the...how do you say it here? *Bewegung*."

"*Bewegung?*" Johan repeated before hearing the translation.

"Yes," Wallace continued. "This Derek Schroeder told my client that the *Bewegung*, what we English speakers call the National Sovereignty Movement, was trying to protect her pregnant daughter."

The girl translated. Johan spoke, and she interpreted, "Protect her from what?"

Wallace replied, "The Charlemagne Award Agency."

***

The computer on the corner of Dr. Herzog's desk beeped, and its monitor turned on with the broadcast of *Köln Augesetzt!* Technicians had programmed his computer to search the airwaves for any mention of his organization. If one was located, it was quickly brought to his attention. Dr. Herzog stopped what he was doing to watch the show. With great interest, he heard Wallace say, "Most people know them as the group that gives away the famous Charlemagne Award in Aachen every year, but I've learned that the prize is just the tip of their iceberg. They've been involved in everything from orchestrating the Maastricht Treaty to creating the euro. They dominate the EU from behind the scenes and set policy in every member state."

Dr. Herzog removed his phone from its charger. He opened his contact list, located a number, and called the head of the studio from which the show was broadcast.

***

In the studio, Wallace continued his explanation by saying, "It's not those activities that should concern your viewers so much as the human experiments they've been conducting, just like the Nazis before them."

Shock and surprise filled the studio when the interpreter finished translating. Wallace surveyed the reactions. He was no dummy. He knew that Nazis and human genetic experimentation were emotional topics in Europe, especially in Germany.

Johan fired off an immediate response, and the interpreter said, "That is a strong accusation. Are you prepared to support it with details and evidence?"

"I am," Wallace replied. For the next ten minutes, he made his case that Agency scientists spent the better part of the last decade studying human genetics and cellular composition as well as experimenting on human cadavers, some of which had been illegally obtained. Heidi listened to her lawyer's argument and wondered why he had never told her any of it. She found herself wondering about Josie's claims to be carrying a clone, but again dismissed them as being too ludicrous to be believed. Wallace concluded by asserting that Agency scientists were using forbidden substances and performing procedures that had been outlawed by every civilized nation.

Johan replied, and it was translated as, "Every powerful organization has its detractors, and people often make false claims for fortune. What proof do you have that The Agency abducted her daughter for these purposes? If that is what you are saying."

Tired of being a silent participant, Heidi blurted out, "Derek told me so."

After the translation, Johan spoke, and the interpreter asked, "Derek? The terrorist who visited you in America?"

Wallace was surprised by the host's response. This was not the arrangement they had worked out. The show was supposed to spin the story in favor of his client.

***

Dr. Herzog watched the broadcast and smiled as the American lawyer tried without success to argue that Derek was not a terrorist. He saw Wallace look into the camera and say, "People of Germany, ask yourselves this...why would the head of the Charlemagne Award Agency, Dr. Clement Herzog, himself a famous geneticist, spend a fortune to send international authorities on a manhunt for a pregnant girl? Is it because the young woman is pregnant with his child, his genetically engineered child?"

Relief washed over Dr. Herzog, and he laughed. He had feared that the American would reveal the truth about their cloning program. Fortunately, he didn't know anything about what they were really doing. But he had come too close for comfort. Dr. Herzog picked up his phone to place a call that would end all future aspersions by the American.

***

Heidi and Wallace occupied a luxurious hotel suite that was a far cry from the conservative image they portrayed on the show. A four-poster bed sat in the center of the suite, and hand painted artwork and a large, mounted television adorned the walls. A retractable partition allowed guests to separate the bedroom from the social quarters, which featured a stocked bar, recliners, and a sofa bed. Heidi sipped vodka from a high-ball glass. She still wore her black skirt, this time with a black lace bra and nothing else. A shower had just ended in the bathroom, sending a mist of warm vapors into the remainder of the suite. "If that host was your friend, I'd hate to see your enemies," she said loudly.

"He must've been afraid of The Agency," Wallace responded from the bathroom. "But that's okay. I'll convict them so well in the court of public opinion they'll wish they'd never met your daughter."

"I just want her back safely," said Heidi.

"You'll have that and more," he assured her. "Do you have any idea what an abduction and impregnation could cost them? When I prove that

Clement Herzog held Josie against her will on more than one occasion and got her pregnant, especially if he raped her..."

"I don't want to hear this," Heidi said. She looked at the liquor and ice in her glass and mumbled, "Yesterday was her birthday."

Wallace came to stand in the doorway of the bathroom. He was naked and soaked, with soap suds trailing down his short, rotund body. "Trust me," he urged. "We'll get her back. And millions of dollars to boot."

The front door flew open and took a shattered frame with it. Two men, nearly three hundred pounds each, followed the momentum of their door-opening kicks to step into the room. They carried automatic weapons and moved aside so Pavlov could enter between them.

"Heidi, mother of Josie Ersman?" asked Pavlov. "Come here."

Heidi didn't know what to do and looked to her lawyer for guidance.

"Now wait," Wallace ordered. "Heidi, don't go any further. Who the hell..."

The giant man to Pavlov's right aimed his gun and squeezed the trigger, sending countless bullets into Wallace's body. The lawyer flailed about, and his blood hit Heidi in sprays and spurts. He finally fell back, hit the commode, and dropped like a sack on the wet floor. Heidi was too frightened to scream, but her body quivered. It looked as if half of her had been dipped in blood. Her wide eyed gaze shifted to Pavlov. With two fingers, he gestured for her to come forward.

GUY COTE

CHAPTER TWENTY-ONE

A small fire warmed Derek as Vanderhoff put the finishing touches on a lean-to made of branches, bark, and the linen strips once attached to the ironing board. The coverings stretched from the ground to a tree, not unlike the way a hypotenuse joins two sides of a triangle. The two men were surrounded by forest, and smoke from their fire hovered in a mid-air fog. The light of the day gradually gave way to the dark of night.

"I feel good," said Derek. "I don't know why. I...what did you do to me?"

"Nothing I hadn't done a dozen times before," Vanderhoff mumbled.

"Whatever it was, it was a miracle. The last thing I remember, I was dying."

"Well, you're not now," responded Vanderhoff. "But you need to dry or you'll freeze out here. I'm going to get some more firewood."

"You're wet too," observed Derek.

"I'm fine," said Vanderhoff as he walked off. The fire did need more fuel, but he mostly wanted to get away. He hated to be reminded of what he had done. To add time to someone's life was to bestow upon them a great deal of power. Experience had taught him that most people couldn't be trusted with even a slight amount of power. He thought back over the years to people he had known, some famous, most of them not. Each had shown him in their own way that people were inherently greedy, especially when it came to power. He knew now that the way he thought when he was King Charlemagne was wrong. One Great Man, no matter how well intentioned, could never be trusted with the welfare of others. That was why he opposed The Agency's plans to re-unify Europe under one government and one leader. It was also why he worried that he might have created monsters with both Derek and Kristina. Why did he have such a bleeding heart for suffering people? He cursed himself for it. The only thing he could think to do was to trivialize their healings and make them believe that nothing out of the ordinary had happened to them.

He returned to the lean-to with logs in his arms, only to find Derek stretching and running in place.

"I feel great," declared Derek. "I could take on the world."

Vanderhoff dropped the wood. He stared at Derek, with irritation building over what he had done. He finally said, "I should not have saved you."

***

Pavlov and his two huge assistants escorted Heidi into the study of Dr. Herzog's home. She was coated in her lawyer's dried blood. The room they entered was richly-appointed with hand carved furniture, bronze statues, and a mahogany shelf built around a wall-mounted television. The screen displayed an image locked in freeze-frame.

Dr. Herzog sat on the corner of his desk with a remote in his hand. "Do you know who I am?" he asked Heidi.

"An asshole, by the looks of it," she replied.

Dr. Herzog aimed his remote at the television and pressed a button. A home video montage played, showing Hans in happy times. He smiled like a child at Christmas as he caught a trophy marlin off the end of a boat. Dressed like a pastry chef, he removed a soufflé from an oven, drank wine, and winked at the camera. He rode on horseback and danced a waltz with an invisible partner. He ate a croissant and read a book on a couch. The video narrowed to a close-up of the smiling, relaxed man, then cut to him in a meat freezer with swollen, greenish-black flesh. His head was partially collapsed. The video lingered on that image. Then it switched to a shot of Josie in bed. She was lying in a position eerily similar to that of the dead, frozen body of Hans.

"Josie," exclaimed Heidi. "You have my Josie! You're Dr. Herzog."

"You're correct on one account, but I don't have your daughter," he said.

"Who does? Who's the man in the video?" she demanded.

"The man was Hans. He's dead," Dr. Herzog replied. "I rather hoped you could help me answer your other question."

"That's bullshit," she said. "You've got her here in this place."

"I assure you, I don't," he responded. "I want to find her as much as you do."

"Of course you do," snapped Heidi. "She's carrying your kid!"

"Not in the way you think," he answered. "Someday I hope to tell you the truth about your daughter's pregnancy, but right now we need to work together to get her back. The question is are you going to be a willing partner or a hostile one?"

After what seemed like an eternity, Heidi said, "I'd partner with the Devil himself if that's what it took to get my daughter back safely."

***

Vanderhoff's admitted regret over saving Derek's life caused a tension for the two men as they tried to share the lean-to. Derek left to wander the forest at night.

He fumed over Vanderhoff's comment for a long time, but his thoughts eventually turned to his near demise. He had survived, but he didn't know how, and the same could be said for Kristina's recovery. He wondered if Vanderhoff had discovered some mysterious drug. And where was Kristina now? He had a lot of questions and no answers, but the issue that bothered him the most was Josie. He knew The Agency had her. He hoped they weren't treating her harshly and tried hard not to think about what was happening to her at that moment. He longed to see her beautiful face again and tell her how sorry he was for failing to protect her. But there was more to it than that. Was he prepared to reveal how strongly he felt about her? How often he thought about her? He wasn't sure.

***

Derek didn't return to the lean-to until the early morning hours, and he was not alone. He was accompanied by a dead boar, which he dragged behind him.

Vanderhoff awoke and glanced at the kill. "You've been busy," he said.

"I had some extra energy," Derek replied. "I hope you like ham."

"What did you kill it with?" asked Vanderhoff.

"I made a spear," Derek replied. He looked at the boar's underbelly. "I don't know how we're going to clean it out, though. Maybe I can cut it with a sharp rock."

Vanderhoff extracted his folding knife from his pocket and tossed it to Derek.

Derek touched the blade to the dead animal's belly but didn't cut it. His mind was on something else. "Where do you think they're holding her?"

"I don't know," Vanderhoff admitted. "She's probably back underground."

"That's what I was thinking," said Derek. "How do we get in there? We had many more people with us last time, and we still failed."

"Maybe that was where we went wrong. Two can be covert. More cannot."

Derek lost himself in thought for nearly a minute. Then, in a sudden burst of energy, he stabbed the knife into the belly of the dead boar and made an incision that ran up to the breastbone. "The odds would be more in our favor if we had a hostage." He turned to Vanderhoff with his hands soaked in blood. "I know where Dr. Herzog lives."

***

Heidi despised Dr. Herzog, but she decided to tell him everything she knew about her daughter's disappearance. He was the best shot she had at retrieving Josie. Pavlov sat in the corner of the study, listening. The door opened and Yuri, one of Pavlov's huge assistants, entered with Kristina. Her face was cut and bruised.

"This young lady is Kristina Troy," Dr. Herzog told Heidi. "She's Derek's one-time girlfriend." To Kristina, he added, "What are you to Josie, I wonder."

He rose from the seat behind his desk and walked to the door. With some difficulty, Pavlov climbed to his feet and followed him. Stopping in the door jamb, Dr. Herzog said, "If the two of you can't come up with some useful information, I'll have to view you as excess. And I don't usually keep what I don't need."

Both Heidi and Kristina knew that a threat from Dr. Herzog was not an idle one. They exchanged glances as he and Pavlov left the room.

The two men didn't have far to walk before the other giant guard met them in the hall. Speaking with a Russian accent, he said, "Excuse. One man you look for has come here."

***

Dr. Herzog's sitting room was an offshoot of his living room. It housed leather sofas, a full-size chair with ottoman, an antique table, and fully stocked bookcases. Dr. Herzog sat on the chair. Once he was comfortable, Pavlov and the large Russian led Steve Cousins into the room.

Pavlov handed Dr. Herzog a pistol and said, "He was carrying this."

"Sit," Dr. Herzog told Steve while using the gun to gesture to one of the couches.

Steve took a seat and said, "I'm not sure if you know who I am, but..."

"I know who you are," replied Dr. Herzog. "Now why did you come here?"

"I have what you're looking for," Steve said. "Or should I say, I know where she is."

Dr. Herzog glanced at Pavlov. "Get the girls."

"What girls?" Steve asked.

Dr. Herzog inquired, "How is it that you come by this information?"

"I know people," Steve said. "But I want to talk to you about a finder's fee."

Dr. Herzog waited until he heard Pavlov, Yuri, and the women returning. Then he responded, "A finder's fee? For turning over your girlfriend?"

"She's not my girlfriend anymore," said Steve.

Spotting Steve, Heidi exclaimed, "You have Josie? You son of a bitch!"

Dr. Herzog watched with amusement as Heidi charged Steve and punched, cursed, clawed, and scratched at him. When Steve maneuvered into a position to defend himself, Dr. Herzog ordered the guards to stop the attack. One man pulled Heidi back, while the other sent a punch into Steve that made his forehead spew blood like guts expelled from a smashed tomato.

"If you lead me to her," said Dr. Herzog. "And she and the baby are unharmed, then I'll let you live. That will be your finder's fee."

"Uh...you can't kill me," said Steve. "In fact, you might already be in trouble for what you just did. My partner's got her. And he doesn't care if she lives or dies."

"You piece of shit!" exclaimed Heidi.

"What does he...what do you and your partner want?" asked Dr. Herzog.

"Did you see our video?" Steve asked while dabbing the wound on his forehead.

"Yes," replied Dr. Herzog.

"What video?" asked Heidi. "The one with the dead guy in it?"

Steve glanced at Heidi and said, "Our demands are simple. We want money. And we want you to clone Hans."

"What?" asked Heidi. To Dr. Herzog, she added, "What's he talking about?"

Dr. Herzog ignored her question. Steve's financial demand didn't surprise him, but his second requirement did.

"Listen jerk-off," said Heidi to Steve. "If you don't tell us where my daughter is, we'll rip you apart piece by piece."

Steve laughed. "Are you working with them now?"

"Yes," she answered.

He turned his attention back to Dr. Herzog. "Five million dol...uh, euro. Five million euro, payable to me. And you have to make a clone of Hans."

"What's this bullshit about clones?" demanded Heidi.

"They didn't tell you?" asked Steve. "I see how important you are to them."

Confused, Heidi looked from face to face, until Kristina revealed, "They treated your daughter like a lab rat. Josie's pregnant with a clone."

Heidi stared at her in perplexed silence. Finally, she said, "I don't believe it."

"Of course you don't," taunted Steve.

"You knew about this all along?" Heidi asked Steve.

"I wish," he replied. "I'd have ransomed her long ago if that was the case. No. My partner told me what's what."

Dr. Herzog interjected, "So you and...I assume your partner is Petra?" Steve nodded and Dr. Herzog said, "You want us to clone a man who's been dead for months."

"How are we to know you even have the pregnant girl?" inquired Pavlov.

"Well, there's the video, and..." He slid his hand into the crotch of his pants and withdrew a small white box. He set the box on the table and said, "Open it."

Dr. Herzog gestured for him to do it, so Steve slowly lifted the lid. Heidi leaned forward, as did Kristina and the Russian guards. A tiny cotton pillow sat within the box. It was stained dark red and the severed upper digit of a white pinkie finger rested upon it.

Heidi gasped. Kristina recoiled back.

"If you don't believe it's Josie's," said Steve, "you can check the DNA."

***

Steve didn't get any money. In fact, he left Dr. Herzog's residence with his life barely intact. The Russians beat him bloody. They chained him to a gurney, and without using anesthesia, slit his abdomen in two places. They made small arterial cuts inside his body which yielded a steady flow of blood into his stomach cavity. They then sealed his flesh wounds. If left untreated, the bleeding arteries would cause his death in ten hours. His blood fed into his abdomen like sand passing through an hourglass. It was Dr. Herzog's insurance policy to compel him to carry a message to Petra expediently.

Steve grew weaker with each passing moment, but Dr. Herzog didn't send him off on his own. Pavlov, the Russians, eight Interpol agents, twelve German police officers, and more than a dozen members of Dr. Herzog's personal security detail took him to a remote cabin where he was supposed to rendezvous with Petra. He was wired with a microphone and a miniature camera that fed Dr. Herzog's home computer. As his escort disappeared into the woods, Steve staggered toward the cabin.

***

The television in Dr. Herzog's study showed Steve's perspective as he entered the cabin. It was a simple, rustic building with an old couch, table, lamp, and ragged rug. Otherwise, it was empty. Steve's voice emanated from Dr. Herzog's television, saying, "He's...not...here. It's...no...not my...fault. You can't let...me...die...like this. Fix me up."

Dr. Herzog stepped around his desk and spoke directly into his computer. "You will deliver my message, or bleed to death in that cabin."

He pressed a button on the remote, and his television divided into six separate images that showed different views of the cabin as well as Steve's interior perspective. Heidi, Kristina, and three Interpol agents watched along with Dr. Herzog.

***

The cab driver who deposited Derek and Vanderhoff near Dr. Herzog's residence had no idea where he was taking them. The estate was surrounded by forest and locked up like a fortress. After creeping through the trees and disabling cameras, Derek and Vanderhoff were about to fill the guard house by the south entrance with an aerosol form of 3-Methylfentanyl, which they had acquired from one of Vanderhoff's black market contacts. To their surprise, the guard house was empty. Dr. Herzog had dispatched most of his security detail to serve as support for the operation at the cabin.

***

Steve was worried and anxious, but the loss of blood from his arteries made him weak. He dragged a chair from the kitchen to the center of the cabin and sat down. Each passing moment and trickle of blood into his abdominal cavity brought him nothing but deeper fears. If Petra was on his way, he seemed in no rush to get there.

***

Derek and Vanderhoff severed the wires of an alarm, picked three locks, and entered the estate through the south portico. They incapacitated a butler, a chef, and two guards at various intervals, and muffled and bound the hired help in different locations.

"This seems extraordinarily easy," Derek whispered as they approached a curving staircase which led to the upstairs bedrooms.

"Yes," Vanderhoff agreed. "Deceptively so."

Gingerly stepping on the first stair, they heard Dr. Herzog say, "Your complaints will do nothing but tell Petra we're monitoring you. Stop talking."

Vanderhoff gestured for Derek to follow him to the sound of the voice.

***

In the woods surrounding the cabin, Pavlov scrambled as quickly as his fragile hip would allow. He needed to get closer to the building in case Petra made a surprise appearance. Yuri and the rest of their team watched from various hiding places.

***

Holding a gun in each hand, Derek followed Vanderhoff to the study. The two men heard Heidi ask, "What if he doesn't show up?"

No one answered her question.

Heidi made another inquiry, "Are you really serious about this clone thing?"

"Yes, unfortunately," answered Kristina.

Derek's eyes shot wide as he recognized her voice immediately. He and Vanderhoff hid on each side of the jamb. They exchanged glances and nodded, ready to make their move in three, two, one...

"Come in, gentlemen," said Dr. Herzog. "I've been expecting you."

***

Steve could feel his hopes fading with his consciousness. He was at the point of no return. Even if Petra arrived and Steve was able to complete the task Dr. Herzog gave him, his survival would be in question. He had bled a lot, perhaps too much to make it.

***

Derek and Vanderhoff kept their guns raised as Dr. Herzog explained the ransom situation and showed them Josie's finger. Extreme anger, worry, and a haunting fear coursed through Derek's body.

"How do you expect to meet his demands?" Vanderhoff asked Dr. Herzog.

"I'll do it," announced Heidi. Everyone in the room turned to her. She added, "I'll give birth to the dead guy's clone if that's what it takes to get Josie back safely."

Dr. Herzog rushed to his computer to speak a message to Steve. "Did you hear that?" he asked. "You can tell him that her mother has agreed to bear the clone of Hans."

Camera feeds playing on the television showed a surprised expression cross Steve's otherwise droopy face.

"Tell him we will begin when Josie is returned safely to us," added Dr. Herzog.

"He'll never agree to that," observed Vanderhoff.

Everyone looked at the television to see Steve's reaction. He searched for the words to express his thoughts while fighting to stay awake and remain alive. "Tha...that sh...sh...should work," he managed to say. "Sh...she was a goo...good mother t...to J...Jos..."

Glass suddenly broke. Three of the television feeds showed a bullet strike Steve between the eyes and explode out the back of his head. He and the chair fell backward.

"Oh my God!" exclaimed Heidi.

GUY COTE

CHAPTER TWENTY-TWO

Dr. Herzog's study became the de facto control center for the frenzied activity that erupted around the cabin. Dr. Herzog conversed with an Interpol agent via cell phone, while another agent aimed his gun at Derek and Vanderhoff, who still held their guns. Heidi and Kristina watched as six feeds on the television showed authorities scouring the cabin and woods in search of Steve's killer.

"I can't believe he's dead," Heidi said. She hated him for what he was attempting to do to Josie, but she had known him for a long time. They'd celebrated Christmases together. He and Josie babysat Josie's siblings. He was a friend of hers before he ever took up with Josie. Now he was gone. She wondered how Josie would take the news.

"You should tell her who you are," Derek whispered to Vanderhoff.

Vanderhoff wondered which of his aliases Derek was referring to but soon realized the answer. He stepped closer to Heidi and said, "I'm Dante Caroli."

"You?" she asked. "You're...what do you have to do with Josie's disappearance?"

"I'm also Karl Vanderhoff," he added.

"Who?"

"I'm the person Josie's father came to see when he met you."

Heidi stared at him. "What the hell?" she said.

"My thoughts exactly," added Kristina.

"Me too," said Derek.

Dr. Herzog ended his call, and said, "I don't know what we'll do now. Steve was our only link to Petra."

"He'll contact you," Vanderhoff replied. "Josie's nothing but a means for him to get what he wants from you."

"Another clone," said Heidi.

"But you won't be able to fool him," added Vanderhoff. "You're really going to have to clone Hans. Can you do it?"

"We may not have to," Dr. Herzog replied. "I have a plan."

He moved closer to Derek and Vanderhoff and said, "The only condition is that enemies are going to have to work together." He extended his hand to Vanderhoff.

***

Though his mobility was limited and he had no formal rank in any law enforcement agency, Pavlov was in charge of the investigation. It was an unofficial activity. The authorities were searching the grounds around the cabin for two reasons—to rescue Josie and kill Petra.

A German police officer shouted, "*Ich fand das Gewehr!* (I found the gun!)"

Pavlov and others dropped what they were doing to approach a tree, upon which was mounted a remote controlled .44 caliber gun.

"*Hole es für mich* (Get it for me)," commanded Pavlov.

He knew that the range on a remote of that nature wasn't great, so Petra or someone working for him had to have been in the vicinity when they fired the weapon.

***

An underground bunker sat beneath a mound of vegetation, near the tree-mounted gun. On the surface, it looked like any other part of the forest, but it was a functional room ten feet below the earth. It contained cots, a desk, a lamp, and a computer bank powered by a silent generator. It had been modeled on The Agency's compound, though on a much smaller scale. Josie was tied to one of the cots. She was on her back and her belly extended like a mound beneath the blanket that covered her. Her face was swollen and flush. The pinkie finger on her right hand was bandaged and missing its upper digit.

"I gotta go to the bathroom," she said.

"Hold it," Petra said from his seat before the computers. He used one monitor to view activity on the surface while another received a feed from Dr. Herzog's computer.

"I can't," informed Josie. "The baby's pushing on my bladder."

"Then you'll piss your cot," he replied.

Josie narrowed her gaze on the back of Petra's head. She longed to see him dead, like Steve, who he had killed earlier. She saw it all go down and mourned in her own silent way. It wasn't enough to say that his death was a mixed blessing, though it was. He was a man with whom she had spent many formative years. He was also her violent abductor, the reason she was in her current predicament, and Derek's murderer. She glanced at her bandaged pinkie finger and her rage boiled. Refocusing on Petra, she said, "He led them right to you. Do you really think they won't find this little room?"

"That's why he's no longer breathing," replied Petra. "Fortunately, I expected that."

"You don't have much of a conscience, do you?"

"Never have," Petra admitted. "I dispatched your father without thinking twice about it."

"Why?"

"Orders."

"Whose orders?" she probed.

"We discussed this already," he said.

"No," she corrected. "We didn't."

"It doesn't matter now anyway," he answered. "Keep your mouth closed. I'm about to send a message."

"I'll scream until my voice runs out if you don't tell me what I want to know."

"This is a sound proof bunker," he replied.

"Maybe so," she conceded. "But I'll mess up your message."

"And I'll cut off another one of your fingers."

"I've got nine more," she snapped. "Tell me the truth. What are you afraid of?"

"We were ordered to do it by Clement Herzog," he said flatly.

"Why?"

"Michael Ersman was a threat to him," he told her. "He was popular with The Agency's directors and the common ranks."

"That's all?" Josie asked. "That's the reason he had him killed?"

"No," answered Petra. "Ersman was closely allied with Karl Vanderhoff, a man dedicated to destroying The Agency. I should know. I worked for him too."

Josie contemplated what she heard and asked, "Did your orders have anything to do with The Saint-Denis Manuscript...uh, a really old book?"

"Yes," he agreed. "He went to America to show it to Vanderhoff. Me and Hans were supposed to keep that from happening and to take out Ersman."

"But you failed, 'cause Vanderhoff got the book," said Josie.

"We got your father."

Josie's eyes again narrowed on Petra, but she said nothing. She wondered why Dr. Herzog tried to prevent her father from giving Vanderhoff the Saint-Denis Manuscript. Did it have to do with the clone? If they were planning way back then to make a clone of whoever was in Charlemagne's tomb, the Saint-Denis Manuscript would have put a stop to it. The Manuscript revealed that Pippin, not Charles the Great, was in the tomb, and who besides Dr. Herzog would have any interest in cloning a traitorous, deformed prince? It all made sense to her. "My poor dad," she whispered to herself.

***

Vanderhoff and Derek reached the same conclusion as Heidi when it came to partnering with The Agency. They would have to endure the alliance for Josie's sake.

Petra's voice spoke through Dr. Herzog's computer, causing everyone in the study to perk up. "You surprised me, Clement," said Petra. "And disappointed me."

Dr. Herzog pressed buttons on his keypad and the broadcast appeared on the television. It showed a close-up of Petra with someone in the darkness behind him.

"You should have returned my messenger without an escort," Petra scolded.

"You should not have taken the girl," replied Dr. Herzog.

"And you should not have killed Hans!" Petra shouted.

Vanderhoff scrambled around the desk to stand beside Dr. Herzog in the computer camera's view. "I understand your rage, son. I honestly do," he said. "You and Hans had something that is not easily replaced."

"Well, this is a treat," answered Petra. "I never would have thought to see the two of you side by side, unless you were in coffins."

Dr. Herzog didn't appreciate Vanderhoff's involvement but tried to focus on Petra. "Josie is in her last trimester," he said. "She needs medical care."

"Then you better address my demands right away," Petra responded.

"We will," Heidi declared to the television. "Just bring her back to us."

"Who is that?" asked Petra.

"It's my mother," Josie shouted from the darkness behind Petra. "Mom! You're there! I can't believe you're there."

"Of course I am, baby!" yelled Heidi. "Are you hurt? What did he do to you?"

Everyone watching the transmission saw Petra turn to tell Josie, "Not another word! Not one!" Returning to his audience, he said, "You'll find directions to a freezer in that box my messenger brought you. It has Hans in it, preserved for your procedure. The girl doesn't come back to you until I get his clone. Alive and healthy."

"She'll give birth before the next clone comes," explained Dr. Herzog.

"Then I'll be a babysitter with a gun until you deliver what I want," answered Petra. "I'll contact you in two days." He reached to turn off the transmission, but hesitated. "I also want the five million euro that was discussed."

He ended the transmission, leaving everyone in the room staring at screens that returned to the six picture feeds of people scouring the cabin and wilderness.

Turning to Vanderhoff, Dr. Herzog exclaimed, "That was great of you, simply superb. Now he knows that we're working together, and my plan is ruined."

"Yes. Your plan is," agreed Vanderhoff. "But mine isn't."

***

The Agency's subterranean compound was selected as the site in which they would attempt to clone Hans. Heidi and Kristina moved into Josie's former residence, and Derek and Vanderhoff settled into another set of rooms. Technicians readied the laboratory and scientists joined Dr. Herzog and Madeline, Josie's former doctor, as they extracted cells from Hans' frozen body. They gave Heidi gonadotropin, a drug which stimulated multiple follicles of a woman's ovaries, and human chorionic gonadotropin, which initiated ovulation. When Heidi's body was ready, they extracted some of her eggs, removed their DNA, and fused the empty eggs with DNA taken from Hans' cells. As with the previous clone, they had to stimulate the dormant DNA from the dead person's cells and wait for the fusion to develop into an embryo. It was a difficult procedure, with much potential for failure.

It became Pavlov's responsibility to communicate every development to Petra, as the kidnapper demanded constant updates. Dr. Herzog was uncomfortable about revealing so much of the procedure for fear that it might be used against The Agency when all was done. But Pavlov reassured him by explaining that every contact with Petra brought them that much closer to finding his whereabouts. The transmissions helped them set the trap that would eventually spring Josie.

It took five weeks to reach the embryonic stage of the cloning process and the optimal time for impregnation. In that period, Heidi and Kristina developed a bond that was based on mutual plight and a desire to save Josie. Heidi realized that her daughter was quite extraordinary, and it pained her to think that it took her twenty-three years and dire circumstances to come to that understanding.

The day which Dr. Herzog and his team selected to be Heidi's impregnation date was not the most optimal time, but Madeline assured them that Heidi's body would still be receptive to implantation. The patient entered the laboratory wearing a white robe. She climbed onto the table and placed her legs in the stirrups. Madeline raised Heidi's robe to expose her nakedness to more than a dozen people. It was an unnerving position for anyone to be in, even someone who made her living in the nude. To make matters worse, Pavlov operated a camera and focused it on her exposed vagina.

As Heidi waited for the procedure to begin, she was afflicted with a serious case of second thoughts. She doubted that she was ready to go through another pregnancy and wondered about the person they intended to clone. He was a criminal, she knew that much, and she would be the mother of his exact replica. She pulled her legs out of the stirrups.

"What are you doing?" asked Dr. Herzog.

"I can't do this," replied Heidi. "Turn off the camera."

"This is a live transmission," Pavlov replied.

"I don't give a shit!" snapped Heidi. "Shut it off."

The Russian looked at Dr. Herzog, who nodded his agreement with Heidi. Pavlov turned the camera on himself and explained to Petra that there would be a brief delay.

***

In a motel room nearly sixty miles from The Agency compound, Petra sat up in a double bed while Josie lay on her back in another. Her head was elevated by pillows. Her stomach was overly large, and her entire body was swollen. She was perspiring and terribly uncomfortable as both of her legs were shackled to the bed.

From a laptop computer sitting on the room's dormant television, they saw Pavlov's transmission come to an end.

"You better hope your mother changes her mind," said Petra.

Josie was conflicted. Her survival instincts screamed for Heidi to resume the procedure, but her better nature didn't want her mother to suffer for her.

***

Derek and Vanderhoff watched Heidi and Kristina huddle away from eavesdropping ears. "This doesn't surprise me," commented Derek. "Josie comes from poor stock on her mother's side. It's a miracle that she turned out as well as she did."

"No, it isn't," replied Vanderhoff. "I've always kept an eye on her."

"I know," observed Derek. "I've often wondered why."

"I owed it to Michael," Vanderhoff answered. "I feared her grandfather would lure her into The Agency, as he did Michael. Regrettably, I was right."

"You could have disposed of her grandfather," Derek replied.

"I'm not a murderer, despite what you may have heard."

"In the very least, you could have selected better guardians for her," Derek persisted.

"Is this a reproach?" Vanderhoff asked. "A child belongs with its mother. As for Steve, the weasel made Josie fall in love with him. There wasn't much I could do after that."

Derek nodded but said nothing more.

As people observed them, Heidi and Kristina continued their private talk. "I won't be able to change my mind and abort it," Heidi said.

"Probably not," Kristina agreed.

"The world's got enough wicked people in it without us making another one on purpose," Heidi added. "Can't we just pretend and make him think we did it?"

"You know we can't. He'd find out eventually and then he'd kill Josie."

"What am I supposed to do?" asked Heidi. "I don't want to get pregnant again. Why did I have to open my big mouth?"

"Because you love your daughter," Kristina responded.

"I do. Having that girl was the best thing I've ever done," Heidi admitted. "The best...oh, hell." She shook her head and turned to face Dr. Herzog and the scientists. "Okay. Let's do it," she said. To Kristina, she added, "Maybe it won't turn out so bad."

***

Petra and Josie watched the impregnation procedure from their respective beds. Pavlov's camera work chronicled the insertion of a lubricated speculum into Heidi's vagina. The close-up video showed the opening of the tool and the inside of Heidi. It was a sight Josie immediately wished she hadn't seen. Petra watched the video intensely, but there were no sexual thoughts on his part. He cared only about the procedure and intended to monitor it closely to avoid being duped by Dr. Herzog. The final phase of the implantation consisted of a plastic catheter entering through the speculum. It made its way to Heidi's cervix and deposited an embryo into her uterus.

The picture on the monitor panned across the laboratory and settled on Pavlov. He explained that the procedure was done, but it didn't guarantee a pregnancy.

Petra saw enough. He climbed out of bed and terminated the connection.

***

Sixty miles away, beneath the earth, a Welsh technician monitored the transmission to Petra. He turned to others and said, "He's logged off."

Derek asked, "Was he on long enough to determine his location?"

"I'm afraid not," the technician said. "He's actually quite savvy. He sends the transmission through a series of locations, maybe ten or fifteen of them."

"What?" asked Dr. Herzog. To Pavlov, he said, "You told me the data was going directly to Petra."

"That is what I was told," the Russian replied.

All heads turned to the Welshman. "Uh, technically, that's true. He's bouncing the transmissions off different networks, but he's the only one to access them."

"These networks are absorbing and retaining the images?" asked Dr. Herzog.

"In part, perhaps," admitted the technician.

"Are you able to give us any idea of their location?" probed Derek.

"I'm trying," answered the Welshman. "The best I have at this point is somewhere within ninety square kilometers."

Dr. Herzog was still focused on the open transmission of cloning secrets. "I want you to find out precisely what data has been absorbed by these networks."

"He must concentrate on finding Josie," Vanderhoff interjected.

"This is my operation," declared Dr. Herzog. "I'm not about to let the world know what we've done or how we did it!"

"That's why you'll ultimately fail," said Vanderhoff. "You try to do too much."

"He is not wrong," said Pavlov. "We must first get the girl back."

Dr. Herzog was like an angry tiger, but he took a moment to rein in his emotions. "You're right," he admitted. To Vanderhoff, he added, "Thank you for that perspective."

***

Three days later, Petra received an email from Dr. Herzog that simply said, *Heidi's pregnancy is confirmed. See attachment. We are fulfilling our part of the arrangement. Now you must do the same. Josie is due at any moment, and she must have medical care. Bring her in before it is too late. Clement.*

Petra glanced at Josie, who was lying in bed as she had been doing for over a month. He knew that she would be giving birth soon, and he had no idea how he would handle it. But the girl and her baby were his only bargaining chips. He typed, *Not yet,* and sent his short response to Dr. Herzog's email.

Being so close to Petra for so long gave Josie insight into his thoughts and behavior. She knew that he had communicated something to Dr. Herzog, and she could tell that her pregnancy left him confused about what to do with her. Capitalizing on these weaknesses, she waited until he was deep asleep, and poured a glass of water over her panties and pelvic area. She hid the cup on the far side of the bed, and used her teeth to rip enough skin from her hand to cause bleeding. After smearing the blood around the water-soaked area, she screamed, "Oh, my God! Wake up. Wake up!"

Petra sat up in bed and grabbed the gun from his nightstand. "What?" he exclaimed. "What happened?" He turned on the light.

"My water broke," Josie said. She pulled the blankets back to show him.

Petra saw that the area where the baby would come out was soaked with a fluid that was mixed with blood. "What does this mean?" he asked.

"It means the baby's coming," Josie replied. She wanted to add the word "stupid" to the end of her response, but thought it would be best not to provoke him unnecessarily.

"All right...how...uh, how much time do we have?"

"Not much," she answered. "I gotta get to a doctor. Or you'll have to deliver it. Do you know what to do?"

"No!" he exclaimed. "Can you slow down, or hold it, or..."

"Are you serious?" she replied. "I thought you had a plan."

"I didn't expect it to happen this soon," he admitted. "I have a doctor I was going to bring you to, but he's in Japan right now. He'll be back in four days."

"The baby's gonna be born before that," said Josie.

"I...I can call him," replied Petra. He grabbed his phone and searched for the doctor's number but stopped when he saw her bleeding palm and noticed that the glass was missing from her nightstand. He lowered the phone. "That was good," he said. "Convincing."

"What are you talking about?"

He grabbed her bleeding hand and raised it.

Her ruse had failed. She opened her mouth to speak, but a sudden movement jarred her abdomen. It was unlike any of the other "kicks" she had experienced. She felt something pass out of her body and saturate her underwear. "Oh God," she exclaimed. She pulled her hand away from Petra's and reached into her underwear. This was for real! She felt a slimy substance coming out of her. "Get me to a doctor now!"

"I don't think so," he calmly replied.

Josie grabbed his hand and slapped a lump of brownish red mucus into his palm.

***

Petra was pale as his foot buried the gas pedal of a 2011 Smart microcar. He acquired the car several weeks earlier, thinking that it would work to his advantage. What law enforcement officer would suspect a fugitive and his prisoner of using a three cylinder microcar as a getaway vehicle? As he taxed the machine's engine and raced it over a desolate road, however, he regretted his decision, and so did Josie. The car was too slow and too small for a late-term pregnant woman to utilize.

"If you run or do anything desperate," said Petra. "I'll shoot you dead."

"Do I look like I can run?" Josie asked.

"All right," he agreed. "This will be a simple exchange; you for your mother."

"What will you do with her?" she probed.

"That's not your concern."

"She's my mother," Josie exclaimed.

"Didn't you steal from her? And she tried to kidnap you?" he asked. "I think your file said she was a prostitute or something."

"Don't talk about her like that!" she yelled and cuffed him across the jaw.

The steering wheel jerked in his hands, causing the car to swerve sharply. Petra quickly brought the vehicle under control and slammed Josie in the face. She felt cartilage shatter in her nose. Blood splattered and her eyes instantly swelled with tears. She cupped both hands over her nose. There was no doubt that it was broken.

***

The Agency's control center was overcrowded with agitated, active people. Every computer was manned. Pavlov, Dr. Herzog, and Interpol agents scoured maps and the global positioning imagery displayed on two large screens.

Vanderhoff and Derek stood in a nearby corridor. Pavlov's two Russians watched them from a distance. "You said you had a plan," Derek whispered. "What is it?"

"It's irrelevant now," Vanderhoff admitted. "You and I were going to contact Petra and convince him that The Agency was staging Heidi's pregnancy."

"I don't see how that would've worked," Derek said.

"Well, it doesn't matter," answered Vanderhoff. "We need to get to Josie before this exchange is made."

"You can bet Dr. Herzog will line every route to the exchange site with police."

"Yes," Vanderhoff agreed. "But you can also expect that Petra has something more than just a straight prisoner exchange in mind."

"I think Josie will have something else in mind too," said Derek.

***

Josie stuffed fabric torn from her shirt into her nostrils to stop the bleeding. Her face throbbed, and her eyes repeatedly filled with tears. She trembled in pain and anger.

Petra ignored the condition of his captive and kept his gaze fixed on the dark road ahead of him. He saw a set of headlights round a corner and speed toward him in the opposite lane. He noticed another set following the first. It was the police, he realized.

Josie saw that Petra was nervous about the approaching cars. Her mind flashed back to the swerve their car made when she struck him. That's it, she thought. The first police car was twenty feet away and approaching rapidly. She had no time to lose. She shoved the steering wheel to the left, and Petra jerked it sharply back to the right.

281

The microcar swerved erratically before the first police car, nearly running it off the road. The second vehicle skidded and swayed to avoid the mini-car.

Inside the Smart car, Petra punched Josie's nose again. She screamed as fabric flew from her nostrils and blood flowed like a faucet after it. Looking in the rear view mirror, Petra saw both police cars make skidding U-turns. Their lights and sirens sprang to life. He pressed the gas pedal to the floor, but his car couldn't outrun the police. He pumped the pedal, trying to get his microcar to move faster.

One of the police cars pulled alongside the Smart car and the other rode close to its bumper. "*Halt das Auto an* (Stop the car)," ordered the driver of the first car through his external speakers.

"You can't beat 'em," Josie said.

Petra didn't need her to state the obvious. Left with few options, he slowed the microcar down and coasted it to the side of the road. The police matched his speed, and the three vehicles came to their respective stops. One police car parked in front of the Smart car, and the other was behind it.

Petra aimed his pistol at Josie's abdomen and ordered, "Don't do a thing."

A policeman ordered, "*Heben Sie Ihre Hände hoch und kommen Sie aus dem Auto raus! Beide von Ihnen* (Put your hands in the air and step out of the car! Both of you!)"

Petra replied, "*Ich werde die Geisel töten, wenn du näher kommst!* (I'm going to kill the hostage if you come near!)"

Josie was afraid he would pull the trigger, but she could see that he was distracted by the police. She discreetly disconnected her seatbelt and slid her hand around her door handle.

Petra maneuvered his mirror to watch the officer behind him. The man hid behind his open car door and aimed his gun. "They don't think I'll shoot you," he told Josie. He saw that she was opening her door and lunged to close it. The first officer fired his gun. The windshield shattered, and the bullet barely missed Petra.

Petra fired four retaliatory shots, and every one hit its mark. Struck in the face, chest, and twice in the throat, the policeman in front of them collapsed onto his car. Josie threw herself out of the microcar and Petra shot at her, as she kicked the door closed.

The first policeman collapsed and the second opened fire through the Smart car's rear window. Glass shattered and bullets assaulted the vehicle. Petra fired back.

Josie scrambled to her feet. Her excess weight threw her off balance, and she stumbled into a forest. It was an hour before dawn, and the light enabled her to make out the shapes of trees and logs. She tried not to trip as branches stabbed her. One limb slapped her broken nose. She recoiled from the pain but stayed silent. Her legs were heavy, and gravity pulled her forward, causing her to lean back and clutch her belly.

A gunshot suddenly rocked the forest, and a bullet spit bark and splinters from a nearby tree. Josie looked back and saw through the water of her eyes that Petra was entering the woods after her.

"Stop," he ordered, "or I'll shoot you dead right here!"

She looked frantically about and saw that she was on a ridge with a sleepy village below her. She hurried down the slope, toward the settlement.

Petra won the gunfight with the police, but his victory came at a price. He had a bullet in his shoulder, and another passed through his left lung. He staggered through the trees with his eyes locked on Josie.

Her legs shuffled to keep their balance as she descended the last of the slope and scrambled past a clapboard house. Petra hobbled after her but paused to gasp for breath. When he looked up, he saw her hurrying toward the village store.

A white bread truck was parked in front of the store. Its two rear doors were open, and its driver wheeled a hand cart full of crated deliveries into the market.

Josie was tortured by pains but strode toward the truck, knowing it could be her only hope. The baby within her suddenly made a discernible shift into her lower pelvis, and she stopped running. "Oh my God!" she screamed and buckled over. Liquid poured from her crotch and saturated her tan, loose-fitting pants. Looking up, she saw the driver of the bread truck exit the store with an empty hand cart. "Help! Help me!" she cried.

The driver was shocked to see a pregnant woman in agony. He was even more surprised to see a man running after her with a gun in his hand. Petra fired his pistol, and the bullet shattered a light on the rear of the truck. Startled, the driver ran around his vehicle, climbed into the truck, and started the engine with a roar of ignition.

"No," Josie pleaded. "Wait!" She staggered after the truck, but it was no use. She floundered and collapsed to the ground.

The bread truck's tires squealed and kicked up smoke, but they were spinning in reverse. The vehicle raced backward. For a moment, Josie thought it would run her over, but its tires locked up and brought the truck to a screeching halt two feet from her face.

The driver rushed to help Josie as another gunshot ricocheted off the truck's bumper. Josie allowed the stranger to guide her into the back of the truck.

Petra fired again and the shot hit the driver's hand as he closed the back doors. He screamed but scurried into the truck. He shifted it into gear and gunned the engine.

Petra took aim again, but it was pointless to fire. He leaned forward and gasped for breath, his forearms on his knees and his eyes on the retreating bread truck.

CHAPTER TWENTY-THREE

It seemed that everyone in The Agency's command center was running on adrenaline, caffeine, or nicotine. Messengers scrambled frantically about and technicians double-checked one another's reports. Pavlov hobbled up to Dr. Herzog with a British technician in tow. "Tell Dr. Herzog what you have," he ordered.

The technician stammered, "It...uh... appears...uh..."

"Quit your stuttering and spit it out," ordered Dr. Herzog. "What is it?"

Impatient, Pavlov tore a paper from the technician's hand and read, "Dispatch Six for Aachen District reports gun shots in Walheim. Dispatch Seven says there was a gun fight and there are two dead police on Schleidener Strasse outside of Walheim."

Derek and Vanderhoff remained in the corridor outside the command center and listened as Dr. Herzog asked, "No other bodies? Just the two police?"

Derek muttered, "He sure cares about the lives of his men, doesn't he? It's a wonder anyone follows him, my former self included."

Vanderhoff glanced at his associate, but said nothing. He watched the Lord Mayor of Aachen walk by as if they'd never met and enter the command center.

***

The sun was beginning its morning ascent as the bread truck raced over a paved lot outside University Hospital Aachen. The massive lot surrounded a medical facility that resembled an oil refinery with rectangular towers extending from its roof and huge gray and yellow striped pipes running into and out of its structure. An ambulance swerved to allow the bread truck to skid to a halt before the hospital's red frame entrance.

The driver hurried out of his vehicle. His wounded hand was wrapped in a bloody rag, but it didn't deter him from opening the truck's back doors. He found Josie sprawled on a pile of bread. Her pants were soaked with clear liquid and blood. Her hands cupped the backs of her legs as she inhaled and exhaled rapid breaths. The driver yelled, "*Hilfe! Hilfe! Beeilen Sie sich!* (Help! Help! Hurry!)"

A nurse and an orderly rushed out of the hospital with a wheelchair to meet Josie as she exited the truck. "Where am I?" she asked them.

The driver guessed at her question and replied, "*Krankenhaus* (Hospital)."

Josie realized that she was at a hospital and hoped it wasn't affiliated with The Agency. But the pressures in her pelvis wouldn't let her linger on those thoughts for too long. She sat in the chair and let the orderly wheel her into their facility.

The emergency room was a hub of activity despite the early morning hour. It had eight stations manned by professionals who asked questions of patients while typing on computers. The orderly deposited Josie in the short term waiting area while her nurse spoke to a receptionist.

A powerful cramp gripped Josie's pelvic area like a vice. She squeezed her eyes shut, a move which agitated her broken nose. It was as if she was having a severe menstrual cramp, worse than she ever had before, and it lasted for nearly a minute. When the pain subsided, she opened her eyes and saw a very pregnant woman sitting in a nearby wheelchair. The woman spoke to her in German, and Josie responded, "English?"

The lady shook her head, and her husband, a man with a Scottish accent, said, "She asked, 'how far apart are your contractions?'"

"Uh...I don't know," she replied.

The husband didn't translate for his wife right away. He waited for her contraction to pass and told her what Josie said.

"Do you know if you'll be having a boy or a girl?" Josie asked.

"No," the husband answered. "We want to be surprised. Do you know?"

"Yeah," Josie said. Another contraction seized her lower body. She could feel it constricting her insides and pushing them downward. Her lower back ached, and the contraction seemed to last longer than the previous one. When she was again able to open her eyes, she saw an orderly wheeling the other pregnant woman away.

Before following his wife, the husband told Josie, "We wish you good luck."

"Wait," Josie said. "What are your names?"

"We are Jason and Greta Blackburn," he replied. "And you?"

"Josie," she answered. "Just Josie."

With a smile, Jason Blackburn said, "Perhaps we will cross paths again." And he hurried to catch up to his wife.

Josie watched the couple and their attendants depart. Pleasant sensations washed over her as she imagined the loving family the Blackburns were creating. It was something she frequently imagined for herself but knew she wasn't destined to have.

In an attempt to avoid giving personal information which would allow her enemies to find her, Josie feigned a contraction when her nurse came up to her with questionnaires. She didn't have to pretend for long. A real labor pain hit her, and she nearly fell out of the chair. The nurse hastily wheeled her into an elevator.

The bread truck driver and a two hundred and sixty pound security guard watched the elevator door close behind Josie. "*Ich denke, der Mann mit dem Gewehr ist hinter uns* (I think the man with the gun is behind us)," the driver said.

The guard nodded and replied, "*Ich werde sie schützen* (I will protect her)."

In the hospital's birthing unit, Josie's nurse handed her off to another nurse, who pushed the patient's wheelchair into a private room. She asked Josie questions, but they were all in German and, as such, received no reply. Frustrated, the nurse stepped into the corridor and called for help. She returned to the room and handed Josie a hospital gown.

Josie accepted the offering. She climbed out of the chair, but an excruciating pain caused her to buckle over. Her body felt as if it was splitting from the inside out. "Ahhh," she cried and dropped to her knees on the green floor.

***

Petra teetered as he drove the scooter he acquired after Josie made her escape. He had lost a lot of blood and wheezed through his punctured lung. He struggled to resist fatigue but was still able to focus on his objective of reacquiring Josie. Using logic and deduction, he guessed that the delivery man would bring her to University Hospital Aachen. When he saw the bread truck sitting in front of the hospital's emergency entrance, he knew that his reasoning hadn't failed him. He abandoned his scooter and made every effort to appear composed as he walked into the giant building.

***

As busy people rushed about the command center, the Lord Mayor of Aachen noticed that one of the computers had a peculiar blurb hidden among regional updates. Posted in German, it was translated as *admitted to University Hospital Aachen thirty-one minutes ago, an unidentified English speaking woman in labor and appearing to be in her early twenties. Patient was found in Walheim, Aachen District, pursued by a man with a gun.*

Making a snap decision, the Lord Mayor etched a note on a scrap of paper and walked casually into the hall. Pretending not to see Vanderhoff, he nearly collided with him and slipped the paper into his hand. *"Oh, entschuldigen Sie* (Oh, excuse me)," he said. He walked past the two large Russians who were watching Derek and Vanderhoff. The Lord Mayor continued down the corridor and Vanderhoff discreetly read the note.

***

Josie was in a bed with her legs spread, a tube running out of her arm, and her gown folded back onto her belly. A male doctor in his late-forties, wearing scrubs, gloves, and a surgical mask, peered between her legs while her nurse used a stethoscope to listen to the baby. A younger, English-speaking nurse dabbed Josie's forehead with a wet sponge. The doctor spoke in German, and the younger nurse translated, "You are five centimeters dilated. He does not think he can perform a...uh...how do you say in English...uh, epis...episi...he does not believe he should perform the surgery to make wider your vagina before the birth."

"How many centimeters do I need to get to?" Josie asked.

"You will be dilated in full at ten centimeters," the nurse told her.

"I still have five to go," Josie replied as a way of saying that he had time to perform the surgery, but another contraction hit her and she grabbed the rails of the bed.

"You are contracting too quickly for the surgery to be done," said the nurse.

No epidural. No drugs. No surgery to make the birth easier. Josie was going to have to do it the old fashioned way, the way Pippin the Hunchback was originally born. As she cried out in pain, the door to her room opened slowly. A man with Mediterranean skin entered. He wore an overcoat and a surgical mask. A stethoscope dangled from his neck, and he held a clipboard. He stayed out of the way, unnoticed.

***

Despite the alliance they made with Dr. Herzog, Derek and Vanderhoff had no illusions over what their "partner" would do once the clone was born. He would use his considerable resources to eliminate any rivals he had for the child's affection, especially its mother. Therefore, they had no qualms about dissolving their association with The Agency's leader, and they made sure that he was not informed of their decision. They crept out of the compound, "borrowed" a vehicle, and subsequently abandoned it. Using the Lord Mayor's note as their guide, they took three different cabs in a hard to follow route to University Hospital Aachen. They kept their guns concealed on their persons and entered the hospital in search of Josie.

The first room they entered was Greta Blackburn's, and they walked in as a baby emerged from between her legs. A nurse exclaimed, "*Es ist ein Junge!* (It's a boy!)"

Another nurse and Jason Blackburn looked at the intruders.

"*Oh...uh...verzeihen Sie uns* (Oh...uh...forgive us)," stammered Vanderhoff, and he pulled Derek out of the room.

In the corridor, Derek exclaimed, "We can't do that again."

Further down the hall, Vanderhoff saw a guard standing outside another delivery room. "That's it," he realized.

***

The man with the mask and overcoat stood in the back of Josie's room, jotting notes in his clipboard. Because the patient refused to give her name, everyone assumed that he was an administrator of some kind. If they had taken time to look closer, they would have seen a patch of red seeping through the chest area of his white coat.

He turned sharply as he heard something slam the door and make a thud on the floor of the outside hallway. The door suddenly flew open and Vanderhoff entered. The man reached for the weapon he had concealed beneath his coat.

Vanderhoff scanned the room, appraising the situation. He saw two nurses and a doctor, who peered between Josie's legs as she screamed in pain. In his peripheral view, he noticed that the mysterious man with the clipboard was reaching into his overcoat. He turned to face the man and saw a patch of blood on his coat of white.

Derek barged into the room after Vanderhoff and charged up to Josie. The younger nurse tried to stop him but couldn't.

Josie's eyes flashed wide at the sight of Derek. "You're alive!" she exclaimed, but another pain seized her from within. She screamed, feeling that her pelvis was about to burst open.

The doctor spoke in German, and the younger nurse translated, "Who are you?"

"We are frie...we're here for her," answered Derek. "How're you doing, Josie?"

A gunshot exploded and everyone, including Josie, saw the man in the overcoat stumble with a fresh wound in his chest. He fell to his knees. Vanderhoff fired a second shot and the man's head splattered blood, bone, and flesh onto the dull, white wall of the hospital room.

The nurses screamed, the doctor fell backward, and Derek looked surprised.

"That was Petra," said Vanderhoff, as he thrust a chair beneath the door's handle.

Derek checked the victim's face, but the gunshot made it unrecognizable. "Are you sure?"

Josie screamed as muscles in her pelvis forced the baby's head into the birth canal. She felt pressure on her rectum, and her vagina burned as if it was on fire. She pushed as hard as she could, but no one helped her. "Ahh...it's coming!" she shouted. "Why isn't anyone down there? Somebody get down there!"

The nurses and doctor were frozen with fear. Derek yelled, "Deliver the baby!"

Still, no one moved, until Derek pointed his gun at the doctor and commanded, "Take care of her! Now!"

Vanderhoff heard shouting outside the room. The handle turned and fists pounded on the door. The propped chair held it in place but not for long. "You have to hurry, Josie," he said.

Josie gave him a glare of pure rebuke. The baby was lodged in her normally narrow cervix, just waiting. Another contraction hit, and she screamed. She could feel her flesh ripping apart. Blood and amniotic fluid seeped out of her. The nerves between her thighs roared in agony, as if they had been set ablaze.

Reaching and peering into Josie's opening chasm, the doctor said, *"Der Kopf ist unter dem Schambogen!* (The head is below the pubic arch!)"

Vanderhoff wanted to see the clone of his son enter the world, but he knew he had to keep others from barging into the room. He dragged a heavy dresser before the door.

"Ahh," Josie gasped. She pushed, ignoring the gross and normally embarrassing sounds which emanated from her pelvic area. The cone-shaped head of her child emerged from within her, and the doctor guided it out.

The younger nurse said, "The baby is...crown...making a crown!"

"Crowning," Derek exclaimed. "It's coming, Josie. Just a little more."

The muscles in Josie's arms were rock solid as she squeezed the bed rails. Her face strained with such intensity that her nose bled again. More of the flesh between her legs ripped as the baby's head fully emerged. The older nurse handed the doctor a plastic suction bulb. He used the device to remove mucus from the infant's airways. The baby's neck and shoulders followed its head, a birth lubricated by blood and other liquids.

"I can see him," Derek declared.

Though she was in horrific pain, Josie knew that she didn't want Derek to see the baby come out of her. She yelled, "Get up by my head! By my head!"

The doctor guided the glistening baby into the world. It was a boy! The umbilical cord ran from the child's abdomen to the now-empty womb, like a lifeline for him to find his way back home. The doctor removed more mucus from the infant's mouth, but it didn't cry. The nurses exchanged worried glances.

Two gunshots suddenly shattered a window, and three men on the outside catwalk ran away from the room. Everyone but Vanderhoff startled, and the baby wailed.

Vanderhoff watched the catwalk for more danger. He slowly lowered his gun and looked around the room at angry faces. "We had company," he explained.

The doctor and older nurse reprimanded him in rapid-fire German while the younger nurse covered the newborn with a towel and said, "Cold air kills babies!"

Josie ignored the shattered window, the chill, and everyone but her crying child. She tried to reach for it, but her pain prevented her from moving too much.

Vanderhoff ignored the voices to gaze upon the clone of his first-born child. The infant was full of life with strong lungs and a loud cry.

He had a full head of wet, black hair. He couldn't tell if the babe's back was hunched or not, but he didn't care. The boy was a miracle, brought back to his father twelve centuries after he had originally died.

***

The black Bentley joined nine police and Interpol vehicles as they arrived at University Hospital Aachen. Officers charged into the facility with little regard for patients and staff. The Lord Mayor exited the Bentley with Dr. Herzog, Pavlov, and the two large Russians. He had given Dr. Herzog the intelligence about Josie's location after secretly passing it to Vanderhoff. He didn't want to but felt it was the only way to prevent Dr. Herzog from discovering his true loyalties. As the others rushed into the hospital, he lagged behind to type a quick warning text on his phone.

***

The baby cried on Josie's chest, as people outside the room attacked the door with voices and fists. Derek hovered over mother and child like a vigilant guardian, his gun ready for action. Josie's face bore an expression that was both elation and exhaustion. The realization that she had given the infant life filled her with pride. It made all the pain she had endured worthwhile, and a love that she had never experienced before welled within her.

"Pip," she said to the baby. "I'll name you Pip. Pip Michael Ersman."

Derek said, "That's a perfect name, Josie."

"We need to check his eyes, his muscle structure," informed the younger nurse. "We have to weigh him and clip the rest of the cord."

Josie gave Pip to the nurse and watched her carry him to a plastic tub that sat on a scale. She glanced at Vanderhoff and could see the man's ancient eyes become misty. He was Charlemagne, she reminded herself, her child's original father. Turning to the nurse, she said, "Let him cut the cord."

The younger nurse translated Josie's command for her co-workers.

Reluctantly, the doctor handed Vanderhoff a pair of scissors. He wanted nothing more than to push the old man through the window he had broken with his bullets, but his profession obliged him to save lives, not take them. Furthermore, he knew he would have to sacrifice his own life in order to end the old man's.

Stepping toward the baby, Vanderhoff accepted the snips and reached for the remaining eight inches of umbilical cord. Like any proud mother, Josie watched her baby's father cut the last of the cord that had once connected the infant to her. An annoying beep in Vanderhoff's pocket brought the tender moment to a close. He checked the message on his phone and declared, "They're here."

"Who?" Josie asked.

"Dr. Herzog and his crew," Derek answered.

"Can't I ever get a break?" Josie asked. She pulled the tube from her arm and tried to climb out of bed, but she was far too weak to even sit up. The doctor, both nurses, and Derek quickly restrained her.

***

A taxi stopped in front of the hospital, and Heidi and Kristina scrambled out of it. When they were at the compound, no one told them anything that was going on. A frenzy of activity, however, raised their suspicions, and Heidi employed her seductive powers to glean information from a low-level technician.

The two women charged into the building with their thoughts on Josie.

***

Vanderhoff and Derek worked feverishly to drag the furniture away from the door. As they labored, the doctor looked at the dead body on the floor and saw what appeared to be a gun inside the man's bloody coat. He stepped cautiously toward it.

"The doctor," warned Josie.

Vanderhoff saw the doctor approaching Petra's body. He aimed his gun at him and said, "*Machen Sie keinen Schritt weiter* (Do not take a step further)." Turning to Derek, he commanded, "Get the child."

"You're not taking my baby," declared Josie.

"It's the only way to keep him safe," Vanderhoff explained. "We must hurry."

"He's right," Derek reassured her. "It's the only way."

Josie didn't know what to do until Derek stepped closer to her. Their eyes searched one another's. He leaned forward and kissed her gently on the forehead.

"I'll die before I let anything happen to him or you," he said.

GUY COTE

CHAPTER TWENTY-FOUR

Hospital employees stumbled back as the door to Josie's room opened and her doctor exited with a gun pressed against his head. Vanderhoff held the pistol and matched the doctor step for step. A cart followed with a tub and the baby upon it. It was pushed by Derek, who aimed his gun at the younger nurse as she walked beside him.

"*Macht Platz. Macht Platz* (Make way. Make way)," Vanderhoff directed the crowd. "*Oder der Arzt stirbt!* (Or the doctor dies!)"

Derek noticed a patch of red on the bottom of the baby's right foot. Was it dried blood? He tried to rub it away, but it didn't diminish or change at all. It was a birthmark. How strange, he thought. Did Pippin the Hunchback also have that mark?

Vanderhoff saw the door to the Blackburn's room creep open, and a gray-haired nurse peered out with a baby in a tub on a cart beside her. He then saw Dr. Herzog, Pavlov, the Lord Mayor, and an army of officers enter the birthing center. "We have to change our plans," he told Derek. "Take Baby Pip to the nursery."

"Where's that?" asked Derek.

"Do it!" Vanderhoff ordered. "Now!"

Derek and the nurse saw Dr. Herzog approach with men who had their weapons drawn. "I know where the nursery is," said the nurse.

Police and other officials peppered hospital employees with questions, and several nurses pointed in the direction of Josie's room.

Vanderhoff guided his hostage to the Blackburn's room. When he reached the door, he threw the doctor aside and grabbed the cart with the tub and the Blackburn's baby lying upon it. He heard a chorus of screams but ignored them to push the newborn toward the birthing center's exit. He feigned shock when he saw Dr. Herzog and his men and quickly reversed direction.

"There!" shouted Dr. Herzog while pointing at Vanderhoff.

Jason Blackburn charged out of his room, followed by the gray-haired nurse. They met Vanderhoff and the baby as they neared an emergency exit.

"Give me my baby!" Jason yelled.

Gun in hand, Vanderhoff turned to Jason and quietly said, "No harm will come to you or your child. I need to borrow him for a moment."

"Drop the gun, Karl," commanded Dr. Herzog. He and his entourage quickly surrounded Vanderhoff and aimed powerful weapons at him.

"Thank God!" exclaimed Jason. "This man stole our baby."

Dr. Herzog ignored everyone except Vanderhoff and the infant. Pavlov, however, found what Jason said to be of great interest.

Gazing at the child, Dr. Herzog approached the tub. "You lost, Karl," he said.

Vanderhoff suddenly thrust the muzzle of his pistol beneath Dr. Herzog's jaw. "I might lose," he replied, "but you won't live to see it."

With the two old men in a stand-off and the police swarming them with guns, Pavlov asked Jason Blackburn to explain what he said moments before. Jason repeated his claim about his stolen son, and the doctor who delivered Pip corroborated his tale. He added that the baby they were looking for was in the nursery. Pavlov grabbed an officer and said, *"Erist im Kinderzimmer! Beeilen Sie sich!* (He is in the nursery! Hurry up!)"

***

Derek waited for the young nurse to clear the nursery of adults and prepare a crib that would blend in with the twenty others that filled the room. Babies of different sizes and races were dressed in white outfits with blue or pink caps to distinguish their genders. Each baby had an identification bracelet on its wrist, and Derek realized that Pip had neither a cap, nor a bracelet. He was about to steal the items from another infant, when the nurse arrived with a blue cap and a bracelet that had been worn and discarded. She fit them onto Pip, and Derek carried the child to a crib. With Pip safely ensconced in a tub on a crib in a room full of babies, Derek allowed himself to take a relieved breath.

***

Heidi and Kristina emerged from an elevator and stopped as they saw two armed men guarding the entrance to the birthing center.

"Do you think we're too late?" asked Kristina.

"Let's hope not," Heidi replied. She led Kristina up to the guards but froze when she saw Vanderhoff, Dr. Herzog, and men with guns surrounding a baby cart. "My grandson!" she exclaimed. Fueled by maternal instinct, she thrust her knee into the groin of the nearest guard. He yelled and buckled over, causing his gun to fire.

The shot spooked an officer and his gun went off, striking Vanderhoff in his right, pistol-holding arm. Vanderhoff's gun arm dropped to the left, and he fired a shot at point-blank range into Dr. Herzog's clavicle. The doctor roared out in pain. Blood burst from his collar and saturated baby Blackburn, whose feet were kicking in the air.

The birthing center erupted into mayhem as artillery flew from the weapons of Russians, police, and Interpol agents. Their automatic guns filled Vanderhoff with bullets, and he shook with every impact. Screaming hospital employees dropped to the floor, while Jason Blackburn protected his baby by laying over it. Vanderhoff's gyrating body collapsed into a bloody heap, twitching and quivering.

Heidi ignored all danger to run up to the massacre site. "Oh my God!" she exclaimed, and pushed Jason Blackburn aside to grab the baby.

"Give me my son!" Jason yelled and tried to take the child.

"He's my grandson," Heidi shot back and jerked the infant away from him.

"Hand me the child," Dr. Herzog commanded. His order was followed by eight guns, which were turned on Heidi. Reluctantly, she gave him the baby. Dr. Herzog's right arm dangled lifelessly. He cradled the child in his left and asked Jason, "Why do you think this baby is yours?"

"Because that man," he said, pointing at Vanderhoff, "took him from our room."

As Dr. Herzog pondered Jason's claim, more of his flowing blood soaked the baby. The doctor who delivered Pip repeated what he had told Pavlov, and Dr. Herzog gradually realized that the baby he held had no value to him.

***

"The man my friend killed in the delivery room was a murderer," Derek told the young nurse. He wanted her to understand who the true villains were. "He came to kill the child's mother and steal her baby," he added. "He would've killed the rest of us too."

"Be quiet," the nurse said. "There is someone...police! Get down!" She directed him to hide between cribs. "Come this way," she whispered.

Like a toddler, Derek crawled between rows of sleeping babies. He looked back to see six men with automatic weapons enter the nursery. The nurse pulled him into a side room. "Your baby should be safe," she said. "He looks like all the others."

"Why are you helping me?" Derek asked.

"Because I know the man you are running from. I dislike him very much."

"Dr. Herzog?"

Nodding, she said, "He has experimented on many women from this hospital. And they have suffered for it."

Derek wondered if she was referring to other cloning attempts. He didn't think Josie was the first woman they tried to inseminate with a clone. As he heard police in the nursery, he realized that the nurse could be more of an asset than he had anticipated.

***

Two orderlies wheeled a stretcher holding Petra's corpse out of Josie's room, and a nurse rebuked them for not covering it with a sheet.

"Get me out of here!" screamed Josie from inside her room. "I want my baby! Does anybody speak English? Where...is...my...baby?"

Heidi and Kristina entered the chamber to find Josie highly agitated. Three policemen milled about and a fourth tried to get a statement from her. A nurse and a doctor attempted to sedate her. Heidi rushed up to the bed and pushed the nurse aside to wrap her arms around her daughter. "My baby girl," she cried. "You're safe!"

Kristina's hand flew in front of the doctor as he tried to add a sedative to Josie's IV bag. The doctor and Kristina argued—he in German, and she in French. He made a second attempt to give Josie drugs, but Kristina shoved him back.

***

The young nurse led Derek in a crawl into a storeroom packed with medical supplies, diapers, and instant formula.

"Where are we going?" Derek whispered.

"Out," the nurse replied.

They heard one of the men in the nursery adjust his gun with a click.

"I need to stay," Derek insisted.

"If you stay, they will know the baby is here. And you will die."

Derek knew she was right. If they found him in the storeroom, they'd know Pip was in the nursery. With great reluctance, he followed her to a door, which led to an adjacent hallway.

Inside the nursery, one man guarded the entrance and Pavlov directed five other men to search for the clone.

"Hurry," the nurse implored while opening the door.

Derek followed her, and police stepped into the storeroom he had recently left.

Pavlov hobbled between rows of infants, inspecting each child closely. One baby caught his attention. It wore a blue cap and a bracelet that identified its gender as female. He checked beneath its diaper and saw that it was a male. It had to be the one, he decided. Nurses don't confuse genders on bracelets. He picked the child up and the bracelet fell off its arm and back into the crib, a sure sign that the adhesive on the band had been reused.

***

The Lord Mayor of Aachen felt flush as he struggled to restrain the tears which threatened to saturate his cheeks. He had known Dr. Karl Vanderhoff for most of his life. In fact, it was Vanderhoff, more than anyone else, who helped him to get the position he currently held. The man was the rock that others broke themselves against, and now he was gone, slaughtered in a hospital by men who had taken vows to protect and serve.

Unable to watch as orderlies set Vanderhoff's bullet riddled body on a stretcher and covered it with a sheet, the Lord Mayor walked toward Josie's room. "God help us all if Clement Herzog gets his hands on that clone," he muttered.

***

Dr. Herzog felt light-headed and dehydrated from loss of blood. His gunshot wound had rendered his right arm useless, but he willed himself to walk to the nursery. He stumbled, and one of the Russians caught him before he fell.

"We must take you to a doctor," the Russian said.

"No," Dr. Herzog countered. "Get me to the nursery."

The Russian glanced at his partner, Yuri, and the two officers who accompanied them. Dr. Herzog was too weak to go on, but no one dared to countermand his orders.

"I don't care about...the other babies," Dr. Herzog stammered. "But we don't l...leave tha...that room without the clone. Just be...sure to get the right child."

He collapsed again, and this time he lost consciousness.

***

In the elevator, two orderlies stood with the stretcher which held Vanderhoff's body. They watched the numbered lights count down. Suddenly, an arm fell out from beneath the sheet and hit one of the men in the leg. He startled and jumped forward.

The other orderly burst out laughing. "*Es ist lebendig! Seien sie vorsichtig* (It's alive! Be careful)," he mocked.

The first orderly felt slightly humiliated until the corpse suddenly sat up and the sheet fell to its waist. "*Holen Sie bitte den Aufzug zurück* (Take the elevator back, please)," said Vanderhoff.

The orderlies screamed in horror.

***

Derek and the young nurse hid in a janitor's closet a short distance from the nursery. Derek checked the bullets in his gun and said, "I have to go back there."

"They will shoot you for sure," the nurse replied.

"Only if I'm careless," he countered.

"Do not expect me to go with you," she said.

"I wouldn't dream of it. I need you to get the baby's mother out of this hospital."

"How would I do that?" she asked.

"I don't know," he admitted. "But Dr. Herzog will kill her if you don't."

The young nurse studied the intensity in his eyes. "I will try," she told him.

"*Danke*," he said with relief. He reached for the door handle but turned back to her. "I don't even know your name."

"Olive," she replied.

"Olive," he repeated with a smile. "Please take care of Josie."

"If I am able, I will take her out by way of the Learning Center in the rear of the complex," she said. "You may meet her there."

Derek squeezed her hand in thanks and opened the door.

***

Jason Blackburn pushed the cart which held his newborn and followed the gray-haired nurse. Though his baby was painted with someone else's blood, it looked perfect to him. The child slept as if it hadn't a care in the world.

To their surprise, Jason and the nurse found the nursery to be devoid of adults. "*Wo sind die Schwestern?* (Where are the nurses?)" Jason asked.

The nurse had the same question, but no answers. "*Das ist seltsam* (This is strange)," she observed.

Realizing that she should fill in for whoever was supposed to be in the nursery, she told Jason to return to his wife. He opposed the idea, but she said, "*Mach dir keine Sorgen. Ich werde für dein Baby sorgen* (Do not worry. I will care for your baby)."

Having complete faith in the nurse, and wanting to check on his wife, Jason agreed to her suggestion. He kissed his son and walked toward the door. Before departing, he said, "*Ich sehe da eine leere Krippe* (I see an empty crib there)."

***

Two policemen stood guard outside Dr. Herzog's hospital room. The Russians stayed inside the room and watched a doctor examine Dr. Herzog's wound. The bullet from Vanderhoff's gun had shattered his collarbone and allowed a great deal of blood to escape his body. That deeply concerned the doctor, but he was also worried that jagged shards of bone might have pierced the patient's lung and could possibly travel to his heart. They would have to perform surgery immediately or risk losing the patient.

***

With the assistance of the Lord Mayor, Heidi and Kristina ejected all unwanted people from Josie's room. They also prevented the doctor from sedating her, although she remained in terrible pain. As a group, they pondered how best to escape the hospital. Josie's thoughts, however, revolved around her son and the man who swore to protect him. She wanted to search for them, but her battered body wouldn't permit it.

The door crept open, causing everyone to be alarmed. Instinctively, Heidi, Kristina, and the Lord Mayor formed a human shield before Josie's bed. When the door opened fully, their bravery gave way to shock, then fright. Dr. Karl Vanderhoff walked into the room. His clothes were coated with blood, but he had no wounds on his body.

"I...I...I don't believe it," said the Lord Mayor.

"It's a ghost," declared Heidi.

Josie laughed, though it hurt for her to do so. "How are you gonna explain this?"

Vanderhoff closed the door. "Would you believe every bullet missed a vital spot?"

Vanderhoff moved toward Josie, and the human shield parted to let him pass.

"Are you all right?" he asked Josie.

"I'll be okay," she answered. "Where's my baby? Where's Derek?"

"I sent them to the nursery," he told her.

Heidi stretched a finger forward and poked Vanderhoff's flesh. It was real.

Kristina was the first to snap out of her amazement. "Dr. Herzog and the police went to the nursery after you...uh...after you were shot."

"This is impossible," the Lord Mayor exclaimed. "I...I saw you die."

"Do you want to put your hands in my side?" Vanderhoff asked in reference to the Bible's Doubting Thomas.

"You must have been shot over a hundred times," the Lord Mayor persisted.

"Things are not always as they appear," Vanderhoff replied.

"Bullshit," proclaimed Heidi. "We all saw you shot, over and over."

"I'd love to hear him talk his way out of this too," said Josie, "but we gotta get my baby back first...and Derek."

The door opened abruptly and Olive, the young nurse, entered. She was flustered and in a rush. "We must go now," she declared. "I can take you out of here."

"Where's my son?" Josie asked. "Where's Derek?"

"He is trying to retrieve the infant," Olive replied.

Josie's face froze in a look of fear. "Retrieve?" she asked.

***

With his pistol ready for anything, Derek crawled through the nursery. He kept his eyes on a gray-haired nurse who was at work in the side room. He stopped at the crib where he had last left Pip. The child was still asleep. The bracelet had fallen off his tiny wrist and was in the crib beside him. Derek read it to see that it was the same one they had put on Pip earlier. A quick glance also showed him the red birthmark on the bottom of the baby's right foot. He looked again at the nurse to see that she was preoccupied. He set his gun on the floor beside him and reached cautiously into the crib. With a hand securely on each side of the infant, he lifted. A cry escaped from the child's body and turned into a wail.

The infant's shrieks rang like an alarm in the nurse's ears. To her horror, she saw two arms snatching the newborn from its crib. "*Oh mein Gott!* (Oh my God)!" she cried. She grabbed a knife and charged into the nursery. "*Legen Sie das Baby zurück!* (Place the baby back!)" she commanded.

Derek set the baby back in its crib and grabbed his gun. He didn't want to do it but had no alternative. He took aim at the woman and shot the knife out of her hand. The explosive gunshot turned every resting child into the purveyor of screams. Derek snatched the baby he held only seconds before and ran from the room. In his haste to flee, he left his gun behind.

Clutching the baby close to his chest, he stumbled into the adjoining corridor. He sprinted down the hall with the child wailing incessantly.

The little guy must be horrified, Derek reminded himself. His introduction to the world had been violent and traumatic. Derek slowed his pace and cradled the baby more gently in his arms. "There, there, Pip. You'll be back with your mum shortly."

It took another ten minutes of comforting for Derek to turn the infant's cries into a whimper, then silence. Rounding a corner, he saw an emergency stairwell that led to the lower floors. He also found two policemen with guns. He retreated into the jamb of a nearby door and prayed that Pip would remain quiet. Several heartbeats later, he looked back and saw Pavlov hobbling behind the police with a baby bundle in his arms. Why did he have a baby? Did he snatch one he thought to be Pip?

"*Nicht bewegen* (Do not move)," a deep voice commanded.

Derek turned to see a man pointing an automatic pistol at his face. He urged Derek and his baby to join Pavlov in the middle of the corridor.

"What is this?" Pavlov asked.

The man responded in German, and Pavlov turned his cold eyes to Derek. "Put the child on the floor," he commanded.

Derek had no viable alternative but to do as instructed. The infant began to cry as soon as it touched the floor. Derek stood upright and fully expected Pavlov to order his men to kill him. Instead, the Russian set his baby on the floor beside the other. Pavlov and Derek looked at the newborns lying side by side. They were remarkably similar. Each had black hair covered by a blue cap. They wore white outfits with no bracelets. Both babies had red markings on the bottom of their right foot, and neither one had a hunched back. Derek and Pavlov were mystified. How could it be?

Pavlov leaned closer to inspect the infants, and Derek saw his only opportunity. He thrust a kick into the man's damaged hip. The Russian screamed as his socket snapped and he collapsed. Pavlov landed with an arm on each side of the infants, his upper body straddled over them. Derek snatched the newborn closest to him, the one he had been keeping his eye on the whole time, the one he was sure was Pip. He scrambled down the hall as surprised police sent artillery soaring after him.

Derek raced with the child in his arms and bullets streaking past him. A shot struck his shoulder. He staggered to a stairwell and fell through its door.

***

Derek escaped the hospital to meet the cool night air. He held the crying baby close to his chest while blood seeped from the wound in his shoulder. He searched the darkness but didn't see anyone waiting for him. Josie must not have escaped. He knew the police were sure to be on his trail, so he hunched over the child and walked out into the night in search of sanctuary, looking every bit like the title character in Victor Hugo's novel.

A car's engine growled, and earth and pebbles crunched beneath rolling tires. Derek turned as headlights captured him in their glare. Beyond the lights, he could see rooftop flashers. It was a police car. He ran, but the vehicle was upon him in seconds.

The police car's back door flew open, and Vanderhoff said, "Get in."

EPILOGUE

Josie, her baby, Derek, Vanderhoff, Heidi, Kristina, and the Lord Mayor of Aachen were all fugitives. Their destination was Vanderhoff's remote hideaway in North America. To get there, they would have to pass from shelter to shelter in the dark of night. They would be hunted across borders and pursued by international agencies.

Josie thought little of their dangerous future as the sun began its morning ascent. She held her child to her chest and was enveloped in the protective cocoon of Derek to her right, the Lord Mayor to her left; and Vanderhoff, Kristina, and her mother occupying the vehicle's back seat. She looked down at her son and felt unbelievably blessed.

Heidi, on the other hand, couldn't find such peace. Her stomach felt uneasy, and she could feel its contents rising in her esophagus. "Pull over," she commanded.

"What?" asked the Lord Mayor.

"I'm gonna be sick," she said. "Pull over."

The Lord Mayor brought the car to a stop on the side of the road. Heidi threw a rear door open and practically fell out of the vehicle. She stumbled several steps and heaved vomit onto the grass at her feet. Kristina approached her to offer support.

"Damn morning sickness," Heidi muttered with moist eyes. "This is bullshit."

"Hey, Pip can hear you," Josie exclaimed and covered the baby's tiny ears.

"Sorry," said Heidi, wiping a string of vomit laced saliva from her mouth.

Vanderhoff waited in the back seat. He would soon have to explain his miraculous resurrection to his companions. He would also have to get them safely to North America. His most important concern, however, was for the babe in the front seat. How would he raise the child in this age? He wasn't sure, but he wouldn't make the same mistakes with young Pip that he made so long ago with Pippin the Hunchback. He thought about the second chance he'd been given, and realized how fortunate he was.

With his shoulder wound clean and bandaged, Derek's body was on the mend and his spirits were high. He stroked the baby's hair, touching Josie's hand as he did so. She responded in kind, and the two of them felt like a mother and father, a family with their little son Pip.

"What do we have here?" Josie asked, as she noticed the patch of red on the child's foot. "Do we have a birthmark?"

Derek looked on as Josie rubbed the red patch, and it flaked off.

"It's blood," she realized. Turning to Derek, she asked, "Why does he have dried blood on the bottom of his foot?"

***

It was early in the morning, and open blinds allowed slices of light to stretch across Dr. Herzog's hospital bed. His right arm was in a sling; his shoulder was wrapped. The door eased open and Pavlov entered the room in a wheelchair pushed by Yuri. A special present sat in the arms of the seated Russian. Dr. Herzog slowly opened his eyes, and said, "Bring him to me."

Yuri guided Pavlov and his little bundle closer to the bed. Leaning forward, Pavlov set Pip on the mattress beside Dr. Herzog. The child squirmed, but did not cry. He kicked his feet in the air, his red birthmark plainly visible. Dr. Herzog looked at the baby for a lingering moment, and a triumphant smile slowly crept up his face.

AUTHOR'S NOTE

As a student of history, I'm fascinated by most eras and many individuals, but the one who has always held a special attraction for me is Charlemagne. He was a mighty conqueror and a penitent man, a magnanimous monarch and the executioner of thousands. He was the illiterate champion of mass education. He saved the papacy and installed Pope Leo III on his throne, but knelt before the Holy Father. He was a pious adulterer who had many concubines and bastard children. He was a devoted son and the likely murderer of his only brother. He was the first Holy Roman Emperor, though he was not Roman at all. In short, Charlemagne was a man of contradiction and the ideal figure for me to craft my novel around.

Many people have asked me what inspired me to write this story. While most of what you read came from my active imagination, I must admit that the legends and real history of Charlemagne also helped to give birth to *Long Live the King*. This story is a work of fiction, but much of it is plausible and nearly all of the clues and artifacts Josie encounters are real. Anyone who is interested in learning more about these things should read *Charlemagne and France: A Thousand Years of Mythology* by Robert Morrissey, *Charlemagne: Father of a Continent* by Alessandro Barbero, *The Enthroned Corpse of Charlemagne* by John F. Moffitt, *Charlemagne: The Formation of a European Identity* by Rosamond McKitterick, and, of course, *Two Lives of Charlemagne* by Einhard and Notker the Stammerer. For my scholarly readers, these volumes will provide you with a wealth of fascinating material that will stir your imagination and broaden your understanding of Europe's lesser-known history. Of course, an Internet search for Charlemagne and the clues mentioned in this story will also enlighten the more casual student of history. And for both the scholar and the casual historian, I would like to recommend a wonderful rock opera entitled, *Charlemagne: By the Sword and the Cross* by famed actor Christopher Lee.

For those of you who are curious about what is real and what is not in *Long Live the King*, I shall now endeavor to fill you in as best I can. First of all, the WWII Charlemagne Division mentioned in the documentary that Steve used as target practice was very real. Hitler idealized Charlemagne as one of the first great Aryans and named his most prized division after him. The cloning process that became the basis of Josie's adventures is most certainly real, and it is true that the animals mentioned in the story have, or are currently being, cloned. While scientists haven't yet attempted to clone a dead human, it is not unrealistic to think that if they will be able to clone an extinct woolly mammoth, they will devise a way to clone a deceased human. The Rathaus, the Grashaus, Aachen Cathedral, the imperial treasures, the bones of Charlemagne, and Charlemagne's throne are all on display for anyone who wants to go to Aachen to visit them. There was, in fact, a plot involving Pippin the Hunchback which was hatched at Regensburg and Charlemagne's response to it was precisely as I explained in the book. The carving of the word *REGENSBURG* on the side of the throne, however, was my addition, though there is a Nine Men's Morris board etched on the throne, and many scholars believe it was used by Charlemagne and Einhard, his friend and biographer.

The central legend of *Long Live the King* is that Charlemagne faked his death, buried Pippin the Hunchback in his place, then mixed his blood with the blood of Jesus to live forever in anonymity. And that is true.

Just kidding.

Charlemagne died on January 28, 814 after lingering for one week on his deathbed. As far as we know, no one was buried in his place, and Pippin the Hunchback died three years before his father and was buried at the monastery at Prüm (the dates of Pippin's birth and death are debatable). But Charlemagne really was buried in a seated position and his remains were exactly as I described them in the book when Emperor Otto III explored his tomb in 1000. The painting by Rethel which depicts this scene is in the Coronation Hall of Aachen's Rathaus (and viewable on the Internet). The testimony by Emperor Otto III's fellow tomb visitors, Otto of Lomello, Bishop Thietmar, and Ademar de Chabannes, is accurately repeated in *Long Live the King*, as is the account of Tolomeo da Lucca, who viewed Charlemagne's remains in 1300. What most struck me (and Josie) about this testimony is the fact that Charlemagne's corpse appeared to be lifelike hundreds of years after his death. In the case of Tolomeo da Lucca, it was nearly 500 years after Charlemagne's death. How could the Emperor's body not have deteriorated into dust? The most likely explanation would be the one I gave in the book, which is to say that Charlemagne's body was excessively prepared for burial (not unlike the remains of ancient Egyptian monarchs) to the point that it essentially became a wax effigy of itself.

The testimony which particularly caught my attention, however, was that of Ademar de Chabannes. He maintained that the amulet which bore fragments of the True Cross was found in Charlemagne's crown when they first entered his tomb. I recalled reading many stories and seeing numerous associations between Charlemagne and the True Cross of Jesus. The ones I mentioned in the book are actual accounts, including the story of how Charlemagne acquired fragments of the True Cross from a pilgrim returning from the Holy Land. The pendant/amulet mentioned so frequently in the story and shown on the cover of this book is the actual talisman of Charlemagne. Many writers attest to the fact that Charlemagne had it fashioned from the True Cross fragments he acquired from the pilgrim, and that he wore it every day of his life and was buried with it. Why it would have been put in his crown as Ademar de Chabannes claimed is beyond me, but it gave me fuel to create my own myth about Charlemagne's immortality. Following along the same lines, the True Cross procession in Saint Guilhem is accurately described in the book, although it doesn't happen as regularly in real life as I suggest in the story. And the abbeys which I claim received fragments of the True Cross from Charlemagne are said to have really received them from the Emperor.

In creating the backstory of Charlemagne living forever in anonymity, there were two issues which I had to consider. First, he was a political animal and a man of action. Would his character even allow him to disappear into obscurity? The answer to that question was no. Second, there would have to be some accounts or images somewhere of him appearing in the historical record. Fortunately, my research provided the evidence I needed to address both of these issues. I learned that there really is a window in Chartes Cathedral which depicts Charlemagne fighting in the first crusade in 1099. It also portrays Charlemagne with fragments of the True Cross. Similarly, the writing by Pierre Dubois which claimed that Charlemagne ruled for 125 years is also real. The tapestry which depicts Charlemagne escorting Anne of Brittany (1477-1514) into Paris in 1492 is mostly real. Although the scene isn't portrayed on any tapestry, it is described in detail by Jean Nicolai in the *Chroniques de Notre-Dame*, just as I wrote in the book. In an uncanny coincidence, I also found the Vatican fresco entitled *The Coronation of Charlemagne in Rome*, which depicts the scene of Charlemagne's coronation in 800 with François I of France (1494-1547) taking the place of Charlemagne. François was in fact, the cousin and son-in-law of Anne of Brittany. The woodcut etching which portrayed Charlemagne as a wild woodsman standing beside Emperor Charles V (1500-1558), François' arch enemy, is also true. It seemed only natural for me to tie all these elements together and have the anonymous Charlemagne serve as a behind-the-scenes puppet master pulling the strings of Anne of Brittany, François I, and Charles V.

The story of the Joyeuse Sword is a mixed bag of real legend and my invention. *The Song of Roland* claims that Charlemagne's sword, named Joyeuse, changed color thirty times a day. History also records that the sword led the coronation procession for every French king from 1270 until 1824. It currently resides in the Louvre, although the one on display today doesn't change color. Like King Arthur's Excalibur, the Joyeuse Sword was said to bestow special powers of invincibility upon its bearer. I took dramatic license with the Office of the Keeper of the Sword, but it seemed to me that if that position didn't exist, it should have. With a sword of such importance, it should be someone's duty to watch over it.

Although Saint Denis Basilica and the tombs of Carloman, Pippin the Short and Bertha of the Big Foot (what chroniclers really called Charlemagne's brother, father and mother) exist and can be viewed by all who wish to see them, the Saint Denis Manuscript and the capitulary which detailed Charlemagne's death bed convalescence at Saint Denis, were invented by me. Abbot Waldo was really in charge of Saint Denis at that time and Charlemagne's heir Louis the Pious was on campaign in Brittany then, but the rest of it was my creation. Carloman's grave in Saint Remi Basilica really was exhumed and his remains were reinterred in Saint Denis as I described. And the leaders of the French Revolution did, in fact, remove bodies from the tombs of Saint Denis and cover them with lime.

Most of what I wrote about Pippin the Hunchback came from real history. By all accounts, he was a likeable child, but that changed when his father disinherited him and gave his name to his brother. As previously stated, he participated in a plot to overthrow his father and murder his family, and was exiled at Prüm, where he died. The manuscript which describes his conversation with Charlemagne at Verden (where he pled for the lives of 4,500 Saxons) was my invention. There is no account of him being at Verden at that time. Likewise, the 1832 newspaper which claimed that Pippin was in Thionville at the time of the Verden massacre was also the product of my imagination. Many people, however, have speculated that Pippin the Hunchback was the inspiration for Victor Hugo's famous novel *The Hunchback of Notre Dame*.

By all accounts, Einhard was a close friend of Charlemagne's. As I already stated, the two men were known to spend hours together over games such as Nine Men's Morris. And Einhard was really known as Bezaleel, which means metal worker and gem cutter. With that basis in reality, it wasn't much of a stretch for me to have Einhard be the creator of Charlemagne's famed talisman and the architect of his immortality.

Lastly, I would be remiss if I didn't mention the Charlemagne Award Agency. Although there is an organization similar to it, my Agency is fictitious. The real organization actually does a great deal of good. I took dramatic license with my Agency, and in no way do I assert that the real organization is nefarious and hell-bent on taking over Europe. Anyone who is curious about the similarities and differences between my Agency and the real one need only conduct a rudimentary Internet search.

In the course of your research you may also realize that cloning Charlemagne and installing him at the head of the European Union isn't really all that farfetched. As I've previously stated, if cloning a sheep or even a woolly mammoth is possible, then how far are we from cloning a real person, even a dead one? Some may say that's exactly what Europe needs. Others might consider it the realization of Hitler's nightmarish vision of a thousand year Reich. I'll let you decide that for yourself...then again, I might explore it in Book Two of the Charlemagne Saga.

Until we meet again, I wish you happy reading.

GUY COTE

ABOUT THE AUTHOR

Guy Cote spent his formative years in Sanford, Maine pretending to be an adventurer and marching up and down Main Street waving an American flag while wearing an army uniform (his youthful response to the Iranian Hostage Crisis). As his body grew and his maturity followed, Guy played sports and emulated fictional characters he saw on the silver screen. He eventually tired of living vicariously through other people's creations, so he began writing his own screenplays. He completed his first script, *The Magic of a Lifetime*, shortly before graduating from The University of Maine.

With a script and a freshly minted Bachelors Degree in hand, Guy moved to Florida to work in the Sunshine State's burgeoning film industry. In the process, he wrote five more screenplays: *Tried and True* (currently in pre-production to become a feature film), *G.I. Joe: The Making of a Hero, The Paper Trail, Soulmate* and *The Widowmaker*.

Guy's fascination with other times and other places eventually drew him back into academia where he earned his Masters Degree in history from The University of South Florida. Thereafter, he took a teaching position in a public school and dedicated himself to the creation of his first novel. *Long Live the King* is the culmination of that effort. It is Guy's hope and belief that you'll enjoy reading this novel as much as he enjoyed crafting it and he looks forward to the two of you meeting again in the sequel.

Like most authors, Guy relishes feedback from his readers. Feel free to visit and leave him a message at www.guycotebooks.com. See you there…